Quid Pro Quo

Manna Francis

CASPERIAN
BOOKS

The author wishes to thank her husband and her editor, both of whom are once again at the top of the list. She'd also like to thank Kimberley at Casperian Books, for having the faith to put the Administration in print, and for giving her the push to write "Quid Pro Quo" itself.

www.casperianbooks.com

Cover illustration by Orit "Shin" Heifets

ISBN-10: 1-934081-09-4
ISBN-13: 978-1-934081-09-9

Table of Contents

Quid Pro Quo 5
Friday 129
Pancakes...137
Surprises...173
Family...212
Mirror, Mirror...253

Quid Pro Quo

Chapter One

❖

God, it hurts. Hurry *up*."

Toreth tried the lock on the cuffs again, without much hope of success. His pessimism proved justified. "Sorry, it's stuck."

"Don't fuck around, Toreth." Anger masked the pain in Warrick's voice.

"I'm not. I'm serious. They won't open. The lock must've fritzed when the chair went over. That's the problem with electronic controls. At work I'd just get a mechanical override key, but they're sign-out, sign-in, and tagged so they can't leave the building."

While he knelt there, he cast a professional eye over the damage to Warrick's wrists. In the five months they'd been fucking regularly this was the first serious accident, which Toreth considered to be a decent enough record considering Warrick's tastes in fun. All inside the damage waiver. This time, though, things couldn't be glossed over with an analgesic spray and a long-sleeved shirt, which might prove awkward.

Warrick shifted on the chair, and then swore under his breath. "Can't you break them?"

"No." Toreth stood up. "They're long-term restraint cuffs, designed to be left on unsupervised prisoners. If it was that easy, there'd be no fucking point using them, would there?"

Warrick closed his eyes. "Think of some other way to get them open, then."

"I'll have to call an ambulance. They'll be able to cut you free at Casualty."

His eyes flew open again. "No! Can't you do *something*?"

"Nothing I can think of, not unless you've got a hacksaw and a few hours. I can't chew through alloyed steel. We could always wait until your wrist swells up, the cuffs cut off the circulation, and you get gangrene."

"Compared to being carried out of the hotel stark-naked and handcuffed to a chair? I think I'll take the gangrene." Warrick stared down at the floor for a moment, then up again. "Yes, all right, call. Maybe I'll be lucky and I'll die of shock before they get here."

"Of course you won't. You've broken your wrist, that's all."

"*All?*"

"Yes, all. It's not going to kill you."

He found the comm earpiece, but before he could make the call, Warrick said, "Wait a moment. Couldn't you break the chair?"

Toreth considered. The chair seemed solid enough that he'd thought it would be okay to cuff Warrick to it in the first place, although in the end it had turned out to be rather badly balanced. Still only wood, though, and therefore an improvement over the cuffs. He'd been looking at the wrong part of the problem. He moved back behind the chair and examined the structure. The linking bar of the cuffs went behind a thick brace between the legs. That left an obvious weak point in the system. "Grip the bar with your good hand."

"I don't have a good hand."

"Yes, you do. The left one's just bruised. Probably."

Warrick's fingers closed tentatively around the wood.

"Harder."

A hiss of indrawn breath. "I can't do better than that."

"Okay." Toreth put his hands on the chair back. "Now, tilt forward, just enough to take the back legs off the ground. I've got you, so you won't go over. Perfect." Unpleasantly precarious, actually, but Toreth wasn't the one with the broken wrist. "Right. I'm going to kick the chair leg away from me, and try to split the glue, or whatever's holding it together. The first one probably won't do it, but hold on as hard as you can, because when it breaks you don't want the bar pulling downwards. On three. Ready?"

Silence.

"Ready?"

"Yes. Get on with it."

"Okay. One, two, *three.*"

With a splintering crack, the leg gave a few centimeters, unexpectedly enough that Toreth almost overbalanced. He slammed the chair back down onto its legs, and Warrick screamed.

"Jesus!" Toreth said. "Shut up!"

"Sorry." Warrick breathed harshly, panting. After a few moments, he nodded. "I'm all right."

"Good. If hotel security kicks the door in, you can explain to them that you do this for fun."

Warrick laughed weakly. "Carry on."

He'd misjudged the kick, or the joint had been weaker than it looked, because he'd freed the bar. With one hand Toreth eased the splintered end away from the leg; with the other he slid the cuffs along it, taking it as slowly as he could. Warrick's heavy breathing modulated into whimpers of pain every so often, but he didn't scream again. "Right, you're free."

Warrick stood up, and immediately headed for the bed. Toreth caught his shoulder. "Don't. Sit down on that and your hands'll end up pressed into the mattress. And if you lie down, you'll regret it when you have to stand up again."

Toreth grabbed the second chair in the room, and sat Warrick on it sideways to keep his wrists away from the back. He couldn't help thinking that Warrick looked pretty fucking good, even—or maybe especially—pale and sweating and biting his lip hard. Toreth crouched down beside him. "Okay?"

"No. I don't think anything has ever hurt so much in my life."

"Yeah, most people are surprised by how bad it is, even with small bones."

"And you know that because . . . ?" Warrick asked with a glimmer of his usual iciness.

Sometimes, the 'no-mention-of-the-Investigation-and-Interrogation-Division' rule was a pain in the neck. Toreth shrugged. "You know how. Pull yourself together, and then we'll get you dressed and over to Casualty." Where there would be a lot of tricky explaining to do, in the unlucky event that someone started asking questions.

"I'm going to need a few minutes, I think." Warrick shook his head. "And I thought I liked pain."

"You do. More than you think, in fact." An idea occurred—a challenge, rather. He loved a challenge. He reached up and smoothed Warrick's damp fringe back away from his face. "Actually, I bet you could get off on this, with enough buildup."

Curiosity worked better than painkillers where Warrick was concerned. "Do you really think so?"

"Yeah. Or at least possibly. Much more difficult starting from this point, of course." Toreth gave it a few more seconds' thought, then said, "Close your eyes."

"What? Why?"

"Because I'm going to make you come, and it'll never work if you've got your eyes open."

"Come?" Warrick snorted. "Rubbish."

"Want to bet? Loser pays for dinner at the place of the winner's choice?"

After another extremely skeptical sound, Warrick closed his eyes. "Very well."

Toreth stood up and moved around behind the chair. He closed his eyes briefly, pulling up a game voice, then said, "I know I'm going to win, because I know you've thought about this kind of thing before, plenty of times."

"I don't—"

"Shut up. I wasn't asking a fucking question, I was telling you. Don't think I don't know what you get off on. Don't think I don't know why it matters that it's me. I know what you fantasize about. This is just games, it's not what you dream about, is it? How does it start?"

Warrick said nothing, but his breathing already came easier, and faster.

"All right, I'll guess." Toreth crouched down again. "I ignore the safe word, don't I?" A quick intake of breath, cut short, and Toreth smiled. "I told you I knew." It had been a guess, but a likely one. "I hurt you, I go too far, and then I ignore the safe word. You tell me to stop, and then you beg me, and it does no fucking good, does it, because the only reason I ever stop is because I want to. If I didn't, there's not a fucking thing you could do about it. Especially not now. Right now, you're mine, and you're exactly how I wanted you."

He ran his palm gently down Warrick's unbroken arm, but the reflexive jerk jolted Warrick's wrists and he swore softly.

Toreth leaned closer, mouth nearer Warrick's ear. "So, when you're lying there on your own, thinking about begging for your life while I rape you, are you already tied up, or do you get to fight back? Tell me."

No response, so he moved his hand to the injured arm, resting it lightly on Warrick's bicep. "Tell me."

"It depends." Warrick's voice sounded deliciously controlled. "If I want to make it last, then forcing me into the cuffs or ... whatever, is part of the fantasy." Pity the control didn't reach everywhere.

"You're getting hard already. I'm going to win my bet." He shifted around, sliding his hand down Warrick's chest, hair slick with cooling sweat. "Just from hearing about it. That's nothing."

Warrick whimpered as Toreth's fingers closed around his cock. The impromptu scene meant that he had nothing worked out, and under the circumstances, improvisation was best kept limited. Fucking Warrick, while incredibly tempting, offered too many ways of things going wrong. Still, no reason not to make use of the idea. "I can do whatever the hell I want to you, and you can't stop me. Bend you over that chair, have you kneeling on the floor. Make you beg for it. You can't fight me, not like this. Not that you ever could. I'm stronger that you, I'm trained— what could you do? Scream?"

Warrick moaned, and Toreth lengthened his strokes. He was hard himself now, although not any harder than Warrick. Much too easy. "I could really give you something to scream about, if you like. If *I* like. I could put you on your back on the bed and fuck you, lying on your wrists. And keep you quiet while I do it— there's a gag right there in my bag. Add some cloth, just to make sure, because I don't care if you fucking choke. If you pass out, I'll just bring you round ... "

Warrick was sweating again, pale except for the flush of arousal on his lips and spreading over his chest. Every involuntary twitch, every shiver, jolted his wrist. They needed to finish soon, or it would aggravate the fracture too badly and increase the chance of trouble at the hospital. Luckily, it wouldn't take much longer. Toreth leaned down, licking salty skin, tongue tracing over a nipple, and Warrick gasped.

"Clench your fists," Toreth whispered.

"I can't."

"Don't argue. Do it."

"I—" Warrick's eyes flew open, lashes glistening. "Ah, fuck. *Fuck.*"

10

A glance down showed that Warrick had obeyed his instruction. Toreth began to move his hand faster, fisting tighter around Warrick's cock. He twisted his other hand into Warrick's hair, pulling backward. "More. You can do better than that."

"I can't." His head went back, tears wetting his face. "Please...stop. Enough."

"*Do* it." No threat, no compulsion required. The muscles in Warrick's arms tensed, and he nearly screamed, choking the noise back.

God, how tempting to drag him off the chair and fuck him. But there were limits to how much pain could still be erotic, and they were on the edge of it now.

"Please," Warrick gasped. "Stop. I can't—"

"If you relax, I'll break your other wrist," Toreth breathed.

"No! Please, I—Christ. Ah, *Christ*."

Pain modulated into ecstasy as his shoulders went back and he jerked up out of the chair. Toreth released his hair, steadying him with an arm across his shoulders. Another scream and Warrick came hard, shuddering against him, sobbing for breath.

Toreth sat back on his heels, giving Warrick a few minutes to recover. And it took minutes, shivers running through him occasionally as he leaned sideways against the back of the chair. Still looking good, Toreth thought. Incredibly fucking good, in fact.

Eventually, when he judged there might be a chance of an answer, Toreth asked, "Well?"

"God." Warrick's head hung forward, his breathing heavy. "Oh, God, that hurts. Sometimes...that's so wrong. That shouldn't happen. I knew how much it hurt and it still...so much. Crossed wiring, somewhere." He breathed out slowly. "You were right. I didn't think I could, but...God. Crossed wiring."

"Good?"

"Unbelievable." Warrick looked up, lashes still wet with tears. "Amazing."

"Better than the SMS?"

"A great deal."

Toreth laughed. "You have no idea how hard I am. I should make you get down on your knees and suck me."

Warrick shook his head. "Plastic duck." A brief smile flickered, composure returning. "Sorry. Selfish, I know, but this really is spectacularly painful, now that I'm in my right mind again. I think a hospital is an excellent idea."

The easy confidence that, previous scene notwithstanding, Toreth would respect the safe word, made him smile. "I can wait. It'll pass the time at the hospital, once they've given you something to take the edge off."

As they walked through the main hospital doors, Warrick said, "Pull my jacket up, would you?" The best they'd been able to manage for Warrick was dressed

11

from the waist down, and a jacket over his shoulders. At least that hid the cuffs, even if it hadn't done much to protect him from the late April night. They'd garnered enough stares on the way through the hotel as it was.

"Want me to sort things out?" Toreth offered.

"It's quite all right. I'll talk to them."

Toreth took a seat in the well-appointed waiting area as Warrick made his way over to the reception desk. It would, on reflection, look better if Warrick did the talking. Now that they were here, the worries he'd had earlier flooded back. Justice would *love* this. An I&I senior, doing something both technically illegal and pruriently entertaining, and doing it with stolen I&I property. No chance of them letting that one go past. Fucking Warrick might be great fun, but it wasn't worth screwing up his career or worse. Too late now to do anything other than hope Warrick could sweet-talk the staff. The positive side was that this was a corporate hospital, and they had to be experienced at keeping things quiet for their clients. Warrick wouldn't want this information out and about any more than Toreth did.

"Mr. Toth?"

It took him a moment to respond to the name. Then he looked up to find a uniformed young man. "Yeah?"

"This way, please."

They were escorted to a small, private room. No shared wards or thin curtains in this place, naturally. The escort settled Warrick onto a chair, while Toreth leaned against the wall and inspected the décor. Considerably better furnished than any hospital he'd ever been treated in.

"What does this place cost a night?" he asked when they were alone again.

Warrick shrugged, then paled. "Mm. No idea. But they recognize the SimTech insurers, so that's good enough for me." He sighed. "This will do my premiums no good at all. Although I don't recall a box to select for dangerous sexual practices, so they can't complain about incomplete disclosure."

Time to mention the potential problems, since Warrick had no reason to spontaneously develop a concern for Toreth's promotion prospects. "Warrick, when they ask you about—"

The door opened. Toreth's long-standing dislike of hospitals had been strengthened a couple of years ago when he'd begun to notice how young some of the doctors seemed. It disconcerted him to be treated by someone younger than himself, even though most doctors were little more than skilled technicians following the dictates of the expert systems. The woman who entered looked to Toreth barely old enough to have completed a school first-aid course. Not a good start. He'd been hoping for someone old and world-weary enough not to want the hassle and form-filling generated by reporting an assault to Justice. Maybe she wouldn't be too keen.

Her frosty expression suggested he was shit out of luck, and her first words were, "Excuse us, please."

Toreth considered arguing, but in the end he simply nodded and left the room. The door closed firmly behind him. He lingered outside for a while, listening and not bothering to hide it, but could make out no more than a low murmur of voices. After a few minutes, he heard a yelp of pain. Well, they'd obviously passed the level one interrogation phase and moved on to the examination. Good sign, or not? He couldn't tell.

As a distraction, Toreth went in search of something to drink. The first restaurant he found made him wonder briefly if he'd wandered out of the hospital and into a leisure complex. The food smelled good enough to tempt him into buying a meal, until he saw the prices, clearly not subsidized by the per diem charges. Scanning the room, he saw rich patients and rich visitors, but no staff eating in there. No doubt they had a less salubrious place somewhere else.

A few minutes' searching found it. A sign on the door barred entry to nonemployees of the hospital, but, of course, with the right attitude of confidence, no one questioned him. He'd planned to have dinner with Warrick after the fuck, and he was ravenous, so he bought a plate of chicken and bacon sandwiches to go with his coffee.

Corporate hospital staff apparently rated better catering than I&I staff. As he ate, he wondered how long the medics would take to cut through the cuffs, assuming that they couldn't find a way of forcing the lock. Depended on whether they had the appropriate kit to hand. He couldn't imagine that corporate hospitals had to deal with many pairs of jammed long-term restraint cuffs.

The doctor had obviously evicted him so that she could quiz Warrick over exactly how he'd ended up there. Toreth felt torn between hoping that Warrick would come up with some convincing lie (although what that might be, he had no idea) and that he'd simply tell the truth and make it sound very consensual. After that, it all depended on her attitude. Nice of Warrick to remember Marcus Toth, but if the woman decided to involve Justice, a false name would provide little protection.

Ah, well... if he was about to be arrested, he might as well enjoy himself while he could. He had time for another coffee, anyway. When he returned to his seat, carrying a fresh cup, he found a woman sitting at the table. As he slowed down by the table, she looked at the empty plate, looked at him, and said, "I'm sorry. I thought whoever was here was finished."

Toreth gave her a basic three-second appraisal. She scored well on the fuckability scale: nice height, nice weight, with short, wavy brunette hair and a relaxed, friendly openness to her voice. Nothing special about her face, but that was more than compensated for by the pleasantly curved body beneath the blue technician's uniform. He smiled. "Please, don't move." He sat down quickly, not giving her a chance to retreat, although she didn't look like the bolting type. "I'd like the company."

While he poured milk into his coffee, she studied him, not hiding the scrutiny. "I don't recognize you," she said when he looked up.

13

"It's a big hospital."

"Where do you work?"

He thought about spinning it out, but in the end he couldn't be bothered. "Not here, actually—the Department of Medicine. My name's Marcus Toth."

"Carri Fenwick. Why are you in here, then?"

He lifted his cup. "I couldn't afford a drink in the patients' place."

She paused, smile hovering on her lips, then said, "No, I meant in the hospital."

"I was fucking a guy, and I broke his wrist." Her eyes widened, and he shook his head. "It was an accident. He fell off a chair. Actually, the chair fell over, and he was handcuffed to it. Still an accident, though."

"Oh." Her shoulders relaxed. "How embarrassing!"

He grinned, trying to project honesty and casual friendliness. "Not for me."

"I suppose not. Is he all right? Apart from the wrist?"

"As far as I know, yeah."

A short silence before she said, "You don't seem very upset about it."

He shrugged. "We're not serious—it's just sex. Besides, accidents happen, especially if you like the kind of thing he gets off on."

"So what do you get off on? Breaking wrists?"

He considered his response while he drank some coffee. "Not really. I top for him, and with other people, I usually just fuck. Male or female."

She raised an eyebrow. "Flexible."

"Oh, yeah. Very flexible."

"Was he still in the chair when you brought him in?"

"No, luckily. But I bet you've seen things far more entertaining than that, working here."

She smiled impishly, which improved her face no end. "Oh, you should hear some of the stories."

"Yeah?" He set the cup down and leaned his elbows on the table. "Go on."

"I shouldn't, but . . . okay. Last year we had a couple in. They had some kind of game going—him dressed as a superhero, I forget who—and he tied her to the bed." Toreth raised his eyebrows, and she grinned again. "I know. You'd think he'd be dressed as a villain, but there you go. Anyway, he'd jumped from the top of the wardrobe onto the bed. He slipped as he jumped, horrible crunching noise when he landed on her—this is what they said—and he cracked a couple of her ribs and did something to his back. He'd had a muscle spasm, but he thought he'd broken it. They couldn't move, so they just lay there until his wife came home."

Toreth laughed. "Really? What did she do?"

"Called the medics. I'd have left 'em there, myself."

"Heartless woman. Go on, tell me another one."

He listened with half an ear, commenting when necessary, making plans for the rest of the evening, assessing as she moved from friendly to interested. He definitely wouldn't mind something to relieve the tension from the interrupted fuck. Eventually, she finished a story involving the inventive use of a home appliance as an impromptu sex toy, and sat back. He took his cue. "Listen, it's been great, but I've got to go. He'll be wondering where the fuck I disappeared to." And I need those bloody cuffs back.

She sipped her tea. "Do you want my comm?"

"Sure. Or—" He paused, considering, finally deciding that Warrick wouldn't be in the mood for anything more tonight. "What time do you finish?"

Carri raised her eyebrows, but all she said was, "Nine."

"Know any good bars near here?"

"A few." She was smiling now. "But I'll have to change out of uniform first. Have a shower."

"Suits me. I'll wait for you at the main entrance, shall I?"

She hesitated a moment, then nodded.

When he reached Warrick's room the door was still closed, so he took a seat outside. No point barging in and upsetting the medics.

Eventually, a technician carrying a scanner case came out of Warrick's room and walked down the corridor without giving Toreth a second glance. A few minutes later the doctor emerged, stopping when she saw him. "He'd like you to go back in," she said. Her manner, although still cool, seemed slightly friendlier. The continued nonappearance of Justice added to Toreth's optimism.

Warrick was sitting up on the bed, arm encased in a protective plastic sheath and held across his chest in a sling. Judging by his color and the set of his shoulders, pain relief had been administered a while ago.

Toreth looked around the room. Shit. No cuffs.

"Looking for these?" Warrick lifted his good hand, revealing the mangled cuffs concealed by a fold in the sheets. "I slipped them under there while everyone was busy. I thought you might like them back, bearing in mind their provenance."

Genius. "Too fucking right." Toreth examined the cuffs, which were completely ruined with both bands cut in half. "What did you tell them?"

"The truth, minus the bet." Warrick adjusted the sling slightly. "Awkward in places, but it seemed by far the easiest, and she was sympathetic enough."

"She didn't mention Justice?"

"Once or twice." His mouth twitched. "And an abuse counselor. And after that, a psychiatrist."

"Fuck. Listen, if they—"

"Don't worry. Persistent cheerfulness on my part seemed to put her off the idea. Ideas. She did mention that she wouldn't like to see me back in here, and I promised to be more careful in future."

"Thank fuck."

"Easy for you to say. I'm going to have a fascinating entry in my medical file."

Toreth almost said, "until you get home and fix it." However, Warrick's over-familiarity with Administration systems remained almost as forbidden a topic as interrogation. He glanced at his watch. Five to nine. "Right, I'll be off. I've got a date."

Warrick's eyebrows shot up. "A date?"

"Yeah. Met her while I was sneaking a coffee in the staff canteen."

"Good God." Warrick's half-smile mask set firmly in place. "Is there anywhere you can't find an opportunity for casual sex?" He didn't sound at all happy.

Toreth lingered, knowing that when he walked out Carri would be waiting for him. It felt quite irrationally enjoyable. "Did you want to carry on tonight, then?"

"Not really. But—" Warrick shook his head, then leaned back. "Never mind. Off you go."

"Do you want to cancel next week?"

Warrick considered, looking down at his hand. "No, I don't think so," he said eventually. "I'll call you if I don't feel up to it, but it's not a bad break." He grimaced. "Allegedly, anyway, and it should be a lot better by then."

"Good." He dropped the cuffs into his pocket. "Because, in case you'd forgotten, you owe me a fucking expensive dinner and a blowjob."

Chapter Two

❖

"I don't see what the problem is," Chevril was saying as Toreth joined the group of senior para-investigators in the coffee room on Thursday morning. "If Corporate Fraud wants to do our job for us, good luck to 'em."

"It's the principle, Chev," Mike Belkin said. "Let them take one case, then they'll find another one they like the look of. Political Crimes will start sniffing around, then the other vultures, and the next thing you know we'll have no cases at all except the duds that no one else wants to touch."

"You're overreacting," Chevril said.

"No. General Criminal's an open invitation to poachers. Almost everything we get could be argued into another section."

"What are we talking about?" Toreth asked.

"The NTS kidnapping. It's obviously General Criminal. Kidnapping usually is, if it's not Justice work. But CF came up with some bullshit about it being an internal insurance fraud, and bang, they got it. Tillotson's not doing his job."

That generated a murmur of agreement. No one really wanted extra work, Toreth knew, but no one wanted to be stuck in a second-rate section either.

"Actually, Tillotson's doing okay for once." Toreth looked at his watch. "I've got a meeting in half an hour with Liz Carey. Senior finance specialist in CF? CF wants to make it a joint investigation and I'm our half."

Belkin sat in silence for a moment while Toreth made a bet with himself about the senior's next comment. "I always have first refusal on the inter-sections," Belkin said. "And I've got free caseload. Why the hell did you get it?"

Toreth awarded himself an imaginary twenty euros, and smiled. "My name was on the request from CF."

"Yeah?" Belkin smirked. "Before or after Tillotson put a word in for the golden boy?"

"Tillotson had nothing to do with it." In fact, the section head hadn't sounded at all happy about the demand for Toreth's time. Probably expecting grief from

17

Belkin, which Toreth was delighted to encourage. "Liz Carey suggested me, apparently. Must just think I'm better than you."

That cleared the smile from Belkin's face. "Bloody data-crunching specialists. What the hell would she know about a real investigation? You're welcome to it, anyway. CF has had it for over a week, and they've made fuck-all progress from what I hear. If they're begging for help, it's probably a shite case and they're hoping to spread the blame when it dead-ends or blows up."

Very possibly true. "I'll handle it."

"That's what I've heard." Belkin leaned forward. "Narr, didn't you say you saw Tillotson coming out of his office with a smile on his face this morning?"

Always slow to spot a windup, Narr looked blank for a moment, the vacant stare emphasizing his normal resemblance to a not-overly-bright frog. Then he glanced at Toreth and nodded. "Yeah, that's right. Looked very happy. Like someone had just given him a really good...piece of news."

Toreth stood up. "Excuse me. If I could have everyone's attention for a moment." Conversations stilled and the occupants of the coffee room, mostly General Criminal staff, looked around. "I don't fuck Tillotson to get cases. Never have, and I don't intend to start now or ever in the future. Thanks. Carry on."

He sat down again. Chevril was choking on his coffee, turning purple while everyone ignored him. Mike Belkin grinned again, obviously delighted to get a rise. The rest of the seniors around the group of low chairs ranged between amused and bored. They'd all heard it before.

"Besides," Toreth added, "if I fucked anyone for cases, it'd be Jenny, not Tillotson." And the section head's admin wasn't interested—Toreth had tried.

Belkin picked up his mug and heaved himself to his feet. "Good luck with CF," he said as he walked off. "You'll need it."

"You know Finance Specialist Senior Investigator Liz Carey, of course."

While Phil Verstraeten talked, he kept his gaze fixed in the center of Toreth's chest. If he did the same thing with women, Toreth thought, he must collect a lot of knees to the groin. Probably why the man was so pale.

"And this is Senior Investigator Au-yong Heng." Verstraeten gestured towards the woman with only the briefest glance in her direction. She nodded to Toreth across the table, clearly used to Verstraeten's manner.

Liz Carey sprawled in her chair at the head of the small conference table. Tall and solid, she made the furniture look slightly undersized. She twirled a thick strand of her vivid red hair back and forth between her fingers, watching Verstraeten with vaguely predatory consideration. Toreth wondered why the hell she'd asked the junior specialist to carry out the introductions. Sadism, probably. While wondering, he missed the exact assignment of the names Verstraeten gave for the two junior investigators: Abel and Brown, appropriately enough. The pair were interchangeable anyway, solidly built men in their late twenties, with brown hair in personality-free short cuts, and matching vaguely bovine expressions.

When Verstraeten mumbled, "Junior Para-investigator Chris Doyle," Toreth took a better look. The man had caught his attention as soon as Toreth entered the room. Judging by his seated height, he was taller than Toreth by a good few centimeters, and his uniform fitted snugly across his shoulders. He sat staring down at his bitten nails—the only physical flaw Toreth could see—and his posture suggested he had somewhere better to be. Doyle provided something easy on the eye, anyway.

The straight-backed man next to Doyle wore a senior para's badge and a look of wary appraisal as he returned Toreth's inspection. Seated beside Doyle he looked slight, but that was only in comparison. If possible, Verstraeten pulled his chin even further in. "Senior Para-investigator Stefan Benz." Toreth had heard the name, but never worked with him before. "He's the senior in charge of the investigation."

Benz shook his head, causing his long black fringe to flop forward into his eyes. He flicked it back left-handed, the gesture clearly automatic but still affected. "The investigation is now joint between CF and GC."

Verstraeten reluctantly glanced up and around the group. "Of course. I meant that Senior Para Benz was initially assigned the case."

Sounded like Belkin had it pegged right, and this marked the beginning of an attempt to dump an investigation that wasn't moving.

"Run us through the case basics, Phil," Carey said, shooting a quelling glance in Benz's direction. Toreth would rather Carey had done the summary. She had a low, gravel-edged voice that tripped some primeval switch in his brain and connected his aural nerves straight to his groin. Might be worth taking a joint CF-GC case just for the chance to listen to her.

Verstraeten coughed, with considerably less erotic effect. He had expanded his hand screen, and the wall screen now blinked into life, showing a teenage girl. "The victim, Sofie Kenward," Verstraeten said, gaze now locked on the screen in his hand. "The kidnapping took place twenty-four days ago. Her father, Paul Kenward, works for New Travel Systems, which is where the ransom demand was delivered. Minor corporation, they didn't even have a proper threat assessment in place. Actually, we had a retrospective assessment done and found no significant predicted threat. The corporation is small and in deep financial trouble."

"So where does the fraud come in?" Toreth asked.

"Uh—" Verstraeten hesitated at the interruption, then pressed on. "A demand arrived for one million euros. NTS is signed up to the standard corporate blackmail, kidnapping, and extortion policies, but they played along to give Justice time to find the girl."

19

Something out of the ordinary there. "They didn't use their own security to look for her?"

"They couldn't afford it," Carey said. "They'd already cut back to the bare bones. About three months before the girl was taken they sacked the bulk of their corporate security." She paused, then added, "Carry on, Phil."

"So NTS was stalling, and Justice claims they had one or two leads. The kidnappers seemed happy to keep the negotiations going and extended the deadlines. Then, two weeks ago, while they were still talking, the girl was found."

"Alive?"

"Barely. She'd escaped, but badly injured. She survived, though. She's in hospital. They—" Verstraeten flicked a quick glance at Benz, then back down. "I mean we, have interviewed her. No solid leads."

Sounded messy, but not obviously financial. "So how *does* that make it fraud?" Toreth asked.

Finally Verstraeten looked up. "Paul Kenward was important at NTS—not a director, not even exceptionally highly paid, but very highly skilled, and the key technical figure on their major project."

"The one that would save the corporation," Benz drawled.

"The one that would save the corporation." Forcing himself to look Toreth in the face rather than the torso, Verstraeten had developed a rapid blink. "So NTS bought key-personnel insurance on him. An unusually large amount, but the insurers assessed his value and agreed it. Since his daughter was kidnapped, he's been unable to work. Medically, the insurers can't argue with it; their own experts agree he's mentally unfit. So they've been forced to pay out on the policy, and are likely to have to keep paying continued support for some time. But even the initial cash injection proved significant. Our assessment is the corporation may pull through now."

Toreth looked at Liz Carey. "That was it? That was enough for Corporate Fraud to take the case?"

She shrugged. "The insurers have been happy to cooperate with us."

Which probably meant they'd shopped their own client to the Investigation and Interrogation Division, via some backdoor route. He turned his attention to Benz. "That's what you think? A fake kidnap gone wrong? Or that someone at NTS had the girl abducted to tip her father over the edge and bilk the insurers?"

Benz shook his head, following up with the fussy hair-flick. "There just isn't enough evidence. We had a tip-off with some persuasive allegations, but unfortunately we've been unable to substantiate any of them. So with the recovery of the girl, we've decided to open the case up."

"Not transfer it? Joint cases are a pain in the arse for everyone. Why not let us take the lot? Or send it back to Justice, if the tip-off washed out."

Liz Carey straightened up in her chair. "It could still be fraud."

Oddly, Toreth got the distinct impression that she didn't believe that. Benz certainly didn't; he shook his head again, and Toreth found himself watching the man's left hand, waiting for it to go up. Flick. However, Benz seemed to be disagreeing with Toreth, not Carey. "The CF head of section would like to keep an interest in the investigation. Of course, if you want to ask your head of section to request a full transfer, that's up to you."

Toreth had expected an eager agreement to dump the case. Glancing around, he found Carey and Verstraeten both watching him. Whatever she and Benz were deadlocked on, Toreth caught a strong whiff of something unpleasant kept out of sight. He gave them his most noncommittal shrug. "I'll take a look at the case, see what I think. What about Justice?"

"They've ceded all interest in the case; without a fight, for once." Benz turned to Carey. "Why not tell him your alternative theory, Specialist?"

The question held a definite edge of sarcasm, and Carey's lips thinned. "A similar case happened fifteen years ago. Very similar. The kidnappers took a young girl, demanded one million euros in a drawn-out negotiation, and the victim was mutilated ten days after she was taken, exactly like Sofie Kenward—her right hand cut off, and a recording sent to her family. The major difference is that in the earlier case the victim didn't escape."

"Killed by the kidnappers?" Toreth guessed. The description had triggered a vague tickle of recognition deep in his brain.

Verstraeten nodded. "Dismembered. The postmortem suggested that it was probably done—that she was still alive when it happened. The pattern of the non-severing injuries to the limbs was consistent with her moving while—" Verstraeten cleared his throat again and, out of the corner of his eye, Toreth saw Benz smile. "It was never solved."

"We don't have any direct evidence that the same people are behind it, but I think it's a coincidence worth looking at," Carey said.

"Or just a copycat," Benz said. "It's common enough for corporate sabotage professionals to pick out old crimes and use the methods."

"It's been done, true," Toreth said, but Benz was still looking at Carey.

"And there are differences to the previous case, anyway," Benz added. "Our girl was raped. There's no mention of that in the other case."

"Which surely makes it less likely to be a copycat," Carey said, while Verstraeten nodded in silent support of his boss.

Toreth didn't want to grow old listening to CF bickering among themselves. "Did you reopen the first case?"

Benz shook his head firmly. "The dead girl's name was Louise Ann Selman, and her father is very much against the reactivation of the investigation." In a variation on the theme, he smoothed back his fringe without a flick. "So far we have no reason not to honor the request."

21

Ah. The nagging familiarity abruptly resolved. "Let me just check, here. We are talking about *the* Selmans, aren't we? Selman-Sterntech?"

"That's right," Carey said. "Her father is Joseph Selman."

A man who probably possessed more euros than the Central Bank, and kept a sharp claw in every departmental pie. Even worse, while Joseph Selman's mother, Theodora, had stepped down from actively running her vast corporation, she filled a corporate seat on the Council of the European Administration. If any member of the Selman family was very much against something, then the odds of it happening were low to nonexistent.

"So what do you want me to do?" Toreth asked.

"Find out who kidnapped Sofie Kenward," Benz said. "If they also make a confession to the murder of Louise Selman, then of course everyone would be delighted, including her father, I'm sure. But don't upset him in the process. That's not a suggestion from me. It's from the head of section and way up beyond that. Remember which case you're looking at, and that any connection to other cases is pure speculation." Benz stood, and the silent Heng stood with him. "I'm afraid I have to go," he said. "Your section head said you had a full caseload, so Doyle, Abel, and Brown are assigned to you for the investigation. Enjoy them; we're paying, for now."

When Benz had gone, Toreth asked, "Are you three from Benz's permanent team?"

"No, Para," Doyle said. "Heng is, but we're all from the pool." Abel and Brown nodded in dumb confirmation.

Carey smiled sourly. "Benz wants this as far away from him as possible, so long as he can keep an eye on me. There's an old, ugly rumor that Louise Selman wasn't a kidnapping at all. The family didn't contact Justice until it was all over and they found the body. There're rumors about the authenticity of the negotiation records, too, but it was all supposed to have been hushed up. I've heard it put down to a boyfriend, or a family vendetta, or even old man Selman in person, but anyway, not corporate sabs."

Toreth sighed. "Liz, I thought we were friends."

She raised an eyebrow. "That's why I asked for you."

"So you could get me on the shitlist of some insanely powerful, potentially axe-murdering corporate who could have us all assigned to I&I Reykjavik by snapping his fucking fingers? What do I have to do to you for a promotion to enemy?"

Verstraeten made an odd noise, something between a croak and a snort that took Toreth a moment to identify as laughter.

Carey shook her head. "I don't think Selman killed his daughter. It's just one of those departmental rumors that came over from Justice with the old guard. But someone nearly killed Sofie Kenward, and if Benz gets his way, the case'll never go anywhere because he's too paranoid about Selman."

Thereby suggesting that the man had been promoted to senior for a solid reason. "But if there's no fraud, then it's not a CF case anyway. So why do you care?"

Carey stared at him. "Why do I *care*? Other than that someone took an axe to two innocent young women?"

"Unlucky for them, but I don't think that's any reason to sink my career down the recycling."

"You've never been scared of corporates before, Toreth."

Cheap, obvious manipulation. But Toreth being perfectly well aware of that did nothing to remove the pool witnesses from the room. Some rumors he couldn't live with. "I didn't say I was scared. I'm saying that I won't screw up my career for it, and that you'll owe me a hell of a big favor if you want me to do anything other than follow orders and leave Selman well alone."

Carey didn't say anything. Toreth contemplated the girl's picture on the wall. A plain-looking teenager, wearing her long light brown hair in an unfussy plait, smiling somewhat nervously at the camera during her last yearly medical. An absence of makeup made her eyes look small, and she lacked the arrogance Toreth expected to see in privileged corporate kids. Probably because she wasn't one. Her only value to the kidnappers lay in her father's technical importance at NTS. On its own, the case wasn't too bad. No big corporate players were directly involved, so any arrests he could make would probably stick, and if it all came to nothing there would be no one important to kick up a fuss. As long as he kept Carey in hand and away from Selman—a job that probably required a team all by itself—he should be able to score some points.

"Will you do it?" Carey asked.

He blinked, pretending surprise. "Of course. I get assigned a case, I take it."

"Good, because I can't run this alone. I'm a finance specialist. Benz handled the kidnapping part of the case, but after I raised the Selman connection he backed off so fast I thought he'd fall over." She lowered her voice a little, appealing in more ways that one. "That's why I need you."

He wondered idly what chance he had of hearing "I need you" in a different context. "You should've kept quiet about Selman. Is that why Benz wants to offload the case?"

"He doesn't. He wanted to bury it. I had a word with Chean, and he had a word with Vaughn and persuaded her to open the investigation up to include General Criminal."

The news dampened Toreth's brief optimism. Chean was Carey's boss, head of the financial investigation specialists. Vaughn was the Corporate Fraud head of section. Tillotson would no doubt also be jockeying for influence over the case. That put the whole investigation in the middle of a mess of inter-section politics, even before Joseph Selman stuck his influential axe in. Toreth turned to the others. "I presume there's some kind of active Investigation-in-Progress?"

"Yes, Para," one of the investigators said.

"Senior Para Benz is very strict with his IIPs," the other added.

"Well, good for him. Right. You three go away and carry on doing whatever the IIP says you're doing, while I get to grips with the files. Then we'll have another conference at eleven tomorrow morning and work out how to run this thing." Belatedly, he remembered to turn to Carey for confirmation. However, she nodded amicably and the junior para and investigators filed out. After the door closed, those left behind sat in silence for a while. Finally Toreth said, "Which one was Brown?"

Carey frowned. "The one on the right."

"The left," Verstraeten muttered.

Toreth sighed and stood up. "Send me the files."

"How did it go?" Sara asked as Toreth approached. He pointed to his office, and she followed him in. "Well?" she asked again as he sat down, curiosity plain on her face.

"Liz Carey hates me, and she's hatched an elaborate plan that probably ends with me being beaten to a pulp by corporate heavies in some back alley. I agreed to take her case because her voice turns me on. Of course, I'll have to fuck her in the dark, but it's a sacrifice I'm willing to make if she keeps talking."

Sara grinned. "Thinking with your dick?" She sat down and leaned forward over the desk. "Come on, cough. All I could get on the admin network was personal gossip about Investigator Carey, nothing about the case."

"Really? What gossip?"

"*Toreth.*"

Relenting, he ran through the assignment. To his surprise, by the end she looked impressed rather than horrified.

"So you mean you could end up cracking the Selman case?"

"Well . . ." That wasn't quite how he'd been looking at it.

"Wow. I mean, I don't go for all that True Crime crap, working here and everything, but it's famous. One of my exes must've had a dozen books about her." She frowned. "Along with a lot of other stuff that was frankly creepy and the whole reason I dumped him, not that we were ever *really* dating seriously anyway. He used to ask about work a lot. I mean, that's always a bad sign, isn't it?"

"Does this have anything at all to do with anything?" Toreth asked.

Sara, however, was happily caught up in reminiscing. "Thinking about it, he got himself in trouble over the Selman thing while I wasn't exactly dating him. Poor Cris. He's a bit of an idiot, really. He had an illegal copy of a documentary about Louise Selman which had been withdrawn from circulation."

"Let me guess—because Joseph Selman threatened to sue the bollocks off the production company and bankrupt them?"

Sara's expression fell a little. "Maybe. Do you think he'll make trouble for us?"

"According to Senior Para Benz, he already is. Should be okay, though, as long as we stick to the new kidnapping and don't dig too deep."

"But then you won't solve the Selman case, will you?"

"Sara, have you ever been to Iceland?"

She tilted her head. "No. Why?"

"Me neither, and I want to keep it that way. This is a favor for Liz Carey, not some bullshit action film where the hero takes on the corrupt corporation and wins." He'd had enough of that kind of truth-digging stupidity with Marian Tanit and Psychoprogramming. Still . . . cracking the Selman case. That would be something for his record.

Toreth pushed the thought to the back of his mind. "Okay. I promised Carey a case plan tomorrow, so we need to get cracking. Her theory is that it's the same people, so that's the first thing we try to rule out. Other cases—I want files for any corporate kidnapping that fits the profile, and any corporate kids found dead and hacked up, too, just in case the kidnapping itself never made it onto the systems."

Sara nodded, looking more eager to start trawling for files than he'd ever seen her. "Is this a priority?"

"Not for you," Toreth said. "But there's a pool junior and two investigators who are probably sitting about in a coffee room somewhere, picking their noses. Haul them in if you need help. I'll take Mistry along to check out the victim. I need to know if I can trust her statements, because by the sound of it, she's all the evidence we have right now."

Sofie Kenward sat in the hospital bed, looking much as she had in her security file pictures, except that her right arm ended abruptly halfway down her forearm. A protective plastic sheath capped the stump. She was watching something on a screen, but before they got far enough into the room for Toreth to see what it was, Sofie said, "Screen off."

Toreth went over to the bed. "Good morning. My name is Para-investigator Val Toreth. This is Investigator Mistry."

Toreth fought the reflex to offer his right hand; beside him, he saw Mistry make a small aborted gesture that suggested she'd had the same impulse. Sofie seemed to be watching their hands, too. Then she looked up and smiled, holding out her left hand to shake instead. "Hi. From I&I? Please sit down." She sounded surprisingly cheerful for someone who'd been abducted, assaulted, mutilated, and repeatedly interviewed.

In fourteen days the deep cuts on her face had healed to thin lines only visible now that they were closer. Clear sealant covered them in stripes, more obvious than the cuts themselves. With adequate treatment the wounds wouldn't even scar, and the Union General Infirmary seemed a competent enough medium-range corporate operation. Nothing near the same standard as covered by SimTech's insurance, though.

"How are you feeling?" Toreth asked as he and Mistry pulled chairs closer to the bed.

"Armless?" She shook her head. "Sorry. I don't have much entertainment here. I feel...pretty much like you'd expect me to feel. I'm trying not to think about it. Any of it. Sometimes it hurts and they give me some more tablets. And I have some nightmares, but they give me tablets for that as well. I can't—" She stopped abruptly, then took a slow, deep breath, in through her nose, out through her mouth. "God, I really wish I could go home."

Although maybe she was safer here. A hospital security guard on the door had checked Toreth and Mistry's IDs with professional care. Toreth wondered what Verstraeten's threat assessment said now.

"How long do you have to stay in?" Mistry asked.

"They're growing me a new hand." She lifted her arm. "It takes a while because hands are so complicated, and they have to keep the graft area receptive until then. They should be ready to stick it on in a couple of weeks. Then a few more weeks for all the nerves and things to start working properly." She shifted in the bed. "I smashed my ankles when I fell. They say those might need grafts, too, if the treatments don't work."

"Who's paying for it all?" Toreth asked.

She frowned. "It's on Dad's corporate health plan, as far as I know. Did you want to ask me about anything in particular?"

Mistry started to speak, but for once Toreth cut her off. "We're increasing the size of the investigation team. I'm the new senior para-investigator in charge of the case. All I really wanted to do was meet you and ask if you have anything you'd like to say to me. 'Piss off and leave me alone' is perfectly okay."

Shock widened her eyes, then Sofie smiled. "No, really, I'm okay to talk. But I can't think of anything that I haven't said already to Senior Para-investigator Benz. Or to...I'm sorry, I've forgotten her name. The woman with the red hair and the lovely voice."

"Specialist Investigator Carey. If you do feel up to talking, I have a couple of points I'd like to check."

"Yes." Sofie took a deep breath. "Okay. Ask anything you want."

Arriving at the hospital, Toreth hadn't known how many questions he'd get. So, reluctantly, he'd lined up first the one to which Liz Carey would want to know the answer.

Mistry leaned forward, taking care not to obscure the camera she'd set up on the table beside the bed. "Do you recall anything, at any point, which might suggest he'd done the same kind of thing before?"

Sofie looked surprised. "Do you think he had?"

"It's always possible, with a corporate kidnapping like this. Might he have said something, perhaps?" Mistry prompted gently.

"No. But like I told the others, he almost never talked to me. Just to give orders, sometimes. I tried to talk to him, but—" She shrugged, the gesture oddly lopsided. "He never answered. If he spoke, he spoke first. He told me right at the start that my life wasn't worth anything except what he was asking for it. Until someone paid him, every breath was on credit." She turned her head away. Toreth could just see the corner of her eye, as she blinked rapidly.

"Is there anything you remember about him that you didn't tell Para-investigator Benz?" Mistry asked. "Anything at all. It doesn't have to be a specific fact, just an impression, or a feeling."

This time, Sofie stared down into her lap, twisting the bedspread between the fingers of her left hand. "He was...distant," she said at last. "He didn't touch me unless he had to. When he—" She glanced up at Toreth. "Did you see the recording he sent to my family?"

Toreth shook his head. "I haven't read the whole case file yet. I wanted to talk to you first."

"Without your words being filtered through a lot of other people's interpretations of the facts," Mistry added.

"Oh!" She smiled. "Thanks. Sometimes—well, I guessed that there must be more than just me in the case. Corporate things. I heard my dad tell someone that I&I wouldn't be here otherwise."

"I promise, you're what matters to us," Mistry said with absolute sincerity. "You were saying something that sounded very interesting?"

"Was I? Oh, yes, right." She looked down again. "Near the beginning, he made a recording of me, to show I was still alive, I think. He gave me something to drink, with a drug it in, so I couldn't move. And then he raped me. Not with—not him. I didn't know what it was then, just how much it hurt. But when he did it...it was just like when he fed me, or cleaned me up. Like he was just doing it because it needed doing." Her breath caught in a sob, and then she had her control back, breathing slowly, still looking down.

Toreth considered the account, then tapped his comm and subvocalized a new question to Mistry. The investigator nodded, and held up a finger. One minute first. "Do you want to stop?" Mistry asked.

"No." Sofie raised her head. "Just—ask me now. I'd rather get it over with."

"Did he tell you he was recording what he was doing?" Mistry asked with a glance at Toreth.

27

"No. I didn't know until I woke up here. And everyone knew what had happened, and I had no idea how, until Dad told me." Her voice softened, distant. "He was recording himself cutting off my hand, too, I think. They would've had to watch that, too."

"How did you get away?" Mistry asked. Toreth had wanted to hear Sofie describe her escape, as the explanation in the case report summary he'd glanced at in the car over seemed so incredible.

"After he drugged me the first time—" She swallowed, then before Mistry could say anything, she added, "I'm all right. I was so scared he was going to do it again, you see. And then when he gave me the drink, I remembered the taste. So I faked it. Or I tried. Just lying there, limp, not moving when he pinched me. Then he untied me, and put me on the floor, and stretched my arm out. And then..."

When she stopped, Mistry opened her mouth, but Toreth shook his head. No prompting.

"The axe broke as it hit the floorboards," Sofie continued. "I couldn't—I could hardly feel anything. I didn't think I could move any more, I thought it had been too long. But I heard the axe head clatter off across the floor. And then he turned away after it. I suppose he was sure I couldn't do anything, so it was safe to leave me. But somehow I managed to get up, and I pushed the blindfold off and I just— I threw myself at the window."

"Did you know where in the city you were?" Mistry asked.

"No. I didn't even know how far down it was. But I decided it was better than staying put." She smiled, tears in her eyes, but the comment sounded well-worn probably because she'd repeated the story multiple times, to investigators, doctors, family, and counselors. Even without any kind of neural scanner in the room, he'd bet a month's salary that she was telling the truth.

"You're very brave," Mistry said. "Thank you; I know this must be hard to talk about."

Not so much brave as incredibly lucky, Toreth thought, watching Mistry run through her sympathetic, soothing routine, getting the girl ready to talk some more. A breaking weapon, followed by a one-story fall. And the axe wound and lacerations from the glass would still have killed her in minutes, if she hadn't fallen almost under the wheels of a car carrying a medic with trauma training. Coincidences sometimes were what made the difference between a useful witness and a far less useful autopsy.

As they left the room, Toreth almost bumped into two men standing right outside. One had his head bowed, and the other—taller, younger, and with blond hair tied back in a short ponytail—stood in front of him, hands on his shoulders as he talked.

"—go in there now that you've come this far. She wants to see you."

"I can't." The older man took a deep, shuddering breath, then repeated, "No, I can't. Please don't tell her I'm here."

"All right. Sit there and wait for me, then." He gave his companion a gentle push towards the chairs across the corridor. Only then did he turn to look at Toreth and Mistry. "Hello." His gaze flicked from them to the door behind. "Have you been interviewing Sofie?"

"Briefly, yes," Mistry said.

"I told the hospital I didn't want anyone talking to her without me present."

"She's above legal age," Toreth said mildly. "And the medic said she was fit to answer questions."

His mouth thinned, but he let the question drop. "You're not the para-investigator we spoke to before."

"No. Senior Para-investigator Val Toreth. I'm taking over the running of the case. You are?"

"Pieter Ryersen. I'm one of Sofie's fathers."

He had more of the air of a lawyer than a parent, but Toreth knew from experience that people reacted to stress in different ways. "I understand your concern, Mr. Ryersen, but you must understand that we need to keep the investigation moving."

"Of course." He smiled tightly. "If you'll excuse me, I'm here to see my daughter."

Toreth took a slight step back, between Ryersen and the door. "Just one thing, if you don't mind. I know Justice was running the negotiation, but were you aware of any independent approaches made to the kidnappers? Real or fake. I know the corporate accords—"

"Accords?" Ryersen snorted. "If there'd been any way to lay my hands on the money I would've taken it to them myself. I would've done anything to get her back. *Anything*. Fuck the corporate accords."

The vehemence silenced Toreth for a moment. Pieter Ryersen looked like the kind of respectable midlevel corporate who would never dream of swearing freely in front of Administration officials, but he certainly didn't follow the standard corporate line.

"But no," Ryersen added after a moment. "We had to let Justice handle everything, unfortunately. Was that all?"

Holding him to answer one question underlined Toreth's authority; more would piss Ryersen off needlessly. "That's fine, Mr. Ryersen. We'll be in touch."

"Okay." He walked past Toreth, then stopped with his hand on the door. After a few seconds he turned around again. "I'm sorry, Para-investigator. I hate having to rely on strangers, especially with something this important. If you want a new statement, I'm happy to give one. Or anything else, if it will help catch these people."

29

"Thank you."

The door swung closed behind him, giving them a brief snatch of Sofie's cheerful greeting. That left Toreth contemplating his other witness. The man he presumed to be Paul Kenward sat, his head in his hands, apparently oblivious to the whole conversation between Toreth and his partner. "Mr. Kenward?" Toreth asked.

He looked up sharply, and when he saw Toreth he flinched. "Para-investigator?" He sounded as though he hoped the uniform might be a mistake.

Toreth stepped back, and Mistry moved smoothly forward and sat down. "Mr. Kenward, we're very sorry about what's happened to your family. I promise we're doing everything we can at I&I to catch the people responsible."

While Mistry explained the increased case resources, and introduced the two of them, Toreth examined Kenward. If nothing else, he could believe an insurance company paying out vast sums on a psych assessment. Where Ryersen had been smartly dressed in classic corporate business casual, Kenward wore a mismatched assortment of rumpled clothes. Pale, hollow-eyed, and hunched over in his seat, he had the air of stupefied confusion that went with long-term sleep deprivation. The last time he'd seen anyone look so bad, Toreth had been working down in the interrogation levels helping out a team running an experimental level seven protocol.

"Is there anything you'd like to tell us?" Mistry finished. "Anything we can tell you?"

After a moment he said, "Have you seen her?"

"Sofie? Yes, just now. She was very brave, Mr. Kenward. She's a remarkable girl."

He shuddered. "They told me what happened."

Mistry put her hand on his arm. "But you don't want to go in? I'm sure she'd like to see you."

"I can't. What they did to her..." Kenward shuddered. "I can't even think about it. I'll never forgive myself. Never. Even if she can. All I can do..." He shuddered again. "Pieter thinks I'm weak. He doesn't say it, but I can see it in his face. He doesn't understand that this is my fault. They took her to get at me."

"Corporate sabotage is always a risk," Mistry said.

Kenward shook his head.

"Is there anything you can tell us about—"

To Toreth's surprise, Kenward cut her off. "No, I'm sorry. NTS. They said everything has to go through them."

How hard had the corporate lawyers drilled that into him to produce such a quick response? "We might need both of you to come in and talk to us again," Toreth said.

"No. I gave—I gave statements, to Justice and to the other para-investigator. I already told them everything I can remember." Kenward hesitated, then added, "Pieter. He can tell you it all again, if he wants. I don't—I can't talk about it."

30

Another time, with someone else, Toreth might've reacted to the flat refusal. Instead he signaled to Mistry that it was time to go. Interrogating Paul Kenward would be a waste of a damage waiver. The man was already as broken by events as any prisoner Toreth had worked on.

In the car on the way back to I&I, Toreth tried to call Sara. Irritatingly, she'd turned off her comm. When he checked his watch he realized she must be at lunch. He left a message instead, asking for security files on both of Sofie's fathers, and for fuck's sake not to miss anything. Since the SimTech case, paranoia about doctored security files had dogged every investigation. The (theoretically complete) files Toreth had access to told him that Pieter Ryersen had indeed been a corporate lawyer, proving his sixth sense for slime still worked. Ryersen had given it up, though, to take a much lower-paid job with a charity to help homeless indigents. How nice and wholesome. Maybe it was penance. He called Sara again, and added a check into the corporations Ryersen had worked for to the list of requests.

"He raped her with the axe handle," Mistry said suddenly. She'd been reading the case file as the car drove.

"Yeah, I saw." Toreth tapped his comm and closed the connection to I&I. "Colorful. I bet copies of that one'll be all over the building before too long."

Mistry shrugged, disapproving but resigned by experience. "Probably, Para."

"Interesting thing to do, though, don't you think? The object rape. In a corporate kidnapping."

"Yes, Para." She sounded surprised. "The system flags it up."

Toreth grinned at her. "I have done this before, you know. And most corporate kidnapping is kid-gloves stuff. This looks more like a vendetta, but maybe they wanted to chivvy along whoever was supposed to cough up the goods. Didn't work, though, if they took her hand off later, too."

Toreth made a note to ask Sara about payment statistics and specific acts against victims. Getting hold of the information usually proved damned hard, that was the problem. Frequently the kidnappers demanded intangibles: information, influence, or the application of subtle sabotage. Corporations which paid up in any way broke the strict rules laid down in the corporate accords. Payments only ever came to light when made by private individuals not bound by them, or when things went wrong and those capitulating were caught. Knowledge that a kidnapping had even happened often never made it outside a corporate security division.

Everyone was too afraid of breaking the accords. Or at least, most people were. Someone as powerful and impeccably connected as Joseph Selman might be able to get away with flouting the rules once or twice, provided that he didn't do it in too public a manner. A minor corporate of, say, Warrick's level, even with important friends, would be in real trouble. Self-regulation could be brutal.

The Confederation of European Corporations had written the corporate accords, the body of civil law that largely defined how corporations operated and behaved. The Administration reserved some areas for itself—regulation of taxation, laws about defrauding the Administration, a superficial skim of laws designed to protect the public—but for the most part, the large corporations set the rules that governed them. Toreth had always thought it was a nice system if you could afford to get away with it, and the corporations could.

"He definitely sounds like a sabotage pro, Para," Mistry said. "What Sofie Kenward said, about him being detached. And that means he was probably following instructions about the specifics."

"Copying the Selman case, like Benz suggested?" Toreth considered the idea. "It's still going to piss people off. Why not pick a less messy case? And why add in the rape?"

"So someone with a grudge?" Mistry offered. "Maybe there is a vendetta in progress, and Corporate Fraud just doesn't know."

"If Liz Carey couldn't find it, it doesn't exist. Still, it could be personal. The money isn't the point, killing the girl is. But then why not just kidnap her, rape her, and dump her in pieces in some contaminated marsh in the old city? That's where they usually end up. Why take all the risk of keeping her alive and sending out the demand? No, that just pushes it back towards CF's theory that it's an insurance job. Trying to make it look realistic."

"Maybe, Para." Mistry closed her screen. "In that case, I think it looked pretty realistic to her."

Toreth spent the rest of the day reading the Corporate Fraud IIP and the steady stream of files Sara sent his way. One file he didn't receive from either source was the original Selman investigation. When he tried to fetch it himself, it came up as restricted. Irritated, Toreth called Verstraeten.

"Are you absolutely sure, Para?" the investigator asked, surprised into unusual boldness.

"Of course I am. Check it yourself if you don't believe me."

Verstraeten ducked his head. "Sorry, Para. If you could just wait..." Toreth tapped the edge of the desk, whistling between his teeth, until Verstraeten reappeared. "I don't understand it, Para. We had access to the file before. L—Investigator Carey is in a meeting with the section head at the moment, but I'll talk to her about it as soon as she gets back."

Between kidnap files, Toreth checked progress on his other ongoing cases and put in as much future planning on them as possible. Barret-Connor, recently promoted to senior investigator, and the rest of Toreth's regular team seemed to be coping, but having wangled his assignment Liz Carey would probably stake a major claim on Toreth's time.

On his way out of the building with Sara at the end of the day, Toreth caught a glimpse of ginger hair out of the corner of his eye. "Incoming weasel!" Sara whispered, then ducked into the lift, leaving him behind.

"A quick word in my office, please, Senior?" Tillotson called before he could follow.

They hadn't spoken much since the end of the SimTech case. Toreth didn't entertain for a moment the idea that Tillotson felt guilty about the fuckup. More likely, he didn't enjoy the reminder that Toreth had associates powerful enough to make Psychoprogramming back down.

Tillotson didn't offer him a seat. He didn't even sit down himself, just stood by his desk with his arms folded. "Head of Section Vaughn tells me that one of the specialist investigators is trying to broaden the scope of the case." He waited until Toreth nodded. "Carey doesn't have the experience of working this kind of investigation. She might be an excellent finance specialist, but she's still just a data analyst. Vaughn granted the request to bring you onto the team, but she doesn't want her investigators getting themselves into any corporate trouble." His voice suggested that Toreth would be his absolute last choice for stopping trouble of any kind.

"I see." *Fuck you, and your spineless arse-covering.* "I'll do my best to see that she keeps focused on the case in hand, sir."

Tillotson looked at him sharply. "And you do the same. No reopening of old cases without my explicit authorization. And I can tell you now that the Selman files in particular won't be released."

"Thanks for making it clear. Is there anything else I ought to know about this case, sir? Anything particular I should watch out for?" *Any reason someone in it might want me dead? Colleagues fitting me up for a mindfuck and execution?* Toreth held Tillotson's gaze, until the section head looked away.

"No. Just don't upset Selman, or anyone else with that kind of corporate status. No one likes kidnappings; they can be very tricky. I understand this is a small corporation, without much in the way of a security division?"

"That's right. They went straight to Justice the moment the target was taken. No influence to speak of."

"Good. That should keep things simple. You went to meet this Kenward girl today?"

Had Tillotson read the IIP already? Toreth had submitted the file only half an hour ago. "Yes. She seems like a good, reliable witness, which is a pity since they were careful not to let her come in contact with much in the way of evidence."

"She's getting a lot of attention in the news, so I've been informed. Sympathetic, of course." Tillotson sniffed. "I should've said 'no one likes a kidnapping, except the media when it happens to someone young and pretty.'"

"Are they making the Selman connection, too?" Toreth asked innocently.

Tillotson's nose twitched. "There is no Selman connection. Just don't forget that all contact with the media will be handled by the appropriate section, as usual. If you want any statements made, pass them on."

"Of course."

"By the book, Toreth. Everything strictly by the book."

Toreth resisted the urge to ask "which edition?" "Yes, sir."

Sara had waited for him downstairs, and they went to her flat together. Toreth wanted to talk the case over somewhere away from I&I. Besides, it was her turn to buy dinner. They stopped off for a takeaway, where Toreth watched with amusement as Sara flirted for free extras. He enjoyed the show; he'd never bothered to tell her that his uniform probably had at least as much effect.

"What did you think of the junior and the investigators?" he asked as they went up in the lift in her building.

"A&B are useless, but they're on someone else's budget, so I suppose they fill a couple of chairs. Doyle was nice."

"Nice as in you want to fuck him, or nice as in he can actually do his job?"

Sara glared at him. "Toreth."

"Sorry, sorry. Not at work."

"And *never* with paras."

Which made her a liar on two counts. *If* she remembered their one drunken night. If Mindfuck hadn't tried to kill him recently, maybe he could've talked Ange into squeezing her in for a session to find out if alcohol had really dissolved the memory or not.

"Well?" he asked.

"He's decorative," Sara admitted with a smile, the skin around her dark almond eyes crinkling. "But, yeah. He seemed competent. When I told him you'd said I could rope them in to help, he didn't argue. And he knows how to run searches, I'll give him that. In fact, he found most of the files I sent you. I was busy checking arrest warrants for B-C."

"Huh." Competent rated as high praise from Sara, especially in less than a day. Perhaps she just felt grateful for the assistance. Five months after Belqola's ignominious departure, Toreth's team remained short of a permanent junior.

Their arrival at the flat's door interrupted the conversation. Sara handed him the bag of food as they went in, releasing a waft of Indian spices that reminded Toreth that he'd skipped lunch.

"There's stuff for us to read while we eat," Sara said as she brought plates through from the kitchen. "Here—I'll copy it to your screen."

He read the book list as it arrived. "*Too Beautiful to Live*? *Victim of Riches*? *Twenty-Two Days in Hell*? They sound fucking awful."

"Books on the Selman case."

Every sensationalized piece of crap produced, by the look of it. While Sara found them beer and portioned out the takeaway, Toreth scanned the openings of half a dozen books. By the time she'd finished, he'd reached a firm conclusion.

Toreth swapped the screen for a plate. "This is rubbish," he said through a mouthful of meat pathia.

"Really? They're usually pretty good. Maybe there's a new chef."

"The books. We'll never find anything in there."

"No?" Sara looked up from her plate. "Why not?"

"Because we're looking at the publishing survivors. Lawyers exterminated anything useful long before they saw daylight. I mean, listen to this." Balancing the plate on his knee, he flipped back to the opening screen of *Corporate Sabotage: Blood and Power.* "'After a year in which unfounded rumors of production problems had failed to halt the impressive growth of Sterntech, the abduction and tragic murder of the daughter of corporate genius Joseph Selman,' blah, blah, blah, bollocks. They've ripped out all the best stuff and qualified the rest to death. Where the hell did you find all this junk? Central records?"

"No. First thing after you told me to start finding files, I called the creepy guy I knew and borrowed it all from him. He was happy to help. Took me out for lunch, too."

"So that's where you were. I thought you said you were the one who dumped him?"

"Oh, that was years ago." She ripped off a length of chapati. "But I keep in touch with all my exes. Just in case any of them turn into multimillionaires."

"And has he?"

"No. Cris is still living with his parents. But he found a job at a production company, researching based-on-a-true-story crime dramas. Just been promoted to assistant producer."

Toreth snorted. "Talking about making a job out of a hobby." He paused. "Is that why he wanted to take you out? They're not looking at the NTS case, are they?"

Sara grinned, like she'd been waiting for him to get there. "Investigator Carey isn't the only one who can spot a pattern."

"Sara..."

"I didn't tell him anything. I just smiled and let him buy me real fresh sushi."

"If you show up as a source close to the investigation, and Selman picks up on it, Tillotson will give me grief until I retire. Or I leave for Iceland."

She waved her beer bottle across her chest. "Not a word. Cross my heart. Cris told me plenty, though."

"Such as?" Toreth prompted when she paused.

"Such as, the Kenward kidnapping isn't the only reason the Selman case is popular again. Someone's touting information around. Supposedly they know all about the original Louise Selman investigation—not the Justice one, the corporate investigation. This person wants to sell their story."

"I'd hate to be the lawyers writing that contract." Toreth dug out a forkful of curry. "But not as much as I'd hate to be the informant when Selman finds out. Who is it?"

"No one knows. They're being very cagey, and they want a *lot* of money, up front, and a guarantee of total anonymity." Sara shrugged. "If I was blabbing things I knew about Joseph Selman, I'd want the same."

Toreth nodded. In fact, selling out the personal secrets of someone like Selman verged on suicidal. "It sounds like a scam to me."

"Maybe. Apparently, all the media corporations are waiting for someone else to risk a serious offer. Cris has written six bid proposals, but the legal department hasn't let him offer one of them. So he's worried either Mr.-or-Ms. Anon will get cold feet, or some other corporation will take the plunge first. That's why he told me about it in the first place, even though it's supposed to be a huge secret." Sara paused to help herself to more food. This time Toreth just waited. She loved drama enough without encouraging her. Finally she sat back in the chair, fork poised over her plate, and looked at him. Toreth raised his eyebrow. "Oh, fine. He told me because he wanted me to help him find this source. He asked if I could trace comms for him. I told him no, of course."

"Good. This case has enough fucking trouble attached already." Toreth thought it over for a minute or two while he ate. "What's his name, again? Your ex."

"Crispin Cole."

A made-up media wanker name if Toreth had ever heard one. Or his parents had had a psychic moment when they named him. "Has he actually met this source? He really thinks there's something to it?"

"No, and yes. They exchanged messages and he says the details look good. That's why Cris is so excited. He went on and on about it—greatest scoop of his life, a chance to do some real factual investigation, and the lawyers are going to ruin it. But no, he wouldn't tell me what the details were."

And according to Tillotson's strict orders, Toreth shouldn't be trying to find out either.

"Set me up a meeting with him as soon as you can. With Cole. I think I'd like to have a word with him about his scoop."

36

Chapter Three

❖

Toreth held the case conference in a General Criminal meeting room. It didn't hurt, he thought, to make it clear which section was in charge of the case now. Carey had brought her shadow along with her; with Benz absent, Verstraeten looked positively relaxed. Doyle, early to the meeting, seemed more alert and interested than the day before.

Carey had left a message that morning suggesting that they swap in more *competent* investigator help. After some consideration, Toreth had admitted to himself that the suggestion had merit. The sooner they cleared the case away, the less trouble they could attract. He tapped Mistry to stay with him, and sent Abel and Brown to help (or hinder) Barret-Connor with the other cases.

"So how did you get mixed up in the kidnapping part of the investigation, Liz?" Toreth asked, while they waited for Sara and Mistry. "Not your usual line."

"No. Justice ran that at first—NTS doesn't have the clout to get I&I involved. Our investigation focused on finding evidence that someone in the corporation knew in advance that the key-personnel insurance would kick in. Then the girl turned up alive, and that's when I pushed Justice to hand it all over to us."

"Why?"

She shrugged. "I went along to the hospital the first time Benz interviewed her there. I just happened to be in his office when the call came through." She frowned, looking almost embarrassed. "It's—she's seventeen, Toreth. Her life's been ruined, and why? Some nasty corporate games she never asked to be involved in. I don't give a damn about corporates cutting each others' throats. Sabotage is a way of life for a good minority of them. But this..." She shook her head. "It's not just illegal, it's *wrong*. It makes me sick."

He'd always thought of Carey as tough. She certainly wasn't sentimental. But he knew from experience that the oddest things pushed people's buttons. Mutilated teenagers obviously hit hers. "Like I said, I'll do what I can," he said. "But I already have Tillotson breathing down my neck, demanding I don't piss off Selman."

A polite tap on the door announced Sara and Mistry's arrival. "Sorry I'm late, Para," Mistry said. "B-C wanted some information."

Toreth nodded. If it hadn't been important, Mistry wouldn't have done it. "Any joy with Tillotson?" he asked Sara.

"No. He said not to bother asking him again. The investigation is into the current kidnapping only. No access to the Selman files, not even for comparative analysis." Sara hesitated in the doorway. "Shall I stay?"

Toreth hid a smile. "Sure. Sit down. Keep your comm open, though, in case B-C needs you."

"Okay." Sara slipped into a seat.

"I don't suppose you kept copies of the files?" Toreth asked Carey.

"Unfortunately not." She looked sour. "I didn't guess they'd pull them like this."

Keeping him away from the old case files most effectively curtailed the risk of the investigation upsetting Selman. It was hard to do a comparative analysis with nothing to compare.

"Fine. So, from what you remember, what similarities did we have with the Selman case?"

"The points I told you before," Carey said. "Age, ransom, cutting off her hand."

"But I bet the system said none of that is a definitive perpetrator match. And that's all you have?"

Verstraeten nodded yes to both questions. "The file was very sparse anyway, Para. Not even a full autopsy, just a summary. Selman cooperated minimally with Justice beyond filing the report. Although it all happened before I&I was created, so it's possible we lost some of the evidence in the reorganization."

"And Selman never turned anyone over to Justice for any part in the kidnapping," Carey said.

That wasn't uncommon for corporate sabotage, if a corporation preferred to deal with things on its own, but more unusual with the death of a family member. "Could mean the identity of the kidnapper would embarrass the family." He nodded at Carey. "Back to your axe-wielding corporate theory."

Doyle spoke up. "I don't think we can discount a copycat, Para."

"There's one more thing," Carey said, sounding reluctant. "Something Benz didn't know about. Doesn't know about."

"Because you didn't put it in the IIP?" Toreth asked.

"Yes. Tell you the truth, I didn't trust him not to panic and try to close the investigation down. Why do you think he didn't want to let the case go completely? Arse-covering. He's got no fucking spine, Toreth. He's too paranoid about his own career to risk letting the investigation he started piss off someone like Selman."

Now he also guessed why she'd wanted him to get rid of Abel and Brown; if nothing else, they might just be capable of reporting back to Benz. They'd probably both forget half of what they heard, but maybe different halves. Beside Toreth, Sara and Mistry had politely blank expressions, as if they hadn't heard a word Carey had said against the other senior para. Verstraeten mirrored them. Toreth turned to look at Doyle. "Well? Are you going to keep your mouth shut?"

The direct challenge seemed to surprise him. "Me, Para? Of course. You're my senior now—I do what you say."

Toreth studied him. Pretty, yes, but also a smooth, unreadable, untrustworthy little bastard. Still, he had one excellent reason to believe the pool junior: Benz had a full regular team, and Toreth didn't.

"Good. Sara, when we're done here, open a team-only IIP for anything related to Selman. No one has access but us." Toreth turned back to Carey. "Well, Liz?"

"Kenward and Selman have a prior connection. Twenty-six years ago, Kenward joined a Sterntech subsidiary called Control Guidance Systems which—go on, take a guess—developed guidance and control systems, for road traffic. At that time Joseph Selman ran CGS alone, trying to impress his mother. Kenward worked there for seven years."

It hardly seemed worth all her precautions to keep it away from Benz. "That's pretty thin."

Her voice sharpened. "It's more of a connection than a lot of other people in the city have with Selman, and Kenward's the one with a 'copycat' kidnapping."

Some kind of a point, Toreth supposed. "We'll keep it in mind. Now," Toreth continued, before Carey could protest, "can we forget Louise Selman for ten minutes? I need to be able to put something in the official IIP for today that Tillotson can actually read." He paused until Carey nodded. "Let's assume it's a genuine sab attempt, not fraud. My first question is: how widely was it known that NTS was in big trouble? Because they seem like a poor choice to sting for a million euros."

Verstraeten cleared his throat. "Not widely, Para, but it's not hard to find out. In the past they were financially secure, but they lost some major Administration contracts in the last couple of years. Any professional sab team would turn that up while they were picking targets."

"Which points towards amateurs," Toreth said. "Fits with the excessive damage to the girl."

"Maybe that's a deliberate provocation to start a vendetta," Doyle suggested.

"Same objection as before," Toreth said. "NTS couldn't pay the rent on the office, still less afford a pro sab team to go to war. If someone kidnapped the girl so NTS could use the insurance money to pay for a vendetta...well, that's twisted, even by corporate standards."

Carey laughed. "Oh, Toreth, you have no idea. But in this case, I agree. The other option is that they planned to switch to a noncash payment demand when they'd softened NTS up. NTS does own some interesting proprietary technology. Rumor is they were already thinking about selling it, although they were damned if they did, damned if they didn't. The tech's all they have that's worth spit, but sell it and the corporation has nothing left."

"I see your point." And he appreciated Carey's effort to drop her pet theory. "But if they were going under anyway...?"

"People don't respond logically in that situation, Para," Verstraeten said, mouth tight with disapproval. "They hold on to any hope that things will get better, however unlikely, because the alternative is worse. By the time they're willing to face the truth it's usually too late anyway."

"Like it was for NTS, pretty much," Carey said. "For them this kidnapping was a miracle. Unfortunately for Sofie Kenward, they had more incentive not to pay than to pay."

"Something else any half-competent sab team would discover quickly, and then probably release the girl. And that takes us back to fraud again," Verstraeten added apologetically.

No one followed that comment up. Toreth noticed that Sara had a slightly abstracted expression, and when he watched more closely he caught her lips moving. Probably talking to Barret-Connor.

"The forensics report came in this morning, Para," Mistry said after a moment. "It's very short. Basically, they found nothing evidential in the building where Sofie Kenward was held. I'd say it's an impressive nothing, Para, since the kidnapper on the scene must've cleared out in a hurry."

She stopped, leaving the conclusion to him. "Which tells us that it's highly likely to be a pro sab team," Toreth said.

"Same with the messages sent for the negotiations, including the files," Carey said. "I've carried out a lot of comm analysis, and this was well done. If the kidnappers were in touch with anyone else, family or corporate, Justice never caught them."

"Well. Justice." Toreth spread his fingertips on the edge of the table and rocked the chair back a few centimeters. A stack of forensics would be better, but a lack of evidence told them something. "Hm. Back to fraud. Where would NTS find the money for corporate sabs? I assume you didn't find any suspicious payments linked to any of the NTS directors?"

"Nothing obvious, but I'm still looking." Carey glanced at Verstraeten, who shrugged slightly. "Yes. Phil's suggestion—it's possible NTS offered a premium rate for delayed payment, if they could find a team willing to work on that basis. We're watching the accounts. One cent goes walking somewhere it shouldn't, we'll nail them."

Toreth didn't doubt Carey's analysis of NTS's finances. Which left them with... what? Not much at all, and few new places they were allowed to look. Selman's security file—now that would make interesting reading. But Toreth had as much chance of seeing it as Crispin Cole had of getting his contracts past the lawyers, and for much the same reason. Not even Sara's hoard of codes would help. The old Selman investigation file also lay out of reach; Tillotson had made that perfectly clear. For a moment, Toreth wished he still had access to Warrick's facility with Data Division files.

He'd have to make do with a more oblique approach, instead. Oblique, and boring, and therefore not for him.

"Doyle, I hear you're good with searches. Do you like True Crime stories?"

"Para?" The man looked at him in confusion.

"Sara, pass all those books you showed me to Doyle for him to work on."

After a second Sara tapped her comm, and raised her eyebrows. "I thought you said they were useless?"

"Yes, I did, but a lot of useless is better than zero useful. I want to know what's public knowledge about the Selman case." He turned to Doyle. "Pull out every single supposed 'fact' in there, compared across the set for consistency and number of appearances. And date-filter everything. They're all bound to be fucking cribbing from one another, because they're too lazy to get real jobs. Find out when the facts appear, how they propagate. Complete evidentiary value analysis."

"How many books are there, Para?"

"I don't know—a couple of dozen? Throw in all the media reports you can find."

Doyle nodded, but despite the dissatisfaction plain on his face he managed to make his comment sound like an observation and not a complaint. "That's a lot of material, Para."

"I know. But I'm curious about where our supposed copycat kidnapper found his information to copy, and where any differences come from. And who knows, maybe you'll find some diamonds buried in all that shit." While the rest of them kept chipping away at the Kenward case proper until someone hit a vein of useful information. "Okay. Unless anyone else has anything earth-shattering, let's get to work."

On the way back to his office, Sara fell in step beside him. "Cris called during the meeting. He's keen to see you. He says, how about tonight?"

"Did you tell him yes?"

"Well, it's Friday, so I didn't know whether..."

Oh, hell. Friday meant Warrick. For a moment, Toreth considered canceling their session. But having missed out the week before due to the accident with the chair, he found himself looking forward to the evening. Especially since he had a bet to collect. "Find me a bar I can meet Cole at on the way." At least he could charge some drinks to informant expenses. "I'm heading for Greenwich Towers," he added casually.

"Don't be—seriously? You're eating there? Not Meridian?" When he nodded, Sara sucked her breath in with an exaggerated whistle of surprise. "Hey, if you've started taking bribes, I want a cut."

Toreth grinned. "I'm not paying. I'll let you know what the view's like."

Nothing about the man seemed obviously creepy. A little shorter than Toreth, and a lot thinner, he wore his long medium brown hair held back in a ponytail by a silver clip. Sara's description of him as 'living with his parents' had led Toreth to expect someone obviously prolonging his adolescence—scruffy, maybe, or wearing too-young clothes. Cole wore casual clothes, certainly, but the kind of casual that came from careful shopping and an effort to coordinate. That made sense. If he'd attracted Sara's attention without a large bank account then he must have reached her minimum standards of attractiveness.

"Mr. Cole?" Toreth asked.

A slightly too strong wash of spicy scent made itself known over the bar smells as Cole turned and, after a brief inspection of Toreth, stepped forward and offered his hand. "You're Sara's boss?" His handshake started off firm, but clung on rather too long.

"Yeah, that's right. Senior Para-investigator Val Toreth."

Cole smiled. "A para-investigator. I don't think I've ever spoken to one before." Another touch of creepy broke through in the more lingering appraisal. "I've had a lot of requests for interviews turned down by the media relations people at I&I. But, hey, that's their job, right? I'm Crispin Cole. What should I call you? I've heard your people referred to as paras."

Your people. Exotic freaks from behind the Int-Sec wire fences. Toreth suppressed a smile. "Toreth will be fine. Sara said you were interested in a case we're looking at."

He looked around the bar. "Isn't she here? I thought—"

"Just me, I'm afraid."

"What do you have to tell me, then? Let me buy you a drink, and we can find a place to talk."

Cole picked a quiet side table, out of sight of most of the bar and out of earshot of nearby tables.

Toreth felt safe enough sipping his drink—he'd watched the bartender pour it, and taken it from his hand before Cole got anywhere near it. "It's not so much what I have to tell you," Toreth said.

"Oh? I was rather hoping that you might be able to help me. Something we could use in a documentary we're making about corporate kidnappings."

"Sorry, I can't do that." Belatedly, Toreth realized he was breaking Tillotson's injunction to avoid unofficial media contact, in fact if not in spirit. "I wanted to ask you a few questions."

"Perhaps a little reciprocal arrangement? Quid pro quo—something for something." Cole smiled. "Or nothing's for nothing, as my producer always says."

"I said, forget it."

Cole gave it one more try. "If it's a question of, ah, paying expenses..."

"No. I don't give out I&I information." Especially during this case.

"So why did you want to talk to me?" Now he looked genuinely confused, and Toreth wished he'd asked Sara exactly what she'd told the man to get him to the

42

meeting. Had she suggested Toreth might be able to run the comms trace he wanted?

"I heard that you had a new source on an old investigation," Toreth said.

Cole's expression closed down immediately. "I'm afraid *I* don't give out information about our contacts. And I should warn you that our legal department has had a lot of practice at fighting off forced disclosure orders."

Toreth considered asking what the legal department would think of Cole blabbing the existence of his secret source to Sara and asking for an illegal comms trace. Antagonizing him would be counterproductive, though. "Well, then," Toreth said. "I'd be interested in hearing any information this source has already passed on. No attribution needed."

"I didn't think that unsourced hearsay was validatable evidence?"

"No, but it might still be useful."

Cole shook his head, the tip of his ponytail flipping over his shoulder. "And by that you mean you could use it to work out the identity of the source and interrogate them?"

"Interrogate? Why? Unless what you know means you think they're a suspect?"

"No."

"Then there's no reason why we'd even want to, and no way we'd get a waiver if we did. We're only interested in the Kenward kidnapping. We're trying to eliminate copycat elements, that's all."

This time Cole didn't even answer, frank disbelief in his raised eyebrows. Time to change the line of attack. "I checked your company's production record. Half your output mentions us in one way or another. How about if I could arrange to give you some background flavor? A look round I&I, maybe?"

The poised disdain didn't waver. "You mean the citizenship class tour? I had one of those at school."

"There's plenty that goes on at I&I which isn't suitable for kids. If you'd like to look at some of that, I don't see why not. No cameras, obviously. No way I could get the security clearance. But if you'd like a personal guided tour, then that would be no problem at all."

Cole licked his lips. "The whole building?"

"Well, no." Toreth smiled, tweaking the possibility away and watching the tension tighten in Cole's shoulders. "It's a big place. But if there's something particular you want to see, I'll do my best."

Now Cole leaned forward unconsciously, like a bored husband hearing the call of no-strings cocksucking. "How about interrogations?"

"If you like."

"Really?" Cole closed his eyes for a moment, then leaned back in his chair, shoulders pushed back, faking composure and doing it passably well. "If I told you anything, it would have to be unsourced and unsourceable. Nothing that would even hint at identity."

"I understand."

"Okay. Give me the tour, and I'll see what I can do."

Collecting on his bet put Toreth in a generous mood. Meridian, at the summit of one of New London's tallest buildings, provided an unmatched view over the city improved by a spectacular sunset. While he ate, Toreth wondered who in the corporate world had suffered a bruise to their dignity by being bumped from this west-side table. Very few I&I employees earned enough to eat there, but Meridian still responded favorably to the I&I name; better, in fact, than some places which felt the pressure more often.

Warrick paid uncomplainingly, without even a flicker of reaction when the breathtakingly attractive waitress presented the bill. Maybe he'd enjoyed the excuse, and the expensive dinner had almost been up to the standard of the blowjob that followed.

Now Warrick knelt, naked, on the lush deep pile carpet of a Greenwich Towers bedroom, one arm still in the plastic cast and the other held obediently behind him, fingerprints branded red on his cheek. There'd be a bruise there tomorrow. Faint and quick-fading, but he'd be marked. Toreth knew this from experience. Not merely from the mounting weeks of games with Warrick, but from previous years of skillfully applied persuasion. Still dressed, Toreth stood over Warrick, rubbing his thumb over his fingertips. His hand tingled faintly from the blows to Warrick's face.

He wondered suddenly what Crispin Cole would think of this. Probably not enough blood and pain. And he wondered what Cole would think of a real interrogation, in the flesh, as it were. Most people, even interrogator junkies, found them hard to take, however much they got off on the fantasy. Might be worth showing him a high-level session, just out of curiosity.

"Can you snap your fingers?" Toreth asked.

"Yes." The surprise showed in Warrick's voice, but he didn't open his eyes, or question why Toreth might want to know.

"Good. Because we'll be playing a new game tonight. If you snap your fingers I'll look at your hand. If something's wrong, spread your fingers out straight. The more fingers, the more urgent it is. One or two, I'll tone it down. Five is stop dead. If you've changed your mind, or if I ever ask you if everything's okay and it is, show me a thumb and I'll carry on. Understand?"

"Yes. Thumb is carry on. A couple of fingers is back off. Five is stop. I understand."

Toreth fished the new toy out of a pocket before he took off his jacket and dropped it on a chair. The paper wrapper crinkled as Toreth opened it. A printed notice warned of the asphyxiation hazard and cautioned against use on unsupervised prisoners in the absence of an appropriate damage waiver. The grey plastic strap had a fastener and a central guard to hold a prisoner's teeth apart and stop them from biting themselves or anyone else. Single use, disposable and sterile. Not many workplaces offered such entertaining opportunities for stealing office supplies. He held the gag out, dangling it in front of Warrick's face. "Look," Toreth said.

Warrick's eyes opened, and Toreth concentrated on them, following his reaction there. A few seconds of blinking at the light, then he focused on the unexpectedly close object. A frown—what is it?—followed by understanding and a fascinating mixture of revulsion and excitement.

"It's from work," Toreth said, knowing that Warrick had guessed. "Theoretically they're for the safety of guards and prisoners when we're moving someone difficult. Actually, we have masks that are easier to fit and more effective. These are mostly useful for the humiliation value. Transforming interrogatees into objects. Have you ever read any depersonalization theory?"

Warrick looked up, expression suddenly cold. "I don't want to hear about it."

"I know. I met someone today, though, through a case. Now *he's* interested in interrogations. Real ones."

"Plastic duck." Every syllable distinct and bitten off.

"Okay, okay. But you don't want to hear about interrogations, you don't like the idea that they're happening at I&I, right now, and yet you're fucking a trained interrogator. Am I the only one here who thinks that's a bit strange?"

"If the situation bothers you, you are welcome to leave. I believe the terms of the bet have been fulfilled."

The arrogance, the effortless tone of command from someone in such a vulnerable position, made Toreth feel suddenly overdressed and impatient. "No, I don't think so. Just making an observation."

"Good." Warrick lowered his gaze, waiting, breathing slowly.

"And what about this?" Toreth moved the gag back into his line of sight. "Do you want it?" He'd expected hesitation, or at least a show of it. Warrick surprised him by simply nodding. "Even though you know where it's from?" A sharper nod. Toreth decided to abandon that line of questioning. "You have to ask for it. Tell me what you want."

"Please." Deep breath. "I want you to gag me."

Toreth dropped it on the floor and started unfastening his shirt buttons. "Fine. Then you can put it on."

This time there was a fractional delay, before Warrick reached out and picked up the gag.

45

Chapter Four

❖

Toreth detoured to the Corporate Fraud section on Monday morning for a friendly, cooperative, cross-section visit, hoping to be there early enough to miss Benz. Unfortunately, he found the senior already in his office, forcing Toreth to make an actual report on the case. Benz, however, seemed primarily intent on making sure the investigation steered well clear of Selman.

"You tried to access the old case files," Benz said.

"Of course I did. They're referenced in the IIP."

"I know. And not long after I opened them I had the word passed down from above to leave them the hell alone. I thought I made that clear?"

Cooperation was one thing; being told how to run his own investigation was something quite different. "You know, if you want a job working for Selman's security, you could just send him a fucking CV."

After that, the conversation went rapidly downhill. Corporate Fraud spent too much time trying to think like corporates, Toreth reflected as he walked back to his own office. Couldn't be good for anyone.

He found Doyle waiting for him outside his office, chatting to Sara. Braced by the argument with Benz, Toreth kept walking and waved Doyle right in, ignoring Sara's muted eye roll. Overeagerness in new juniors often irked her, especially if it interfered with her Monday-morning routine, but in this case she seemed more annoyed with Toreth for interrupting.

"Good news?" Toreth asked as he hung up his jacket.

"That depends, Para."

Toreth sat, and grabbed the insulated coffee mug that Sara had left on the desk for him. The unusual attentiveness must mean either she'd screwed something up (unlikely, because normally she'd confess right away), or that she was keen to keep him in a good enough mood to humor her delusions over solving the Selman kidnapping. When he'd almost burned his mouth on the first sip of coffee, he said, "Okay, find a chair, and let's hear it."

"It's about the books you gave me." Doyle swung a chair over and sat, snapping open his hand screen as he talked. "The evidence system spat a lot of content right back at me, and I don't blame it. Recycled speculation, random unconnected facts thrown in to fill up space, re-sourced interviews—by the later books, there's virtually nothing new added except totally unsubstantiated theories. Probably the only reason a few of the writers weren't sued is that they could plead insanity." Toreth smiled politely at the joke; juniors usually liked the encouragement. "But I did find something slightly interesting. The big standout difference between the two kidnappings, on the surface, is the rape. With the axe," Doyle added.

"Yeah, I remember. What about it?"

"At first glance there's nothing explicit to tie that to the Selman case. But when I got the system to trawl for anything even slightly similar, there are just two mentions of 'violation'—both in early news reports. Nothing about the detail, and nothing at all about a recording."

"Could be anything. Someone wanting to spice things up. Tillotson was right that there's nothing people like better than some sex with their dismemberment."

Doyle nodded. "I thought the same, Para, so I pulled some strings, and I managed to get hold of a first-draft copy of one of the oldest books." He grinned. "And it's in there, spelled right out: the axe, the file sent to the family, just like the new case. It looks to me like the writer somehow got a glimpse of the recording, or heard from someone who had. Then Selman must have had it suppressed. If the Kenward girl is a copycat, then whoever is copying knows more about the original case than most people."

Toreth raised his eyebrow. "You pulled some strings?"

"Yes, Para." Doyle shrugged. "I checked the employee registers of some of the publishers, and I found a couple of names with thirdhand resister links statistically weak enough that they'd never been brought in and questioned. I called one, and he was willing to do I&I a favor in return for keeping it that way."

"Good work," Toreth said. "Really—well done."

"Thank you, Para."

"Of course, when you're filling in the IIP, remember that we're still not looking at the Selman case. Not officially."

"No, Para. And I wasn't." The junior had a particular smile that radiated trustworthiness. Toreth didn't believe him for a moment, but it probably came in useful with witnesses. "Just confirming an evidence pattern, like you said. Although I used that new common factor of the rape to sweep old kidnap cases here and at Justice, and I didn't find anything."

"Did you search Central Medical, too?"

"Para?"

Toreth ignored the question and opened the IIP. Doyle filed evidence well; it only took Toreth a few moments to locate the analysis and start his own related search. "Not all kidnappings make it onto the system. The official estimate is that somewhere between 'lots' and 'most' are dealt with by corporate security before we or Justice get a sniff of them."

"But if someone was killed, Para, isn't that usually reported?"

"Usually still isn't always. And—" Toreth scanned the results and grinned. "Here we are. What do you think of these?"

Doyle looked at the results on his hand screen. "Coincidences of distal right arm grafts and internal injury repairs. Oh, I see."

Together they looked through the files tabulating fifteen years of medical treatment in the Administration: assaults, small-scale illegal pharmaceuticals traffickers squabbling, indigents, intra-family incidents both corporate and noncorporate. Boring, Justice-level stuff in the main, quickly filtered out, along with the few marked as the medical consequences of official interrogations. Toreth filtered again and again, like cutting cards, looking for the aces. When Toreth had made his own selections, he said, "Doyle?"

"These two look the most promising, Para: one male and one female, nine and seven years ago. Nineteen and twenty-two at the time. Neither case says anything in the notes about what happened. Bare minimal Central filings from private corporate hospitals, but the amputations were approximately ten to fourteen days old when first treated."

Same ones that Toreth had marked. "But no record of a matching kidnapping or connections to any monitored vendettas."

"No, and no, Para. But like you said, there doesn't have to be. Unlikely there would be, even."

Toreth nodded. "If those two were kidnapped and released because someone paid up, no one will admit it ever happened. Not on any witness waiver we could get, anyway. Fucking corporate accords. Oh, well. See if you can find any other connections to Kenward. Check out families, close friends, anyone they were fucking, all the usual."

"And links to Selman?"

"Did I put that in the IIP?"

Doyle grinned. "No, Para. And nor will I."

For the rest of the day, Toreth abandoned the kidnapping with a sense of relief, and went with Barret-Connor and the rest of the team to supervise arrests on another case. With help from I&I branches across Europe, they picked up the key figures in a network of importers and distributors shipping illegal pharmaceuticals around the Administration. After a long and tedious time spent tracing contacts and movement patterns, a sudden flurry of activity among the suspects had suggested it was time to bring them in. Ultimately the network might or might not be tied to funding resister activity—that was what the interrogations would find out for certain—but either way it would make a nice, solid case. Before he went home, Toreth ran through the security files for everyone arrested. Only a handful with corporate status among them, thank fuck.

Sara opened the office door. "Sorry to bother you, but are you still okay to see Cris in the morning?"

"Cris? Oh, shit. Him."

"I did send you a note. Meeting first thing tomorrow. If you're busy with the arrests, I can cancel it."

Toreth considered a moment, then shook his head. "Leave it. I can kill two birds with one stone; three, even, if I'm lucky."

Chapter Five

❖

Some interrogation rooms had an attached observation room, for purposes such as teaching, inspection, and salutatory lessons. The immediacy of watching an interrogation separated by just the thickness of soundproof one-way glass could never be matched by a screen, and few interrogators liked to have a line of gawking students inside the room.

Standing beside Toreth, Cole stared, palms pressed to the glass. Sweat misted a halo around the edges of his hands.

Toreth had asked Doyle to help Parsons with initial interrogations of some of the drug-runner prisoners from yesterday. They'd brought in a good haul, and Toreth wanted to see the junior at work down here, as well as upstairs. Any investigator could hit a lucky combination of searches. Very informative it had proved, too. The prisoner twitched in the chair, uncontrollable tremors juddering through him, the movements limited by the restraints. Sweat streaked his hair dark, running down his face. Toreth recognized the symptoms from long experience. Doyle had overdosed the prisoner, and probably deliberately, trying to work around the limits of a low waiver.

The junior had taken a break, leaving the prisoner there. He'd be watching a feed on a screen nearby, but all the prisoner knew was that he was alone in the room, with his body slipping terrifyingly out of control. Shakes moving on to spasms, bringing agonizing cramps. Soon he'd be convinced he was dying, and then he'd start begging in earnest.

The man's head snapped back, pinned against the neck brace by a sudden contraction of his muscles. "I can't breathe," he gasped, the words jerking out. "I can't—can't—ah!"

Toreth had stood in front of prisoners, holding the injector of antagonist where they could see it, waiting until he heard the information he wanted and the neural scans confirmed it as probably true, or he felt satisfied the prisoner knew nothing. When hard-pressed for time the technique could be a case-breaker, but he didn't like it. Too many deaths or close calls on low waivers, too many fatal accidents without the sanction of an annex order, and questions were asked. Valuable prisoners wouldn't be entrusted to someone with a reputation for sloppy interrogations.

A negative mark against Doyle, then, after his solid work the day before. Toreth sighed. Some days juniors were a punishment for making senior grade.

"Oh, God," Cole said softly. "It's *real.*"

"Uh-huh." Toreth leaned on the wall behind him. "What were you expecting?"

"I didn't—I know a couple of people who've had official tours here. Journalists. And—" He flinched slightly as the prisoner in the chair jerked and cried out again, but his face was flushed. "And someone who wanted to make a documentary on the justice system. They only saw interview rooms. I didn't think you'd really show me . . . that you could . . . "

"You think I'm ashamed of what we do here? We're protecting the Administration." Toreth stepped forward, right up close. "And most people out there don't care what we do, as long as they don't have to see it. They just want to be safe." Cole didn't respond. Toreth leaned on the glass, his hand right beside Cole, thumb touching his little finger. "They especially don't want some fucking maniac kidnapping their daughter and cutting her arms and legs off with a fucking axe. Understand? It's the kind of case which makes people appreciate why that—" he nodded at the prisoner, "—is necessary."

"I can't tell you anything about the source." Cole sounded husky but resolute.

"Just something to think about," Toreth said. "Come on: time's up."

Cole barely seemed to register the two guards waiting in the corridor outside. He stopped, taking deep breaths of the antiseptic-laden air, and glanced back over his shoulder as if he couldn't decide whether he felt happy to escape or not. Toreth beckoned the guards over, and put his hand on Cole's shoulder. "I want him searched, thoroughly. Don't trust the scanners. Anything on him, or in him, you find it for me."

"I—" Toreth caught the flash of naked guilt, followed by panic. Cole's voice jumped higher. "No! You can't. I'm not under arrest."

"You should've read the clearance you signed a bit more carefully. You agreed to any and all necessary precautions; the search methods are listed in the small print. I have reasonable grounds to suspect a violation of security."

"What grounds? I haven't—"

"Your security file. Now, I suggest you go with the guards and don't make this any more unpleasant than it has to be." Toreth squeezed his shoulder. "If you cooperate, they might even warm the instruments first."

While the guards searched Cole, Toreth drank his morning coffee and read his IIPs. He stayed down in a level D interrogators' coffee room, with his comm switched off. Sara would probably kick up a fuss about him ordering a cavity search on her ex.

The results proved worth the potential annoyance when he caught up with Cole in an interview room. A tiny camera and recorder lay in a plastic bag on the interview table. Toreth had been quite prepared to plant evidence, but just as he'd hoped, Cole had been stupid enough to make things easy.

"You do know what this is?" Toreth said.

Cole nodded sullenly. Stripped of his designer gear and wearing the interrogation suit thoughtfully provided by the guards, he had already spent an hour waiting. His long hair hung loose, disordered by the search, the clip confiscated.

"Really?" Toreth said. "You do? I don't think so, because you don't look anywhere near worried enough. This—" Toreth tapped the bag, "—is a political crime."

Cole's head snapped up. "What?"

"The whole of Int-Sec is a high-level security-restricted area, as defined by Administration department law. And the interrogation levels here are designated data-sealed." Toreth sighed, mock weary. "There is a notice at all the entrances. Bringing concealed recording or surveillance devices of any type down here without clearance is prima facie evidence of resister activity."

"That's bullshit!" Cole rallied well, Toreth would give him that. "You know perfectly well I'm nothing of the kind."

"Do I? Well, I suppose we could sort that out in an interrogation room. But I don't need to bother. In fact, I checked your security file and your employer doesn't extend corporate status automatically to all employees, so I don't even need to submit the form to have it suspended for criminal political activity. You're just an ordinary, unprotected resister."

"I'm not a—"

"Which means I can pass this on right now to the Justice sentencing system as a category five offense. Now that you've had a tour of I&I, how about a close-up look at a re-education facility? You'll probably get one of the lower-grade ones, for a first offense like this. Although, taking into account the cautions on your record from Justice for attempting to record inside corporate security areas, maybe you won't be so lucky."

Cole glared at him, fear betrayed only by his quick breathing. "This is harassment; it's ridiculous. I'm going to file a complaint."

"Go right ahead. Of course, it might take you a while. Justice won't process the complaint until after the sentence, and political criminals don't have independent legal access. Your bosses might make an approach, but...well, you'd be surprised how many corporations just deny all involvement and hang their people out to dry. Taint by association. My guess is they'll say you did this all on your own initiative, against policy." Toreth smiled. "Look on the bright side. It won't matter if they sack you, if you're in a re-education center."

Cole stared at the camera from a moment, then shook his head. "Fine, you can have the information."

"I beg your pardon?"

"You can have the detail I was given about the Selman case. That's where this is leading, isn't it?"

Toreth leaned back in his chair and smiled. "It would certainly be good evidence of your standing as a loyal citizen. But I'm not interested in whatever scraps they're feeding you—I want the name."

"I can't!" Cole's eye widened. "I can't—I don't have it! I swear!"

"You exchanged messages, didn't you? We can start there." Toreth stood up and leaned over the table. "And you'd better hope we can trace them, or you're going to make news in a way you really won't enjoy."

Sara caught up with him outside the room booked for the case conference. "Want to sit in on this one again?" Toreth asked.

"*Did* Cris have a camera on him?" Her emphasis made the implication clear.

"Absolutely. He makes a habit of pulling crap like that—ask Justice. Or I can show you his file."

"Oh. Oh, the *moron.*" Sara shook her head. "Look, you aren't really going to bust him, are you? Because that will look amazing on my file, what with him being my ex and me signing him in here."

"Were you ever registered partners?" He hadn't considered that.

"No." Sara shrugged. Despite her attempt to be casual, she couldn't hide the mix of nervousness and annoyance underneath. "But you know how it goes."

"Don't worry. He's being very cooperative. Mistry's getting the comm traces set up now."

"Good." The vane of anger snapped around. "Then I hope whoever was holding the speculum shoved it up there hard. He deserves it, the idiot. Now I remember why I dumped him in the first place. He never thinks about other people."

"I thought last week it was because he had a creepy interest in dismembered women?"

"Well, that too." Sara sighed. "God, where do I find them?"

"We've hit gold," Toreth said as soon as everyone had taken their seats around the table. "And when I say gold, I mean 'more kidnappings and severed limbs.'"

Carey and Verstraeten looked at him in surprise. "You found another case?" Carey asked.

53

"Not just one." Toreth smiled. "See, this is why you need me."

Doyle put up on the room's screen the two cases they'd found.

"So these look like strong possibilities," Toreth said after he outlined the background to the discoveries. "Same sab protocol. The only problem is, we'll have a hell of a time proving they were ever kidnapped in the first place. Unless these kidnappers are the least competent outfit in the history of corporate sabotage, I doubt they let two more escape like the Kenward girl, or that they were both rescued."

"Paid up, then." Carey sighed. "And there's no official time limit on infractions of the corporate accords."

Verstraeten was scanning the files, lips pursed. "Excuse me, Para-investigator, but what's the confidence on these? Only one of them has close relatives rich enough or of high enough status to flag them as obvious profit-based sab targets, and that's marginal."

"You mean, just like Kenward?"

After a moment, Verstraeten nodded. He could hardly do otherwise without rubbishing his own boss's theory. "I suppose looking at it like that, it's another similarity, Para."

"Doyle," Toreth said, "did you manage to find any connections between those cases and Selman or Kenward?"

"Yes, and no, Para. In the first case there's a good solid link because the father worked directly for Selman at the same time as Kenward, in corporate security. In the second the best connection I could find is pretty tenuous. The girl's grandfather was a director at Parallel Flow, which also works in the traffic monitoring industry, and that's it."

"Okay. Leaving that—"

"Excuse me, Para." Doyle managed an appropriately respectful interruption, so Toreth sat back and nodded. "I found something else, too. Looking at the past association links, I realized that we were using the Selman case as the copycat reference, which meant we were only searching forward. When I opened it up..."

Another case appeared on the screen, key points in the summary timeline neatly highlighted. Fantastic job, except that Toreth hadn't seen any of it before. And he'd looked at the IIPs, official and unofficial, right before the case conference. Out of the corner of his eye he noticed Sara wince. Her favorite wasn't performing so well today.

"Natasha Patterson. Rape...right hand...dismemberment. And she's eighteen." Carey gave a low whistle. "That's not just similar, that's virtually identical."

"Yes," Doyle said. "But this one definitely isn't copycatting the Selman methods. It happened five years before it—twenty years ago. Smooth, efficient operation, according to Justice. The sabs put someone inside the corporation, picked their target, and lifted her with no fuss at all. Last message her parents had from her said she was going out after work with friends."

"Friends at CGS or Parallel Flow?" Carey asked hopefully.

"No. At a corporation called Avendiax. It ran a student sponsorship program for tax breaks, and this Patterson girl went there for a year between school and university. Avendiax was in the traffic control field, but I couldn't find a direct connection to CGS or Parallel Flow."

Could the corporation be a new suspect for Sofie Kenward's kidnapping? "Is Avendiax still active?" Toreth asked.

Doyle shook his head. "It collapsed not long after the kidnapping."

"Why?" Verstraeten asked.

Doyle smiled. "The CEO, Alan Huddleston, was caught breaking the corporate accords during negotiations, trying to pay off the kidnappers with information. He denied it, of course, but the Confederation investigation found against him. The file strongly suggests he was—" Doyle hesitated, obviously picking the appropriate description. "In a relationship with the girl. Anyway, half the board was downgraded for possible complicity, and all their financial backers withdrew support, as dictated by the accords."

Carey was frowning. "Doesn't make sense. In cases like that the sab team usually cuts their losses and pulls out. Why kill the girl?"

"Possibly due to panic, Investigator, or to stop her from identifying them. Justice somehow got onto the place they had her stashed. The details don't seem to have made it over here—the case file is missing a lot of documents. But I called a couple of people at Justice, and found one of the original case officers. Apparently the kidnappers went out the back door as Justice was kicking in the front. Justice officers pursued, but the sab team's car crashed. All five of them were killed. The Department of Transport investigation, which we do have, concluded they'd tampered with the system to disable tracking and override, and that caused the guidance to fail."

"Which makes at least one set of copycats, then," Toreth said. "If they're dead, they didn't take Louise Selman."

"True," Carey said. "But whoever took Sofie Kenward could still be connected to any of the previous cases."

Doyle still had his screen in his hand. His self-satisfied expression gave Toreth a strong urge to smack it off his face. "There's one more possible case pre-Selman—here." Doyle brought up a fresh set of files. "Now this is an interesting variation. Seventeen years ago, Gena Finn, twenty-two, went missing, taken off the street on her way to work. The girl's a nobody, but she was engaged to a very rich bloke called Jerrold Rankin. Somehow he got hold of the kidnappers' contact information, and he went into business with them privately."

"In the open?" Toreth said, surprised into the question. "What about the accords?"

"Rankin resigned from all his directorships and voluntarily renounced his corporate status. I know, I didn't think it was possible either, but I checked the accords and there's a clause to deal with it. So after that, technically, he was free to do what he liked."

"But did they get her back?" Carey asked.

"Yes. Rankin arranged payment exactly as requested, left it at the drop, it vanished. Then—" Doyle checked the file. "Five days later, after everyone had given up expecting a return, Finn was found alive in a park, drugged unconscious. But the odd thing is, the kidnappers took payment in negotiables, mostly antique jewelry. None of the pieces have ever turned up again. Not one. For all anyone knows, the kidnappers could just as well have melted the lot. Either they had the most phenomenally flawless laundering system ever devised, or—" He shrugged.

"Or?" Carey asked.

"Or something happened we don't understand yet," Toreth said, trying to sound in command of the situation. "Kidnapping corporates is a hell of a lot of trouble to go to, if you don't want the money."

"Especially what...six times?" Carey said.

"Five, anyway," Toreth said. "Although you'd think they'd pick a template which worked out better for the first team."

Toreth pulled up all the cases on his hand screen (five files, plus his own notes on Louise Selman) and sorted through them, scanning the summaries for the new cases. Everyone waited; he was the senior in charge of the case, after all. That didn't make him any less irritated with Doyle. Bloody grandstanding juniors.

Once he'd found what he wanted, he gave it another thirty seconds, then laid the screen down. "So what do we have? Six victims so far, five female, one male. All young. Current oldest case, victim died, apparently without a payment made. Next time we have new kidnappers, and after the rape and handjob—"

Carey gave him the same look she'd shot at Benz in the first meeting.

"Sorry," Toreth said. "Anyway, the fiancé paid up once he'd seen the recordings, and got what he paid for. Third, Selman—full works, obviously, and no payment so far as we know. Fifth and sixth are the presumed cases, with rape and mutilation, and probable payment since the victims have current files in Central Medical. And finally Sofie Kenward, at least one of whose fathers would've paid up if he'd had the money, but he didn't."

"That's a likely fifty percent positive completion rate for payments over all six cases," Verstraeten said. "Possibly more. Very high indeed, as far as the statistics go. And three million in total, assuming all the demands are the same."

"And they happened twenty, seventeen, fifteen, nine and seven years ago."

"There has to be a connection," Carey said. "Some logic behind it. Some reason why this group picked these particular kids."

Toreth nodded. "Now I'll buy it. We can look for corporate links, and comb the sab database for teams active over that period, try to narrow down the field. And if we can't dig anything conclusive out of the files, we'll need to interview whoever the hell will talk to us until we find out what the link is." Or until Joseph Selman found out what they were doing and had the lot of them fired.

Carey obviously had the same idea. "But at least this means we can work round the Selman case now. That's four other cases currently unconnected to him. Technically unconnected, anyway. Officially, there's still no sexual assault recorded in the Selman IIP."

Toreth doubted Selman would be interested in that kind of hairsplitting, but his only other option was to punt the whole case back to Corporate Fraud. And if he did that now, right after a positive avalanche of fresh evidence, the whole building would be talking about how he bottled out. "Get Abel and Brown back from B-C to help," he said to Doyle. "Don't let them near any mention of Selman. Mistry's in charge of organizing interviews, and if she needs help you do exactly what she says." The junior nodded without any sign of dissatisfaction at being told to defer to an investigator. "You'll be searching the files, since you have such a magic touch."

His expression didn't change. "Yes, Para."

"Liz, speaking of magic, can you do some financials? Whoever these people are, they've made themselves a small fortune, and I don't believe they gave it all away to widows and orphans. Or if they did, the widows and orphans know the best fucking fences in Europe."

Carey nodded. "Maybe there's a trail. And I can look for solid connections between Selman and this—" she checked the file, "—this Parallel Flow." Before he could protest, she shook her head. "You're getting as bad as bloody Benz. Okay, I'll be careful, nothing in the IIP."

The new leads divided up, Toreth sent everyone on their way. Just outside the conference room, he stopped Doyle with a hand on his shoulder. He felt the junior tense up, but he didn't let go until everyone else had gone. When the others were out of sight, including Sara, who showed signs of wanting to linger, Toreth dropped his hand and looked the junior in the eye. "I don't appreciate case-conference surprises from inside my team. Not that kind, anyway."

"I was down in interrogation all morning, Para. And I couldn't file it in the IIP when..." The excuses petered out, and Doyle shrugged. "No, Para. Sorry. I just wanted to—"

"I don't give a fuck why you did it. Don't do it again, or you'll be helping Benz polish his badge for the rest of the case, or whatever they do for fun at CF. Or I can just send you straight back to the pool, if you prefer?"

"No, Para." He squared his shoulders. "Won't happen again."

Toreth nodded. "And by the way, you missed something in the second case you found. Gena Finn's mother had worked for Parallel Flow for a short while, as a security consultant. That ties it to one of the later kidnappings."

"Had she, Para?" For a moment, Toreth thought Doyle might pull his screen out to check. "Sorry, I don't know how I missed that."

"Too busy focusing on the rich fiancé. Money isn't always everything. Now go put it in the IIP, and tell Liz Carey about it. In person. Apologize to her for rushing the summary and not noticing it before."

The junior didn't even blink. "Yes, Para. Sorry again, Para."

Toreth considered mentioning the overdosed interrogation he'd seen that morning, then decided he'd like to hold something in reserve for later. "Other than that, good work."

Doyle frowned slightly, hesitating like he expected a sting in the tail of the compliment. "Thank you, Para."

Leaving the others to deal with the boring routine work, Toreth looked in on Barret-Connor and the others to check progress on the other case. B-C seemed happy enough that Abel and Brown would be gone again for a few days, but clearly disappointed at not getting Mistry back in return. "You'll have to make do with me for a while," Toreth said. "I can spare some time."

"Couldn't possibly be better than that, Para," B-C said, deadpan. "And to be honest, I wouldn't mind losing them even if you couldn't. I have to say, I'm afraid those two almost contribute negative effort."

A pretty damning indictment from Barret-Connor, who generally kept his opinions to himself unless pushed. Either his promotion to senior investigator had made him more confident, or the investigators were just that useless. Probably the latter, Toreth decided, watching while B-C organized the case summary.

Abel and Brown were clearly the types who bumped along the bottom of a career at I&I, never rising above junior status. No surprise, then, that the two investigators hadn't found themselves a permanent place in a team. Why Doyle was in the same situation, eighteen months after qualifying, might merit further investigation. Rushing casework to chase down the juicier details was a minor issue that any half-competent senior could train out, and Doyle had never benefited from the prolonged attention of a single boss. Being an arrogant, devious little fucker couldn't entirely explain why he was still floating around in the pool. Toreth made a mental note to look at his file.

Thinking about Doyle reminded him of the junior's highly effective investigation skills, and his string-pulling. "B-C, doesn't someone in your family work at the Department of Transport?"

The investigator looked up, startled. "Yes, Para. My mother."

Read enough personal files at enough appraisals, and something was bound to stick. "Anything to do with traffic control?"

"No, 'fraid not. Infrastructure planning. She's the division head," B-C offered, as though to make up for the defect.

58

"Huh. Is it a lively department? Do they get a lot of corporate sabotage around it?"

"Some, I think, Para. The Administration regularly places huge contracts, and I know my mother has formal risk assessments at least once a year. But Administration contracts are like taxes. They're entirely regulated by Administration law rather than the corporate accords, so the corporations have much less wriggle room in all areas."

"I suppose that doesn't stop them entirely?"

"I suppose not, Para. But to be honest, with Administration staff it's more likely to be a bribe than anything nasty. We're pretty cheap, or so I hear. I know my mother's never had an actual targeted threat." Barret-Connor paused. "At least, not one she told us about. If there's anything you want me to ask, I can call her."

For some reason, Toreth hadn't expected the offer. "God, no. Bad enough I have Sara's ex down in the cells, without getting someone's bloody mother involved."

B-C grinned. "Yes, Para."

"Right. Now, show me the new network matrix, and let's see who else we need to pull in."

59

Chapter Six

❖

The next day Toreth busied himself with illegal pharmaceuticals—unfortunately in the sense of catching their smugglers, rather than enjoying them. Barret-Connor had done his job as thoroughly as ever, and the case was shaping up well. The network wasn't being used exclusively to fund resisters; perhaps it had been intended to do that, but so many people were creaming off so many percentages that any resisters ultimately involved must be running a shabby outfit. Still, it remained enough to classify whole swathes of the arrests as political, which streamlined processing beautifully.

He'd told Mistry to report in person when she finished arranging the first round of interviews, and she arrived first thing on Thursday morning, with a hand screen and an apologetic air. Toreth hoped it was because she'd interrupted a conversation with B-C, not because she had nothing to report. The IIPs, official and unofficial, had been depressingly thin. "Any luck with Cole?" Toreth asked.

"No, Para, sorry. Systems worked through all the comm traces for the messages he gave us." She shrugged apologetically. "There's nothing, I'm afraid. Whoever it is really doesn't want to be found."

"Can't say I blame them." Disappointing, but less so now that they had more, and safer, cases to look into. "What about the other kidnappings?"

"A lot of people wouldn't talk to us at all," Mistry said. "Most of those involved in the original kidnapping have their corporate status back now, and they directed us to their lawyers who are preparing formal statements, probably to say that it was twenty years ago and none of them remember a thing. Likewise with the two cases where we suspect someone paid up. Shorter time frame, but even worse memories."

Toreth nodded. He hadn't expected anything else.

"We didn't approach anyone involved with the Selman kidnapping, obviously. But Jerrold Rankin agreed to an informal interview, and I spoke to him over the comm." Mistry gave a small shrug. "The only problem was that he knew almost nothing about the background to the case. He claims that all he did was follow directions from the kidnappers. But . . ."

"Well?" Toreth prompted.

"I don't know, Para. He's . . . " Mistry frowned, and looked down briefly. Toreth noticed she was fiddling with the end of her long plait. At the same moment, she flipped it over her shoulder, as though the tic annoyed her. "He's hard to read, and bizarrely laid-back considering what we were talking about. But something else about him definitely didn't gel. When we talked about the drop-off, about finding Gena, he seemed fine. But I'm sure he was holding something back about the negotiations." The slight frown vanished, and she shrugged briskly. "Most likely there was someone else involved and he's protecting them."

Toreth nodded. Representatives of the Confederation of European Corporations would've been watching everyone involved at the time, and had apparently seen nothing. But anyone with corporate status who'd broken the accords and evaded notice then would still suffer if exposed now. Gena Finn's mother, trained in corporate security, seemed an obvious possibility.

"But I can't say for sure it's only that," Mistry added. "Not yet. He's coming in later today to talk to us."

"Good. I'll interview him," Toreth said. "And what about the others? Worth bringing them in on witness warrants?"

"I'd say not until we have some specific questions we can warrant for. They're going to fight hard against anything, and in cases where all we have is medical records, it'll be almost impossible for us to prove that a kidnapping even happened."

Toreth nodded. After all, the families involved had had years in which to perfect their stories.

Toreth sent Abel and Brown to collect Rankin, as a courtesy and to make sure he didn't change his mind on the way to I&I. When they handed him over, they showed the first evidence of unusual emotion Toreth had ever noticed in them: relief.

Toreth had contemplated booking an interrogation room, but without even a witness warrant he couldn't back up the implied threat. He did the best he could by having Rankin escorted to an interrogation-level interview room and left there alone to contemplate the cheerful I&I décor.

Toreth watched him on the monitor for five minutes. Once Rankin lifted his hand and brushed his undistinguished brown hair back from his forehead with a gesture that reminded Toreth of Benz. Once he leaned down and scratched his ankle. Otherwise he sat quietly, not even glancing at the door or the guard standing by it. He looked much younger than forty-two, and whatever he was thinking didn't show on his smooth, oval, slightly pudgy face.

As Toreth opened the door he made a mental note not to try to outstare the man. "Hello," Toreth said, and Rankin looked up. "I'm Para-investigator Val Toreth."

Rankin nodded. "Your name was on the warrant."

"How's life without corporate status?" Toreth asked as he sat down.

"Not as bad as most corporates think." Rankin cocked his head. "Don't you know?" It sounded like an honest inquiry, not the usual bluff and bravado.

"We're Int-Sec," Toreth said, and Rankin nodded.

"Ah. Same privileges, less profit."

"Not quite the same." Toreth paused. Rankin regarded him with the same steady and oddly detached calm. No curiosity, apparently no apprehension. Toreth wondered briefly whether it was worth running a drug screen on the man. "You don't have a registered partner," Toreth said. "What happened to Gena?"

"She left me." His placid voice didn't change. "Which with hindsight I suppose was inevitable. How would you like to come home every day to someone who bought your life? Not a relationship of equals."

"And not really worth a million euros, then," Toreth said.

"Worth it every day to know that she's alive and happy."

"Alive just because of you?" Toreth asked, keeping his voice casual. "Or was there someone else involved in the negotiations?"

"No, just me." Rankin smiled. "With the scrutiny given to the payment, do you think anyone else could've contributed a cent?"

"What about contributing in other ways?"

He didn't even blink. "Other ways? I'm afraid I don't understand. What did you have in mind?"

Toreth wondered if the man knew how irritating most people must find his serenity, and whether he cultivated it for exactly that reason. Thinking about how quickly he'd be able to break that serenity down if he could use some of the drugs and equipment downstairs took the edge off the annoyance. "Perhaps information about a previous kidnapping?" Toreth asked.

Rankin's lips parted, then closed again quickly. A moment later, he said, "The demand was for one million euros."

Toreth had been probing for a response, and in someone so contained the tiny hesitation might as well be a wailing siren. "A million euros and something else, yes."

"I paid," Rankin said. "That's all. Anyone else involved would've broken the accords."

"Mr. Rankin, as you said, I'm not corporate. I don't care about the accords. Every corporate in the Administration could break them every day and twice on Sundays, and it still wouldn't make my case list. I care about kidnappings." Toreth called up the pictures of the other kidnap victims, less Louise Selman, and pushed his screen across the table. "I care about these kids, who all went through exactly what Gena did, or worse. And I care even more about the next one these sabs are going to pick, unless I can stop them."

Liz Carey would be proud of him, Toreth thought, as he watched Rankin stare

62

at the pictures. If they didn't work, he'd throw in a couple of gory images of Sofie's severed hand at the Kenward crime scene. A nice bit of blood often did the trick.

"There may have been other information. From Angelina—Ms. Finn," Rankin said, gaze still on the screen. "Gena's mother. But what, I have no idea. Angelina gave me a data stick, and I hid it inside one of the ransom items that shielded it from screening. But that's all I know."

"So the money was just a cover for you to pass on the information?"

"Definitely not. They told me that if I didn't pay every cent, then Gena... well. We wouldn't see her again."

Odd then that no items had resurfaced. "So they got what they wanted?"

"I honestly don't know for certain. I did my part—I paid. If they asked for something more, either it was on the stick, or Angelina told them she didn't know. Or maybe it was a bluff, a distraction."

Toreth nodded, although he knew which he didn't believe. Nothing so far suggested the kidnappers were people who bluffed. "And did you ever find out who was behind the kidnapping?" Toreth asked.

"If I had, don't you think I would've reported it?" When Toreth didn't respond, Rankin's shoulders dropped slightly. "No, I didn't. Even corporate sabs are wary about dealing with someone who has renounced his corporate status. I had no contacts, no resources I could draw on beyond money."

"I didn't think sabs cared about anything beyond money."

"From my limited experience, they seem to envy corporates as much as they despise them. Odd, but true."

It made a certain twisted kind of sense. Like the corporates they preyed upon and were paid by, sabs supposedly prided themselves on their group loyalty and codes of conduct. All equally bollocks, too. Toreth would rather trust a pack of starving old city rats than either sabs or corporates.

After he'd sent Rankin home, and noted a city-limits movement restriction on the man's security file, Toreth called Mistry and Doyle into his office, and showed them the relevant part of the interview. "Now we have a possible motive," Toreth said. "The kidnappers may still be after information as well as money, and for some reason they thought Paul Kenward had it."

"That would explain why the kidnapping has hit him so hard," Mistry said. "It makes it a personal attack, not directed at the corporation. If only NTS would let us talk to him."

"Still, Para," Doyle said, "it's a long time to look for the answers to any question. Why's it so important?"

"We'll have to ask the sabs when we find them." Toreth leaned back in his chair. "And they may have more than one question. Gena Finn's the connection to the old case. Or rather, her mother. If she did exchange information, I bet she hasn't forgotten it."

"She's one of the people who refused an interview. We could reopen the case," Mistry suggested. "Arrest her as a witness."

"We'll have to convince Tillotson that Selman won't object." And Tillotson tended to be unfortunately conservative when it came to upsetting major corporate figures. "Of course, we could always ask her again to volunteer. Maybe she'll feel public-spirited." Neither Doyle nor Mistry commented. The idea had the same problem as ever: paying off kidnappers was a breach of the corporate accords, not an arrestable crime. Anyone involved had every incentive in the world not to talk. He doubted that Rankin's claims about the joys of noncorporate life would help. Toreth sighed. "Doyle, go check all their files anyway, see if the evidence analysis system can pull up anything we can use for leverage this time."

Toreth leaned back and looked up at the ceiling. The light panels had switched themselves off, outcompeted by the sunlight.

The case felt as fragile as a spider's web. Gena Finn was linked, via Parallel Flow, to one other kidnapping. Three cases tied together via CGS. Tempting to put Selman in the middle of the web, but was that just the attraction of a big corporate name? Ultimately, none of that might be connected to Sofie Kenward's kidnapping. But how could he prove or disprove the links without risking a one-way ticket to career suicide? Another thread to consider: someone with secrets about Joseph Selman for sale. That morning Toreth had been willing to drop that line of investigation, but if he were lucky that secret could cut through swathes of tedious witness warrants and wrangling with corporate lawyers. And Toreth still had one lawyer-free lead that might be worth a few more euros of CF resources.

Doyle had gone. Mistry still sat there, waiting patiently. Toreth held up a finger. "One minute. I have another interview for you."

Crispin Cole looked distinctly unhappy to see Toreth on the comm. "Is everything all right?" he asked.

"You ought to be asking, 'is my file at Justice yet?'" Toreth said.

"My—" Cole shook his head. "Now wait a minute. You said you wanted the messages. I already gave you everything I had."

"No, I said I wanted the person who sent them, and I haven't found them yet."

Cole gave him a heart-rending look of despair, which must've worked a treat on Sara. "I don't know anything more. I can't help you."

Toreth smiled. "Oh, yes, you can. Jasleen Mistry will be along soon to make the arrangements. How are you as a salesman, Mr. Cole?"

64

Chapter Seven

The pool was always quiet on a Friday lunchtime, only a handful of people, all swimming seriously. Toreth dove in, down, kicking forward, eyes closed but acutely aware of the pressure of water against his face. Another kick, and his jaw clenched involuntarily. If he opened his mouth, if he breathed in—and then he broke the surface, the shock of adrenaline buzzing through him. It lasted for two fast lengths, and then he settled in for forty minutes of steadier swimming.

More people at I&I knew of his drowning phobia than he liked to think about, including Sara. She'd asked him once why he went swimming, and he'd shrugged. Because he could. Because the fear never went away, but he refused to let it beat him.

When he finally hauled himself out of the water, breathless, he spotted Liz Carey right away, her red hair standing out clearly behind the glass wall of the observation gallery high up on one wall. He waved, and she waved back and held up a plastic bag, mouthing something that looked like "lunch."

"Two minutes," he said, and held up the fingers to illustrate, making her laugh.

❖ ❖ ❖

"Sara told me where you were," Carey said as he came out of the changing rooms.

"What's up? You should've asked them to call me out of the pool."

"It wasn't important. Besides," she grinned at him, "I was only there for five minutes, and I didn't mind watching for a while. I brought sandwiches. Not from the canteen—I sent Benz's admin out for them."

"Why?"

"You're a suspicious bastard sometimes. Because I thought we could go eat them outside, away from both our sections." And away from Tillotson, and Benz, and Doyle, and the useless pair of investigators. Toreth nodded.

The Int-Sec leisure complex had an outside area with tables, surrounded by trees. Toreth remembered the paving stones in their original white, matching the

65

building. In ten years they'd weathered to a patched pale gray. The late spring sun shone warmly, but most people seemed to have finished eating and left. They picked a quiet table, well away from the few small groups still lingering. The sandwiches certainly beat lunch in the I&I canteen: thick slices of real bacon in crispy white rolls, still hot inside a warming wrapper.

"Sara heard a rumor that you're screwing Verstraeten," Toreth said. "Now that he's off probation and it's not a disciplinary."

"I heard that one, too." She gave him a sly, sideways grin. "Lucky me, it's all true, every word of it."

"Jesus. He's a bit limp, isn't he?"

She chuckled richly. "Not where it counts." Carey tore her sandwich in half and took a bite. "Now, be serious for a minute. I've been looking at the new cases your junior found, and the interview with Rankin. The only way the target selection makes any sense is if there's a motive beyond money. And if these people want information connected to the first case, then I can see one obvious motive."

"Revenge." Toreth swallowed a mouthful of sandwich. "Paying back whoever killed the girl."

"Natasha Patterson." Carey nodded. "Or rather, paying back whoever ordered the sabotage hit. The sabs smeared themselves across an underpass wall long before the other kidnappings started."

"And with the whole team dead, they can't talk about who hired them, so anyone who wanted to know would have to try their luck somewhere else." Sab teams who wanted to maintain any kind of reputation kept silent about the identities of previous employers under any circumstances. Or so the sales pitch went, anyway. Half of Toreth's job was based around demonstrating that, under the right circumstances, everyone talked. Toreth picked out a sliver of bacon and nibbled the crispy rind thoughtfully. "Corporation, family, partner, they're the usual three for a vendetta."

"And the corporation went the same way as the sabs, and almost as fast."

"Family or partner, then. Someone who cared enough to keep this up for twenty years." Toreth licked his fingers, and fished his comm earpiece out of his pocket. "Mistry," he said when she answered, "have you talked to the parents of the first girl who was killed?"

"Not yet, Para. Although they're one of the few positive answers we had back. I was planning to go there this afternoon. I'm afraid I've been held up with Crispin Cole."

"I'll save you a job, then. Liz Carey and I will do it. You keep at the rest."

"Very good, Para. Thank you."

The car drove them to a bland, lower-corporate building in a lower-corporate area, respectable enough but teetering on the edge of a slide down. Could go either way, Toreth thought as they walked over to the entrance. If the right developer came along and decided to splash some investment euros around, things would improve, and then no doubt the current residents would find themselves priced out. All in all, Toreth liked the security of I&I paying for his accommodation.

Yvette Patterson had the same air of clinging to respectability in the face of lack of funds. Deep lines grooved her dark skin, setting her expression in bitter unhappiness. "Austin's making coffee," she said as she showed them through to the living room. "He was watching for your car. We don't see many I&I uniforms around here."

If Toreth had bothered to wonder whether the couple had come to terms with their daughter's death, the flat would've provided the answer. He took out his camera, studying the room around him as he set it up. At least fifty pictures of the girl surrounded him, prints and screens hanging on the walls or standing on shelves and tables. They ran from images of a tiny baby with a wild frizz of dark hair to a pretty teenage girl dressed for a party. One wall held the collection of paperwork amassed in a short life—school exams, citizenship awards, her university acceptance notification. Even a trio of Department of Population documents had been printed out and framed: the reproduction license, pregnancy registration, and birth certificate. Toreth eyed the collection with distaste. Morbid obsession over the dead turned his stomach, especially kept up for twenty fucking years.

Toreth listened to the faint sounds of someone in the flat's kitchen, and hoped the coffee would arrive soon. The faster the interview went, the happier he'd be, and he wished he'd let Mistry deal with it.

Austin McDonald was as unsmiling as his wife, taller than Toreth, thin and slightly stooped, his gray hair showing only a hint of its original reddish color. He gave the impression of something slowly desiccating, as though his parchment-pale skin were shrinking down onto his bones. He filled and handed around the cups almost without a word, then sat beside Patterson.

"You wanted to talk to us about Natasha?" Patterson asked.

It didn't take long before Toreth realized any help they could provide would be highly selective. So long as he and Carey asked about the original case, they got all the response they could want. The couple seemed to have every detail of the case imprinted in their memories, right down to the names of the Justice officers who'd worked on it. Neither half of the couple showed any interest in the more recent kidnappings, though. "They were all killed," Yvette Patterson said when Toreth told her they were looking for connections to other cases. She sounded vaguely surprised he'd even suggest it. "Officer Dhaliwal asked us to look at the bodies, to see if we knew any of them. And we did. One of them had taken a job at Avendiax. Jolie. But her real name was—"

"Jo Rogerson," McDonald supplied without hesitation. Had she forgotten the name (unlikely, Toreth thought) or did he always spare her from having to say it?

Patterson carried on smoothly, as though there'd been no break at all. "She made friends with Natasha, told her all kinds of lies, pretended to be pregnant. Natasha loved babies. When she was at school, she volunteered to work in a creche."

Patterson reached out without even looking to pick a small screen from the table beside her, and thrust it towards him. Natasha Patterson smiled out at Toreth, frozen in time with a fat baby in her lap and more children clustered around her. "She was such a kind girl," Patterson said. "So generous. Everyone would tell you the same. Just watch her." The image began to move as the recording activated. Imagining the other screens around the room also flashing into life, Toreth felt he deserved a damage waiver.

"That's how they took her," Patterson continued. "Because Natasha always kept herself safe. She knew how much we worried about her going anywhere alone. That girl even came here once. We welcomed her into our home. So I recognized her. Oh, yes. But the others, we couldn't be sure. They hit the wall very hard." A tight, mean satisfaction lit her face, wringing out what comfort she could from what must've seemed like swift retribution. Better than they'd ever had from Justice, anyway. She stroked the edge of the screen, then set it back in place.

Carey glanced at him, and Toreth gave a small shrug. "Was there anyone with whom Natasha was especially close at the time?" Carey asked.

"There was her brother, of course." Patterson turned to one of the pictures, where a thin boy with his father's red hair stood half hidden by his sister. "He doesn't come home very often. Simon adored Natasha, you see, and being here reminds him of her."

Yeah, that must be the reason. Nothing to do with their obsession with his dead sibling. Toreth couldn't imagine anyone wanting to come back to them or this mausoleum.

"The case file suggested that Natasha might have had a relationship with one of the directors," Carey said with a surprising delicacy.

Austin McDonald shook his head at once. "You mean Alan Huddleston. No, Natasha always said he was just a friend. He recognized her potential, that's all. She was such an extraordinary girl. And we don't blame him for what happened. He did his best to help her until—until they—"

"What happened to him, that was wrong," Patterson broke in. "He shouldn't have been punished like that for trying to save an innocent girl."

McDonald straightened, casting a nervous look at Toreth. "Yvette..."

She ignored him. "They should've let him give them the money. Then she'd still be here. It's all their fault. They're the ones who killed her, just as much as those five—"

"Yvette, *please*."

The criminal law and the corporate accords formed a clear distinction to I&I, but not always to the public at large. Openly questioning the Administration's laws in front of a para-investigator was apparently stupid enough to break through McDonald's focus.

Carey was making soothing noises, trying to deflect them back to the case.

Toreth sipped his coffee, then gagged a little: far too bitter. How appropriate. He sat back, trying to ignore the fifty pairs of eyes staring at him, and let Carey finish the interview.

"Who'd have kids, eh?" Carey said as they walked back down to the car. When Toreth didn't answer, she added, "So, you think they have anything to do with the other kidnappings?"

"Well, they're obsessed enough," Toreth said.

Carey shook her head. "If they're blaming anyone, it's Justice and the corporate accords. No mention at all of whoever ordered the kidnappings."

"Still fucking demented, though." Demented, and pathetic.

"Maybe. But it's the wrong kind of demented, unfortunately for us."

Toreth nodded reluctantly. The memory of the ranks of carefully dusted pictures clung like dirt on his skin. Carey was probably right about them, but doubt lingered. The only way to end an obsession like that would be for someone to take the pair of them out and put a bullet in their heads (which would make the Administration a saner, and definitely happier, place), or to finally make them feel justice had been done.

"Besides," Carey added, "they don't have the know-how for something like this, nowhere near. Or the money to pay someone else to do it."

"That's true."

The car made a welcome sight in the dreary street. Toreth yanked the door open and climbed in without a backward glance.

Toreth slithered sauce-coated flat rice noodles into his mouth without making too much of a mess. Takeaway Chinese food of the kind he shared with Sara just couldn't compete with the corporate restaurants Warrick favored. Opposite him, Warrick was managing very well despite the plastic cast still on his arm. Even with the distractions of delicious food, and the anticipation of great sex to follow, Toreth found himself thinking about the case. "You don't have any kids, do you?" Toreth asked when he'd swallowed.

Warrick's eyebrow lifted quizzically. "Not the last time I checked. I'm sure someone would have told me."

"Anything close?"

"Ah...I have a niece of whom I'm very fond, if that's the kind of relationship you mean."

Good enough. "What would you do if she were kidnapped? For corporate blackmail."

"Well." Warrick set his chopsticks down and steepled his fingers. "Is this related to work?"

"Yeah. I thought a corporate view might be helpful."

Warrick nodded. "The risk has been assessed—it has been for all key personnel and their close relatives. Security says that the danger is very small, but not infinitesimally so. There are periodic reassessments and monitoring." He smiled briefly. "Only what's legal, I assure you."

"But suppose someone did it anyway?"

"SimTech subscribes to the corporate accords, of course. No payments of any kind would be made."

"Sure? What if they sent you a recording of her being raped?"

"She's five," Warrick said icily.

"So? These people are fine with kidnap and live dismemberment. I don't think they'll give a fuck about the age of consent."

"I..." Warrick leaned back and looked down at his hands, stroking the palms together as he thought. "I don't know. How much money are they demanding?"

"In the case I've got? One million euros."

"Then even if I wanted to, I couldn't produce that kind of money instantly. Probably not at all, without selling shares in SimTech and that would raise too many alarms. I'd be stopped. And SimTech would be legally obliged not to release the funds." He looked up. "Her father would want me to pay."

"Yeah?"

"Tarin's not corporate. He wouldn't understand or accept that we have to present a united front to reduce the overall threat levels. And I don't know what I'd tell him. I doubt he'd be impressed by a signed copy of the corporate accords."

Toreth nodded. Pieter Ryersen had been open enough about his desperation to save Sofie; Yvette Patterson had been clear about where she laid the blame for her daughter ending up in pieces. What was best for the corporation, and the corporate world as a whole, cut no ice with them.

"But whatever he said," Toreth said, "if you didn't have the money, you'd be fucked. So you'd have to stick to the no payment policy."

"Quite so." Warrick nodded slowly. "I'd have to. Or..."

"Or what?"

"I said that I couldn't lay my hands on the money. That isn't strictly true. I couldn't do so legitimately. A million euros would be small change compared to what I could get in return for some of SimTech's proprietary software and hardware."

Genuine curiosity prompted Toreth to ask, "Would you do it?"

Warrick contemplated the table in silence, brow furrowed. "I don't know," he said finally. "I hope I would have the—the discipline necessary to trust our security people could locate and retrieve her in time. But I really don't know. I suppose it would depend on finding someone to collude with me." He smiled wryly. "Not

70

that I will even attempt to pretend there are no corporations out there willing to break the rules, but they would be very unwilling to be caught—they'd have to be convinced it was a genuine approach. The penalties for breaking the accords are severe. Loss of personal corporate status, even delisting of the corporation. The Confederation of European Corporations enforces that part of the accords, at least. But..." He shrugged. "I can't say no, I wouldn't do it. Not for certain."

Toreth found it difficult to believe that anything could score higher than SimTech in Warrick's priorities, but the conversation had opened up a new line of inquiry. Could the scenario Warrick had outlined explain Paul Kenward's reluctance to talk to I&I?

Warrick folded his napkin, and Toreth took the hint. "Want to move on to the hotel? I booked a room."

"Mm." Warrick smoothed the cloth, then shook it out and refolded it. "Actually, I have to say I'm no longer in the mood. Perhaps next week?"

Toreth smiled to himself. Not in the mood, indeed. "No."

The curt refusal drew a sharp look from Warrick. "I said—"

"I heard what you said." Toreth leaned forward. "And I said no. What makes you think you have any fucking choice?"

Toreth had learned the signs. Where other people flushed, Warrick paled slightly, his breath catching. He started to rise, and Toreth reached out quickly, catching his arm. "Sit." Warrick hesitated, and Toreth dug his fingers in, pressing down. "*Sit.*"

He obeyed in a rush, gasping softly as Toreth tightened rather than released his hold.

"You—"

"We're going to pay, then we're going to the hotel. Right? Because that's what *I* want to do and that's all that matters from now on. Right?"

Warrick held his gaze for a few seconds, then looked away and nodded minutely.

"Right." Toreth kept up the pressure for a few more seconds, then let go. Time for a sharp lesson in unpredictability. "Although, on second thoughts, maybe I'm not in the mood either. Bye."

He stood up quickly and walked off, not reacting to the exclamation of dismay behind him. That Warrick had lost control enough to react that way in public told him all he needed about the effectiveness of the tactic. Imagining they understood the rules gave people a powerful illusion of control, and that was why prisoner-handling theories all emphasized the value of intermittent over constant rewards. Toreth laughed to himself as he stepped out into the surprisingly warm night air. His old psychology trainers would be amazed to find he had listened after all.

Chapter Eight

Toreth decided against working over the weekend. He saw no reason to knock himself out over a case which no one but Liz Carey and Sara especially wanted investigated in the first place. Overeagerness would only attract attention from Tillotson, and maybe others. Instead he split the weekend between the gym, shopping for new pick-up clothes, and test-driving his purchases with good results on Saturday and Sunday. Warrick left a message on Sunday, politely neutral, merely confirming that he'd be free the following Friday. Toreth smiled and deleted it without a reply. By Monday morning he felt relaxed enough to be thinking more positively about the case as he walked in to work.

None of the Justice interviews or records of the negotiations even hinted that Sofie's kidnappers had demanded more than money. Had a direct approach been made to Kenward himself? Toreth briefly considered asking for a witness waiver for Kenward, but merely the idea of more tussles with corporate lawyers made his temples start to throb. Perhaps he might be able to get away without. Kenward had blamed himself for what had happened to his daughter. Sometimes, especially when they felt guilty enough about something, all people wanted to do was confess. On that basis, he decided simply to go to the man's house and ask him there.

❖ ❖ ❖

Kenward answered the door in his dressing gown. He hadn't even shaved and didn't look as if he'd slept well. Still, he didn't step back from the doorway once he recognized Toreth. "Is there some news, Para-investigator?"

"Not as yet. I had an appointment for another case out this way, and since I have something I wanted to clarify, I thought I'd save you the journey into I&I."

"Clarify?" Kenward swallowed. "NTS said I shouldn't—"

"It's just a minor point." Toreth smiled, relaxed but trying to make it clear from his stance that he wouldn't discourage easily.

72

After a moment, Kenward nodded, backing down from the confrontation. "Come in."

The place smelled of coffee. While Kenward poured them both a cup in the kitchen, Toreth placed the camera on the table there—keep the interview as informal as possible. When Kenward turned and saw Toreth waiting, he hesitated. "Do you want to—the living room?"

"Here's fine. This won't take long at all."

As Kenward set the mugs down his hands shook, coffee almost spilling. Toreth sipped his coffee, examining Kenward carefully. As nervous as before, maybe even more so, adding creamer to his coffee and enough sugar to turn it into syrup. The coffee tasted slightly stale. Toreth guessed Ryersen had made it before he left for the day.

"What do you want to know?" Kenward asked.

"When the kidnappers made their demands, did they ask for anything other than money?"

Kenward stared at him blankly for a moment. "Like what?"

"Anything, Mr. Kenward. Information, perhaps?"

The question seemed to genuinely baffle him, canceling out his normal air of twitching confusion. "No. Just money. I'm sure—Justice said they'd showed us all the communications."

"The kidnappers didn't make a separate approach to you? Or to your partner?"

"No. I'm sure Pieter would've told me about it."

His utter lack of reaction stumped Toreth. He sipped his coffee again, wondering whether to mention the connection to the previous cases. If Kenward told NTS, then they'd seize on the news as evidence to support their insurance claim, more proof the kidnap was genuine.

The taste of coffee reminded Toreth of his conversation with Warrick at the restaurant. Sometimes a long shot was worth taking. "Which corporation offered you the ransom money in exchange for corporate espionage on NTS?"

With experienced criminals (among whom Toreth counted most corporates by default), the sudden-attack tactic largely misfired. People clammed up or started squealing for lawyers. Here it worked as flawlessly as the highly classified experimental truth drugs never did. Coffee flooded across the table as Kenward fumbled his mug. Toreth stood up and stepped to the side as the flood ran over the edge and started to form a steaming pool on the floor.

Kenward stared up at him, eyes wide and his mouth slack with horror. "How did you know?" he asked.

Toreth hadn't even made it to work yet, and already it was the best Monday he could remember. "Give me the name."

"I don't know. One of our competitors who makes the same kinds of systems. Traffic guidance." He looked down at the table, then waved his hand over the mess. "I should . . ."

73

"Leave it." Toreth moved around the table to a drier spot. The oversweetened coffee made the air sickly, but he didn't want to risk Kenward starting to think through the consequences of this confession. "They made the approach?"

"I was so desperate—I couldn't eat, I couldn't sleep. Sofie. She was the only thing I could think about. Just seeing, over and over, what they might be doing to her. And they'd tried to get hold of our technology before. There'd been a sabotage attempt. Last year. A break-in at the building. We kept the investigation in-house, but these people knew all about it."

"So you guessed it was a genuine approach."

Kenward nodded. "They wanted designs, a promise of future information. I didn't—we were going under. I didn't think it would matter. But then once the insurance started paying out..." Kenward laughed, his voice brittle. "I tried to go back to work, Para-investigator. To kill the corporation. But I was so—I can't concentrate, I can't think, and the directors wanted the insurance money so they wouldn't *let* me work."

"When did you get the money? What happened to it?"

"I never got it." Kenward looked at him, as though surprised Toreth didn't know that, too. "I hadn't managed to deliver the information they wanted, you see. But they contacted me again, before Sofie escaped, and they agreed to give me the money in advance. I told the kidnappers about the deal and I swore that I'd pay as soon as I could. I begged them not to hurt her."

"When was that?"

"The day before she escaped. The day before they cut off her hand." He looked away, his voice a bare whisper. "They all told me that if I didn't pay, if I stuck to the accords, they'd find her and she'd be okay. But I couldn't—how could I risk it?"

"Are you talking about the Justice officers? Or the NTS board?"

"Everyone. I knew how it was going to end..." Kenward bowed forward, his hands hanging limp between his thighs. "Can I call Pieter before you arrest me? I'm sorry—I don't know how it all works."

Toreth hesitated. The corporate accords were civil law, not criminal, so proving Kenward had meant to pay wasn't grounds for arrest. While he'd planned to steal information from NTS, he hadn't gone through with that either. Right now, NTS had no choice but to fight for Kenward. Their lawyers would have a field day with an unwaivered confession of prospective sabotage from a corporate whose medical file was plastered with expert opinions about his fragile mental state. But until he had a name for the other corporation involved, he had to keep hold of Kenward.

"Do you have any evidence of this deal?" Toreth asked, trying to keep the tension out of his voice. "Anything recorded between you and these people? Anything that could identify them?"

"No. It was all face-to-face meetings, and verbal contracts. Because of the accords." Kenward looked up, a dawning awareness in his face. "They wouldn't have anything recorded either. There's only my word it happened."

Fuck. All the more reason to get the man into I&I and have him repeat everything in an interview room with a Justice rep properly assigned. "You know, if someone approached you, there's an excellent chance that they were behind the kidnapping." Kenward didn't react. "Help my investigation, and I can guarantee you won't be charged."

Kenward shook his head. "I'll still lose corporate status. NTS will throw me out."

"They'll do that anyway if we charge you with conspiracy to commit corporate sabotage."

"Yes. Yes, of course." He took a deep breath, and then stood up and brushed his hands over his dressing gown. "I'll need to put some proper clothes on. Shower."

From where Toreth sat he had a clear view of the front door of the flat. He listened for a minute, until he heard the shower start to run, then opened his hand screen and started pulling up information. Now that the gamble had paid off he wanted to have everything he could ready before news leaked and he found himself buried in corporate lawyers. Keep the momentum going, and maybe he could reach the evidence before the corporate security cleanup. Nothing immediately discoverable connected Kenward to any of NTS's competitors, and Corporate Fraud listed their prior sabotage activity as low. The alleged break-in had left no evidence in the system. Perhaps, if Toreth kept the arrest quiet and the NTS lawyers at bay, he could persuade Kenward to set up another meeting and produce some solid evidence that way.

A quarter of an hour had passed, he realized suddenly. The shower had stopped running minutes earlier, but he heard no sound of movement in the flat. Could there be another exit? Cursing, he snapped the hand screen shut. He hadn't reached the bedroom when the main door to the flat opened.

"Paul?" Pieter Ryersen called.

Oh, fuck, no. Through the bedroom door, Toreth could see Kenward sitting on the bed, holding his comm earpiece in one hand. Before he could step inside, Ryersen reached him.

"Paul, don't say anything." Ryersen turned to Toreth. "What's going on here?"

"Mr. Kenward and I were talking about the case. He agreed to the interview."

"Did he? Well, that agreement is hereby rescinded. I'm his lawyer, and—"

"I thought you gave that up."

"I did." Ryersen stepped forward, not exactly pushing Toreth aside, but occupying the doorway. "But as I'm sure you know, my license to practice is current."

"And I have twenty-four hours to question him."

Ryersen's eyes narrowed. "What's your evidence for making the arrest?"

"You're late," Sara said when he finally reached the section. If it had been anyone else, he would've taken their head off. Toreth simply glared and stamped through to his office.

Five minutes later, while he was staring out at the courtyard below his window, the door opened. "Coffee!" Sara said, holding the mug out like a shield. "You looked like you needed one."

Snapping at her would only add to the stupidity of the day. Fucking, *fucking* Monday. "Thanks."

She brought it over. "Anything I can do to help?"

"Yeah. You can start preparing a witness warrant for Paul Kenward, which will be a total waste of your time because between his fucking employers and his fucking partner, it will get us exactly nowhere."

"Okay." She paused. "What happened?"

Someone had to know sometime. Toreth burned his tongue on a mouthful of coffee, and told her about his morning so far. "So," he finished, "the bottom line is that Ryersen isn't such an ex-lawyer after all, and NTS will help him bury any suggestion Kenward tried to pay the ransom, to protect their insurance."

"But what about the confession?" Sara asked. "It hasn't come through to me yet."

Toreth grimaced. "And it won't. He spilled fucking coffee on the camera and fritzed it. I should've stopped to check it, but I didn't want to break the flow. He started coming round at the end as it was. *Fuck.*" Never mind that the cameras were supposedly robust enough to survive something like that. He'd made an amateur, fucking *junior,* mistake. If Doyle had done it, he'd already have gone the way of Belqola.

"Well," Sara said. Toreth waited for some irritatingly cheerful suggestion for how he could look on the bright side. This time, though, even Sara's optimism seemed to be faltering. "Well . . . at least *we* know what happened, right?"

He didn't even bother to tell her to get out.

After he'd finished the coffee, though, he had to admit that she had a point. The evidential value might be zero, but at least they knew. Maybe he could worry at the information from the other end, find an evidence trail leading back which would let him sidestep the awkward issue of the missing interview record. Kenward had said that they'd only talked face to face. That meant meetings, but where? Surely not the mystery company's offices, or Kenward's house.

Toreth called up Paul Kenward's credit and purchase records and analyzed them in more detail. The kidnapping had disrupted his usual movement patterns considerably, but eliminating work, family, and Justice locations helped thin it to manageable proportions for the ten days in question. It took another few minutes to set up a search to track other car and taxi journeys terminating in the same locations in a reasonable time frame, and cross-reference them with names of people and corporations from the case files, and then he let the system run. He'd picked up the trick from a senior para called Uche, who'd run a profitable sideline catching straying spouses for high-level corporates. He'd since left the division and set himself up as a private detective. In theory that was a step down, and the approved reaction was contempt. Some days, like today, Toreth thought it wouldn't be a bad life. No Tillotson, to start with, putting impossible limits on his investigation and then complaining about the result.

Oh, fuck. No doubt once Tillotson read today's IIP, he'd have some choice words about technical proficiency and carelessness.

The first run came back blank. Toreth broadened the criteria and tried again. It took four attempts, each search taking longer as the complexity grew, and Toreth had slumped low in his chair before one of the hits grabbed his attention. He sat up abruptly.

Parallel Flow. One journey route, moving through three anonymous prepaid taxis, had left Parallel Flow's headquarters and arrived at a backwater nowhere part of the city within ten minutes of a car from Kenward's house. The departures, twenty minutes later, were almost simultaneous. He called Carey.

"What can I do for you?" She squinted ostentatiously down at the bottom of her screen, and grinned. "Is that a cup of coffee? Be careful!"

Record time, even for the office gossip network. "Fuck off," Toreth said. "I don't know why you're laughing. This is your fucking case."

"Laugh, or you'll cry. And at least it wasn't me," she added callously. "Me, with my lack of field investigation experience. I probably would've really bollocksed it up."

"No, Liz, I mean it. Fuck off."

She ran her hands back through her hair, composing herself. "Sorry, sorry. What do you want?"

"Did you ever get anywhere with Parallel Flow? Links to Selman?"

Carey shook her head. "Benz has been all over us, making sure we don't step out of line, so we kept away from Selman and stuck to looking for the Finn case money, where the fiancé paid up. Not that we're getting anywhere with that either. A million euros of ransom, worth a hell of a lot more now, just—" she snapped her fingers. "Gone."

"Start working on Parallel Flow. Their name just came up again independently, linked to Kenward."

"Will do. Oh, by the way, it might take a while longer than normal. Your girl Mistry borrowed Phil first thing this morning. Do you know what she's doing with him?"

"No idea." Toreth hadn't yet caught up with the IIP. "Something more useful than screwing him, I hope."

Carey chuckled, an astoundingly dirty sound even over the comm. "Just tell her I want him back in the condition he left."

Just before lunch Mistry called, wanting to make a report in person. She had an air of quiet excitement that gave him hope she might have something to take away the lingering taste of embarrassment. She brought Phil Verstraeten with her to Toreth's office. He seemed to adopt an identically respectful attitude with the junior investigator as he did with his own boss. When Mistry pulled up a chair, Verstraeten did the same, sitting a little behind her.

"So Cole's been a good boy?" Toreth said.

"Very cooperative indeed, Para. And very convincing. He was here all Friday, and the messages certainly sounded desperate enough." She hesitated. "I had to authorize a good-faith payment, to help him convince the seller he was serious about the negotiations."

"I don't care," Toreth said. "CF is paying case costs. Where did the payment go?"

"Blind account," Mistry said. "It's locked up there for ninety days, or until someone arrives with both halves of the withdrawal code."

He'd stopped believing in lucky breaks for this case. "Of course it is. Did you manage to crack the comms?"

She smiled. "It wasn't easy. We tracked all the negotiations through our systems, and by the time they cut off the negotiations to wait for the payment to go through, Systems still couldn't pin it down to less than a few tens of thousands of possibilities on traces alone. These people are very good. But the evidence analysis system picked a name out of the list right away."

Toreth sat up straighter. "Does he sound plausible?"

"Oh, yes, Para. His name is Marcos Barrow, and he had charge of Selman's personal and family security when Louise Selman was kidnapped."

Suddenly the sun seemed to shine a little brighter into the office. The only shadow was cast by the same cloud he'd faced with Kenward. "Is there anything we can pull him in with?"

"Not for selling secrets. He's breaking a confidentiality agreement, but that falls under the corporate accords, nothing we can specifically arrest him for. I didn't think a witness warrant would do much good, so this morning I asked CF for help checking up on him."

"Good thinking." Toreth nodded. "You found something?" he asked Verstraeten.

"Certainly, Para." Verstraeten looked even more pinched than usual. Probably offended that his highly trained finance skills were being wasted on trawling for minor infractions. "He has a lot of debts, Para, and those are just the official ones. From the way money moves through his accounts, I'd say that he's servicing unregistered debts, too, and that often means illegal gambling."

"Can you make a warrant out of that?"

"Oh, yes, Para. It's reasonable suspicion, at least. Um . . ." Verstraeten peered at the screen. "Yes. No corporate status, so he has no rights to financial privacy at all. Just having an unregistered debt is a category two offense."

"Category two financials. Jesus fucking Christ." Toreth hoped this didn't mark the peak result for the whole case. At the moment, it looked like an excellent contender for the section's "Feeblest Arrest Of The Year" award (not one of Tillotson's official recognition incentives, but probably far more effective at motivating the paras). Maybe he could put the warrant in Benz's name. "Okay, we'll bring him in. But don't apply for a damage waiver. We wouldn't get it anyway and it'd only attract attention."

Barrow lived in a one-room flat in a block of subsidized social housing, paid for by one of the many corporations that offset their taxes by supplying accommodation or health care for unfortunate citizens unable to provide for themselves. Often a debatable step up in comfort from living on the street, a registered sub-soc address provided the minimal level of respectability required to avoid indigent classification. Toreth always suspected the main point of the system was to provide a strong incentive for people to stay employed and healthy in the first place.

Most crimes which took place in sub-soc accommodation were Justice affairs, and only rarely anything important enough to draw the attention of I&I. Toreth stepped carefully through the rubbish littering the stinking entryway. It made his own building look like the height of corporate luxury. Doyle poked at the lift controls, then brightened when the light came on. He pressed the button again, then cocked his head. "I can't hear the lift moving."

"We'll take the stairs," Toreth said.

"We could give it a minute. He's on the fifteenth floor, Para."

"Exercise is healthier. You should talk to Senior Para Millet from Political Crimes Marseille about taking lifts. Although you'll have trouble, as she's being spoon-fed and having her arse wiped in some facility somewhere."

Doyle paused, finger still over the button. "Sorry, Para?"

Toreth headed for the stairs, talking back to Doyle over his shoulder. "She went into a place a lot like this to pick up someone who'd been organizing local demonstrations against bad housing. The lift stuck on the way up, or possibly someone disabled it deliberately, and not long after that there was a lovely riot in progress. By the time they'd called in the Service to deal with it, three investigators and a junior para were dead and Millet was a fucking vegetable." When Toreth had heard the story the first time, it had taken him an embarrassingly long time to realize why that was funny. He blamed the pronunciation. "It's famous."

"Never heard of her, Para."

"The Martigues riots?" Toreth looked back as he turned a corner in the stairwell, and Doyle shook his head. "Fuck. Don't they teach juniors anything in training these days?"

On the fifteenth floor, they found a corridor slightly cleaner than the entryway, but which still stank. A tang of cigarette smoke and at least a couple of even more illegal drugs cut through the less savory smells. A door opened as they passed, and a barely clad woman half fell through it, grabbing the wall for support and missing. She took another stumbling step, reaching for Doyle's shoulder instead. Doyle sidestepped smartly.

"St'n still you fucking—" The abuse cut off abruptly when she finally focused on their uniforms. She pulled up short and retreated backward, slamming the door closed.

"Nice," Doyle said.

"Yeah. You know, this is the kind of place you'll end up if you keep pissing off your seniors."

Doyle glanced at him, then said, "This is the one, Para. 1507."

When Barrow answered their knock on the door he was at least shaved and sober, which at barely after lunchtime probably put him in the top few percent of the building's inhabitants. He was shabbily dressed, though, in clothes that had seen too many washes over too long to hold their shape. They looked tired, like they'd given up, and the same weariness weighed down Barrow's face. He looked every year of the forty-nine claimed in his security file, and then some. He took in their uniforms in one glance, and then simply stood there, one hand on the door frame, waiting for them to speak. Self-possession intact, then, even after however many years of living in places like this.

"We're from I&I, Mr. Barrow," Toreth said.

The man nodded, like he'd been expecting this for his whole life.

"We need you to come with us, please."

While he waited for the prisoner to be processed and brought to the interrogation room, Toreth scanned the case files. Why, he wondered suddenly, hadn't he heard from Tillotson or Benz in the last couple of days? The double IIPs kept up the thin fiction that they were steering clear of the Selman kidnapping, but Tillotson and Benz both had enough experience to read between the files. Maybe Selman genuinely did only care about his own daughter's case. Was the big secret the fact that she'd been raped? Whatever the truth, things should get livelier when Selman found out they'd arrested his former security officer.

When the guards showed the prisoner in and seated him, Toreth didn't look up from the hand screen. The lack of damage waiver rather limited his opening options. Never make threats you can't carry through, that was one of the first things his trainers had taught him. Not unless you are a hundred percent sure you won't be required to follow through, anyway, and something about the man opposite him, a stolidness underneath the shabby exterior, made Toreth disinclined to bluff.

Toreth glanced up, then back at the screen. "Mr. Barrow," he said, in a voice meant to imply that he had every minute detail of Barrow's life laid out before him. "Now that you've been processed into I&I custody, do you have any questions?"

"How did you find me?" Barrow asked.

"That's our job, Mr. Barrow." Toreth set the screen aside. "To find people who've broken the law."

He shook his head. "Not people like me. Unregistered debts? Why aren't I at Justice?"

"I think you know why. We intercepted some interesting messages you exchanged with Crispin Cole."

"Who?" Barrow said.

"The financial corporations don't like unregistered loan transactions taking place. Cuts into their business. And the public needs to be protected from unscrupulous sharks."

Barrow's eyebrow twitched. "Sharks," he said.

"There's a minimum re-education period per offense, just so people know the Administration takes it seriously, too. A good enough lawyer might be able to talk the Justice system into running some of them concurrently. Do you have a good lawyer?" Barrow held his gaze, but he didn't reply. "Well?" Toreth prompted.

"All right." Barrow looked down for a moment, then shook his head slightly. "It doesn't matter now, I suppose. There's nothing you can do with it. The truth is, Selman paid up to get Louise back. Every cent. That's what I was selling."

And possibly the last thing Toreth had expected to hear. "Paid? But—she died."

"Something went very badly wrong. We delivered the ransom as arranged, and someone took it, and then a week later we found her body."

"How was the ransom paid?"

"Exactly according to the demand. Easily saleable items: gold jewelry, other antiques."

Another tick against the list of potential similarities. "And what about anything else? Information passed along with the ransom?"

That won a microhesitation, which would be ringing alarm bells on the analysis system. "What kind of information? Corporate secrets?"

Playing for time, if Toreth was any judge. Toreth kept his face blank, watching Barrow levelly.

"Mm, okay. Information..."

A long silence followed. Toreth didn't press. He had leverage on the witness, but not enough to get a decent damage waiver. Plus it could only be a matter of time before Tillotson, or Selman himself, found out that Barrow was here. When someone like Selman paid close attention, leaks were inevitable. Finally Barrow rubbed his chin. "You know...maybe there was, yes. I was in charge of personal security, but I didn't handle all the negotiations. Selman liked to split things up, not to let any one person have too much power. But right before I set off to deliver the payment, Selman himself added another small box to the bag. I assumed it was more valuables, but it could've held a data stick."

"You didn't look?"

"I was concentrating on my job. And besides, Selman was always watching." He smiled thinly. "If you really want to know about it, you'll have to ask him."

Using the highly trained I&I squad of flying pigs to run the interview. "The investigation isn't focused on Louise Selman." Might as well get that firmly on the interview transcript. "We're looking at a recent kidnapping. I don't suppose you've

81

ever heard anything which makes you think the same team was at work again?"

"No." Barrow took a deep breath, then shook his head. "Although I can't say that I exactly have my finger on the pulse of corporate security these days."

Toreth thought of the squalid building where they'd picked Barrow up. "Thin fifteen years?"

Barrow's expression soured even more. "Selman's personal safety was my responsibility. Including his family's. I'd only been in the job a few months, not enough to claim any loyalty from him. How long do you think I lasted after we found his daughter? How many people do you think would hire me with that on my CV?"

"Selman sacked you, even knowing what you know?"

"Have you met him?" Barrow asked.

"No." And not likely to, either. "As I said, we're investigating a completely different kidnapping case."

"Right." Barrow leaned forwards slightly. "I've worked for some ruthless people, but Selman matches any of them. He doesn't give second chances, and he doesn't tolerate risks if he can eliminate them. Believe me, it's safer not to be noticed by him at all. And don't ever be something he finds inconvenient."

"So you never tried to apply any leverage?"

"To be honest, back then I was grateful he just sacked me." Now Barrow sounded resigned, like any resentment had worn down over the years. "Besides, you'd need to be a braver man than Marcos Barrow to try to blackmail Selman."

"Yet you're selling your story now."

"I need the money. As you know." Toreth caught the veiled flash of resentment. "Right now those debts are a bigger threat to my health. I'm not doing anything illegal—the information is mine to sell. My personal notes and recordings."

"Recordings?" Toreth asked.

"The drop was filmed beginning to end, to prove that I'd done what we were supposed to do. And that probably saved my life. At least Selman knew I hadn't bollocksed it up."

"Technically you might not be breaking the law, but you're breaking the confidentiality agreements you signed."

"And what are they going to do? Take away my corporate status? Fine me? They can try." He slumped down in the chair, looking suddenly tired. "Look, is there some kind of accommodation we can reach here? If I give you the recordings, can I go? I have them hidden. I'm sure you'd find them in the end, but it'll save you a lot of trouble, and they're useless to me. I can hardly make an anonymous sale now."

Toreth ignored the (probably true) implication that I&I would either leak the information, or simply turn it over to Selman. He could afford to look generous, because right now everyone would win, except possibly Barrow who was fucked anyway. "That sounds fair enough," Toreth said. "You hand then over, and I'll find you somewhere nice and comfortable to stay until Systems have authenticated them."

The file detailing the authentication of the recordings had barely arrived for Toreth's inspection when Sara put her head around his office door. "Toreth..."

"What do you want?"

She grinned, unabashed. "Just to ask if I can file Cris as no charge. Since he found you what you wanted."

Toreth smiled. "Okay. You can—no, wait. No need to bother, I'll call him."

Sara eyed him suspiciously, then nodded. "Don't forget, please?"

"I'll do it right now. It'll be a pleasure."

Cole, if possible, looked even less happy to see him than before. "Oh. Hello, Para-investigator."

"Well?" Toreth prompted.

Confusion flickered over his face. "I—you called me." When Toreth didn't answer, his expression cleared to bitter recall. "Oh, right. Did you send my file to Justice yet?"

Toreth smiled. Got the little fucker nicely trained. "I'm just this minute about to officially close the file, no submission."

Cole managed an almost gracious smile. "Thank you very much."

"No, thank you, Mr. Cole, for your public-spirited assistance. Sorry about your scoop."

"There'll be another one along." Cole smiled wryly. "I'm thinking about submitting an outline for a piece on the wonderful job I&I does protecting corporations and corporates."

"Sounds fascinating," Toreth said. "If you need any help, send the request to Media Relations. And try not to take any cameras into restricted areas this time."

"Don't worry, I've learned my lesson. Strictly aboveboard methods from now on, I promise." He rubbed his chin. "You definitely found the source, then?"

Toreth ignored the question. "There's just one more thing before you go."

Cole tensed. "What? I thought we were done."

"I don't appreciate people trying to persuade my team to break the law."

Cole leaned back slightly, frowning. "Break—I don't understand."

"Try this, then. If I ever hear again that you asked a member of I&I to make illegal comm traces for you, then I'll personally take you down to level D and make sure you come back up in more pieces than Louise Selman." Toreth smiled pleasantly. "Now do you understand me?"

"I—" Cole swallowed, his face suddenly flushed. "Yes. Yes, of course."

The correctness of his decision to trade for the recordings was confirmed later that day, when Toreth was watching a much-younger Barrow walk along a narrow alleyway on the screen for the fifth time.

The door opened, no knock, and Tillotson said, "Toreth?"

"Right here." Toreth flicked the picture off the screen. Why the hell couldn't the section head stick to summoning paras to his office?

"Why did you arrest one of Joseph Selman's ex-employees?"

"We had reason to believe he possessed information relevant to the case, sir," Toreth said blandly. "Comms analysis combined with the evidence analysis system picked his name out. It's in the IIP, unless the new junior forgot to put it there."

Tillotson frowned. "I thought I was clear about this, Toreth. Joseph Selman does not want any investigations into his daughter's death."

"I'm not investigating that. Like I said, I had reason to believe Barrow might have information relevant to the current case. Sofie Kenward, you remember?"

"And I suppose that reason's in the IIP, is it?"

Some days Toreth truly understood the meaning of job satisfaction. "Want to know why Selman's so scared of an investigation?"

That stopped Tillotson dead. Then his pointed face sharpened even further with curiosity. "What do you mean?"

Toreth grinned. "Come here and watch this."

Looking like he expected Toreth to bite, Tillotson came to stand beside him. Toreth started the recording again. Tillotson watched in silence as it ran. "Is that authentic?" he said when the screen went blank.

"Yes." When Tillotson didn't answer, Toreth said, "If I might make a suggestion, sir, why don't you tell Selman that you have everything under control? Barrow knew nothing, we'll let him go right away, you've slapped my wrist and I won't do it again. All the usual. No need to upset him. And then if he ever tries to make trouble in the future, we know a lot more than he thinks we do."

After a long silence, Tillotson said, "Send me those recordings."

"Of course, sir."

Tillotson moved around to the other side of the desk and frowned at Toreth. "All of them. And don't keep copies."

Toreth smiled just a little. "Of course not."

This time the silence lasted even longer, before Tillotson turned and walked out.

"Good job, well done," Toreth said to the empty office.

Carey might only be a specialist investigator—although questions of relative rank between senior paras and senior specialists were always tricky—but she had a nice office. Better than anything in General Criminal. CF and Political took all the attention and budget perks.

"When did you get redecorated?" Toreth checked the pile of the new carpet with his heel, hoping it would leave a mark. "I remember Chevril whinging about it, but he whinges all the fucking time so that hardly pins it down."

"Last year. That was quick," Carey added.

"Sorry?"

"I called you about two minutes ago and you didn't answer. I left a message with Sara."

"I was already on my way here. I'm avoiding Tillotson for a while."

"Why?"

Toreth handed her a data stick. "That's why. Don't put it on the system. And definitely don't file it in the IIP."

Carey watched the partial interview, and then the old recording, interest slowly changing to amazement, and finally a broad grin. All she said at the end, though, was, "Selman himself isn't in the recording."

"No, but half his personal security staff are. And his name certainly is. Watch it again, and count the references to 'Mr. Selman.' I don't think he'd like to have to explain it to a CEC investigation at any rate."

Carey set the stick aside. "And I have something you're going to like about Parallel Flow. Nothing criminal, but it's a link. I had to trace through a maze of subsidiaries and holding companies, but guess who owns a large minority stake in Parallel Flow?"

"Selman-Sterntech."

Carey stared at him. "How the hell did you know that?"

"Why the hell else would you be so excited about it?" Toreth grinned at her disappointment. "No, you're right. It's still good. It doesn't prove anything, though. Selman-Sterntech has a lot of interests in traffic control."

"But if Selman paid his own daughter's ransom, then maybe he was willing to risk paying someone else's, too. He could've used Parallel Flow as a front to make the approach. You know who we need to talk to."

"Fucking Kenward." Toreth contemplated kicking the edge of Carey's nice new desk. CF would probably claim for the damage. "Shit. This is what comes of trying to find a way round the paperwork. We've got the witness warrant in now, but I don't rate our chances of getting it back soon. If at all. NTS and Ryersen will fight every fucking syllable."

Pity all the corporates in the Administration weren't as helpful in a case as Warrick. Mind you, they weren't as much of a handful to control, either.

Carey shook her head, mock sympathetic. "Maybe tomorrow will be better, eh?"

Chapter Nine

When the comm chimed, long experience meant Toreth could feel the time before he checked the clock. Too fucking early to be anything other than very good or very bad news.

"Senior Para-investigator Toreth? This is General Criminal."

He didn't recognize the individual, just the solid, emotionless tone of a night-shift admin who had called out every imaginable incident, and whose entertainment derived primarily from waking up people not yet suffering a night shift. "What's happened?" Toreth asked.

"Report linked to an IIP in your name, Para. Person or persons unknown have kidnapped a Sofie Kenward from the Union General Infirmary. That's Kenward, Sofie, K-E-N—"

Toreth groaned. "I know who it is, and where. I'll be right there."

❖ ❖ ❖

Over on the other side of the city, up on higher ground, the rising sun dyed the white stone of the Int-Sec complex buildings a bright pink. As Toreth's taxi drove to the hospital, he hoped the day wouldn't get any bloodier than that before the end. Media Relations would have a hard time finding the positive in this story. Maybe he should ask for a suppression order right away.

Mistry and Doyle, both living closer to the scene, were waiting for him in the hospital reception. "No chance she just discharged herself?" Toreth asked as he buttoned his jacket. "Decided to go home after all, or go into hiding?"

"No, Para," Mistry said. "Sabs, no doubt about it. Late last night someone brought in a patient, supposedly with extensive burns, to use a neural scanner. Apparently it's routine enough that no one was suspicious. Half an hour later, the patient was wheeled out again." Mistry raised her eyebrows eloquently.

"Oh, no. Where was the fucking security guard?"

"Unconscious in a closet, Para," Doyle said. "He's awake now, but I talked to him for a few minutes and he claims he doesn't remember anything that happened since about last Thursday. I believe him. I sent samples to the lab, but he's been dosed with something, no doubt."

"And the burn patient?"

"Was lying in Sofie Kenward's bed, equally unconscious," Mistry said. "She's a good match for age and hair color, enough to fool a casual glance in from the corridor. The system says she's an indigent. She hasn't come round enough to make a statement yet, but..."

Toreth nodded. "But why would he give only half his witnesses amnesia." No hope there, unless they were incredibly lucky and the decoy had some kind of natural resistance to whatever drug she'd been dosed with. And Toreth wouldn't bet against the kidnapper having been careful enough to screen her for exactly that.

"Why would he take her back from here, Para?" Mistry shook her head. "The risk is ridiculous. Insane."

Toreth contemplated the question. "Either he is crazy, or he's trying to get caught, or there's some kind of a time constraint. Something serious enough that he couldn't wait until she was out of hospital again and lift her somewhere easier."

"Although he made it look easy enough," Doyle said.

No question about that. Snatching the subject of an I&I investigation was just taking the piss. The web of the case suddenly felt a lot stronger, and Toreth had the unpleasant feeling of being the fly stuck in it while the spider ran mockingly around him.

"Right." Toreth squared his shoulders, trying to shake off the early morning gloom. "All the usual. Forensics are on their way. Start interviews. And the car won't show up on the systems, I'm sure, but let's see how far we can track him on cameras."

The trouble with working against pro sabs was that they knew the routine as well as anyone at I&I.

Toreth found Liz Carey waiting for him in his office when he finally made it back to I&I. He threw his jacket at the hook and missed, so he left it on the floor.

Carey looked actually upset, her bright hair in even more disarray than usual. "We should've left an I&I guard there," she said.

"Why? He'd only be lying in a cupboard, too. Whoever these sabs are, they're good. Plus there was no reason to think it would happen. No one would waste the budget on guarding someone like Sofie Kenward just on spec."

Carey grumbled, then finally shrugged. "I suppose so. What next?"

"Next?" Toreth sat down at his desk. "We try to find her."

"I remember the days of tagging." Carey sighed. "Shame that's long over."

Shortly after Toreth had qualified as a para, there had been a brief vogue for corporates to chip their children with trackers, to deter kidnapping and to keep an eye on their whereabouts. For a while, how strong a signal the tiny devices produced had become a status symbol. After a couple of cases where kidnappers had tossed their prizes into a Faraday cage and started digging with scalpels, the fashion had reversed itself quickly.

"Yeah," Toreth said. "The hospital uses bracelets, but somehow he swapped it off onto the indig girl. Again, technically he's fucking good. We can hope for something from forensics, but since he wasn't even in a hurry this time, I wouldn't rely on it. I'll call Media Relations, get them to add an appeal to all the news feeds."

"You think there's any chance someone connected to the previous kidnappings might start feeling altruistic now that the poor girl's life is in danger again?"

Toreth snorted, at the idea and at Carey's dry tone. She and he shared a pretty harmonious view on the priorities of corporates. "They didn't in the last decade or so. But Kenward could know something. If he's part of the pattern, there must be *some* link. He's got every fucking reason to talk to us now."

Carey shook her head, at the possibility rather than the principle. "I'm sure you're right, if we can get him away from Ryersen and the damn NTS watchdog lawyers."

If. Toreth sat up, sudden inspiration sending a prickly jolt down his spine. Risky, but... "I'd say we have good reason to believe that Sofie Kenward is in imminent danger of death or life-threatening injury, wouldn't you?"

Carey looked at him blankly. "Yes, of course."

"I don't suppose it comes up much for finance specialists. Death, life-threatening injury, acts of sedition likely to harm the Administration, treason—they're some of the circumstances allowing unwarranted actions. Arrests, interrogations, you name it."

"We can interview Kenward?" Carey asked.

"Liz, we can call in a fucking Service riot suppression detachment just so long as we can justify it afterwards to Internal Investigations."

"How about Selman?"

Toreth hesitated, wishing he'd thought ahead before he blurted out his idea.

"Well?" Carey demanded.

"*You* can arrest him, if *you* can justify it to Internal. You're on your own with that."

"How about asking for an interview? At his offices." Carey could put a rich depth of pleading in her voice when she wanted to. "Toreth, it all leads back to him, and I bet the bastard thinks he's untouchable."

"He doesn't just think it. We don't have any evidence he ever broke any real laws. Just Barrow's statement that he probably violated the accords, and I don't want Joseph Selman pissed off at me personally over something that isn't even going to make it onto my case record."

"No evidence?"

"Okay. No evidence that I want to try to convince Internal with."

"Fine." Carey shrugged and stood up. "I'll go on my own, then."

No bluff involved, that was clear. And with Tillotson making it equally clear Toreth's neck was on the line, no way in hell could he let Carey loose on Selman unsupervised. For a moment he contemplated asking Benz to bring his specialist into line, but that he couldn't stomach. "Wait. Give me a couple of minutes. And find a car." Despite himself, Toreth grinned, feeling a kick from the sudden jump to action. "This time in the morning we should get a new one, and if we're going to commit suicide we might was well go out in style."

Before he left, he called Mistry at the hospital. Her comm was off, but she called back after a minute. "I'm sorry, Para. I was busy with the surveillance recording. What do you need?"

"As soon as you can leave the hospital, I want you to go pick up Kenward and bring him in. We're calling this imminent danger, okay?"

"We're—yes, Para. Imminent danger."

"Take a few guards with you, even if you leave them in the car. I don't think NTS and Ryersen will hand him over without a fight. We have to deal with Internal whatever happens, so we don't fuck around and waste our chances."

Toreth had half hoped that Selman would simply send them away. Then maybe he could persuade Carey that they had more productive things to do elsewhere. Instead they were left for almost an hour in a private waiting room clearly intended for visitors far more important than I&I. Toreth paced the spotless deep-pile red rug, distracting himself by trying to calculate how much the room's décor must have cost relative to his salary. Carey, more relaxed now that they'd made it inside the building, sprawled in a deep chair, picking out chocolates from the incised crystal bowl set on the table.

"Want some?" Carey offered. "The ones with the gold leaf on top are good."

Toreth shook his head. "I don't like sweets."

"Relax. Sit down. If we made it this far, they'll talk to us." Carey smiled. "Trust me. This is what *we* do in Corporate Fraud. Damage waivers and interrogation rooms don't solve everything," she added.

"But they make life a hell of a lot easier."

The door opened, admitting a neat, slender young man. His short-cut black hair and almond eyes made him look like Sara's corporate admin double, and he had a high-paid admin's flawlessly polite smile. "Please, let me apologize for the delay. Come this way."

Selman also apologized, with equal insincerity. Just to prove how much he meant it, he'd come out from behind the vast desk to shake their hands. The admin he dismissed with a nod, leaving the three of them alone together. The absence of lawyers or security advisers meant little when any number of them could be watching the meeting, but it made a polite gesture.

After the waiting room, the office seemed austere, if Toreth ignored the cost of each severe, carefully placed piece of furniture and the size of the place. The floor was the most highly decorated part of the room, with lines of darker wood set into the pale-grained background. They formed interconnecting loops, dotted with circles in polished silvery metal, each one inscribed with *ST.* Toreth didn't recognize the design. The Sterntech logo was silver, but a different shape, and the rest of the somehow familiar pattern seem unrelated to it.

"Do you like it?" Selman took a few more steps, out onto a curve. "It's the plan of the new underground system. Sterntech won the contract for the infrastructure and transport control systems."

"Of the northern and western segments," Carey added politely.

Selman's smile didn't waver. "We're heavily involved in the whole system. It will be our contribution of the final restoration of New London." And so, the floor reminded them, Joseph Selman was a politically powerful figure who couldn't be embarrassed without in turn embarrassing the Administration. "Although, of course, it's a little inconvenient. Whenever there are the inevitable alterations in the plans, someone has to come in and relay the appropriate section. I seem to spend half my life in my second office."

As Toreth took out his camera, Selman shook his head. "I don't think so, Para-investigator."

Toreth didn't argue. "We don't want to waste your time, so I'll get to the point, Mr. Selman. Sofie Kenward has been kidnapped again."

"I heard." When Toreth's eyebrows went up, Selman smiled. "I have my sources. A private news feed, if you like. I heard in the car on the way here in the morning." His voice deepened a little. "The poor girl. I hope you find her soon. I imagine NTS security won't be much help."

Information went both ways in encounters like this. As Toreth fished, so did Selman. And Selman almost certainly had a clearer idea of what he wanted to hook. "I'm glad you appreciate the urgency," Toreth said. "We have some questions we'd like to ask you. Under the provisions for imminent danger to—"

"I understand the circumstances," Selman said. "Our lawyers reviewed all the details of your request for an interview, and deemed it acceptable."

Acceptable? Toreth had been woken up too early to fuck around with game-playing corporates.

Carey stepped forward. "Thank you, Mr. Selman. We're here because we suspect these sabs have carried out the same plan before, including when they took your daughter."

Selman moved away, around behind his desk, and sat down. "If that's why you're here, I'm afraid I can't help you."

"Mr. Selman," Carey said. "We're confident the connection is there, but we can't find enough information about the team to hope to locate Sofie quickly."

"I'm sure you can't. You've been looking for a few days. I've had fifteen years." The crisp finality of his voice didn't entirely hide the bitterness underneath. "If I knew anything which would let you find the individuals who took Louise, then I promise you I would've used that information myself, a long time ago, and they would be in no position to kidnap anyone."

"As you might know, we interviewed Marcos Barrow recently," Toreth said. "He told us that you arranged payment for your daughter's kidnappers, and he delivered it."

"How interesting," Selman said flatly. "Of course, that was a long time ago, and he could be said to have a reason to bear a grudge."

"Although it wasn't his daughter who was killed," Carey said, and Selman looked at her sharply.

Toreth wished he could manage a discreet kick to tell her to tone it down, but Selman had left them standing, in clear view of his desk. "We also know that Parallel Flow attempted to pass money to Paul Kenward for his daughter's release, in exchange for NTS secrets."

"And an altruistic lot they are," Carey said. "They were willing to pay him in advance, with no practical way to make sure he delivered. They could hardly sue him if he didn't, could they?"

"And do you have Paul Kenward's claim on record?" Selman asked. "Because if not..."

"Imminent danger," Toreth said with satisfaction. "We're taking him in to I&I right now. The NTS lawyers can do what they like, but with Sofie gone again how long do you think it will be before we persuade him the best thing for her is if he answers any questions we ask?" Selman didn't answer. "He'll name Parallel Flow. The Confederation will investigate the breach of the accords. If we can find parallels to old cases, so can they. There are two other kidnappings we know about, and we believe you arranged payment for them, just like you tried to do for Kenward through Parallel Flow." Toreth caught himself just in time to avoid leaning over the desk. If Selman was remotely likely to be intimidated by that, he would

91

never have sat down. "Look, I'll be blunt. We don't care about the accords. They're not in our jurisdiction. Kidnapping, now that is. So is murder."

Selman looked up quickly. "Murder?"

Discretion being the better part of a continuing career, he'd let Carey volunteer to deliver the ultimatum. "If Kenward can't pay," she said, "then these people will kill his daughter. And if that happens I'll turn everything we have over to the Confederation of European Corporations."

Toreth didn't look at Carey. They'd discussed the plan on the way over, but bluffing someone like Selman meant zero margin for error. If Selman kept denying the connection they'd have to tell him about Barrow's old recording, but Toreth hated playing all his cards.

Selman stood up again, and for a moment Toreth thought he was about to dismiss them. Then Selman gestured over to a collection of small armchairs. "I think we can discuss this more comfortably over here. Please, sit down."

Carey grinned at him as Selman led them over. *We win,* she mouthed silently, and Toreth frowned at her.

The chairs were a lot more comfortable than they looked. Toreth settled in, giving Selman the courtesy of some breathing space now that they'd forced his hand.

"So tell me more about these kidnappings you've linked to Louise's," Selman said.

Toreth had the screen ready, with the names of the three kidnap victims taken after Louise. He saw no need to let Selman know they'd discovered the older cases. He handed the screen over, watching Selman's face carefully.

"That's a provisional list," Toreth said. "Only the ones we're certain about."

"I see. Interesting." Selman scanned the list again, then handed it back. "If my security team finds anything out about them, I'll be sure to let you know." No request for permission for that, but it hadn't taken Selman long at all to memorize the names, either. He plainly knew them already, and he didn't seem to care if they knew it, too.

"You remember Paul Kenward, then?" Toreth asked.

"Of course. One of the most brilliant engineers who ever worked for us, if somewhat highly strung. Corporations are built on people, and his technical skill helped push CGS to the front in its field. When my mother moved on into public service, CGS's success showed her to whom she could best entrust all this." He gestured to the map spread out around them. "I owe him a lot."

Carey's eyebrows were eloquent enough that she didn't need to put any sarcasm in her voice. "Enough to take a risk as big as paying off kidnappers?"

"You have no evidence that I did anything of the kind. Supposition and coincidence. Potentially, the word of a man suffering severe mental stress." Selman brushed the words aside with a flick of his fingers. "Nothing the Confederation would find conclusive. They're no more all-knowing than I&I."

92

"Still, I'm sure you don't want them to look," Toreth said. "And again, we don't care if they don't—or do."

Selman nodded. "Of course. So, your current theory, if I understand it correctly, is that after I failed to save Louise, I used Parallel Flow to arrange corporate espionage as a front to pay the ransoms of several kidnap victims, because their parents had no other chance of getting their children back alive?"

"We never speculated on a motive," Carey said.

Selman ignored the qualifier without a flicker. "Hypothetically, if I wanted to help someone I knew who found him- or herself in such a terrible situation, then of course I'd need to circumvent the accords in the least suspicious fashion."

"By helping them in ways which resulted in you getting information you wanted, without having to pay for sabs?" Carey asked.

"It would be necessary to have a convincing layer of protection." Selman shrugged slightly. "Who said altruism has to be a one-way street? NTS possesses some extremely interesting technology. In view of their financial problems, our strategy has been to wait until they go under and buy them out."

"But the situation changed?" Carey said.

"Hypothetically, it could have done so. And I have a great deal of sympathy for Paul Kenward's situation. More than sympathy. Empathy."

"Or perhaps you're being blackmailed into paying these ransoms?" Toreth suggested. "By the kidnappers, or someone else who knows what happened with your daughter?"

"Perhaps you should think that suggestion through in a little more detail." Selman's mouth drew sharply down. "The consequences of paying up would be worse than of coming clean. If I chose to quite anonymously help one or two unfortunates avoid the loss I suffered, I would need no other motive."

The firmness seemed slightly at odds with Selman's previous demeanor. Could Selman be telling the truth about his quasi-altruism? If so, did he primarily use the corporate espionage to justify the ransoms to himself, or vice versa?

"All the people involved in these cases are linked to Selman-Sterntech or Parallel Flow," Carey pointed out.

Selman acknowledged it with a shrug. "If, hypothetically, I were to pay any ransoms, then naturally they'd be in cases I came to hear about in time to make an anonymous approach. How else would I do it? Corporate sabotage is by its nature secret."

Toreth wondered how much of the hour they'd spent waiting Selman had used up in preparing answers to just these questions. Then he laughed silently at himself, because, no, that was ridiculous. Whatever his true motives, Selman would have had the responses polished for years. Still, and despite the repeated reiteration of the hypothetical nature of the conversation, they'd learned more than Toreth had ever expected. More than their evidence justified. He'd expected flat denials, and the minimum length of interview to let it be seen that Joseph Selman was co-operating like a good citizen. If he was willing to say so much, what was he hiding?

"And what about the information wanted by the kidnapper personally?" Toreth asked. "How does your supposed anonymity fit with that?"

He hadn't expected much of a reaction; he couldn't be lucky more than once a case. Selman frowned. "I have no idea what you're talking about, Para-investigator."

"Hypothetically," Toreth said with some irritation.

"Not even hypothetically."

"Suppose that *hypothetically* someone told us that they saw you add a small object to the bag holding the payoff for your daughter's ransom? A data stick."

"Barrow?" Selman snorted. "Do you think I ended up sitting here in this office today by being that careless and stupid? If—*if*—I decided to authorize any such payments, then I'd take care to be somewhere a long way from where the transfer happened. I certainly wouldn't have touched the ransom, or anything in it. Suppose it had been intercepted? What's this information supposed to be?"

Toreth hesitated. Bluff, or not? "That's something I can't disclose."

Selman smiled slightly. "What a pity. I'd like to know what's valuable enough that I'd take such a ridiculous risk over it." He looked between them. "Was there anything else you wanted to ask?"

"The Justice files on your daughter's kidnapping are very thin," Carey said. "If you have any more information, we'd be keen to see it. And as quickly as possible—every minute matters for Sofie Kenward."

If Selman knew they'd been forbidden access to the Justice file, he didn't show it. "Sterntech will, of course, give you every assistance. I'll have the full details of the security operation from when Louise was taken sent to you. Maybe you'll be able to find something in it that will help. Which is something my security teams have never been able to do."

Toreth gave it one more try. "If they demanded information from Paul Kenward in exchange for his daughter, he will tell us about it."

"I hope you'll be considerate of his situation when you question him. I know what he's going through." The balance had shifted back away from them again. Either they'd told Selman what he wanted to know, or he'd decided they knew nothing of interest. "If there's nothing more for now..." Selman reached for his comm without giving them a chance to disagree. "Tam, could you escort the officers out of the building?"

Almost immediately, the same admin who'd shown them in opened the office door. "This way, please."

Toreth lingered, the last to leave. As the heavy door swung closed behind him, Toreth set his heel on the threshold, stopping the door just a fraction open. Selman's voice came clearly from inside the room. "Ambrose isn't answering her comm. Find her and send her up." A pause. "Then get her out of the meeting. Immediately."

94

Tam cleared his throat. "Please, let me show you out." Toreth had the feeling that if he wore anything other than an I&I uniform, the invitation would be nothing like as polite.

In the lift, Carey leaned in towards him. "Rowena Ambrose," she murmured. "Sterntech head of security. Sounds like the cat's well in amongst the pigeons."

Her voice rippled pleasantly down Toreth's spine. "Well and truly," he agreed.

As soon as the lift opened, Toreth strode out across the cream marble foyer of the Sterntech building, ignoring the glances from the receptionists and security guards. He had the feeling back that they were still in the dark, but at least they were moving.

"Where next?" Carey asked, keeping pace with him easily.

"I want to talk to Barrow. Almost everything he told us tallied up, except for Selman denying he'd put a data stick in with the ransom. Which means that one of them isn't being entirely honest with us."

Carey smiled. "Naughty."

Corporate Fraud investigators had even less experience of subsidized living than most of I&I, but Liz Carey didn't show any surprise when they entered Barrow's building. She walked smartly through the detritus on the floor, sidestepping the worst without blinking. "Looks a lot like the place where I grew up," she commented.

Must be the case for it, Toreth thought sourly as they climbed the stairs.

At number 1507, Toreth hammered on the door and gave Barrow a minute. He didn't like the idea of forcing his way into a room owned by an ex-corporate security officer, not in a building where there must be a strong incentive for residents to protect their belongings by whatever means they could. When no one answered, Toreth cautiously overrode the security, foot tapping while the system ground through the authorization check. He made Carey stand to one side as he pushed the door back with his foot, but the precautions were wasted. The room looked exactly as it had when Toreth glimpsed it over Barrow's shoulder, right down to the chair pushed back from the table.

Toreth scanned the contents. The bed was made, every surface dust free and clean, and empty containers were stacked neatly beside the presumably broken recycling unit. Nothing suggested a hasty flight. When he'd made certain the room was clear, Toreth bent to look under the bed. An empty suitcase confirmed his suspicions.

This hour of the morning clearly counted as unreasonably early to most of the building's inhabitants. Toreth and Carey banged on doors and roused some of Barrow's immediate neighbors. Of those able to deliver a coherent account, not one had seen him since Toreth and Doyle picked him up the day before.

"There's nothing that says he even came back here after we released him," Toreth said.

"I don't blame him," Liz Carey said. "He's probably still running."

"Maybe. Or maybe something more permanent. Watch the corridor."

Toreth opened his screen and called up a credit and purchase check for Barrow. Nothing since a taxi ride which had brought him from the edge of the Int-Sec complex to the street below. Had Barrow lied to them about the ransom because he didn't think they'd ever interview Selman, or had Selman lied because he knew they wouldn't find Barrow alive?

He'd just shared the information with Carey when his comm alerted him to a message from Mistry. For a moment he expected her to say that Kenward had also avoided them again, but the fast-swoop tactic had worked. "I had to use the guards in the end, but we have Kenward down in the cells."

"Good work. Did you talk to him yet?"

"No." Mistry hesitated. "How long are you going to hold him, Para? He's much worse than he was before—I'd describe him as hysterical when we took him out of his flat. He just kept saying he has to be there in case anyone makes contact about Sofie. I don't think he's realized yet that there's no way Parallel Flow can pay him now. I'd say that when he does then he's likely to break down completely."

"Start the interview," Toreth said. "I'll join you as soon as I can."

The alarm began to sound as he opened the security door into the corridor. No logical reason existed why it should be anything to do with his case, but Toreth lengthened his stride. Up ahead, a flurry of sudden activity marked the site of the trouble, staff hurrying in through an open interview room door. A handful of guards stood around like ugly decorations, useless but attracted by the urgency.

Even before he pushed through to the door, Toreth could smell it. Fresh blood streaked the walls, still dripping and pooling. Paul Kenward lay on the floor, twitching feebly, his throat ripped open. Black-uniformed medics surrounded him, shouting instructions to one another. Away from the frantic focus, Mistry sat on a chair, blood coating her as liberally as the walls, while a medic treated a deep gash across her right palm. Her blood dripped down to mingle with Kenward's. When Mistry saw Toreth she tried to stand, but the medic pressed her firmly back down on the seat.

"What happened?" Toreth asked, raising his voice over the commotion.

"I'm sorry, Para. One minute I was interviewing him, the next he was—" Mistry gestured at her throat with her uninjured hand. "I tried to stop him, but all I did was get in the way." She winced, her shoulder jerking involuntarily as the medic temporarily sealed over the wound.

96

Of course it would be Mistry, someone actually useful to his team. Pity he hadn't put Abel or Brown in with the bastard. He looked back to where Kenward sprawled, still now, the wounds in his throat sealed. A broken piece of something, metal or plastic indistinguishable under the thick coating of blood, lay on the floor near Kenward's hand. Nothing like that should be on a processed prisoner or witness, but Mistry wasn't responsible for prisoner security. That was the job of the useless fucking security staff standing around him.

A machine started an irregular beeping as another medic attached a monitor to the prisoner. Still alive, then, but he might as well be dead. With this much blood around Toreth wouldn't be interviewing Kenward today, or for a while to come, even if he lived. The ragged gashes cut across his windpipe, and the fucker had probably destroyed his larynx. He hadn't even gone for an artery and done the job properly, just slashed away at random.

"Fuck." Toreth slammed his hand against the door frame. "Fuck, *fuck*."

One of the medics looked up and winced. At the edges of his vision, Toreth caught sight of the guards shuffling back, all suddenly thinking of somewhere else they needed to be. Toreth whirled around, grabbed the nearest guard and pushed him back against the wall. The badge on his shoulder, immediately above the handful of uniform clenched in Toreth's fist, labeled him a senior security officer. Probably the useless cunt in charge of the shift. "What the fuck went wrong?" Toreth demanded.

"I'm sorry, Para." The man held his hands up, half apology, half pleading for calm. "I don't know how he got that in there with him. The sensors in the room went off the second he started cutting, even before the investigator called us. He was still on his knees when the medics got here."

"Still too fucking late for my case! If he dies..." All the effective threats Toreth had were fucking bureaucratic bullshit involving disciplinary hearings. None of them were close to what he wanted to do. He swore again, then released the man and turned away.

The medics had loaded Kenward onto a trolley. Toreth smacked the door frame again with helpless frustration as they hurried his witness away down the corridor. Keeping back from trouble, a cleanup crew waited to mop up the mess. Inside the blood-streaked cell, Mistry was still watching him with apprehension. Toreth shook his head. "Not your fault, Jas. Get patched up, and cleaned up. I'll see you upstairs."

Toreth paced his office, stopping every turn to glare out of the window at the courtyard below. Mistry and Doyle sat quietly; Mistry was cradling her injured hand, while Doyle clearly possessed a healthy respect for an angry senior. Sara had brought in a coffee, and she lingered by his desk. She probably had a good excuse, but Toreth knew that she wanted to hear the details of the fresh cockup.

The latest news from downstairs hadn't improved Toreth's mood. Kenward was in the intensive care unit, stable according to the medics, but a long way from useful. The piece of plastic he'd used to open his throat had been torn from the underside of the interview table, and so Toreth had no one to bollock except possibly a maintenance crew. And on top of everything else, they were being battered by a storm of demands and legal submissions from Pieter Ryersen and NTS. Eventually, Internal would arrive to examine the imminent danger claim. The only people not complaining were NTS's insurers. They were probably hoping Kenward would die. No insurance policy in the Administration could be forced to pay out after a suicide in I&I custody.

"Why the fuck did he slit his throat?" Toreth turned with his back to the window. "Idiot. Any half-fucking-competent corporate lawyer could've mitigated him down to light re-education. Probably not even that. If we even pressed charges, which we had no reason to do. Mistry?"

"Yes, I told him we weren't interested in the corporate sabotage," Mistry said. "Although I'm not sure he was listening."

"So why, then?"

"I can think of one reason, Para," Mistry said slowly.

She hesitated, and Toreth waved her to go on. "No need to spin it out."

"Sorry, Para. It's Sofie. If this is some personal vendetta against a specific group of people that includes Kenward, maybe he was hoping that once the kidnappers found out he was dead they'd let Sofie go."

"Do you really think so?" Surely no one, however unhinged, could be that delusionally self-sacrificing?

"If it's true, it could buy us some time," Doyle said. "They might at least keep her alive until they know whether Kenward will be around to see her suffer."

Toreth wondered if they were really so desperate as to clutch at such thin straws. "Or they might kill her immediately. Either way, we're not getting any answers out of Kenward. And the kidnappers aren't getting anything either." Toreth paused.

"Para?" Mistry asked.

"Maybe they will wait. Remember when Rankin paid the ransom? They held Finn for another five days. Now, possibly the kidnappers were getting fresh instructions from their backers."

"Because the plan didn't include a boyfriend paying up," Doyle said.

"Right. Or maybe they were simply sticking to the copycat timeline, regardless of payout. How long would that give us?"

"The first time, they had her for eleven days," Doyle said. "All the other kidnappings were twenty-two. Depends on how they're counting it, I suppose."

"Then we could have ten more days to find her," Mistry said. "That's a long time."

Her optimism sounded forced, and Toreth agreed. Pessimistically, they had the whole Administration and even beyond to comb for the girl. Moving victims added risk, though, so for now the target area was merely New London. That still meant one tiny straw in a giant haystack, working against a demonstrably skilled team. And right now they had very little to go on. They were waiting for the results of forensics at the hospital, which Toreth expected to yield as little as before.

"Let's start with an easier one," Toreth said. "Hopefully. Barrow's run out on us. He has a head start, but at least he isn't a sab team."

The last entry in Barrow's c&p had given Toreth an accurate time. Another minute, and he had the recordings from two cameras on the street outside Barrow's building. Both poorly placed but with a distant view of the entrance, they showed the taxi pull up and Barrow get out. Barrow paused, looking around with the care of a man who had personal security ground deep into his soul. Very sharp, for someone who hadn't had a proper security job for fifteen years.

Maybe Barrow had grounds to be suspicious. Only a few seconds after he'd entered the building, another taxi pulled up. The occupant flung the door open and jumped out, his ponytail whipping back as he ran along the street. He stopped by the other taxi, bending down to peer into the back window, then followed Barrow inside.

"Oh, fucking wonderful," Toreth said aloud.

"What?" Doyle asked.

"Surveillance. Barrow did go home, but guess who was following him?" He looked up at Sara. "Crispin fucking Cole."

"Oh, no," Sara said.

Toreth turned to Mistry. "Was Cole with you when you made the link to Barrow?"

"Um … yes, I think so. It happened late on Friday night, and he was still down in Systems with us, waiting for another call. Para, I'm so sorry, we should've kept him secluded."

"Yes, you should. Still, let's see what we have."

Toreth started to fast-forward through the recording, but stopped almost immediately. Cole and Barrow came out together, climbed into Barrow's taxi and drove off. Toreth checked the c&p again, but the journey had definitely terminated there. Interesting.

Cole failed to answer his comm when Toreth tried. Not surprising, since he'd found his new scoop. Toreth left an irate message anyway, demanding Cole call him immediately.

"Sara, did you process Cole's file yet?"

"I did it right away yesterday."

"Fuck." Now they had nothing to hold over him. Canceling the no-charge submission to Justice would take far more time than they could waste.

"You said you'd finished with him." Sara sounded reproachful.

"Yeah, I did, and I thought I had. Just see if you can track him down. Maybe it's only me he doesn't want to talk to."

Sara nodded quickly, opening her hand screen as she walked a few steps away to make the calls.

Letting Barrow go had been a necessary mistake. In Barrow's situation, Toreth would've been inclined to listen sympathetically to whatever line Cole was selling, too, although if Cole thought a small media outfit could protect Barrow from someone like Selman, he must be taking the bad kind of drugs. Toreth checked Cole's c&p, which, like Barrow's, stopped dead at a taxi charge to Barrow's building. Without much optimism, he put a high-priority alert onto the system for both Cole and Barrow. If either of them swiped a card or passed through a secure point, he'd know. Toreth glanced over to Sara, and she shook her head, still busy on the comm. Doyle and Mistry were watching him expectantly, like they were expecting a miracle.

"When I was on secondment to I&I Mars, one of the hydroponics technicians disappeared," Toreth said. "Not really my problem, but I was so damn bored I helped base security track her down. Now, okay, those off-Earth bases are small, but they're like rabbit warrens. Rooms, corridors, tunnels, access spaces. Plenty of places to hide, and when you include places that'd only be good for a corpse, well..."

"Was she dead?" Mistry asked.

"Oh, no. Turned out someone she'd fucked and dumped had flipped out and decided to lock her in his room until she took him back. I've never worked anywhere people spent so much time screwing. I suppose that's what happens when you set up a dry base. No one has anything better to do."

"But how did you do it?" Doyle leaned forward, clearly hoping for a solution to their problem. "How did you find her?"

"The base administration instituted a lockdown, and metered the oxygen usage room by room."

"Oh!" Doyle sat back. Mistry had a matching accusatory glare. Toreth grinned at them and shook his head.

Sara snapped her screen closed, looking grim. "I'm afraid Cris's gone. He won't answer his comm, not for anyone. I called his mum and dad, but they're on holiday in Rome. They haven't heard from him for a couple of days, but I asked them to try and they can't get in touch with him either. He didn't go to work yesterday or today and no one knows why. I can keep trying."

"Your fucking exes," Toreth said.

Indignation overcame the worry on Sara's face. "Hey, it isn't my fault! Without Cris, you'd never have found Marcos Barrow at all."

100

"And now Cole must've convinced Barrow that the only way out is to sell what he knows and take the money. I bet they're holed up somewhere together while Cole drafts his journalistic masterpiece."

Doyle nodded. "It's a better chance for Barrow than running flat broke."

"I'm glad you approve. I don't think Joseph Selman will be dancing for joy about it, though, assuming he hasn't already had them both killed. We'd damn well better find them before he does." *Three* missing witnesses, and two searches, both equally hopeless. Toreth rubbed his temples, and silently cursed Liz Carey for involving him in the whole mess.

The traffic analysis specialists reported that Barrow's taxi had ID-hopped for miles across the city, illegally switching the identifying signal which should've let the traffic control systems track it to the centimeter, until they lost it in the ants' nest of New London traffic. The news strengthened a vague suspicion, but didn't improve Toreth's mood.

Toreth was alone in his office reading the preliminary results from the forensic assessment of Sofie Kenward's hospital room (nothing, blank, clean, inconclusive, and a dozen other ways of saying "useless") when Tillotson appeared, unannounced. It was turning into a habit Toreth didn't like.

"What went wrong?" Tillotson demanded. "The news about your prisoner is everywhere!"

"Yes, sir," Toreth said. "Everything went through the correct channels, I promise."

"We could've issued a suppression order based on ongoing investigations. Now we have an attempted suicide in custody when we were supposed to be saving the man's damn daughter. This makes the whole section, the whole *division*, look bad. I'm getting memos," he added with grim finality.

"Better memos than a corpse," Toreth said, then hurried on when a dark flush broke out on Tillotson's cheeks. "Look, would you prefer to find the girl chopped up, or would you like the kidnapper to wait while he finds out whether or not Kenward is going to make it and give us the time to find her alive?"

"And why should he care?"

"A million euros?" Toreth suggested. "The evidence analysis system backs up the theory." No need to mention how hard he and Sara had needed to beat the system into submission to force it to agree. Tillotson never looked beyond the number at the top of the screen.

"I see." Tillotson sniffed. "Well, since it's done now, I'll support your decision, of course. I suppose that Senior Para Benz signed off on this?"

"I suppose so, sir," Toreth said, knowing full well that Carey had given the CF approval in Benz's name.

"Then at least that's something. What about these witnesses you've lost?"

Maybe a spell in re-education for assault wouldn't be so bad. "We're finding them as fast as we can."

Tillotson gave him a careful inspection, as though weighing up whether there was any point in saying more. "I see. Well, keep me informed."

When Tillotson left, Toreth gave him a few seconds' head start, then followed him to the door. He leaned on the door frame, watching Tillotson cross the office. All the admins were carefully busy, looking elsewhere, not catching the section head's eye.

"Your fucking boyfriend," Toreth said when Tillotson was out of sight.

This time, Sara didn't rise to the bait. "You mean Cris?"

"I want to know everywhere he's been since he walked out of here on Friday. What does his c&p look like?"

"Very busy," Sara said promptly. "So far I have his home, Justice, the Department of Population, Department of Transport, retail purchases, and a large cash withdrawal. Lots of comms, lots of taxis, and from the journey end points it looks like he walked to other places in between."

Nothing in this case ever produced a clear, simple answer. "Okay, thanks. Get the system to generate a comprehensive list, best guesses for the blanks, and pass it on to Doyle. Tell him to get Abel and Brown to help him cover them as fast as possible, and to keep a fucking eye on the pair of them. Any hint as to where Cole might be hiding now, however slight, I want to hear about it."

Chapter Ten

"Could you meet me at my flat right away?" Rankin said.

Toreth, who had been in his office for ten minutes and barely dented the overnight stack of files and messages, stared at him. A colorful version of "no" sat right on the tip of his tongue, but the man's disheveled, hollow-eyed appearance stopped him. "I'm afraid I'm rather busy right now," Toreth said. Better not to start the new day by abusing witnesses.

"Yes. I saw the news. That's why I'm calling. I have some information but I can't bring it to I&I with me. It's something significant, I think."

"I can send one of my team to—"

"Please. If you could come. It is important."

Toreth eyed the list of files running down his screen, weighing them up against the idea of being legitimately elsewhere when Tillotson arrived looking for another status report, then nodded. "It had better be."

"Thank you." Rankin looked almost apologetic. "And if you could not wear your uniform when you arrive..."

❖ ❖ ❖

On the way out of the building Toreth passed Mistry, and turned her right around and took her along with him, as a corroborating witness and someone to keep an eye on the camera. Right now he had no margin for fuckups. Outside, a couple of maintenance technicians were scrubbing bird shit from the statue of Blindfold Justice. Pity the fuckers didn't apply the same diligence to checking the interview room furnishings.

"What information?" Mistry asked when he'd explained where they were headed.

"I have no idea. Something important, he claims. If it's not, I'll arrest him for impeding." And wouldn't that make a nice replacement for the level two financials charge for which Toreth no longer had a prisoner.

Rankin's money clearly hadn't all gone on his fianceé's ransom. The car took them to a decent enough postcode, albeit one of the areas rebuilt quickly as the rubble of the old city was cleared away. The collection of low-rise buildings showed their age in wired-up cornices and spalling plasterwork. Building speed had been more important that quality, but in the odd housing hierarchy of New London, a home where the radioactivity in the foundation concrete registered slightly above background still held a certain cachet.

Mistry opened the door to the building, reaching for it with her injured hand first and wincing.

"We make this as quick as we can, okay?" Toreth said as they followed the directions up to the flat. "Your job is to make sure anything he says ends up as useful evidence."

"Yes, Para," Mistry said without blinking.

Rankin was waiting at the open door. He looked even more agitated than he had on screen, so at odds with Toreth's first interview with him that he had to check twice to be quite certain it was the same man.

"This is Investigator Mistry," Toreth said, but Rankin was already nodding, ushering them through into the tiny flat.

When they walked into the living room, Toreth realized he'd possibly struck luckier than he'd known by meeting Mistry on the way out. The woman sitting on the sofa Toreth recognized at once from her security file: Gena Finn. For the past week he'd been mentally classifying her as "the second kidnapping victim," listed with the other youngsters, and so it mildly disoriented him to find the woman in the flesh really was thirty-nine. She sat slightly hunched over, with a steaming mug clutched in her hands, and she didn't stand up when they entered. Judging by her rumpled clothes and the fatigue blurring her face, she hadn't been to bed all night. Rankin sat protectively beside her. Ironic, when he was the one in the room with the least legal protection. Gena Finn's file gave her profession as small animal vet, a partner in a corporate franchise whose parent extended corporate status to all its franchisees. Following her mother into security clearly hadn't appealed—presumably the odds of being kidnapped and dismembered in a dispute over a budgerigar were attractively low.

"Ms. Finn," Toreth said as he sat down.

She didn't seem surprised that he knew her name. "You're Para-investigator Toreth?"

"And Investigator Jasleen Mistry." Toreth glanced at Mistry, who was setting up the camera with far more concentration than any of his team would normally put into the task. "I apologize if I seem abrupt, but we're in the middle of an urgent investigation. Do you have some information for us?"

She nodded. "I saw that poor girl on the news feeds. Jerrold told me you thought the sabs who have her are the same ones who took me. And that—that there had been more of us."

"And there might be even more to come," Toreth added. He'd reviewed Rankin's interview in the car on the way over. "You've seen the latest news, I suppose?"

"Yes." She sipped the contents of the mug, then set it down. "There're some things you need to know about what happened to me. What they paid to get me back."

"Gena never knew the details of the exchange," Rankin said, leaning forward slightly. "She had no idea about any payments made other than the money."

"You told us you didn't know the details, either," Toreth said.

"And I wasn't lying. But last night we both talked to Gena's mother and... well, Angelina told us, eventually, what really happened."

"And I decided that we had to tell you, in case it helped you find the other girl. But." Finn clasped her right arm, rubbing around it in a familiar place. "We don't have any proof, you see. Just what she told us."

"That's enough," Toreth reassured her. And with this safely recording, he'd have no problem in pulling in Angelina Finn for interrogation.

Mistry gave one final check to the camera. "Just tell us," she said. "Take as much time as you need."

Rankin was watching Finn anxiously, but she didn't seem to pay any attention to him or to them. Instead she talked to the camera, as if it negated the pairs of eyes on her. "My mother took a contract with a company called Parallel Flow. Corporate security—sabotage prevention and, well. The opposite of prevention. The board brought her in as an expert, because they were under a lot of pressure. And then... a company called Control Guidance Systems contacted a Parallel Flow director with a proposal. Between them, they could monopolize traffic guidance development contracts from the Administration—or something like that. I'm sorry, the details didn't seem important."

"We understand," Mistry said. "Did she mention any names in particular at CGS?"

Finn nodded. "Joseph Selman. He made the proposal. But my mother said that Selman also decided to neutralize another corporation. And that's where it went wrong. They wanted—they hired sabs to stage a kidnapping and force one of the directors into breaking the accords. My mother—my mother handled the contacts." Finn looked up briefly. "It was a long time ago."

"We already know about that kidnapping," Toreth said. "Natasha Patterson was taken, and the CEC caught an Avendiax director trying to ransom her. Tell us what went wrong with the plan."

"The security screen broke down—a missent file or comm details, maybe. Somehow the sab team found out the names of those involved at CGS and Parallel Flow. My mother told Joseph Selman to forget it, that most teams are professional enough to leave that kind of information alone, but she said Selman was afraid his mother would find out."

"Theodora's old-fashioned," Rankin said, and Toreth wondered if he actually knew her on first-name terms. Probably. "She doesn't approve of family-targeted sabotage."

"So my mother said that Selman insisted, and so the team was eliminated.

She thought that would be the end of it. Her contract finished, she moved on. And then—" Finn swallowed. "Then three years later, someone kidnapped me. He wanted money, and he wanted to know who was behind the deaths of the sabs."

"Specifically the sabs?" Mistry said.

"Yes. He wanted to know about everyone involved."

"And your mother told him," Toreth said.

Finn nodded. "She wouldn't tell us the names, just that she gave him everything she knew. Two or three of the directors, I think, from Parallel Flow and CGS, and the corporate security who handled the operation. And someone from CGS who modified the car control system, to allow remote override." She glanced between Toreth and Mistry. "I'm sorry, I can't be any more exact than that."

"That's all we need to know," Toreth said. He didn't think they'd have any trouble filling the names in. All they needed to do was look at the list of kidnappings.

Finn looked down at her hand, folding and smoothing a crease in her skirt. "You can't hold her responsible for what happened. She couldn't know why he wanted the names. Not then. And—he said that if she ever told anyone what had happened, then he'd come back and take me again. She knew what he'd do to me."

"No one would want to have to make a choice like that," Mistry said gently, and Finn gave her a grateful smile.

Angelina Finn saving her own arse at the expense of other people sounded to Toreth like the kind of choice corporates and corporate hirelings made every day.

"And Angelina was right," Rankin said. "You couldn't protect Sofie Kenward, could you?"

Toreth didn't answer. The fact that he hadn't even been trying at the time she was taken didn't change the fact that he'd lost his grip on more than one witness in the case. Kenward, Cole, and Barrow—

He paused. Parallel searches, that was how he'd been thinking of them. But linking the evidence together in a different pattern... "Just a moment." Toreth called up the interview with Cole. "I'd like you to listen to this, please."

Crispin Cole's voice filled the room, a section from one of his interviews with Mistry. *"If this was all aboveboard, the next stage would be for us and them to sign a contract. But personally, I think money on the table works just as well, especially when the fucking lawyers never stop coming up with reasons why we can't make a deal. Look, is there any chance of some coffee? My head is—"*

"Familiar at all?" Toreth asked.

Finn shook her head slowly. "I don't think so. He sounds a little like someone at work, one of the other vets, but only the accent."

Satisfied, Toreth fetched another file. "And how about this?"

"...was my responsibility. Including his family's. I'd only been in the job a few months, not enough to claim any loyalty from him. How long do you think I lasted after we found his daughter? How many people do you think would hire me with that on my CV?"

106

Toreth stopped the recording. He didn't prompt Gena Finn for an answer this time, because it showed in every frozen line on her pale face.

"Who's that?" Rankin demanded. He turned to Finn. "Gena? Are you all right?"

"It's him," Gena whispered. She pressed her arm across her chest, holding it there. "God. It's like it was yesterday."

"You mean—" Rankin put his arm around her shoulders. Anger gave his face a certain animation and made him look abruptly older. "What the hell do you think you're doing? We've been nothing but cooperative—we didn't have to call you. You have no right to treat—"

"No, I'm fine." Finn straightened, shrugging his embrace away without looking at him. "It was a shock. That's all. I'm fine."

"Are you sure it's him?" Toreth asked.

"Sure?" She looked directly at him. "I spent twenty-two days lying in the dark. That was the only voice I heard. He told me that whether I lived or died wasn't up to him, it was up to the people who claimed they loved me. That I was just a tool to him, a means to an end. I was breathing on credit. My life wasn't mine and it meant nothing. I meant nothing. So, yes. I'm sure."

"Do you think she's right, Para?" Mistry asked as they drove back to I&I.

"Do you?"

"I think she believes she is. But that isn't the same thing. It's still seventeen years ago. Or the kidnapper could've altered his voice."

"And just happened to pick Barrow's?" Toreth shook his head. "Corporate security makes a good cover for a sab. Half the time you can't tell the difference anyway."

"He must've taken the job with Sterntech to get close to Louise Selman," Mistry said. "Same method as the very first case. She was the hardest target by far, and who better to get through her security and kidnap her?"

"Especially since it was the one case where it didn't matter if she recognized his voice."

"How did you know it was Barrow?" Mistry asked.

"I didn't for sure, until she reacted. The ID scramble in the taxi made me wonder about him, though—rather high-end for a broke ex-security officer to drive around on spec, but typical sab equipment. And either he or Selman lied to us about Selman giving information to the kidnapper, and there aren't many reasons why Barrow would do that unless he was trying to confuse the timeline. Now we know the kidnapper—Barrow—already had the information he needed, from Angelina Finn. Selman was the one who took the decision to eliminate the sabs, so Louise Selman died."

"And the others?" Mistry asked.

"Revenge?" With a cast-iron suspect and solid evidence, motive didn't matter much. "He targeted the directors and corporate security. And Kenward is probably the one who modified the car controls."

Mistry nodded. "And since Barrow chose those particular targets, Selman would know that another ransom demand was on its way."

"So he could find a way to intervene." Toreth picked his jacket up from the car seat and checked the pockets for his hand screen. "I don't imagine Barrow cared who paid up."

"Maybe he was collecting for the team," Mistry said. "It would be symmetrical. Five sabs killed in the car, five kidnappings we know about. A million each."

Toreth shrugged agreement, then paused, jacket hanging loose from his hand. "Which means if Sofie Kenward is the last, then Barrow's done."

"So maybe he *was* serious about exposing Selman," Mistry said.

"And a lot more, I bet: all the payments, the original kidnapping. He probably has evidence about the lot." He whistled softly. "Everyone goes down together— it would take a miracle to hush that up, even for Theodora Selman's son."

"And Selman knows," Mistry said. After a moment, she rephrased it. "Do you think he knows?"

Toreth thought it through. "He couldn't have known that Barrow was behind it, or Barrow would be dead. But, yes, this has to be why Selman paid the other ransoms. I never believed in his bleeding heart, not even with side benefits. No wonder he's been so interested in the case." He laughed sharply. "And no wonder he didn't like it when Liz and I suggested he was being blackmailed into paying. That's exactly what was happening. We just guessed at the wrong leverage. More than that, though—Barrow has Cole. Not the other way round."

"Direct access to the media." Mistry shook her head. "Selman won't like that."

Had they mentioned Cole to Selman? Toreth felt almost certain they hadn't, but that meant little. If Joseph Selman didn't have contacts at I&I, then he'd be the only major corporate without. Sara's ex-boyfriend was in the kind of trouble that would make illegal surveillance look like littering.

When they reached I&I, Toreth left Mistry to file the new evidence in the internal IIP, while he went over to Corporate Fraud to share the news with Carey in person. To his surprise, he found Doyle in her office with her, standing behind Carey's chair while they both studied something on her screen. "I thought you were supposed to be out looking for Cole?" Toreth said.

"Yes, Para. Abel and Brown are checking every location on the list, trying to find out if he talked to anyone, but it's a lot of ground to cover. So I came back here to try to refine the searches, narrow it down."

Doyle was wearing his expression of earnest truthfulness again. Toreth briefly considered telling him flat out to stop wasting his time. "So what're you doing skulking around in CF? Homesick?"

"He's found something, Toreth." Carey waved him over. "Not out of the c&p, but see what you think."

Doyle and Carey were watching the recording of Cole outside Barrow's building. They had the same section looping, Cole running down the street and stopping by the stationary taxi. Run, pause. Run, pause. "I was trying to find something externally distinctive about Barrow's taxi, hoping to track it through the cameras," Doyle said. "But see, right here. How he bends down? I thought he was looking inside, and he's on the wrong side of the car to be absolutely sure, but if you look closely—there. It seems to me like he ducks down lower than the window, just for a second or so."

"Maybe." Toreth squinted at the dark, fuzzy picture. "Yes. You know, he could almost be—fuck."

Doyle grinned. "Yes, Para."

Toreth straightened up. "And if he did fit a tracker, then there must be something somewhere to pick up the signal."

"He might carry it with him," Carey said.

"It's specified equipment," Doyle said. "And I checked—he doesn't have any valid licenses."

"Then let's hope that just this once, he's not quite as stupid as he seems." Toreth clapped Doyle on the shoulder. "Well spotted. Right. Now you take a team of Systems specialists, and get a warrant for Cole's place of work—imminent danger, don't forget. Make sure you go over the whole place, not just his office. Cellar, store rooms, anywhere he can possibly hide something and get access without anyone noticing. And get the Systems team to rip through all the work equipment. He could have the receiver hooked up to that."

Doyle's mouth tightened for a moment, then he nodded. "Yes, Para. What about his home?"

"Investigator Carey and I will cover that. We don't have time to do them one after the other."

Toreth watched him go, then called through for a somewhat smaller Systems team of his own.

"You think we've got the best chance?" Carey said when he was done.

"Yes. And so does Doyle. I mean, would you keep something that important here?" Toreth waved his hand, indicating the office. "Besides, Sara says he hasn't even been in to work."

The screens on the walls in Cole's bedroom mostly displayed images of attractive young women. Toreth briefly entertained the idea that Cole had more success in acquiring partners that he'd ever have given him credit for, and then he recognized some of the faces.

"Fuck me," Carey said, obviously reaching the same conclusion. "Are those all...?"

"Dead. Yes."

Not just dead, but from what Toreth could recall of the cases, rather dramatically dead.

Noticing the ghost of a square at the bottom right corner of the nearest screen, Toreth tapped it. Immediately the image changed to display a crime scene, as lavishly decorated with blood as Kenward's interview room had been. The screen cycled slowly through more pictures, finally returning to the smiling face.

"That was a postmortem, wasn't it?" Carey said. "Surely some of those are restricted-access investigation files?"

"Let's hope we find the bastard healthy enough to charge, instead of in need of a postmortem of his own." Toreth turned to the Systems specialist waiting outside the door. "Senior Specialist Dale, isn't it? I want you to go through everything in the room, piece by piece. *Everything*. And if you don't find anything, start on the rest of the house. We have a full warrant, so don't be precious about it."

"Yes, Para." The man eyed the pictures with evident distaste. "Everything."

When Crispin Cole's parents returned from Rome, they'd no doubt be horrified to discover just what a determined I&I search team could perpetrate. Toreth, on the other hand, surveyed the wreckage of the small office with great satisfaction. Perhaps it wasn't for Cole's use only (with no one in residence, he couldn't ask), but Cole had certainly been busy there. The Systems team had the tracker receiver activated and displaying results on the screen. Systems Specialist Senior Investigator Dale nodded toward it. "It's hard to be accurate at a glance, because Cole assigns a new code when he reuses them, but looking at the simultaneous records he must have five or six trackers at least, Para."

"And a total of zero licenses for them," Carey said. "Very naughty."

"Yes," Toreth said. "Looks like he didn't learn his lesson."

"He's used it a lot," Dale said. "I'm afraid it'll take us a while to untangle the records and find out exactly who he's been tracking, when and where."

"I'll make it easy for you." Toreth put his hand on the specialist's shoulder and leaned closer to the screen. "Right now we only want one. The car that left Marcos Barrow's building at around six p.m. on Monday."

The sun had just dropped below the horizon when Toreth and Carey found the fresh tire marks leading through a gate which no one had any business using. Carey had already called the location in to I&I when they left Cole's house. Somewhere in the city, reinforcements were on their way.

"Check where they are," Toreth said to Carey. "And tell them if they turn up with the sirens going, I'll rip their bollocks off myself. I'm going to look for another way in." As he walked away, he heard Carey chuckle.

Across the city, a slowly shrinking number of areas still awaited redevelopment after the dirty bombs and subsequent rapid cleanup. Sealed off behind walls and fences plastered with faded warning signs, they were being sat on by corporations with an eye to the very long term, or caught up in Administration red-tape wrangling, or awaiting the invention of economical techniques for their decontamination and clearance. Lacking a handy Geiger counter, Toreth decided to rely on Barrow's good sense not to have chosen one of the latter sites. An access gate a hundred meters away from the tire tracks, clearly unused, yielded to his authority to override. Toreth stayed there, listening, until Carey caught him up.

"Should we wait here?" she asked.

"You wait. I'm going to see if I can find where they are before there's too much disturbance. He's not an idiot; he'll have covered the car from above."

As quietly as possible, Toreth moved deeper into the wasteland. Rubble made the footing uneven, and scrubby plants caught at his trousers. He paused often, listening, scanning ahead for any lights.

"Anything?" Carey said in his ear over the comm.

"Not yet." Toreth subvocalized with scrupulous care. "But it's a good place. No sign of indigs, or anyone else."

"Why didn't he keep Sofie Kenward out here?" Carey said as he threaded through a narrow alley between ruined buildings. "Or the others?"

The lack of traffic noise, unhelpful for covert investigation, also showed how far they were from normal city life. "Back then he was protecting his identity. He can mask traffic tracking all he likes, but repeat journeys out here won't go unnoticed forever. Twenty-two days is definitely a risk. I'll bet he kept all the others walking distance from places he had every legitimate reason to be." Toreth held still, straining to listen, then peered around a corner. "If we're lucky, Cole interfering forced him to pick a backup location."

Toreth scanned the map on his screen, squinting in the low light. Matching the satellite overlay with the broken ground wasn't easy, but the signal from Crispin Cole's tracker suggested he must be within fifty meters of the car's location.

The moon shone, strengthening as the last traces of daylight faded from the sky. The sharp light picked out tumbled walls and the gray shadows of mounded brambles. A pair of unusually straight lines led across a patch of open ground, the pattern in the mud turned into black and white brush strokes by the moonlight. The tire tracks led directly up to the ground floor of a relatively intact building. Toreth couldn't see an opening, only a heavier weight to the shadow suggesting a wide door, but it matched perfectly with the tracker. He looked carefully from window to window, letting his gaze rest on each one for long enough to check all four corners.

He'd already started to ease forward out of hiding, ready to move to the next side of the building, when he caught a tiny speck of light, a transient flash as though someone had swung a torch beam across a crack in a blacked-out window. After a minute, it happened again. Toreth made a note of the location of the room, then retreated silently the way he'd come to wait for reinforcements.

His message about sirens must have made it through the system. As Toreth slipped back out through the gate, he found the last of the cars bringing backup pulling to a silent halt in a side street opposite the gate. Black-clad figures were already swarming out of the vehicles, forming ordered groups. As he crossed the street, though, relief turned into cold shock. The unmarked cars might be part of the effort to avoid alerting Barrow, but the streetlights showed him that none of the armed men and women wore a uniform from I&I, or any branch of Int-Sec. A team who had taken up station at the end of the street looked him over as he approached. They seemed neither surprised nor impressed to find a para-investigator there. Carey stood nearby, looking bewildered.

"What's the hell's going on?" Toreth asked. Before she could answer, Toreth recognized a slightly built man in a plain suit, stepping out of the closest car in the line. "Tam—" he started, then hesitated, realizing he didn't know the man's last name.

"Tam Lee." The man nodded politely to Carey. "Good to see you again, Investigator, Para-investigator."

"What are you doing here?" Toreth asked.

"Offering our full cooperation. As he told you, Mr. Selman is always happy to assist the Administration in any way he can."

"I meant, how did you know where we were?"

"Ah. You'll have to ask Ms. Ambrose." He nodded towards a tall woman in the center of a group of security officers.

"I called I&I for help," Carey said. "They have the location. They'll be here any minute."

Toreth didn't believe in that kind of a coincidence. "Who did you speak to, Liz?"

"Benz, both times. Why does it—oh, no. He wouldn't *dare*." If Benz had seen Liz Carey's face at that moment, Toreth thought, very probably he wouldn't have dared, at that. "Vaughn will have his balls on a plate."

"I'm sure Benz doesn't give a fuck, because next week he won't be working for Vaughn." Toreth turned to Lee. "Let me guess—new member of the security team on the payroll soon?"

Lee shrugged. "Selman-Sterntech staffing arrangements are covered by corporate information privileges. Unless you have a warrant?"

Toreth could call in to I&I himself to order the armed reinforcements, and he and Carey could pull back and wait all over again. He could call the Service and try to get troopers; they might have a unit closer to the building. Or even fucking Justice. But every minute gave Barrow time to spot that something was wrong. The man was too fucking sharp.

"How long can we have?" Carey asked, echoing his thoughts. "How long is it going to take them to come from I&I?"

And how could the two of them stop Ambrose from going in on her own anyway? "Shit. Call Sara anyway, then wait here."

Toreth shouldered his way through the security guards, ignoring the weapons and the dirty looks. By law, corporate security was supposed to use nonlethal force as a first resort, but apparently the last resort had arrived early today. "You're Ambrose?"

An I&I badge didn't seem to intimidate her, but she immediately slung her weapon and held out her hand. "That's right. And you're the para-investigator in charge?"

"That would be nice."

She smiled thinly. "Mr. Selman promised you every assistance, Para-investigator. Well, we're here to assist. Marcos Barrow's personnel file suggests to me that you should use us quickly." She hadn't yet dropped her hand. Aware of everyone watching, Toreth shook it. Reluctantly he had to admit that he liked the firm shake, and the calm way she returned his inspection. Didn't hurt that she had a pleasant enough face, and a fit-looking body under the black uniform.

"Can we reach an arrangement here?" Toreth asked bluntly. "What's your optimal result?"

Now the smile looked much more genuine. "What's yours?"

Ambrose had shared Sterntech security goodies with them, including low-light intensifiers. Their strap itched infuriatingly at Toreth's temple, but they lit up the shadows with a flat brilliance, smearing briefly into white if he looked up at the lights of inhabited New London before the intensifiers adjusted the contrast. Despite the intensifiers, for long heartbeats Toreth felt alone in the darkness. Then the shadows split and moved as the Sterntech security officers slipped from cover to cover. As they ran they made no more noise than rats, but his earpiece crackled with quick-fire subvocalized reports and orders.

His own group of shadows kept close to him, Ambrose at his left hand. Her voice cut through the others, prioritized by the comms. "Team A in position. A."

Movement in the corner of his eyes made him turn his head, but by the time he focused everything was still again. "Team C in position. C."

"Team B in position. B." That came without any warning, from the group sent around the back.

"That's definitely the building?" she asked.

"Probably the building. I think the car's in there, and I saw a light."

"Better hope for the best, then," she said. "We're placing spotters and cameras across the site, anyway. You never know, we might get another chance."

Not unless Marcos Barrow was asleep.

Ambrose scanned the building with a small pair of binoculars, then handed them over to Toreth. The window he'd marked, and the wall around it, glowed faintly with a temperature trace barely above ambient. The heat of a body or bodies inside, incrementally warming the room. He scanned along the building, finding an even fainter second trace three windows along. "What's the background count like in here?" Toreth asked.

Ambrose tapped a monitor clipped to her belt. "Nothing you'd notice, Para-investigator, and definitely not enough to generate heat. I wouldn't lick the soil, mind. Okay, teams, move on. Still following the primary insertion plan."

Doors were out of the question, but by the time they reached their designated access point, the Sterntech security team there had removed a window from its frame, four stories up, and a ladder hung down the side of the building. Toreth hadn't heard a thing.

Carey arrived a few seconds later, escorted by a separate team. Toreth had debated leaving her outside, but assuming that they found Barrow, and assuming kidnapper and hostage survived the discovery, there'd come a point where he'd need all the I&I backup he could muster. At the moment, Carey was it.

Two of her team went up the ladder, then Ambrose followed. Toreth watched her go, climbing easily, the uniform tightening over her arse, and wondered about the Sterntech security policy on fraternizing with Int-Sec employees. He gave himself a quick mental shake. Survival first, fucking second. The plan involved Toreth and Carey going up last, ostensibly to keep them out of the middle of the trained unit. Toreth suspected Ambrose wanted a first look at what might be waiting for them. How long would the agreement they'd made hold out?

"Will you be able to manage the climb?" Toreth asked Carey as the last of the Sterntech guards started up.

One of the reasons he liked working with Carey was because she took questions like that seriously. She weighed up the distance from the ground to the window, then nodded. "Just don't let anyone small and light stand underneath me."

Toreth climbed as fast as he could while staying silent. They were on the opposite side of the building to Barrow, but he might have sentry devices active, despite Ambrose's sweeps. Up in the corridor, he found the security guards had

114

already spread out, watching the access points, with two of them cautiously approaching the stairs leading down. The rooms Toreth had marked were a level below them. The guards moved slowly, stepping around the larger pieces of debris on the floor, and placing their feet to avoid making noise. Toreth split his attention between the corridor and the window, with a sliver of awareness left over for the radio. When Carey appeared, he helped her over the ledge. Despite her joke, she moved better than he'd expected for a finance specialist who supposedly got most of her exercise wrestling numbers. Maybe Verstraeten made a more athletic fuck than he looked.

"Primary stairs are clear," the point team reported.

Toreth and Carey moved down the corridor, following Ambrose. In the odd depthless light of the intensifiers, the plaster made abstract patterns where it had scabbed and fallen. Down the stairs, slowly along the corridor, listening hard for any sound that would announce discovery . . . Toreth would rather have I&I personnel backing him up, but heavily armed corporate security definitely beat a kick in the teeth, and might even prevent one. When a guard reached the first door, though, Toreth wished he could take charge. He waited until Ambrose had gone up to the room herself. Fucking around with someone else's team in the middle of the action was the kind of suicidal stupidity his ego could live without.

Ambrose beckoned him over. "Someone you're expecting?"

A single figure lay sprawled on the floor, with the awkward disjointed look of a man dumped there while deeply unconscious. His long, pale hair spread over the floor. "Yes," Toreth said. "Let me in."

He knelt by Cole, and put a hand over his mouth. Cole didn't react, and through his gloves Toreth couldn't tell if he felt warm or not. Pulling off a glove, Toreth felt for a pulse, finding it at once. "Just unconscious," Toreth said, and added, "pity," even further under his breath.

"I'll leave a guard with him," Ambrose said.

With no other choice, Toreth said, "Thanks."

Sara would play hell if he found Cole alive, only to have him accidentally caught in the crossfire or, more likely, deliberately shot by Barrow. Of course, he could always gloss over the "found alive" in the IIP.

Ambrose tilted her head, and Toreth nodded. Every second they stayed still gave Barrow more time to spot that something was wrong.

Two rooms along, a bright vertical stripe painted down Toreth's vision, a door left ajar. The light inside barely lit the room, but after the pitch darkness of the rest of the building it took a second for the intensifiers to adjust. Toreth lifted them up onto his forehead, trying to get a clearer picture. Through the narrow gap, Toreth saw a glint of metal which resolved into the blade of an axe, leaning against a wall. A sharp-looking axe but also a clean one, and Toreth breathed out in silent relief. Then he froze as a floorboard creaked—someone inside the room moving. When Toreth sniffed, he caught a faint whiff of coffee.

Ambrose's voice came through the earpiece. "Gas him?"

"What do you have?"

She pulled a snub-nosed gun from her belt. "Narcoleptac, with some old-fashioned CC-24 just in case."

Toreth searched his memory, wondering whether he ought to call in to I&I to double-check. "No. I have no idea what he gave Cole, but he's obviously drugging captives again. If he's dosed the girl, too, those might kill her."

"He might shoot her."

In no statement had anyone ever mentioned Barrow using a gun. "I'll take the risk. But if he goes for the axe, kill him."

He caught a dim glimpse of her mirthless smile. "Of course. Let me check that everyone's in position."

While she gave her orders, Toreth directed the comm to Carey alone. "Stay back, out of trouble. I don't want you getting shot." By anyone. Despite Ambrose's overt friendliness, her job would be a lot easier if there were no I&I officers around. Toreth glanced over his shoulder, and found the still, crouching shapes of the guards left behind them covering the corridor. He much preferred it when he only anticipated the criminals shooting him.

"Move in," Ambrose said calmly.

This time Toreth couldn't help moving forward before she called him, to Ambrose's shoulder and right behind the two guards who kicked open the door.

Barrow looked almost comic, caught in the middle of the floor with a half-eaten cereal bar in one hand. Behind him Toreth could see a bed, and a still body lying on it. Halle-fucking-lujah.

Despite the crashing entrance, Barrow reacted fast. He raised his hands, spreading his fingers wide, the bar dropping to the floor. "I'm not armed," he said clearly.

"I&I," Toreth said, and watched Barrow's gaze move from him to the Sterntech guards, finally settling on Ambrose. His eyes widened fractionally in recognition, and Toreth wondered what would have happened if Barrow had realized right away that I&I formed a definite minority that night.

With her men holding the building, Ambrose seemed content for Toreth to take over the official aspects of the operation. Hard to forget, though, who controlled the guns. Toreth switched to subvocalizing, directed to Carey only. "Liz, when I have him cuffed, check the girl. Dead or alive, get her the fuck out of here as fast as you can."

He caught sight of Carey in the doorway. "Got it."

"Hands behind your back," Toreth said to Barrow, and cuffed his prisoner with the Sterntech security guards still covering him. Ambrose was standing well back, out of the line of fire. Only good procedure, but it didn't improve his feeling of being inconvenient in a room full of armed security guards.

"B team, sweep the building," Ambrose said. "Booby traps, surveillance. I want a full report fast, especially any sign of associates."

Dirt and dust streaked Barrow's face and hair, and his eyes were a little puffier, but he had the same weary self-possession he'd shown in the I&I interview room. If only the crazy obsessives were all as easy to spot as Natasha Patterson's fucking parents.

"She's alive," Carey said from the bed. "But she's not waking up."

"And she won't for a while yet," Ambrose said. She'd picked up an injector from a table.

"Were you planning to bring her round before you killed her, Barrow?" Carey asked. Rich contempt thickened her voice. "Your whole team wasn't worth one of these kids, you know."

Barrow said nothing.

"Be quick, Liz," Toreth said, eyeing Ambrose who was studying the injector carefully.

Barrow had made no mistakes this time. Sofie Kenward stayed unconscious, unresponsive to Carey's touch. Carey spent a few seconds working on one of the knots, then took a large penknife from her trouser pocket and cut cleanly through the ropes. The last knot dealt with, Carey lifted the girl easily and turned. Toreth held still—would Ambrose stick to the deal they'd made?

Carey must've felt the tension in the air, too, because she hesitated, looking at Ambrose as though she expected a protest. After a moment, Ambrose stepped back, her team following her lead, clearing a path to the door. "She's all yours, Investigator," Ambrose said, her voice absolutely neutral.

"Go on," Toreth said. "Take her to the car and call an ambulance. I'll catch up."

"Investigator," Barrow said suddenly as Carey reached the door.

Carey stopped. "What?"

"It wasn't just about the team," Barrow said, and Ambrose shot him.

"But don't you want to know what he meant?" Carey asked in the car on the way back to I&I. "Come on, you must be curious."

"No," Toreth said. "We have the girl back, Barrow's dead, and if I have any kind of luck at all, Joseph Selman is going to forget my name, the sooner the better."

After the dust had settled, there'd been a tussle for the evidence. Desired outcomes had sharply diverged: Ambrose and Tam Lee wanted a swift cleanup, Toreth at least the appearance of I&I authority. Toreth had held his ground, betting more heavily than he would have liked on the fact that shooting I&I officers was considered beyond the pale even for the highest-ranking corporates. Finally, the backup from I&I had arrived and settled the dispute in Toreth's favor.

In truth, the scene looked to be as bare of meaningful evidence as the previous locations. The only juicy morsels were Barrow's hand screen and Cole's still-unconscious body. Toreth carried off both as soon as possible, leaving Barrow's corpse in the care of the I&I forensics team. Cole and Sofie were both in an ambulance heading for the I&I medical unit. As Carey said, it seemed like the safest place for them.

"I take it we aren't pressing charges," Carey said.

"Against Ambrose? It was an armed assault. Criminals get shot during those all the time."

"Unarmed, cuffed criminals," Carey pointed out.

"There was an axe nearby." Toreth leaned forward. "Look, Ambrose and I made a deal. We wanted Sofie Kenward back alive, she wanted Barrow dead. Everyone who matters wins."

"I'm surprised she let you take Cole without putting a bullet in him, too," Carey said.

Toreth shrugged. "I wasn't sure she would, either. Cole's just lucky that Barrow left the injector lying around."

"What?"

"Barrow dosed him with the same amnesia crap he used at the hospital. And more of it, the medics said. Barrow might've kept him alive planning to use him later to get his story out, but Cole won't remember a thing when he wakes up." He laughed, as Carey's face fell. "It's a good result, Liz. Better than good. Kenward, Finn—those are solid cases. Selman will probably let us close his daughter's kidnapping, too. Quid pro quo."

"There's still Natasha Patterson," Carey said.

"And the sab team," Toreth added. "But if you want to go after Joseph Selman for those, then for fuck's sake, let me close this case and pack my bags for Iceland first."

"This whole thing is his fault, you know." Carey's voice had developed a gravelly growl. "He called in the sabs, then he started the vendetta by killing them. Then he paid the blackmail every time, even though he must have known more kids would be taken, just to hide what he did from his fucking *mother*."

"Patterson died twenty years ago," Toreth countered. "There's no vendetta now, and the only political angle is that we embarrass a sitting Council member. No, thanks."

"I know." Carey looked out of the car window, then shook her head. "They'd kill the case before we even started the IIP. But he's such an arrogant bastard. And I hated his office. Anyone who needs his ego massaged by his fucking floor deserves some hard re-education."

Toreth laughed. Carey wasn't stupid. Pissed off, yes, but she'd talk herself down. "Come on, cheer up. We cracked the Selman case, Liz. Neither of us will ever put anything like that on our records again."

Chapter Eleven

❖

Tidying up the case took until Friday. A pair of Internal Investigations officers appeared like mean-minded black ghosts first thing on Thursday morning to examine Toreth's invocation of imminent danger. Toreth had Sara make them coffees, and answered their questions with his best air of bland honesty. Even they seemed wary around the Selman name, and besides, the case had a good result with no official complaints. Internal always preferred ends to means.

Then came cleaning up the case files, removing anything which might embarrass any interested parties. Luckily for Gena Finn, they could eliminate her secondhand account of the original kidnapping as low-value hearsay, leaving only her identification of Barrow as her kidnapper to forward as evidence. When Selman's name in the case files sparkled sufficiently white that even Ambrose would be dazzled, that still left a few loose ends. Toreth signed the medical unit discharges for Paul and Sofie Kenward, and Crispin Cole, noting them all as no longer of interest to any ongoing I&I investigation.

When Toreth collected him from his locked room, Cole said almost nothing. I&I Medical often had that effect. It wasn't until they reached the ground floor, and he could see daylight, that he recovered his tongue. "What day is it?" he asked as the lift doors opened. "No one would tell me down there."

"Friday. By the way, what did the medics have to say about the memory loss?"

Cole looked at him sourly. "That it's permanent."

"You should be happy about that."

Cole pounced on the opening. "Why?"

Toreth grinned. "If I told you, then it wouldn't apply any more, would it? Just be happy."

"Look, I don't suppose there's any way that I could get access to the case files, is there? Any legal way," he added hastily.

"I'm afraid that the whole investigation will be classified," Toreth said with satisfaction. "Corporate security provisions, and the wider interests of the Administration."

119

"Don't I at least get my data and systems back?"

"You should also be grateful we aren't processing you for illegal surveillance. Again."

"Oh, come on. Tracking a few cars? It's nothing compared to the stuff that corporations get away with every day."

"Not in my cases," Toreth said.

Cole eyed him, clearly wondering whether to challenge the lie. Then he looked pointedly at the main door. "Can I go?"

"Of course." Toreth smiled, watching Cole scurry across the reception area, and thinking about the man's face when he opened the door to his room and saw the damage done by Systems to his precious collection of screens.

Pieter Ryersen came in person to retrieve his partner and daughter. They departed through a side door, somewhere ambulances could park without cluttering up the front entrance. Ryersen refused to set foot in I&I, waiting by the ambulance for the medical technicians to carry out the transfer. Toreth waited with him.

"I'm talking to NTS's lawyers about filing official complaints," Ryersen said.

They wouldn't get anywhere, Toreth knew, even if they had the balls to carry it through. But on the other hand he didn't want corporate legal bullshit making his case history look untidy. Like unwaivered deaths in custody, people noticed. "Your lawyers would be better advised to keep their mouths shut," Toreth said pleasantly. "Or they're going to find themselves busy explaining the multiple meetings between Mr. Kenward and Parallel Flow."

"You have nothing conclusive to—"

"Not many corporations are brave enough to stand up to accusations of breaching the accords. Most of them drop their employees like a shitty stick. Sometimes even if there is a lot of money riding on it." Toreth ran his hand down the gleaming edge of the ambulance door, then leaned slightly to examine the ranks of equipment inside. "Impressive. Better than I got when someone stabbed me."

"In the line of duty?" Ryersen asked. "Or just someone who didn't like you?"

"A suspect stabbed me in the kidney. Still, I did all right out of it. Time off work, I&I paid for everything, and the I&I medical units are good. Personally, I'd hate to risk the possibility of having to trust, say, critical reconstructive surgery to Administration basic care."

Ryersen looked at him with loathing.

"But, lucky for you, NTS will cover everything, won't they?" Toreth said. "For both of them. How good's your medical insurance?"

"Nowhere near as good as Paul's," Ryersen said quietly.

Toreth got no more than that, but he could see, in the way that the man no longer met his gaze, that the trade-off had been accepted. Quid pro quo. Hiding his smile, Toreth clasped his hands behind his back and breathed in deep. If Ryersen had only known it, the search discovering Parallel Flow's meetings with

Kenward had already been lost from the final case file. Another courtesy to Selman, and one Toreth didn't begrudge. Who cared about penny-ante corporate snooping when he could close three high-profile kidnappings?

He'd expected Liz Carey to have taken charge of Sofie's exit from I&I, but the girl was wheeled through the doors by a uniformed medic. Toreth could guess why. He hadn't bothered to go downstairs, but according to reports, after waking up to find her father lying in the next room with his throat slashed, Sofie Kenward had become rather less appreciative of I&I's heroic efforts on her behalf. The fact that she'd also suffered total amnesia about ever needing the recent rescue probably hadn't helped. She kept her face determinedly averted from him, embracing Ryersen awkwardly from the trolley, while the medics transferred Kenward's still-unconscious body into the ambulance.

"Goodbye, Ms. Kenward," Toreth said.

Forced to acknowledge him, she gave a small, bitter smile. "Everyone tells me I should be grateful. I'm afraid I don't remember anything about it."

"Probably for the best," Toreth said. "In any case, we all wish you a speedy recovery. And the best of care."

"Thank you." She frowned at the phrasing, and then Ryersen took over, moving her trolley closer to the ambulance, taking his daughter out of line of sight and ending the conversation.

Eventually the ambulance pulled away, metal trim flaring brightly as it left the shadow of the I&I building, and turned right towards the nearest exit from the IntSec complex. The sound of the wheels had faded when Toreth's comm chimed. "There's something you should see, Para." Doyle's voice held unmistakable excitement. "Right away."

Carey and Mistry were already in his office with Doyle, and Sara sat in front of his screen. She slipped out of Toreth's chair the moment he opened the door. "Case conference surprise?" Toreth asked.

Doyle shook his head quickly. "I called you the moment I found them, Para, I promise."

With just long enough to call the others in, too. On the other hand, Toreth had had to come across I&I from the side exit. He let it slide, and sat down at his desk. Two long numbers showed on the screen, unlabeled, the format unfamiliar. "You found the ransom money?" Toreth guessed.

"'Fraid not, Para," Doyle said. "CF is still looking for it. Abel and Brown submitted these to the IIP, while they were checking Cole's movements. Cole went to the DoP and made some inquiries. These are what he bribed out of one of the employees. The system says that they're DoP reproduction application numbers."

Toreth made the call to the Department of Population. Even on the internal Administration network he got an anonymous voice asking how it could help him. "This is Senior Para-investigator Toreth, I&I. Just put me through to someone who can answer questions intelligently and without needing to stop to get clearance every five minutes."

That demand won him a face as well as a voice, although not one Toreth would choose to look at for fun. The DoP officer had lank, greasy black hair, which matched well with his unenthusiastic manner. "How can we help I&I?" he asked.

Toreth gave the numbers. "Those are a very old format," the officer said. He sounded as though Toreth had produced them deliberately to make his life harder.

"How old?"

"At least eighteen years. But I'll see what I can do." Despite his pessimistic tone, the query came back in a few seconds. "Yes, they're for two separate applications for open licenses, although they were filed the same day. Successful—twelve-month window conception licenses were granted, no serious genetic flags."

"But not a joint license?" Toreth asked.

"No." The man frowned, as though he suspected Toreth wasn't paying proper attention. "Two open single applicants. It's a more complicated way of doing things, with much higher standards, but it happens. For unofficial surrogacies, say, or if the couple aren't registered partners. Most still notify intent to conceive together, just to double-check genetic incompatibilities, and so on, but if they both have a valid license there's no absolute requirement to do it until the pregnancy's confirmed and registered." He shrugged, clearly resigned to the annoying ways of the fecund public.

"So, do these citizens have names?"

"Marcos Andrew Barrow and Johanna Rogerson."

Carey sucked her breath in. "Barrow? And—don't I know that other name?"

"Do you want their security file IDs?" the DoP officer asked.

"No." Toreth put the DoP on hold, for a taste of their own bureaucracy, and pulled up the case files. He flicked quickly to the list of— "Three guesses." He looked around the office. "No one? Rogerson was one of the original sab team. She died in the car crash."

Carey's face cleared. "Of course! And Yvette Patterson told us the sab who befriended her daughter lied about being pregnant."

"Only maybe she didn't," Sara said.

"Why didn't we know about this?" Carey demanded.

"If you remember, we never had the autopsy files on the sabs," Doyle said. "And if she was pregnant, there wasn't a note on her medical record. Possibly she never told anyone official."

"'It wasn't just about the team,'" Carey said.

They all stared at the screen for a moment in silence.

"I like it." Absently, Toreth canceled the still-open connection to the DoP. "Strengthens the motive, and the Justice systems always give points for that. Much better than a sab spending twenty years in a vendetta simply over his colleagues."

Doyle laughed. "I'm afraid I wouldn't do it. I hope no one's offended."

Sara was the only one who laughed in response. Toreth was busy running through the new evidence in his head, making sure that adding it to the submission wouldn't annoy Joseph Selman. The others cleared out of the office, but Carey lingered, looking at the open DoP files on the screen.

"Liz? Something wrong with the conclusions?"

"No, not as such." Carey shook her head. "I just can't help wondering about her."

"Who?"

"Jo Rogerson. She was part of the sab team. Maybe she wasn't the one with the axe, but still. She brought Natasha Patterson to them. How could she do that?"

"Money?" Toreth considered further for a few seconds, then dismissed the question. "We'll never know, so why worry? It's nothing evidential anyway."

"But she really was expecting a baby. I wonder if Barrow made her go through with the entrapment?"

Toreth stared at her, nonplussed. If ever he'd needed confirmation that the specialists had different psych evaluations to the paras, that was it. "Breeding doesn't automatically make mercenary sabs any less mercenary than they were before."

"I—" She stopped. "I suppose not. But still, doing that to someone else's child..."

"Well, Angelina Finn arranged the kidnapping in the first place. Maybe the sab team came up with the details, but she still authorized it all. She didn't seem to have any problems with it either, until it was her own daughter being raped and chopped up."

"Yes, you're right, of course." But she stared at the files for another moment before she sighed and straightened up. "That's done, then. Ready to submit?"

"Yeah, I think so."

"Good," Carey said. "By the way, I hear Benz is planning to hand in his resignation on Monday."

Toreth laughed. "Subtle. I thought it was standard practice to at least wait until Justice delivered the verdict."

"I suppose with Barrow dead he didn't see the point. Barrow's hardly going to appeal for a Justice review, is he?" Carey shook her head. "Stefan Benz. Even for a para, the man's a shit. It should be you walking into a nice corporate job."

"He's welcome to it. No, really," he added, stung by Carey's skeptical snort. "Who'd want to spend their life kissing corporate arse full-time instead of only half?"

"Just wait and see. One day you'll get an offer and I bet we don't even have long enough to buy you a round of drinks."

"Think what you like." Toreth closed the DoP file. "So, what about you? Tempted to transfer to General Criminal?"

"I don't think so. Too much excitement for me. We don't get to catch many Joseph Selmans over in CF either, but at least no one's pointing a gun at us while we don't. But next time I need help..."

"Please, feel free to ask anyone else."

Carey laughed, and patted him on the shoulder. "Thanks."

Before he left for the night, Toreth called Doyle into his office and waved him to take a seat. "You've done some good investigative work while you've been here, Doyle."

"Thank you, Para."

"I watched one of your interrogations, though. You deliberately overdosed a prisoner."

"Yes, I did." Doyle won marks back for not denying the accusation. "The waivers we asked for were too low." And lost some right away again for arguing. Although Toreth didn't mind juniors with some backbone, at least in moderation.

"They were intentionally low. I wanted them back from Justice without any chance of quibbling, so we could run a fast first set of interrogations and hopefully catch any names we'd missed in the arrests. With that many prisoners, it doesn't matter if one or two clam up and we need to apply for a higher waiver later. Do you understand?"

"Yes, Para." The junior took the reprimand well, again. "I'm sorry. I was frustrated, that's all. I should've gone straight on to the next name on the list."

"You're right, you should. Get a reputation for carelessness—or frustration—and no one will want you on their cases. I finally read your file," Toreth added.

Doyle nodded. He didn't look nervous—more resigned, if anything. He must get a lot of questions about it. When Toreth didn't say any more, Doyle prompted, "Para?"

"You picked up a good permanent junior post straight from training. Six weeks after that you were back in the pool and your senior was drinking his meals through a straw."

"I used to have a bit of a temper on me."

"And now?"

His voice held no inflection. "Now I've still got a temper, but I keep it in hand."

"That's not the only disciplinary note on your file, though, is it?"

"No, Para."

"Fight with another junior, witness complaints...damage to prisoners outside

124

the waiver." Toreth paged up the screen. "Nothing recent, though. Nothing for the last six months. Not since the incident with the corporate security officer."

"That's right, Para." Doyle was staring past Toreth's left shoulder. "I had a psych assessment and the psychologist sent me on a compulsory course. Control of inappropriate impulses."

"Must be the only psych course that ever worked." Toreth sat back in his chair. "So tell me what happened in your first placing."

Doyle folded his arms and straightened slightly. "It was all an accident, Para."

"Bullshit. I've broken jaws and it's not that easy."

He shrugged and looked directly at Toreth. "We were drunk. I punched Senior Para Lewis, he fell over, he hit his temple on the curbstone and knocked himself cold. I called the ambulance. Nothing more to tell." His gaze flicked to the screen. "You can look it all up, if you want to."

Toreth ignored the suggestion. "And the witness who said she saw you kicking the shit out of him while he was on the ground?"

"If you read the whole file, then you'll have seen that she retracted the statement."

"Yes, I did notice. Why did she do that?"

"Decided she'd made a mistake, I suppose. All by herself." His clear blue eyes were absolutely guileless and Toreth knew without a doubt he was lying through his teeth.

"Quite impressive, breaking someone's jaw in five places with one punch."

"I hit him just the once," Doyle said softly. "That was what happened and the inquiry accepted it."

"Yeah, and Lewis still had his jaw wired together when the inquiry panel sat. Must be why his version was so short. Lucky for you he didn't want to press charges." Toreth pointed to his screen. "What the report doesn't say is why you did it in the first place."

"Does it matter?"

"Maybe—and I'll tell you why I'm asking. I'm looking for a new junior. A permanent team junior." The brief flash of naked hope in Doyle's eyes made Toreth smile. "But I'm not taking someone who hospitalizes his seniors unless I know what happened. So if you want the post, you have one minute to tell me the truth."

Toreth waited through a few more seconds of silence, until Doyle shrugged again. "Okay. We went out to celebrate the end of my first case. We were both plastered and . . . well, when we left the bar to find a taxi, he propositioned me. I lost my rag and hit him."

"He . . ." Toreth blinked. "*Lewis? George* Lewis?"

Doyle nodded, his expression tight.

"Jesus Christ." Toreth had always prided himself on being able to assess sexual inclination. If he'd been making a list of fanatically straight seniors at I&I,

125

Lewis would have been second on it, right below Chevril. "George Lewis tried to pull you?" Another nod. "And that was enough for you to kick his teeth in?"

"Yes. I—well, looking back on it, I know I overreacted." At least he'd stopped disputing the kicking part. "Anyway, Para, you can see why I didn't tell the inquiry. No one would've believed I wasn't making it up."

"And I can see why he wanted it kept quiet. Fucking hell. George Lewis." At least the senior showed some decent taste for his sudden aberration. Toreth snorted. "You live and learn. Did he say what he wanted you to do with him?"

He expected the question to rattle Doyle, but the man simply nodded. "Oh, yes, Para. He was very specific. Far more than I wanted to know. I don't fuck men."

"I do." Toreth checked his watch—bollocks. He should've been out of the building twenty minutes ago. "And I will be in about an hour and a half, if I'm not so late that he gives up and goes home. That a problem for you, if you joined my team?"

"Only if you expect it to be me."

"Definitely not." Doyle's expression didn't change; he certainly didn't look as if he believed Toreth in the slightest. "I don't fuck inside my team," Toreth said. "Ask B-C—he's pretty enough to know. Or ask any of them."

"With all due respect, Para, that's not what I've heard in the pool junior coffee room."

Ah. "Harry Belqola was a useless piece of shit who couldn't pull his weight. You aren't. Actually, impatience in interrogations aside, from your casework and the IIPs I'd say you're an outstanding junior. This is a straight offer—" And Doyle smiled briefly at that. "No strings, no probationary period. Do you want the place?"

Doyle hesitated for a second longer, then nodded. "Yes, please, Para."

"Fine. I'll sort out the paperwork later." Toreth was already standing up. "Welcome to the team," he said as he pulled his jacket on. "Have a word with Sara about a desk, and I'll see you on Monday."

"Thanks for the corporate tip," Toreth said, after the waitress had delivered the pizzas to their table.

"What tip?" Warrick asked.

"The idea you gave me, about selling corporate secrets. Very helpful—the kidnapping case."

"I caught a news bulletin today—that was you? I didn't hear your name."

Toreth nodded. "Haven't you ever noticed I&I never connects names to cases? Not officially, anyway. Supposedly it's because it gives resisters someone to aim for. Mostly I think they don't want to have to pay us bonuses."

"I don't pick up much criminal news. I think it was flagged because it was corporate." Warrick cut an exact triangle from the edge of his pizza. "You got her back safely, then?"

"Eventually. Closed the case, and that's the important thing."

"Congratulations."

"Thanks. I could've used your help a few times. Fucking corporates and their fucking confidentiality privileges."

Warrick shook his head. "I'm afraid that's all in the past, now. All my file access is of an impeccably legal nature."

"Really?"

"Oh, most definitely." The small smile could mean anything. "These days I am the most law-abiding of citizens."

"Good." If Warrick were ever caught doing what Toreth felt absolutely certain he was still doing, he wouldn't be the only one answering tricky questions. Dinner and fucking once a week certainly made enough of an association that Toreth would at least have an interview with Internal Investigations. No one wanted that. Lucky, really, that Warrick didn't want to hear about I&I. It would be hard to be disciplined for betraying confidential information to someone who preferred to pretend Toreth's job didn't exist. Of course, if Warrick were ever interrogated, Toreth would be fucked anyway. But that milk was so thoroughly spilled, no amount of crying could fix it. Better to keep a watch on Warrick, and hope for a decent warning if he were about to try something stupid again.

"Are you still satisfied with our arrangements?" Warrick asked in precisely the same conversational tone he'd used to ask about the case.

Following on from Toreth's thoughts, the statement seemed oddly sinister. "What arrangements?"

"This?" Warrick raised an eyebrow as he gestured between them. "And afterwards."

"Oh! Yeah. Yeah, of course. Why wouldn't I be?" Toreth put down his knife and fork. "Aren't you?"

"Yes, very much so. It simply occurred to me that you might be finding it a little too...routine."

Because Toreth had walked out last week, no doubt. Typical fucking Warrick: overthinking and overanalyzing. Toreth frowned, relieved and irritated at the same time.

"There's nothing wrong with that. You know what someone told me once? Order and discipline is what makes the difference between citizens and indigs." Of course, Gee Evans had never seen the inside of Toreth's flat, but then neither had Warrick.

"You have a lot of routines, then?" Warrick asked.

Toreth eyed the symmetrical attack currently in progress on Warrick's pizza, then decided not to mention it. "Well, I try to get to the gym every evening after

127

work, that kind of thing. I don't always manage it, but I try. Except on Fridays, of course."

"I feel as though I should apologize for disrupting your week."

"I go at lunchtime instead. Same at the weekend." Toreth shrugged, and picked up the knife and fork again. "Gym, lunch, shopping or whatever other crap I didn't have time to do all week, out in the evening. Routines, I suppose." No comment came back in return. When he looked up from his plate, Warrick was watching him. "What?"

"Nothing." Warrick smiled slightly. "I tried to imagine you shopping, that's all. It seemed somehow improbable."

"Food and clothes don't buy themselves." Toreth decided to kill the line of conversation. He nodded at Warrick's arm. "Cast's off, I see. I brought some more cuffs, if you're interested."

Warrick hesitated, and Toreth could see the struggle in his eyes, wondering what he should say to make Toreth stay, what might make him walk out again. No need to tell Warrick that after closing a successful case Toreth had no intention of not rounding off the week with great sex. Finally the tension snapped. "Yes," Warrick said. "Please. Very interested indeed."

Friday

❖

Friday, late afternoon. Warrick had an end-of-the-week feeling, something relatively new. Since the foundation of the corporation, weekends had been simply the days when it was quieter at SimTech and he could get some work done without a constant stream of employees, suppliers, and investors eating into his attention. Also the days when he spent a little time with friends or family, although sometimes he found himself resenting even that much distraction from work. In essence, the weekends themselves hadn't changed that much. The difference was Friday evenings. His evenings with Toreth.

Not every Friday, but regularly enough that he'd begun to find himself distracted on Friday afternoons. At first it had annoyed him, and he'd tried to force himself to concentrate. In the end the effort hadn't seemed justified by the benefits, and he'd given up. Instead he simply scheduled things that required less attention. Winding down, preparing for the evening. Another element of ritual that, he had to admit, added to the experience.

Friday wasn't the only day. Occasionally one of them would set up an extra meeting. A couple of times a month they'd also do something in the sim, either a genuine trial, or his own, unofficial experiments into translating his real-world experiences with Toreth into the virtual realm. Unsuccessful, so far, although the failures had been very enjoyable. It was something that the sim couldn't do, and he even knew what was missing.

Fear. The touch of fear he sometimes felt with Toreth, the knowledge of what he was: dangerous, ultimately uncontrollable, and addictively good at fucking. At giving Warrick what he needed. A slightly unhealthy attraction, possibly, but the danger was undeniably and desperately arousing.

There had been no call from Toreth today to announce that he was too busy, or simply to say he wasn't coming, without any reason supplied. That didn't mean it was definitely on. Three or four times over the last seven months he'd arrived at the hotel, waited for an hour or so and then gone home, annoyed and unfulfilled.

Toreth would call, or he'd call Toreth, and they'd set up another meeting. No apologies, no explanations.

Thinking about it, he checked the place and time again, just to make sure—a new hotel, with dinner beforehand this time. Not long now. A few hours, time slipping away, seeming to pass more slowly with every minute until it would be almost a shock when the bedroom door closed behind them and the game started in earnest.

What would it be tonight? Warrick glanced at his watch and smiled. Daydreaming time away, and at SimTech, too, something he wouldn't have believed possible this time last year. Not quite the end of the working day yet, though. He had another meeting, which ought to have started fifteen minutes ago. Cele was late, which didn't surprise Warrick at all. She shared Toreth's erratic timekeeping, although Cele's applied as much to work as to social appointments. At least this time she'd called SimTech to say she'd been held up at the studio. While he waited for her, he considered what he was going to say to her. Businesswise, he had everything planned out. It was the personal side that filled him, if not with dread, then with a certain degree of apprehension.

She had always been his sister's friend first, and his second. But when Dillian had left for Mars, she'd made him promise to keep in touch with Cele—primarily, he suspected, so that Cele could keep an eye on him. In the months before she left, Dilly had tried to persuade him to go on a string of dates with acquaintances of hers, all of which he'd declined. The last thing she'd said to him at the 'port was, "Don't spend all your time in the sim, will you?"

Well, now he certainly wasn't spending all his time in the sim, which ought to make her happy. On the other hand, he'd hardly mentioned Toreth in all the times he'd spoken to Dilly over the last months. Partly it was the investigation—and Marian. Dilly had been contacted by I&I and questioned (although not, he thought, by Toreth in person), and so he'd had to tell her something about it. Not, of course, about how things had ended. He didn't want to get into a conversation about Toreth that would lead too close to dangerous topics.

In addition, there was the difficulty of knowing what to say about him. A weekly or biweekly dinner and fuck (or often plain fuck) wasn't what Dillian would consider a relationship, and in truth Warrick agreed. Just sex, however good, didn't qualify, whatever Marian had thought. While he found it very satisfactory, he doubted Dilly would understand. It would be easier to explain it in person than over a time-delayed comm link.

As for *what* they did, that was none of Dillian's business, or anyone else's, come to that. However, too-obvious bruises had already caused comment and necessitated some explanations—to the SimTech staff medic, for one, and to one of his admins. Difficult conversations, but he understood their concern. The broken wrist two months ago had been the most awkward incident. In the end, he'd frankly

130

lied and attributed it to a slip in the kitchen. Far more palatable than handcuffs and an accidentally tipped-over chair.

The bruises had grown worse, lately, until he'd had to ask Toreth to concentrate his attentions on less visible areas. Toreth had agreed, and complied, mostly. Sometimes they both became too caught up in the game to remember. A case of overexuberance last week was the cause of the current fading marks on his lips and cheekbone. Cele was bound to notice them. She had an artist's eye for detail that picked up on everything. She would worry, as the other people had worried and he'd tried to reassure them that there was no need.

Toreth would stop, if asked. His trustworthiness in this area, if in few others, was the reason the bruises were there in the first place. Trust made it work. When things went well, when he felt his own control starting to slip away, he trusted Toreth to know how far to take things and when to stop.

Danger and trust. A paradox.

There had been plenty of mistakes and misunderstandings, but sex was the one thing Toreth was always happy to talk about. Then, with the rules more clearly defined, the next time would be better. That there had been so many next times surprised him a little. He'd never imagined that Toreth's interest would last this long. Not that he was complaining in the least, but he'd spent so long braced for the day when Toreth would simply stop calling that the expectation had become ingrained. It was one more reason, beyond the nature of the relationship, that he didn't mention Toreth to other people.

The comm broke the spell, reception calling up to say that Cele had arrived, so he told them that he'd be down to collect her.

When the lift door opened, he spotted her at once. The sun caught her polished silver jewelry and picked out the reddish highlights in her brown hair as she leaned over the reception desk, talking to Lillias Brinton. "Cele!"

She looked around. "There you are!" She turned back briefly, patted Lillias on the shoulder, picked up a large folder from the desk, and crossed over to him with her usual quick, confident walk.

They stepped into the lift, accompanied by a couple of SimTech staff returning from a very late lunch, deep in technical conversation. Warrick made a mental note of their names so that he could speak to them later about commercial confidentiality. He disliked having to circumscribe the SimTech staff's days, but they had a canteen in the building for people who had to talk about work while they ate. He doubted the discussion had started the moment the two stepped into the lift, or even into the reception area, which was still classified as public for corporate espionage purposes.

As the lift rose, Warrick caught the scent Cele was wearing—something musky. "Nice perfume," he said.

"I should hope so. You gave it to me for New Year." She laughed at his expression. "Or did you?"

Caught out, he had to smile. "All right, I confess. I was too busy to buy the presents before I got there. I did tell Mother to buy perfume; I just left the details up to her."

"I should've guessed Kate. Much more her taste than yours." It was then, as she looked at him, that he saw her smile lock in place and her eyes narrow. No more was said until they reached his office. When the door closed, she said, "Come over by the window."

The couple of people who'd asked already had taken a while to build up to it, but he hadn't expected anything indirect from Cele. He stood in the sunlight while she examined his face, turning it from side to side with impersonal fingers. He could smell oil paint and turpentine on her hands. "Where'd you get the bruises, Keir?" she asked.

"From a man called Toreth, in an entirely consensual and mutually satisfactory fashion."

Cele looked at his cheek for a moment longer, and then released him. "You've kept that quiet."

One day he'd find something that would actually disconcert her. "I'm full of surprises."

"How long's it been going on?"

"A few months."

She pulled a chair around the desk and sat down. "So, what's he like?"

Warrick joined her, a little reluctantly. It was, he realized, the first time he'd talked about Toreth in detail to anyone. "Well...tall. Short blond hair. Blue eyes. Attractive." Feeling the description was rather too physical, he added, "Intelligent." Personality disordered.

"Well endowed?" she asked cheerfully. "Good in bed? Go on—skip to the important stuff."

Somehow he managed to keep his expression deadpan. "I have no complaints."

"No, you don't look like you do." Another careful examination. "In fact, I will admit you're looking good. Capturing the essential happy glow of the well-fucked individual, as one of my tutors used to say. Anyway, carry on. Is he fit?"

"He certainly spends a lot of time in the gym."

Cele raised her eyes. "Good Lord, it's like pulling teeth. Come on—details, details."

Physique was always the part that interested her most. "Well...broad shoulders, slim waist, long legs. Looks like a swimmer—he does swim, I think. Not overly muscular, though, not like a bodybuilder. Well proportioned is probably the best way to describe him. Very good skin."

Cele had a distant expression, as though there were an incomplete painting of Toreth hanging in midair and she was sketching in details as he gave them. "Thighs? Calves? Backside?" she asked.

132

Now Warrick had an image of his own. "Mm. Definitely all of those."

She laughed. "Sounds fabulous. Do you think he'd let me draw him? Or sculpt him, maybe. I'm looking for a really buff model at the moment."

Would Toreth like to have an attractive woman paying attention to his body? Not a question that required much consideration. Or had it been an indirect way to request a meeting? "I don't know. One thing he doesn't have is a long attention span." For some things, anyway.

"Oh, well. Right—so he's good-looking, fit, smart, he's a great lay . . . and he hits you?"

Inevitable that they'd get back to that. "Only on request."

"Really?" Before he could answer, she lifted her hands, palms towards him. "I know, I know. But—" She held up a finger. "Firstly, I promised Dilly that I'd look after you, even though of course you don't need it, and I only said it so she'd go off to Mars and not spend all her time there fretting over her big brother, screw up her job, and make some terrible engineering mistake ultimately resulting in the grisly deaths of thousands. And secondly—" Another finger.

"Yes?"

She folded her hands in her lap and shrugged. "We lonely singles need to look out for each other."

"I didn't know you were lonely."

"Nope, sorry. We're not changing the subject." Now her tone was serious. "Go on, tell me once more. Humor me."

He looked her directly in the eyes. "It's absolutely, one hundred percent, totally and in all ways consensual. He does what I want, no more."

She smiled. "And no less?"

"Definitely no less."

"Good." She brushed off her hands. "Job done. Okay, I'm a happy camper now. So, when do I get to meet this kinky stud?"

"You don't. The social element of the arrangement stretches to pre-sex dinners, and that's all." Cele pouted, which was always amusing but not so much so that he'd change his mind about keeping Toreth away from his real life. "It's not possible," he said firmly. "If you really want to know more, ask Asher. She met him during the investigation."

"Investigation?"

"Yes. He's—"

"Jesus!" Her eyes widened. "I *thought* the name sounded familiar, and then I thought it couldn't—he's the para-investigator?"

Only a few minutes ago he'd wondered what would surprise her, and now he knew. "That's him."

Now she didn't look so happy. "Ash told me all about him already. She said he had an aura."

133

"Aura?"

"Like he wasn't using extreme violence right that second, but the situation could easily change the moment you pissed him off."

"Mm." Not at all a bad description. "That sounds a bit poetic for Asher."

"I got the feeling he made an impression. She told me what happened to the psychologist as well."

No, she didn't. "Marian died in custody."

"You mean they killed her."

Tactful, for Cele. He'd half expected "your kinky stud killed her."

"No." Warrick managed to keep his voice level. "It was unfortunate, but it was an accident. An unforeseeable accident. We had a report from I&I."

"An accident." After a couple of seconds, she nodded. "Well...accidents happen, I suppose."

"Yes. They do." The memory of that morning at I&I, of watching Marian die, left a sour taste in his mouth.

"So, does Ash know you're seeing him?"

"I'm not *seeing* him. I told you that already." He couldn't keep the irritation out of his voice. "It's purely sexual, so there's no reason to tell her anything. Or anyone else. It's not as if anyone's ever going to meet him."

Except, of course, they had—here, at SimTech, when Toreth had come to use the sim. Even though the private sessions had been out of official hours, there was no way to keep them secret. For one thing, it would be breaking the rules he required others to follow. He wondered now how many people knew, or had guessed, and what they were saying about it.

"So, *does* Ash know?" Cele asked again.

"Probably. I didn't send her a memo, but I don't smuggle him in here under a blanket, either. However, Asher knows when to mind her own business."

Cele was, predictably, utterly unabashed. "You're beginning to sound awfully defensive about this. Sure you want to stick to 'purely sexual'?"

"Yes. Absolutely."

"Fair enough. Have you told Dilly?"

No point hedging around it. "No."

"She's back soon."

"In a fortnight, yes. I'll tell her about it when I see her. I'd rather you didn't mention it if you speak to her before then."

She nodded slowly. "Are you going to tell her everything?"

"I don't really see that it's any of your business."

Her eyes narrowed. "Don't give me that shit. I've known you too long."

"Very well. What I do with Toreth—" he tapped the fading bruise, "—is something apart from the rest of my life. I don't want you, or Dilly, or anyone, to get involved with it. Dilly doesn't need to know, and I don't want you to tell her. Clear enough?"

134

"Crystal, but I don't like it."

"I'm not expecting you to." Time to play his best card. "I'm just asking you, as a friend, not to tell her that one thing."

Cele hesitated, and then said, "She'll see the bruises."

"There won't be any by then."

She shrugged. "Okay. I won't mention it."

"Thanks."

"But—" She held her finger up again—a warning this time. "If she notices anything herself and she asks me about it, I'm not going to lie for you. Not to Dilly."

No more than he'd expected. "And I wouldn't want you to. Would you like some coffee?" When she nodded, jewelry ringing musically, he rose and crossed to the coffee machine. "Biscuits?" he offered. "Homemade. There's ginger or shortbread."

"I'd *love* some. Both kinds. Hey, does this mean you're baking again?"

He frowned at her over his shoulder. "Baking again?"

"Yeah. I mean..." Her expression turned speculative. "You haven't done much baking in years. Since Mel left, in fact."

He looked away. "I cook all the time."

"Not to the extent of leaving tins of biscuits scattered around the place. I had to practically get on my knees and beg for the last lot of gingerbread."

True, he supposed. "What on earth does that have to do with anything?"

"Nothing, nothing. Ignore me. Just thinking out loud."

Obviously not true, but he didn't feel like pursuing it. He picked up the jug of coffee. "So, to change the topic, how's *your* love life? Did you genuinely mean you were a lonely single?"

She waved her hand. "I exaggerated. Single, but not lonely. I've put my second lesbian phase on hold and I'm having a celibate year. Avoiding distractions." It was only when Cele exclaimed, "Whoa!" and pointed that he realized the coffee had overflowed into the saucer while he stared at her. Cele laughed. "Lord, it's nice to know what your friends think of you."

He poured the coffee carefully back into the jug and tapped the saucer on the edge. "It doesn't, ah, seem quite like you, that's all."

"Well, after the first three months I thought I'd make a virtue out of necessity. But really I haven't got time to look, never mind to get down and do the dirty."

"You should make time. It's worth it."

She shook her head, smiling, and took the offered cup. "Listen to you. The man who leaves work only to sleep and shower."

"Not any more." Warrick checked his watch again. "I'm seeing him tonight, in fact, so..."

"Hey, far be it from me to get in the way of the kink-a-thon." Cele set down the cup and opened her folder, bringing out a stack of large sheets of creamy paper.

135

"Did you get the copies? I brought the originals anyway. I always think paper looks so much better than screens."

"Luddite."

She grinned, unrepentant. "Do you want some cheap, autogenerated computer pretties, or do you want Great Art?"

While she spread the sim room designs out on his desk, he stared into his cup, thinking about the coming evening. A lover he wanted to keep away from everyone he knew. A man who smiled while he hit him.

A murderer.

What the hell am *I doing with him?*

Strangely, Marian's death was part of the answer, an unbreakable link between them, something that he could never walk away from. Refusing to see Toreth wouldn't bring Marian back to life, or undo the part Warrick had played in her death. Better to keep Toreth an enclosed, secret part of his life, as segregated as he could make it.

Not as segregated as it had been, though. One more person who knew now—a friend, not a colleague—and Dillian was returning soon. The only certain way to stop this slow blurring of the line was to tell Toreth it was over, and that was simply unthinkable. It was too good to give up.

He'd find a way to handle it, and to keep things in their proper places.

Then he turned his attention back to work.

Pancakes

❖

Toreth found Warrick waiting in one of the side booths. He'd already bought them both drinks, and Toreth knocked back a third of his before he sat down, or even said hello. Warrick looked at him inquiringly.

"I've had the most fucking awful day," Toreth said with feeling. He slid onto the bench opposite Warrick and leaned back against the smooth wood of the booth, closing his eyes. "From the second I arrived it was one bloody thing after another. Sara went home sick and she managed to double-book me a room and lose half my files before she left. And, if you can believe it, Chevril offloaded two cases' worth of prisoners onto *me*, as if I didn't have enough to do with the investigation. Tillotson is a complete fucking idiot. And they were both real bastards, impossible interrogation requests from Justice, no leeway at all for results. And I have to go back in tomorrow morning to finish the fucking job. Fucking Justice interrogations, on a Saturday! Sometimes I think..."

A certain icy quality in the silence coming across the table finally pierced through his monologue and induced him to open his eyes. Warrick regarded him with an expression that might charitably be described as unsympathetic. "I'm not interested," he said bluntly.

Toreth sat up, belatedly remembering where he was. "I was only—"

"You were talking about your job. Specifically, about interrogation. I don't want to hear about it." Warrick took a small sip of his drink and then set the glass carefully in the center of the coaster. "You know I don't want to hear about it. I've told you that before. Several times. And yet you keep doing it." He looked up. "Why?"

"I..." Toreth tried to think of an answer which wouldn't sound stupid, then gave up. He shrugged. "I forgot."

"Mm." Warrick stood up, and picked up his jacket without putting it on. "My sister is arriving back from Mars tomorrow. I'll be very busy for the next few days, so don't bother to call."

And then he walked out.

Toreth stared after him, too taken aback to react. He'd had the whole evening planned out, and the sudden wrench off course threw him utterly. When the fuck had *Warrick* started being the one who could walk out? By the time he'd started to stand, Warrick had pushed open the bar door and left without a backward glance.

So much for a nice, stress-relieving evening of fucking, the prospect of which had been all that had kept him going through the afternoon's interrogation. At least Warrick hadn't finished his drink before he left. Toreth pulled it across the table and drank it. Then he leaned on one arm, watching the ice melting against the side of the glass. For a couple of minutes he tried to be angry, but he was too tired and generically pissed off to focus his resentment on Warrick. It was the perfect fucking end to his day.

Toreth finished his own drink and thought about going home. But, quite frankly, he couldn't see the point. Even looking for another fuck seemed like too much effort. So he had another drink, and then another, and so on until the very last one just before the bar closed, when he was surprised to discover that the tab was larger than it usually was when he was drinking in company. And that he was pissed. Very pissed. Very, very pissed, in fact.

Out in the street, he leaned against a post and waved at passing taxis, and tried to recall the last time he'd drunk so much. He couldn't remember. Actually, he could barely remember his own address. Funnily enough, he found he could remember Warrick's easily, even though he'd never been there. He'd read it in his security file. And, of course, it would be in the old investigation files. So it wouldn't matter if he turned up uninvited. Not that he was going to. Warrick wouldn't want to see him. They'd had an argument, sort of, he thought, although the exact details lay drowned in whiskey. It had definitely been Warrick's fault, anyway.

And Warrick had no right to walk out, either. No right at all.

When a taxi finally stopped, Toreth wasn't quite sure whose address he gave. Luckily, or perhaps not, the taxi was new and the voice-recognition well up to the task of deciphering slurred directions, so he only had to give the address once. Since he didn't recognize the building it stopped at, he assumed it must be Warrick's. Quite a nice building, in what looked like a nice bit of the city.

Nice.

The first problem was that the building was large, and consequently had a large number of flats. Through the reinforced glass door, he could see a guard watching him, but he didn't feel like trying to explain what he wanted. There was a comm screen on the outside, though. After a couple of minutes trying to focus, he entered what he hoped was the number of Warrick's flat and pressed the button. No answer. He tried again. Hadn't Warrick said something about going away somewhere?

Toreth leaned against the wall above the screen, resting his head on his forearm. Then he put his finger back on the button and held it down while he tried to remember what Warrick had said. Yes. He was going to see his sister. Oh, fuck.

The cool night air had chased some of the alcohol from his mind, but his body was as pissed as it had been when he left the bar. More pissed, indeed, because the drink he'd had before he left would be filtering into his bloodstream faster than the earlier drinks were filtering out. Sober, Toreth was good at calculating drug clearance rates. In the state he was in now he was still trying to remember how many milligrams of alcohol the liver could process per whatever when the comm screen flickered into life.

Toreth realized he still had his finger on the button, and released it. Luckily, he could see the screen from where he was. Letting go of the wall suddenly felt like a very bad idea.

The screen showed nothing other than the number of the flat he had been buzzing for the last however long it was, but he couldn't mistake the voice over the speaker for anyone else. "What the hell are *you* doing here?"

He couldn't see Warrick, but clearly Warrick could see him. Which sounded very metaphorical. Or something. "I—" His tongue felt as though someone had injected an extravagant amount of local anesthetic into it. "I jus' wanted to say, you don't have any right..."

"Oh, for God's sake." There was a long pause. "Stay there. I'll be down."

Toreth nodded mutely, then rolled around so that his back was against the wall. The full moon above swam in and out of focus. He had bed-spin, and he wasn't even in bed. Very slowly, he slid down the wall.

Oh. Fuck.

By the time Warrick opened the door, Toreth had managed to rally slightly. He looked around, which wasn't so bad if he did it slowly, and smiled. Warrick stood in the doorway, completely and carefully dressed. He'd even taken the time to brush his hair, Toreth noted absently. Even so, he looked less than thrilled to see Toreth. "Since the odds are very heavily against my being able to carry you upstairs, you'd better stand up," he said icily.

Toreth eventually managed to struggle to his feet as Warrick watched impassively. Once they were inside, he deigned to lend aid to the extent of an arm around Toreth's waist, waving the guard away when he approached. The silence as they went up in the lift was deafening, and continued until they reached the flat. After they went inside, Warrick propped him carefully against the wall while he closed and locked the door. Then he took hold of Toreth again and pointed down the other end of the hall.

"What?"

"The toilet is over there."

"I don't—"

"Toreth, I have unpasteurized curd cheese in my fridge which is less green than you. If you throw up on my floor, you are going back out of that door. Now, move."

He nearly began to protest, but whether it was the power of suggestion, or the change from the cold outside to the warm flat, or simply the night catching up with him, Toreth realized Warrick was right. He made a grab for Warrick's shoulder and missed. Warrick caught him before he fell, muttering something Toreth didn't catch, but which sounded uncomplimentary. "I think I'm—" Toreth put his hand hastily over his mouth and swallowed heavily.

"Oh, hell!"

They made it the length of the hall just in time. Warrick stood around for a few minutes, making doubtless witty and biting comments that Toreth was too busy being miserably sick to appreciate. Then he left him to it.

By the time his stomach had convinced itself there was absolutely nothing left to get rid of, embarrassment had begun to steal over him. He couldn't even remember why he'd thought it might be a good idea to come here. He leaned on the toilet wall for a while, trying to decide whether he was up to creeping out of the flat and finding a taxi. In the end he concluded that if he did he would probably end up spending the night face down in the street. Fine if you were eighteen. Not so good at . . . thirty-two. Instead he made a poorly coordinated effort to clean up the toilet. It was the best he could manage but, he reflected, Warrick was unlikely to be a believer in the saying "it's the thought that counts." At least outside the sim. Toreth washed his hands and face, rinsed the taste of stomach acid and second-time-around whiskey out of his mouth, and went in unsteady search of his reluctant host.

He found him sitting at a table in the kitchen, watching an antique coffee brewer. Steam was beginning to waft the smell of coffee across the room. For a moment Toreth hovered between feeling sick again and desperately wanting a cup. The need for caffeine won out, and he let go of the safety of the wall long enough to make it to a chair. Warrick looked at him with the same lack of enthusiasm he'd shown outside. "Finished?"

Toreth nodded.

"Would you like some coffee?"

Toreth thought about the question, which proved to be harder than it sounded. His stomach was still profoundly unhappy about the idea. "I'm not sure," he said eventually.

The corner of Warrick's mouth crept into a tiny smile. "You should probably start with a glass of water. Or ten."

Toreth rested his head on his arms, closed his eyes. "'M okay," he mumbled.

"No, you aren't. Toreth? Toreth! Wake up." Insistent prodding of his shoulder eventually roused Toreth enough to sit upright. "How much did you have to drink?" Warrick sounded almost concerned.

140

"Don't remember. Lots." There was something else. Something important. Oh, yes. "'S all your fault."

Warrick shook his head. "Come on. Let's get you into bed." He bent down to lift Toreth, and then stopped, wrinkling his nose. "Undressed, and into bed."

Toreth opened his eyes to find the room blissfully dark. He lay very still, assessing the extent of the damage. Head: very bad. Stomach: worse. His mouth tasted as if particularly scrofulous pigeons had been nesting in it. At least he'd managed to get home in one piece. Or had he? Slowly, he became aware of the little presences and absences that added up to the realization that he was not, after all, at home. He rolled over and moaned. The bed beside him was empty, and he wondered what time it was. "Warrick?"

"Good morning, Val Toreth!" a female voice announced with grating cheerfulness. The windows began to de-opaque, letting an increasing stream of sunlight into the room. The computer must have been coded to Warrick's voice, because it ignored his pleas to stop. He squeezed his eyelids shut. "Warrick has gone out," the flat management system continued relentlessly, "but he'll be back. In the meantime, he says, 'look on the table by the bed, don't fiddle with the security systems, and don't use up all the hot water. Oh, and your clothes are in the washer.'"

On the table beside the bed he found a large carafe of water with a glass over the top and two tablets set on a saucer, one buff-colored, one orange and white. He took the tablets and then gathered pillows, propping himself up in bed. He sipped water slowly and ignored the churning in his stomach.

His clothes were in the washer. Warrick must have undressed him, then. Toreth could imagine how happy he would have been about that. In fact, the entire—mercifully hazy—night must have royally fucked him off. He tried to think back, wondering how much of an apology would be required to smooth things over. He remembered the taxi, and the lift, and Warrick locking the door. Then things went blank. But he had an uneasy feeling that there was a fair chunk of time after that missing from his memory.

He finished the first glass of water and refilled it. To his surprise, the edge was already fading from the hangover. He wondered what had been in the tablets, and where they had come from. At least Warrick had been in a good enough mood to leave them for him. "How long is Warrick going to be?" he asked the empty air. The system stayed silent, but Toreth decided that he wanted to be up and dressed by the time Warrick got back. It would be easier to come up with a convincing apology with a little more dignity involved and the option of a fast exit.

He sat on the edge of the bed and his foot touched damp carpet. Damp with water, he decided, rather than anything worse. But there was a very faint, sour smell of vomit in the air, overlaid with disinfectant, which reminded him of work. Fuck. He was late for work. From the look of the sun it had to be midmorning. His watch, on the tray beside the carafe, confirmed it.

He showered quickly, remembering the admonition about the hot water, then started searching for his clothes. He found the washer in the kitchen, which seemed somewhat familiar, so he assumed he must have been in there last night. His clothes from last night were dry and, having been washed here, smelled like Warrick as he pulled them on.

He refilled his glass from the tap and looked around the kitchen. It was larger than most Toreth had been in, with a real hob and an oven, and a refrigerator that seemed excessive for one person. Most people who could afford to live in buildings like this didn't bother with cooking. There was a surprisingly extensive collection of pots and pans, and the first cupboard he opened held a large assortment of jars and sealed packets containing what Toreth assumed were herbs and spices. More cupboards held an impressive array of bottles of oil and other ingredients. Interesting. Just went to show that you couldn't find out everything about someone from his security file. Of course, a detailed credit and purchase check would have got it all. Had he never bothered asking for one for Warrick? He closed the cupboard door and leaned against the edge of the counter, admiring the collection of knives. The flat and its pricey contents helped explain the security Warrick had warned him about. And, of course, Warrick was a corporate sabotage target. SimTech would pay for all the electronics that incidentally protected his expensive hobbies from criminals.

Toreth considered leaving a vaguely apologetic note and going to work, but the idea of being arrested trying to break out of a former murder suspect's flat was unappealing. Warrick had trapped him neatly. Still, he might as well make the most of it while he was here, so he started a tour of the flat.

The rest of the rooms were as neat as the kitchen. Insofar as he'd thought about Warrick's home at all, he'd visualized it as being as messy as his office. Then again, he almost certainly had service here. Toreth couldn't imagine anyone at SimTech daring to touch Warrick's office. The décor was tasteful and unostentatiously expensive. Primarily pale, neutral colors, including rather impractically light-colored carpets. Most of the furniture was wooden; the sofas in the living room were beautifully soft gray-blue leather, toning perfectly with the large, thick-pile rug. It seemed familiar, and eventually he recognized it as the color of the SimTech logo. Making a corporate statement, or did Warrick just like the shade? It wasn't by any means the most opulent home he had even been inside. Indeed, in the course of various investigations he'd visited places in the rarefied heights of the corporate world whose inhabitants would consider a night here to be unbearable slumming. Still, someone wealthier than Toreth's usual run of acquaintances undoubtedly owned it. He'd always known, in an abstract way, that Warrick was relatively rich, but it was strange to see it made real.

There were electronic gadgets and fittings everywhere, but no office. There was a locked room, with a serious-looking door, so Toreth guessed that would be the most likely place. It had its own security, with an iris scan and voiceprint as well as a keypad. Over the top at first glance, perhaps, but not necessarily so, if he kept sim tech in there. It was only as Toreth idly started to open drawers in the living room that he wondered if the security system included video surveillance. It was likely. He looked around the room, found nothing obvious. That didn't mean anything, though. Never mind. He'd be out of here before Warrick could discover his impromptu investigation.

Just then he heard the door opening, so he went to stand at the window, looking out at the sun-drenched street. With the bright light full in his face, it occurred to him that his headache had gone completely.

To his surprise, Warrick didn't say anything. He heard the door close and footsteps going into the kitchen. He waited, and the footsteps re-emerged, then disappeared into the main bedroom. At that point he felt sure Warrick would call his name, but instead, after a minute or so, he heard the shower start to run. He went up to the bathroom door. "Warrick?"

"Ah. There you are. I've put some coffee on in the kitchen—when the top part fills up, switch the heat off and stir the top bowl. I won't be long."

He didn't sound angry. In fact he sounded neutral-to-friendly, which was oddly more worrying. And intriguing. Toreth went into the kitchen, where he noticed a new box on the table, but decided against looking inside. He'd pushed his luck with snooping far enough for one morning. Instead he kept an eye on the coffee brewer, as instructed, while trying to work out how the hell the strange thing functioned. He had a feeling he'd seen it before, last night presumably. Two glass globes, one above the other, with bits of glass piping between them—it forced the boiling water up into the coffee grounds in the top globe, he decided in the end, then generated a vacuum that drew it back down through the filter. An expensive, fiddly toy to do something that could be done in a fraction of the time and with no effort at all.

He'd just taken the coffee off the hob and started looking for cups when Warrick spoke right behind him, startling him. "What do you think of the flat?" Warrick asked.

Meaning "have you had a good look around?" No point in pretending otherwise. "You must earn a fucking fortune."

"I believe in paying my employees well, so I don't see why I should stint myself. Excuse me." He started taking ingredients from the cupboard and refrigerator, and lifted a bowl down from the shelf. "Do you have time for breakfast?" Warrick asked.

Toreth hesitated, thinking about breakfast and looking at Warrick. His hair was damp from the shower and he wore just a pair of loose black trousers. Bare feet, which was how he'd crept up so quietly. A more different look from last night he couldn't imagine. Toreth smiled. To his surprise, he did feel hungry, and he also remembered now why he must've wanted to come here after the bar. Whatever the hell those pills were, they were good. Regretfully, there were more important things in life than fucking. And interrogations, even for fucking Justice, counted as one of them. "No," he said. "I'm late for work. Very late."

"Don't worry about it. I called I&I first thing this morning, when it became clear you were still out for the count, and spoke to the inestimable Sara. Coffee cups are over there." Measuring by eye, Warrick began to mix up a thickish batter from flour and milk and a few other things. Culinary matters were entirely outside Toreth's experience, so after he had poured the coffee, he moved to stand beside Warrick and watched the operation with mild fascination.

"What did you tell her?" Toreth asked as Warrick set a wide, heavy, flat pan on the hob.

He left the pan to heat and returned to the batter, mixing with concentration. "I told her you turned up here at three this morning, unable to stand, woke me up, threw up repeatedly, and finally passed out in my bed without any exchange of bodily fluids occurring. She sounded entertained by the beginning, but disappointed by the conclusion."

Toreth stared at him. "You didn't."

"Oh, yes, I did."

"*All* of that?"

"Yes. Sara said she'd turn it into something acceptable for official consumption." His voice turned a fraction cooler and very precise. "She asked me to tell you that there's nothing worth coming in for this morning, because Justice is still arguing over the latest prisoners. They want an absolute guarantee of no deaths. She told them nothing is guaranteed at, ah, a level six, and if you want her to tell them anything different you should let her know by this afternoon."

Oh, well done, Sara. Just the thing to put Warrick in a better mood. "Sorry about that."

Warrick dribbled pale yellow oil into the pan, swirled the pan to coat it, and shrugged. "I called her at work. I can hardly complain if I heard something I didn't wish to. My problem, not yours." Now that was something Toreth could agree with, although he felt it represented something of a change of tune since the night before. But not one worth mentioning just now.

Without spilling a drop, Warrick quickly poured three ladlefuls of batter into the now-smoking pan. They spread out to form three identically sized, thick pancakes and after a few seconds they began to bubble. It was done with an ease that masked the obvious skill involved. Toreth said, "I didn't know you could cook."

"I like to think there are a lot of things you don't know about me."

There was an edge to his voice Toreth couldn't identify. Anyway, noticing a fading bruise on Warrick's shoulder distracted him. A dark, yellowish ring, still recognizable as a bite mark. Toreth remembered putting it there. He moved around behind Warrick, traced the bruise with a fingertip, considered putting a fresh mark on the other shoulder. Nice idea. Especially the thought of doing it here, in War-

144

rick's own flat. He curved his hand over Warrick's shoulder, rubbing the bruise again with his thumb, his other hand moving without conscious direction to test the strength of the waistband of Warrick's trousers. He had a sudden, delicious image of turning Warrick around, forcing him down on his knees in front of him, of...his grip on Warrick's shoulder tightened. Muscles shifted under his hand. "Plastic duck," Warrick murmured, turning the pancakes with a spatula. They sizzled briefly, and the golden brown side now uppermost began to steam gently.

"What?"

"I'm not in the mood. Actually, I never am in the mood before breakfast."

"Oh." Toreth took his hands away and stepped back a fraction. It occurred to him that, until now, he'd never seen Warrick before breakfast. "Sorry," he said absently, while examining this novel idea.

"No need to apologize. You weren't to know. Unless it's in my security file, of course." Toreth blinked, temporarily caught out by the reference. "You must have read it," Warrick continued. "We've both been pretending otherwise, but now that you've turned up, blind drunk, at an address I've never given you, it's become too obvious to ignore." He stacked the pancakes on a heated dish, covered them with a tea towel, and then started pouring more circles of batter. "You can tell me you got it from the investigation files, if you like."

Toreth, who had just that second opened his mouth to do precisely that, closed it again. "Your file doesn't mention anything about your preferred times of day for fucking," he said eventually.

He caught Warrick's smile reflected in the steel backing of the hob. "I know."

"What? How?"

"Because I've read it. I've read yours as well."

"That's illegal," Toreth said reflexively. Extremely illegal.

"Of course it is. That's why I assumed you'd rather not know about it." He turned the pancakes, which proved to be a very slightly darker shade of brown than the first batch. "Damn. Burned them."

They had strayed into one of Warrick's weirdly elliptical conversations, which always made Toreth feel as if he'd been taking some of the more exotic drugs from the pharmacy at work. Why the hell would Warrick tell him he'd been illegally accessing controlled files? Toreth could crucify him with it. "They look fine to me," Toreth said, meaning the pancakes.

"You can have them, then." Warrick stirred the remaining batter in a careful figure of eight as the pancakes cooked.

"What does it say?" Toreth asked, not bothering to specify the subject because non sequiturs were the basic style for this game.

"It's very flattering, actually. They think a lot of you. Tillotson gives out more praise in secret files than he apparently does to your face."

"Oh." Toreth felt pleased, but thought he managed to hide it rather well.

"Sounds about right—he's probably worried I'd want a pay rise. What else?"

Warrick flipped the pancakes out of the pan and onto the stack, and poured more. He offered one of the allegedly overcooked ones to Toreth, who took it, burning his fingers and then his mouth. "Fucking excellent," he said indistinctly, which it was.

"Thank you." He adjusted the heat of the hob slightly. "I didn't read all of it."

No, he wouldn't have. There would be summary figures in there for the investigations and interrogations Toreth had carried out, and his success rate and death rate and very probably details of some of his cases. Served Warrick right for looking at it.

"You've been recommended for a grade increase," Warrick added after a moment, lifting the corner of one of the pancakes to check the color. "But it's been deferred until the end of your current investigation. There is a cross-reference from that deferral to a file I tried to get hold of but couldn't. At least not yet. It's in the Corporate database at Int-Sec, in one of the ultrasecure sections concerning corporate sabotage."

Toreth stared at him.

"I only mention it because it suggested, to me, unfriendly corporate interest in the outcome of whatever you are currently working on. I thought you might like to know."

"What the hell were you doing in my file in the first place?"

"Old business."

It took him a moment to realize what Warrick must mean. "Tanit?"

A second of stillness, then Warrick nodded. "Keeping an eye out for signs of activity on the part of Mr. Howes and any of his friends. Investigations begun into you or me, interest in the case files, and so on."

"And?"

"And everything was fine." He flipped the pancakes, studied the result. "Better. I'd let you know at once if it wasn't."

"Even though you didn't tell me you were looking?"

Warrick ignored the question. "I check every month or so. I might make it less frequent from now on."

"Why?"

"Howes has resigned from Psychoprogramming. He has an offer of a corporate contract. Once he's gone, I think we're clear. I thought you'd like to know that."

Even though Warrick had to realize it already, Toreth said, "If you get caught inside Int-Sec systems, you'll be more thoroughly fucked than I can even begin to explain."

"Don't worry, I won't be."

Caught, or fucked? Toreth wouldn't have cared, except that he could be in big trouble himself if Warrick were found out. He was the one who had opened the door to Warrick's explorations in the first place. The Administration's Data Division was very proud of their security and the idea of it being violated tended to send them into hysterics. He filed it under "things to worry about later."

Leaving the pancakes, Warrick opened the box on the table and took out a large

146

bag. From it he spilled oranges out over the work surface. Toreth caught one as it rolled towards the edge. He held it up, fascinated by the vibrant color. Warrick must have bought them when he went out. Of course, this sort of residential area would be littered with shops selling corporate delicacies; the oranges weren't even plastic-wrapped. He scored the skin with his thumbnail and smelled the unfamiliar, bitter scent. To have fruit any fresher, Warrick would need to keep a tree in his living room.

Warrick transferred the latest batch of pancakes to the plate, wiped the pan, and added some more oil. "Do you know how to use a juicer?" he asked. Toreth, who didn't really believe in food that didn't come out of a packet or ready-presented on a plate, shook his head. "Then you'll have to do the pancakes. Just pour the batter in and keep an eye on them."

"I'll make a mess."

"Then I'll wipe it up after you." Warrick smiled serenely. "I'm in practice."

Toreth stirred the batter and poured while Warrick sliced oranges in half with one of his wickedly sharp knives, releasing their sweet, sharp smell into the room. Then he took out a juicer that looked to be about the same vintage as the percolator. It had an inverted cup for crushing the oranges, and a long handle. Toreth watched as Warrick worked his way through the oranges, collecting the juice in a clear glass jug.

"Pancakes," Warrick said after a while.

Toreth carefully turned the mildly misshapen pancakes to find them exactly the right shade of golden brown underneath. "How do you do that?" he asked.

"Cooking is very like programming. It requires a sound understanding of basic principles, the patience not to cut corners, and—" he grinned briefly, "—a great deal of talent."

In a modest mood today. Looking at the jug of juice reminded Toreth of something. "Where did you get those pills? And, more to the point, what were they?"

"Standard electrolyte replacement and detox, plus something extra from work. Anti-nausea and so on for the sim. A bad sim experience is somewhat like a hangover, so some genius discovered that the drugs are as good for one as for the other."

"I've never felt like that after the sim."

"You're lucky. Most people do at least once or twice. Maybe it'll happen to you eventually." Toreth drank his coffee and watched the pancakes cooking as Warrick set the table. The shopping box also produced fresh bread, real butter, and pastries. "They should be done now," Warrick said.

Toreth brought the pancakes over to the table and sat down. Warrick sat opposite and lifted his glass of orange juice. "Your continued good heath." Then he yawned, obviously catching himself by surprise.

"Did I keep you awake?"

Warrick helped himself to pancakes and began to butter one carefully. "In a way. The spare bed isn't very comfortable. And I kept getting up to take a look at you, anyway."

Toreth couldn't remember him doing it. "There was no need."

"I had no idea how much you'd drunk, and I thought it would look bad for SimTech if a naked para-investigator were to be discovered dead in the bed of one of its directors," he said mildly. "You were throwing up with monotonous regularity for the first few hours, or I'd have tried to get you sober."

"More drugs from work?"

"No, reminders of a misspent youth. Probably quite out of date, even if you could have kept them down."

"Sorry."

Warrick shook his head. "Stop apologizing. Or try to sound as if you mean it. One or the other." He stretched, then winced and tilted his head, rubbing at his neck. "You could give me a massage before you get off to work, if you'd really like to say sorry."

"Oh." Toreth considered the idea while he chewed a mouthful of bread, then shrugged. That would be an easy enough apology. "Okay."

Warrick smiled. "Lovely. But let's finish breakfast first."

Massages didn't play a major role in Toreth's sex life. He usually found them deeply boring, and tending to get in the way of business proper. After the leisurely breakfast, though, he found he didn't mind very much. It fitted the mood of a stolen morning off work. He wondered about Warrick's sister, and her return from Mars, but decided not to bring it up. Breakfast over, they adjourned to the bedroom, where Warrick surprised Toreth not at all by carefully covering the bed in towels to protect the sheets from the oil. Then he stripped off and lay down. Given Warrick's concern for the sheets, Toreth felt he could use the excuse of not wanting to have to wash his clothes again to justify stripping himself. As it was, no justification was required. Warrick simply watched him undress, smiling slightly.

Toreth was pleased to find the oil wasn't scented, which he hated. Massages were bad enough in themselves, without ending up smelling like a brothel afterwards. His lack of practice was more than compensated for by a thorough knowledge of anatomy. As usual, Warrick was responsive to his touch, but in a different way from their normal games. Mapping out these new reactions, finding which touches produced sighs or murmurs of appreciation, filled up a reasonable amount of time. It wasn't even unarousing, in a relaxed way. Toreth helped that along, touching himself whenever he had a hand spare. Warrick had been right about the towels—the oil got everywhere. He kept half an eye on his watch on the bedside table. Eventually Toreth decided that he had apologized adequately for the previous night. He slapped Warrick on the arse, just hard enough to get his attention.

Warrick rolled onto his side and opened his eyes, focused up at him. "Is that it?"

"Half an hour. That's all you're getting."

"Bored?"

"Yes."

Warrick smiled lazily. "Well, come down here and I'll see what I can do about that."

He lay down, and Warrick pressed up close, slipped a thigh between his, and began to rub against him. Trapped between them, their cocks rubbed together, surrounded by hot, oil-slick skin. After a few seconds Toreth caught the rhythm and began to thrust back. "I thought you weren't in the mood," he said after a moment.

"Mm. No. I said I wasn't in the mood before breakfast. We had breakfast."

"You always have an answer, don't you?"

"Not always. But often. Now, shut up."

Toreth shut up and tried to remember the last time he'd done anything like this, and couldn't. It made a very pleasant change from their usual more energetic fucking. He kept his eyes open, watching Warrick, his face only centimeters away. His eyes were closed, long lashes fluttering occasionally, and his lips were slightly parted. It made Toreth think about the first time he'd seen Warrick, when he'd noticed his mouth straight away. It *was* beautiful. "Kiss me," he said, surprising himself.

Without opening his eyes, Warrick leaned forwards and brushed their lips together.

"More," Toreth murmured into the soft mouth. He felt Warrick's lips curve in a smile against his. Another kiss, still just lips, a teasing touch. He closed his eyes. "More." This time Warrick's tongue swept lightly across his own, startling him into a moan. "More." Warrick laughed softly and complied, kissing him thoroughly and deeply. "More," Toreth said indistinctly when there seemed to be a danger of his stopping. "More."

Eventually the kisses faded out and there was nothing but the slow, steady movement, building pleasure in deepening layers. Beautiful, blissful, but as the minutes stretched slowly past, Toreth felt a faint stirring of unease. It was like the sim in a way: timeless, dreamy, and cut out of normal life. Yet not like the sim, because there was no distance, no awareness of another world somewhere else. It felt sickeningly intimate. There was no plan, no protocol, no roles, and no game. There was no safe word, because this didn't need one. Words meant what they said here. All he had to do was say "stop," and it would.

Without really meaning to, he tried to pull away. Warrick's hand slid down his spine, pressing into the small of his back to keep him in place. The movement made them both moan on the same breath. Warrick drew his breath back in deeply, then pressed his face into Toreth's shoulder. Toreth could feel quick, hot breath against his skin and realized he was breathing faster, too. In fact, somehow, he was getting close to the edge, which was ridiculous because they hadn't even done anything yet. How long had they been here?

149

"Warrick—"

"Shh," Warrick whispered against him. "Just...shh."

Toreth didn't want it to stop, anyway. He nodded and the hand flat against his back pressed him closer, acknowledging the surrender, urging him to move a little faster. Not much, just enough to change close to the edge into right on the edge and then tipping, slowly, deliciously over into orgasm.

As Toreth came, he found himself biting his lip, trying to keep quiet, somehow not wanting to spoil the moment. Warrick must have been pacing him, holding back, because he came only a breath behind, not crying out either but just stiffening in Toreth's arms and then, gradually, relaxing completely against him. Neither of them said anything. Warrick lay against him, breathing slowing, heart settling down to a slower rhythm against Toreth's chest. Part of Toreth's mind, irrationally unsettled, wanted to get up and leave, right now. In the end, the rest of him ended the debate decisively by pulling him down into sleep.

The sound of a drawer closing woke him. He found Warrick standing near the window, fully dressed and packing clothes into a small suitcase. Toreth propped himself up on one elbow and blinked at him.

"Uh?" he managed.

Warrick looked around and smiled briefly. "I have things to attend to, as I think I mentioned. I shall miss Dillian's shuttle if I don't go now. I've set the system to lock the door after you, but it won't let you back in again, so take everything with you."

Toreth nodded.

Warrick looked at him for a moment longer, then finished packing the last few bits and pieces. He zipped up the bag and turned to leave, pausing briefly in the doorway. "I'm going straight on to Mother's house with Dilly, and I'll be away for five days. When I get back you may call me, or not, as you wish." He hesitated, considering, and Toreth might have guessed the next words even if he hadn't said them. "I should like you to call."

Toreth nodded again and lay back down. By the time the outer door of the flat had closed, he was asleep once more.

Hours after Warrick's departure, Toreth woke up to silence, and sunlight slanting onto the pillow beside him. He felt warm, relaxed, and deeply contented, lying there and watching flecks of dust dance in the sunbeam as he breathed. The unscented oil on his hands now smelled of Warrick, and so did the pillow, and the whole bed where they'd...where they'd fucked.

150

Where they'd fucked.

And the contentment drained away, leaving something cold. He felt slightly sick, as though he was standing next to a long drop with no safety railing. That was the hangover coming back.

He showered and dressed quickly, and then, when he got home—because it was too late to go in to work—he had another shower. After that the soap scent on his skin wasn't Warrick's.

More water and something to eat didn't chase the queasy feeling away. So he decided to try hair of the dog instead and went out to a bar he liked—coincidentally, one he'd never visited with Warrick. During the course of the evening he picked up an attractive woman with dark hair whose name he'd forgotten by the morning. They went back to her flat and she proved a very effective distraction from the things he wasn't going to think about anyway.

The next morning he felt fine, until he got in to work and thought: only four days until he gets back.

Toreth didn't call.

The five days went past, and in that time he discovered Warrick had been right. There was corporate nastiness somewhere at the back of his latest case. Toreth backed off from the investigation as far as he could without raising suspicions and waited to see what crawled out of the woodwork. He wanted to be very sure of what answer he was supposed to find before he found it. The success of the Selman case had entirely canceled out the fuckup with Psychoprogramming, and Tillotson seemed once more happy to send the nastiest, trickiest cases his way.

Warrick had mentioned there was a file, and he'd said he hadn't managed to get hold of it "yet." Had he done so now? He should be back from his little family visit by now. But Toreth didn't call him. He didn't know why, and he didn't think about why, any more than he thought about what had happened in Warrick's flat.

I should like you to call.

If Warrick liked it that much, he could call. Toreth had his days filled with Chevril's offloaded prisoners, explaining to Justice representatives why it was possible to seriously interrogate prisoners or it was possible to guarantee they wouldn't die, but it wasn't possible to do both. Or rather that the guarantee wouldn't make them any less dead if things went wrong, which was why he sure as hell wasn't putting his name on it. The representatives listened, and nodded, and went back to their superiors and returned the next day with a carefully reworded demand for exactly the same impossibilities. Fucking annoying internal politics, which put him in a filthy temper and made him snap at Sara over nothing.

He had to put up with it for the five days Warrick was away, and for a couple of days after that, until finally he managed to get the case transferred to someone else. Chevril had had the right idea, because as far as Toreth could tell the prisoners stood every chance of dying of old age before they saw the inside of an interrogation room. It had been an insane waste of time and money all around. Still, it had kept him busy, during the day at least. At night he found other things to keep him occupied, one night blurring into another.

Then, on the first day free of Justice irritations, Sara's voice came over the comm, sounding intrigued. "Warrick wants to speak to you. Shall I transfer him?" She was wondering, no doubt, why Warrick hadn't called him directly.

"No," he said without thinking about it. "Tell him I'm out."

"Oh. All right." Now she sounded piqued. She'd probably been planning to listen in.

An hour or two passed, and then a file arrived unexpectedly on his screen. It had a password requirement, which read: "One guess only. Clue? What don't you want to hear?"

Toreth thought it over, imagining the words in Warrick's voice, then smiled and entered "plastic duck." It proved to be the file Warrick had mentioned. Very interesting reading it made, and best of all, it told him the answer he was supposed to find. When he tried to take a copy, the file vanished, deleting itself so neatly and thoroughly that he could find no trace it had ever existed. Fair enough. He'd been the one who had warned Warrick against getting entangled in Int-Sec files. Warrick had taken a risk to get it, and a risk to send it. So . . . it would only be polite to say thank you. He got as far as putting the call through to SimTech. Then he canceled it.

What don't you want to hear? He dismissed the thought. He had a lot to do.

Sitting in his own office across the city, Warrick waited, unable to concentrate on anything else until the message came back that the file had been read and safely deleted. Interesting, since Toreth was allegedly out of his office. Deciding to carry out a small experiment, he called I&I once more. "Sara? It's Keir Warrick again. Is Toreth back yet?"

He waited, counting seconds, until her voice came back. "Still out, I'm afraid. Do you want to leave a message? I can take it, or—"

"No, no message, thanks. No, wait. Just ask him to call me, please, if he has time. Thank you." He cut off the call. She had been gone for twenty-seven seconds. Longer than she would need to make sure Toreth was out, but plenty of time for him to tell her that he was. His original hypothesis was now confirmed, or at least strongly supported. Toreth was avoiding him. Warrick leaned back, watching his system running a final check to make sure that his illegitimate presence in Int-Sec had evaded notice. He was well aware of the dangers involved, although if he hadn't been confident of success he wouldn't have done it, not even for Toreth. He considered that phrase for a moment. "Not even." Mm.

He started to plan things out. He'd call again tomorrow, after lunch. Then once more, in the evening of the next day, perhaps. And after that... After that the sensible thing to do would be to drop it and not try again. He smiled wryly. Somehow it felt a little late in the day for being sensible. Five days away, surrounded by people he loved, and he had missed spending time with Toreth. They'd gone without seeing each other for much longer than that before.

Something had changed.

He could put his finger on the exact moment the change occurred: as he stood in the darkened bedroom, looking down at Toreth in the light from the door and realizing that he liked it. Liked seeing him asleep in his bed. Liked the idea of watching him wake up. Liked the way that the flat felt different, warmer and more alive. And he'd felt a sudden need to make pancakes, which was a clear warning sign. The last time he'd felt it had been with Lissa. It meant an incipient urge for domesticity, and this time with such an unlikely object.

After all the trouble he'd taken never to extend an invitation to the flat, it had been a strange experience. Before that morning, he'd thought that he didn't want his time with Toreth—and the game they played—intruding into his home. He'd thought it was better kept separate. Apparently, he'd been wrong. He didn't mind admitting his mistake, especially when the process of discovering the error had been so very pleasant. Still, it was definitely not sensible. In fact, it came very close to impossible. Was it worth pursuing? Standing there in the semidarkness, he'd thought so, and so he'd called I&I to tell Sara that Toreth wouldn't be in.

Investigation and Interrogation—that was one part of the impossibility. The rest of it was simply Toreth. Impossibility didn't even begin to describe the idea of trying to have anything that might reasonably be called a relationship with him. However, was it impossible to want something more than... whatever the hell they had?

Eventually he realized that he was staring blankly at the screen, where a message informed him the checks had been completed and no problems reported. He was daydreaming and planning to build on foundations that might not even be there anymore. For now, it was simple. He wanted to see Toreth again. If it was over, then he wanted to hear it, not have things dragged out into a growing list of unreturned messages. And if it wasn't... well, he'd have to see. If the comm proved fruitless, he would find another way.

Anonymous dark hotel room, not one of Toreth's regular places. Anonymous hands on him, anonymous cock inside him. He liked it. He wanted it. Doing, not feeling. A safe, familiar thing and it was good. Or at least it stopped him from thinking.

When they had finished and were dressing, the man whose name he hadn't asked said, "Tell Warrick I said hello."

Toreth nearly choked. "What?"

"After hearing his name so many times, I feel like I know him."

He didn't have an answer to that.

Sara had been unnaturally polite and formal all week. It was probably something to do with the fact that he'd forced her to come in over the weekend, when he knew she had other plans. If he'd had to come in to work, now that his case was active again, he didn't see why she shouldn't. Then, on Wednesday afternoon, she put her head around his office door without knocking and asked, "Are you doing anything tonight?"

"I was planning on going out."

"Well, I'm stunned. Makes a change from the last fortnight. But the married men and women of New London will just have to manage without you. I've got tickets, for the theater." He looked at her blankly. She rolled her eyes, then produced a bunch of lurid pink flowers, which she'd been holding out of sight of the doorway, and said, "It's your birthday."

They had an arrangement about birthdays. On Toreth's birthday, Sara would buy him some flowers, because he hated them, and take him out to some suitably weird venue for the evening, usually a strip club of some kind. On Sara's birthday, Toreth would forget to arrange anything at all, so she would do it for him and he would pay. For her birthday they usually went somewhere classier and considerably more expensive than they did for his. Every year he complained, and every year she told him that if he wanted something cheaper he should organize it himself. This year he'd managed to forget his own birthday as well as hers. "Why the hell are we going to the theater?"

"Good question. The mood you've been in I don't know why we're going anywhere. But a friend had some tickets and couldn't make it. So I'm getting a bargain. Pick me up at seven."

"Are you ready to—" Toreth stopped dead inside Sara's flat doorway and sniffed. "What's that smell?"

Sara appeared out of the bathroom, wearing a robe. "What smell?" she asked unconvincingly.

He pointed to the hall behind her, where the door to the bedroom had opened silently. "And what the fuck is *that*?"

"It's a cat, of course. What does it look like?"

Toreth studied the apparition from a safe distance. "It looks like a badly stitched-together traffic accident in a scabby black fur coat two sizes too large. Why are its teeth sticking out like that?"

"I think he must have been malnourished when he was a kitten."

Toreth doubted it. Nothing could grow to that size on an inadequate diet. A more likely explanation seemed to be that it had evolved in some deserted back street in the old city to hunt something large and slippery. Wet dogs, perhaps.

Sara picked it up and kissed the top of its head between its tattered ears. "Were you, sweetie-pie? Were people cruel to you when you were a baby? But it doesn't matter, does it, 'cause *I'm* going to feed you from now on." The cat looked profoundly embarrassed, then started to purr.

"It's *living* here?"

"*He* is, yes." She proffered him the cat. A near-visible miasma of unneutered tomcat surrounded it. "Here, stroke him. He's really friendly."

Toreth backed away. "No, thanks."

"He hasn't got fleas or anything like that."

"I believe you. They wouldn't be able to stand the smell. Where the hell did it come from?"

"He was waiting by the door when I got home from work on Monday. I've asked around the building and no one knows who he belongs to. Apparently he's been hanging around for ages, poor thing. I think he must have wandered away from home and got lost."

"Or its owners moved to get away from it."

"Don't be so horrible. I think he's lovely."

"I think you're completely fucking insane. It's repulsive. What's it called?"

"Dunno. I haven't chosen anything yet. Come on, stroke him. Say hello."

Dubiously, Toreth reached out in the general direction of the thing's head, hoping that a quick pat would be sufficient to satisfy her. Ears flattening, the cat lashed out and opened a set of four neat parallel cuts from his wrist to his knuckles. By the time they started to bleed, the cat was back in its original position in Sara's arms, yellow eyes fixed on him. The purring revved up a gear. "Fucking *hell!* You fucking evil *bastard!*"

"Oh, dear." Sara hugged the cat. "You must've frightened him."

He licked his hand and the blood welled up again at once. The scratches were surprisingly painful. "Does it *look* frightened?"

"He's never done that to me."

"So now it's *my* fucking fault that it's psychotic?"

And, from her expression, it was. But all she said was, "You should go and wash that."

"Really? I thought I'd just stand here until I died of blood poisoning."

Sara put the cat down. "Go on. I'll get dressed; we don't want to miss the start of the play." Put that way, being maimed by the cat didn't seem so bad.

In the bathroom, Toreth ran water over his hand, watching the faint wisps of blood vanish away into the drain. A couple of minutes later Sara appeared, wearing a rather eye-catching red dress and carrying a bottle of disinfectant and a large drink. "I'm sorry," she said. "He just needs some love and proper attention, that's all."

"It needs putting down. Ouch! Watch what you're doing with that stuff."

Sara slopped more disinfectant over his hand. "Then stop saying things like that. I tell you what, you can choose a name for him."

"What?"

"To make up for the scratches. You can choose his name."

He sipped the whiskey while he thought it over. Since she was feeling guilty, it would be a shame to waste the opportunity by choosing Fluffy, or whatever the fuck people called their cats. "Got it," he said eventually. "You Fucking Evil Bastard."

"No!" Sara looked gratifyingly appalled. "I can't call him that."

"You said I could choose. So I'm choosing." Toreth downed the remains of the drink. "You Fucking Evil Bastard. Might as well let people know what's coming. You can call it Bastard for short."

The play was better than Toreth had expected. He didn't pay attention to the plot. Instead he watched the actors. He liked masks. It was entertaining trying to read the casts' real feelings towards each other underneath their assumed emotions. About three-quarters of an hour in, he could feel Sara shifting next to him, bored. He leaned down and whispered, "The lead's fucking the woman in the purple dress. What do you think?"

After a couple of minutes he heard her giggle. "Yeah. And the guy in blue isn't happy about it."

Toreth hadn't noticed that, but a few minutes' observation convinced him she was right. Sara was good at spotting that sort of thing. He'd told her a few times that she should apply for a late entry into the investigator training program. She said she was happy doing what she did, which was fair enough. But in all honesty she was wasted there, however much easier she made his life. Warrick had said the same thing after he'd met her, although he wouldn't—

Toreth realized where the thought had ended up and squelched it. He checked his watch. Only five minutes until the interval.

The bar and foyer were crowded. By making a rapid exit, Toreth managed to get a drink for himself and Sara before the horde descended, but they finished them quickly and he wished he'd bought two each. Perhaps Sara would agree to skip the second half and they could move to a more usual birthday venue.

Looking around the room, Toreth assessed the crowd. Mostly middle-aged and solidly respectable citizens. Here and there were groups of corporate types on an evening out. Plenty of money around, anyway. He wondered which one of Sara's friends had bought tickets and been able to afford to give them away. He thought back to the last office event but the only details he could summon for her escort that evening were that he had sandy hair and an annoyingly nasal voice. Rich, though, or at least rich enough to keep Sara's semiexclusive interest. He ought to ask her if he was the one who'd funded this evening.

Then he saw Warrick. Toreth was slightly surprised by how easily he picked him out of the crowd, even with his back towards them. He stood with a group of people Toreth thought might be from SimTech. One arm rested casually around the shoulders of a dark-haired woman standing next to him and he had his face half turned towards her, listening. His arm rested comfortably, familiarly, over her shoulder and Toreth felt a twist of something tight and angry in his gut.

"Who are you looking at?" Sara asked, then followed his eyes. "Oh, hey."

"Don't—" Toreth said, too late.

"Hey! Warrick!" Sara followed up with a whistle, which attracted the attention of Warrick and a fair proportion of the rest of the immediate area. Solidly respectable lips thinned in disapproval.

Warrick looked around, lifted a hand in acknowledgement, said something to the group, and then turned towards them. Toreth glared at Sara and made dire silent threats about her next performance assessment.

"Well, this is a surprise," Warrick said as he walked up.

Toreth wasn't quite sure what to say, but Sara, naturally, had no such qualms. "Hello, Warrick," she said brightly. "You're looking good."

Warrick bent to kiss Sara's cheek. At the last moment she turned her head to catch it full on the mouth. She developed the kiss into something rather more than was socially required before Warrick broke it off. "Very nice to see you again, too. You look beautiful. I should call—"

He looked over his shoulder, but the woman he'd been with was already approaching. Seeing her properly now, Toreth felt his mouth drop open slightly.

"Ah! You're here." Warrick stepped aside a little to make room for her. "Come and meet the inestimable Sara, who may or may not possess a last name. And this is Val Toreth."

The woman returned Toreth's gaze with frank interest, while Toreth tried to slam his brain back into gear. "Delighted to meet you," she said. "Both of you."

Warrick gave the situation a moment to develop before finishing the introduction. "And this is Dillian Avens. My sister."

Of course, Toreth thought. She couldn't possibly have been anyone else.

Sara chuckled. Warrick raised an eyebrow. "You're very alike," Sara said, which Toreth knew full well wasn't the reason she'd laughed.

Dillian smiled politely. "So we've been told."

Looking between them, the resemblance was startling in detail, but oddly less compelling in overall effect. They had the same dark eyes and thick dark hair, the same sharp cheekbones and chiseled mouth. The main difference was in their noses. Dillian's was a petite tip-tilt, which he was ninety-five percent sure owed more to a skillful surgeon than a lucky divergence of genes. They were also much of a height, Dillian being only a couple of centimeters shorter, and her voice was low for a woman's, dark and rich. Yet, all features taken together, he was undoubtedly masculine, and she feminine. It was an odd effect, which Toreth found triggered some arresting and hard-to-ignore images. Too fast to be censored, the questions flickered through his mind. Would she taste like Warrick? Smell like him? Would her hair feel like his? Would she scream like he did when she came? All the things he hadn't been thinking about jostled for his attention, escaping into consciousness now that this excuse had presented itself.

Toreth realized he had been staring at them for the best part of a couple of minutes. Warrick was occupied in talking to Sara, but Dillian was looking back at him with a sharp, assessing intelligence that also reminded him of Warrick. When she caught his eye, she smiled, and it was exactly Warrick's cool smile. She held his gaze until Warrick touched her shoulder. "Would you like a drink, Dilly? The crowd's thinned out a bit."

"Please."

"I'll get one, too," Sara said. "Toreth?"

"What? Oh, yes."

The two of them headed over to the area where the wooden front of the bar made a sinuous curve across the plushly carpeted room, leaving Toreth and Dillian alone. "So," Dillian said, after a slightly awkward pause, "Keir told me you met during the business at the Center?"

For a moment the familiar name threw him, then he nodded. "I was in charge of the investigation, yes."

She shuddered delicately. "A horrible thing to happen. Awful for Keir."

As understatements went it was fairly comprehensive, so he changed the topic. "What do you do?"

"I'm a structural engineer, specializing in low-gravity, sealed environments." She laughed at his expression. "I've never understood why that should come as such a surprise to people, but it does."

158

He smiled in response. "It's because structural engineers aren't usually so... prepossessing."

Warrick and Sara joined one of the queues for the bar. She looked back across the room. As she'd expected, Toreth looked hypnotized by Dillian. She could appreciate the fascination. Knowing Warrick only slightly, as Sara did, his sister was still a fairly interesting sight. "How are you enjoying the play?" Warrick asked.

She looked around. "Boring as fuck," she said candidly.

Slight smile. "Then you're doing it wrong, because the play is very tedious."

She laughed. "Boring as not fucking, then."

"Mm. I'm sorry I spoiled your evening, but Dilly wanted to see it."

"And Dilly always gets what she wants?"

The question came out with more of an edge than she had intended, but Warrick didn't seem to mind, or didn't even notice. "Probably more than is good for her. However, in this case I felt like indulging her. We don't get to see each other very often—she's only on Earth for a few months this time, then she's off to Europa to build something else. Besides, this was the best venue I could think of. The most plausible, if not the most entertaining, I'm afraid."

Sara waved the apology away. "I don't mind. As long as it puts *him* in a better mood."

"Better mood?"

"Christ, yes. He's been in a strop for days, which I expect is all your fault."

Warrick smiled ruefully. "Possibly."

"Yeah, well, you should think about other people for a change. He's being an utter bastard at work."

"Oh? I thought that was his job."

"Being one to me isn't, no."

"Mm."

That seemed to mark the topic closed. Sara began to wonder exactly what Warrick was hoping to get out of the evening. This had seemed like such a promising plan when Warrick had proposed it, the objective being, she'd thought, to get them back in bed together and consequently make her life better. She realized that she wasn't even sure why they needed getting back together at all. Warrick had said...no, actually, she'd *assumed* that they'd had some kind of row which had interrupted their exotic round of simming and fucking. He hadn't said anything specific at all. There was something going on that she didn't understand properly, and it worried her.

She looked back across the room. Toreth's attitude had shifted from mesmerized to prowling. Dillian watched, smiling broadly, as Toreth related some story that required extravagant gestures with both hands. Then she shook her head and laughed. Sara nudged Warrick with her elbow. "You ought to be keeping an eye on your sister."

He studied the scene and seemed to find it amusing more than anything else. "Dillian can recognize trouble when she sees it."

"She looks to be having fun to me."

"Oh, no doubt. She's working her way round to asking the two of you to join us for dinner after the play."

"She's in on it, too?"

"Well, I wouldn't say 'in on it,' but it occurred to me on the way here that she would be much better at persuading him than I would. If he doesn't agree, the whole exercise will have been a waste of time."

"Why the hell didn't you just call him?"

"I did, if you recall, and he declined to speak to me."

"You could've called him at home." She decided to plumb his motives with a little strategic gossip. "Not that he's there much."

"No?"

"No. As far as I can tell he's been spending all his spare time fucking his way round the city. I get the latest scorecard at morning coffee. The only wonder is that he can still walk."

Warrick merely smiled again. "I shall be sure to bring it up in conversation."

"Don't you dare." She looked at him closely, wondering if was worth saying anything more. Almost everything she knew about him came from the case, or from Toreth's colorful accounts of screwing him. Seeing him standing there, cool and self-possessed, most of what she'd heard seemed, to put it mildly, unlikely. All she knew about him personally was that he'd always been polite when he'd spoken to her at I&I, which said something because not everyone thought it was worth being civil to admins. She'd met him once or twice away from work when he was with Toreth and they'd seemed, well, happy enough, for two people in a relationship comprised entirely of semicompetitive sex. And, of course, he had gone to the trouble of setting up this silly excuse to see Toreth, including buying the tickets and offering to pay for dinner. Corporate or not, that was a significant investment. There must be something there.

"Listen," she said, before she could change her mind, "this is going to sound incredibly bizarre, I know, and it's none of my business, but—be careful with him."

From his icy expression she saw straight away that he'd misunderstood. "I don't need—"

"No, sorry. That came out wrong. I mean, um, please don't hurt him."

He stared at her for a moment, astonishment replacing irritation. "*Hurt* him?" He sounded as if the idea had never occurred to him, which it probably hadn't. The possibility hadn't crossed her mind until very recently.

160

"Seems unlikely, yeah. But he's human. It could happen." She plowed on, determined to finish now that she'd started. "I wouldn't exactly call him a friend but, glaring faults and all, I like him. Whatever you've half done to him, undo it, or get it done properly. Before I forget what a good boss he is normally, put in for a transfer, and end up working for someone who won't look the other way when I leave early every Friday."

The people in front of them turned away from the bar, murmuring apologies as they squeezed past, and Sara noticed that they had reached the head of the queue. She watched as Warrick ordered for the four of them. He handed two glasses to her, her own and Toreth's. "Well?" she challenged.

He took the other pair of drinks. "I'll bear it in mind," he said blandly.

Smooth bastard, she thought as she followed him back. And then: suits Toreth, I suppose. She decided to forget about her misgivings for the night and just enjoy herself. They were old enough to play their games without a referee.

When they reached Dillian and Toreth, Dillian turned towards her. "Sara, I wondered if you would like to join us for dinner afterwards? I'm sure we can change the reservation. But Toreth said that since you're in charge of the night out, he really ought to let you decide."

Sara smiled, enjoying the thrill of conspiracy. "Sounds lovely!" she said, without looking at Toreth.

The restaurant was one that Toreth had never eaten at before. Still, merely walking through the door gave him the idea that it was likely to more than wipe out any savings occasioned by the free tickets. Sara was paying, though, so what did he care?

To his surprise, he enjoyed himself. Dillian made good company: witty, fun, and relaxed. And so very like her brother that once or twice he almost called her by the wrong name. With Warrick there, he entertained himself by walking the fine line between interested conversation and flirting. Not that it was particularly any of Warrick's business what he said to her. Warrick talked mostly to Sara, but Toreth caught him looking at the two of them more than once, and he enjoyed that too, without bothering to analyze why.

Eventually Dillian looked at her watch, covering a yawn. "I'm awfully sorry, but I'm afraid I'm going to have to call it a night. I've still not really adjusted back from Mars time and I'm supposed to be meeting clients tomorrow. If I don't get some sleep I shall probably end up agreeing to build them something that breaks the laws of physics, never mind the structural codes." Toreth tried to catch her eye, but she cut him out, turning to Sara. "Are you a night owl like these two, or would you like to share a taxi back? If I remember New London properly, I believe I'm on your route home."

Sara grinned. "Sure." She finished her drink and stood. "Ready when you are."

Dillian stood up with her. "See you later, Keir—don't make too much noise coming in. Goodbye, Toreth. It was lovely to meet you." She didn't sound entirely convinced of that.

Warrick watched them go, then turned back to Toreth. "More coffee?"

Toreth shrugged. "If you like."

"Mm. Perhaps not; it is getting late." Warrick nodded at Toreth's injured hand. "That looks nasty."

"Sara's new cat." Toreth rubbed his thumb over the scratches, which despite the disinfectant were red and slightly swollen. "It's fucking psychotic. But apparently I scared it, so it's all my fault."

"Really? Somehow I'm not surprised." Warrick glanced around briefly, as though looking for a waiter, then fixed his gaze back on Toreth. "So. What do you think of Dilly?"

"I think...she's very nice." *And I want to fuck her, because she looks like you.*

Warrick looked as if he'd caught the first half of the thought, if not the second. "Do you want to know what she said about you?"

Yes. "Not really."

"She said you were charming, considering what you do for a living." He seemed to find that rather funny.

Toreth smiled nastily. "Maybe I should give her a call. What do you think?"

Warrick looked at him for a moment, serious again, then shrugged. "I think I'm not sure whether you want me to warn you off from her, or her off from you."

Too wound up to even try to decode that one, Toreth snapped, "Why should I give a fuck what you think?"

"Well, apart from the fact that you just asked me, there is absolutely no reason at all."

Toreth sat and fumed for a moment, not understanding why he felt so angry.

"Sara told me it's your birthday," Warrick continued. "Which I knew already, actually. I apologize for not sending a gift, but I wasn't sure whether you would—" He paused, then said, "Toreth?"

He looked up, looked into Warrick's eyes, and suddenly the anger was gone and he *wanted* him. It took his breath away, dulled the noise of the room around them. A drug hit, delivered straight into a vein and flooding his whole body at once. He fought the feeling down until it was only unbearable, then stood up. "I have to go." He couldn't think of a reason to give, so he just repeated it. "I have to go."

"Toreth—"

But he was already walking away, somehow putting one foot in front of the other and ignoring the sound of Warrick's chair scraping across the floor as he stood up. At the door he almost turned back, but he pushed his way through and

162

into the street. As he stood there, trying to attract a taxi, he wondered what the hell he was going to do if Warrick came after him—and why the hell he didn't know if he wanted him to or not.

Back at home, he went to bed and couldn't sleep. The air conditioning was on the blink again, and the room for once was too hot for him. He opened the window and lay on top of the sheets, pretending he could feel a breeze from the still July night outside. Even after the room cooled a little, sleep seemed no more likely. Lack of sex and an unusually early night, he decided in the end. His body had grown used to the excesses of the last couple of weeks.

Well, the extra sleep might do him good, and the first part of the problem he could solve on his own. Rolling onto his back, he tried to fantasize about Dillian, but every time his concentration slipped, she morphed into Warrick. Eventually he gave up and thought about Warrick. Not the sim, or their D&S games, but about the leisurely not-quite fuck in Warrick's flat.

Just . . . shh.

He put one hand up to his shoulder, to the place where he could almost feel Warrick's mouth against him. The other hand he pressed flat on his cock, trying to duplicate the smooth slide of Warrick's body against his. Unsatisfying and lonely by comparison, but less so, surprisingly, than having another body there who wasn't Warrick.

Shh. Just . . . shh.

He focused on the words, remembering, murmuring them out loud as his hand moved faster. Feeling, not thinking. Warrick moving with him, burning hot skin under his hands, so close. He could taste him now. Soft, generous mouth against his. So close, nothing separating them, wonderful and frightening at the same time. Yes, feeling the same fear he'd felt before, but able to ignore it because this was like the sim, distance dulling the edge. It was only a fantasy. Tomorrow he could tell himself he hadn't done this, or that it didn't matter. And that it didn't matter if he said Warrick's name, over and over, wanting him to be there with him as he came, because there was no one else to hear it.

Then he fell asleep and slept better than he had done since he had been in Warrick's bed.

Maybe it was the good night's rest, but as he walked in to work, he had an idea, which seemed so blindingly obvious that he was sure it had to be wrong. "'Morning, Sara," he said cheerfully.

She looked up. "Christ, what happened to you?"

163

He sat on the edge of her desk, picked up what was probably an important piece of paper, and started to fold it into a bird. It was the one thing he knew that both qualified as a party trick and could be performed in polite company. She watched him without further comment.

"Sara, who gave you those tickets?" he said eventually.

"Which tickets?" she asked, and he knew he was right.

"For the play. For my birthday."

She struggled with the temptation for a couple of seconds. Then she said, "Warrick."

"Why?"

"He said he had a couple spare."

Toreth contemplated the finished bird sitting in the palm of his hand. "Lying cunt," he said, watching Sara's eyes widen with shock. Then he crumpled the figure up, dropped it in front of her, and went off into his office to think about what to do.

Once inside the office he stood by the window and stared blindly at the tiny enclosed courtyard below, feeling the rage build. Part of him almost welcomed it: familiar and focusing, something he understood.

Very neatly planned. It had all been very neat and he had to admit that even as his hands tightened on the window frame until the knuckles whitened and the scratches stood out lividly against his skin. He felt like going back outside and taking it out on Sara, but a tiny voice of self-preservation said: not in front of the rest of the office.

Sara helping Warrick set him up. And Dillian, of course, because she'd been the one who'd asked them to go to dinner. Thinking back, she'd also taken Sara out of the picture at the end of the night. Yes, the two of them had gone off very conveniently so that Warrick could . . . what? Something he couldn't think about clearly because remembering made the dizzying mix of fear and lust he'd felt last night return to catch him like a hammer blow in the chest. He closed his eyes, willing it to go away.

He wasn't scared. He didn't want Warrick, right now, here. No. He was angry. Very angry, because he'd been played like a fucking fish and he hadn't seen it at all. And by Sara, of all people. The anger washed the metallic taste of fear out of his mouth, allowed him to concentrate. He couldn't let this go—or he couldn't let it go on—and that meant seeing Warrick and finding out what the hell he'd been playing at last night. Letting him know how very fucked off he was.

He put a call through to SimTech, his hands shaking almost too much to fit the comm earpiece. On another day he might have asked Sara to call for him. No doubt she'd just love the chance to fucking interfere again, the treacherous conniving bitch. When Warrick answered Toreth somehow managed to bite back the anger sufficiently to sound, if not friendly, at least not homicidal. He fixed his gaze on the wall, trying to listen to the words without hearing Warrick's voice. "I'd like to see you. Yes. That's fine. I'll see you there."

Warrick hadn't sounded at all surprised to hear from him, either. Bastard.

Somehow, he made it through the day. After he'd gone outside and explained in low but serious tones that Warrick had better not hear anything about this, Sara went home with a headache. Toreth did paperwork at random, and then went to the gym and lifted weights until the blood rang in his ears and the monitoring system made him stop.

In the bar that evening, Warrick was waiting for him, looking so relaxed and unconcerned that Toreth felt a near-irresistible urge to punch him. Instead he said, "The inestimable fucking Sara told me about the tickets."

Warrick smiled. "I thought she would. Too much fun to keep it a secret. I hope you aren't too angry with her."

Toreth sat down and Warrick pushed a drink over. He ignored it. "I feel like strangling the bitch."

That produced a pause before Warrick said, "I think she suffered enough having to sit through the play. She was only trying to help."

"Help?" He clenched his fist, the scratches stinging as the skin stretched. "What the fuck does that mean?"

Warrick shrugged. "You'd better ask her."

"I'm asking you. Don't try to pretend it wasn't your idea."

"All right, I won't." He looked away for a moment, then looked back, his gaze very direct. "I wanted to see you. I remembered your birthday and I thought it would be a perfect opportunity." He raised an eyebrow. "I really didn't think that you'd mind."

We play games all the time, his tone implied. Toreth met his eyes, still managing to hang on to the anger that had carried him through the call and got him here. "So why the hell did Sara think I needed help?"

"She told me that you had been keeping yourself occupied with, as she put it, fucking your way through the city. All night, every night." Warrick shrugged, his tone overly casual. "*She* seemed to take it as a sign that you were unhappy about something I'd done."

"And what did you think?" Toreth asked, even though he didn't want to. What he increasingly wanted to do was walk out before something awful and irrevocable happened. He was going to kill Sara tomorrow.

"Well, it's hardly untypical behavior." Warrick grimaced. "All that sets your

165

recent endeavors apart is a certain grandeur of scale. And the fact that I no longer feature in the lineup."

"It's none of your fucking business. You—"

"Isn't it?"

Toreth ignored the interruption. "You don't own me. You don't have any rights over me. And you sure as hell don't have the right to tell me that I can't fuck anyone else."

Warrick shook his head, exasperation replacing the restrained discomfort. "When, exactly, did I tell you not to fuck anyone else?"

This question stopped Toreth dead. He thought it over, and began to suspect that quite soon he was going to feel like an idiot. "You've never been exactly thrilled about it."

"No, I haven't. Why would I be? Would you be delighted to hear from me what a great fuck the latest arrival at work had been? Or, if it comes to that, to hear from a third party that I'd been out bedding anything with a pulse?"

Far from fucking delighted. In fact, if he did hear Warrick had fucked someone else, he'd want to hunt them down and kill them, a realization which did nothing for Toreth's melting self-esteem.

Warrick watched him for a moment, then, when Toreth said nothing, he continued. "Tell me when I expressed any expectations of, or made any demands for, exclusivity."

"Never," he had to admit. "You didn't."

"Right. So what have I done or said that made you think I had?"

"Nothing." It's nothing to do with what *you* want.

"Well, then I think we have the situation straightened out," Warrick said crisply. "I don't think I own you. I don't want to own you. I just want some of your free time and the occasional use of your body." His voice softened. "And anything beyond that is entirely up to you. No demands or expectations."

Toreth nodded dumbly. Silence seemed by far the safest option.

Warrick looked at his watch. "And now I have to get home. I promised Caprice Teffera I'd speak to her sometime this evening. Have fun."

Toreth watched him leave and then rested his head in his hands. He'd been dead right. He felt like a complete fucking idiot and on top of that he never wanted to see Warrick again, because it would only remind him of how big an idiot he'd been. He looked around the bar, at the men and women in various stages of inebriation and availability. Have fun. Except, of course, that now that he had permission, he didn't want to. The very idea of Warrick presuming to give him *permission* for anything should have made him furious, but he found he didn't care. And he didn't particularly want to think about what that meant.

It was the first, basic lesson in interrogation training. No prisoner can resist forever. The absolute best they can hope for is to die, and victories don't come much hollower than that. Otherwise, the only possibility is to hold out for another minute, and then another one, until they reach the minute when they can't bear it any more. Everyone gets to that point in the end. After long and careful consideration he decided: what the fuck. It was easier to break, and he should know.

He sat in the bar for half an hour, to give Warrick time to finish his meeting, or pretend to finish his meeting, whichever was the case. Then he caught a taxi.

Warrick took one look at him, standing on the steps of the building, and shook his head. "No."

No? "Warrick—"

"I meant, not here."

They went to a hotel, not speaking on the way. Despite his frenzied nightlife of the last weeks Toreth felt as if he hadn't touched anyone for months. He watched Warrick sitting quiet and still, looking out of the window of the taxi, and he could've fucked him right there, he wanted him so badly. "Why wouldn't you let me into the flat?" he asked, thinking about what they could be doing this minute if he had.

"Dilly's staying there. She's very broad-minded, but," Warrick said, his smile reflected in the glass, "I doubt she really wants to overhear in that much detail what her brother does for fun."

For fun. *Have fun.* Oh, yes.

At the Renaissance Center—the same hotel where they'd first had dinner and first fucked—there was already a room reserved. 212. He planned this, Toreth thought. He knew that I'd come back to the flat tonight. That ought to have bothered him, but it didn't. Maybe tomorrow, when he could think about something other than how much he wanted the man walking beside him through the endless hotel corridors.

Once the door to the room closed behind them, Warrick turned and looked up at him, his eyes bright with anticipation. "So. What do you want me to do?"

Lots of things. More than Toreth could put into words. Instead he said, "I want to hear you say it." And he did, surprising himself by how much.

Warrick put his hands on Toreth's shoulders, half smiling. "Want me to say what? That I want you? That I want you to fuck me?" His eyes darkened as he listened to himself, a shiver transmitted through his hands and all the way down Toreth's spine.

Toreth smiled back, pulled him close and kissed him. He tasted even better than he'd remembered. "Yes. All that. Again."

He made Warrick ask to be fucked, and then to beg him for it, over and over again, until it stopped being a game and he was hoarse and panting and they were both almost ready to come just from hearing it.

The clearest image he kept from the night: Warrick pressed against him, beneath him, clinging to him, shuddering with desire, bucking against him with every touch and whisper, stumbling over the words. "Please. Toreth, don't. I can't...not any more...I need...now. Please. Now."

Begging for him. Wanting it almost as much as he did. Wanting him.

Wanting *him*.

After that everything was too fast, and the overwhelming need made him clumsy. He thrust in too quickly and too hard and heard Warrick gasp with pain and didn't care because it felt so good. Another deep thrust brought another protesting sound, and Warrick's shoulders knotted as his fists clenched in the pillow.

Toreth slipped his arms around Warrick's chest, buried his face in his sweet-smelling hair and managed to stop moving, because it was going to be over too quickly. He held still for just a few seconds and then he couldn't, couldn't stop himself. Mine, he thought, and maybe even said out loud. Mine. Oh, yes, Warrick. Mine. He'd never wanted to possess anyone like this before, to make them completely his. He wanted it to last forever, not just the few more short, hard strokes until he came; it felt better than the sim, better than the SMS, more intense than ever before in his life.

He was eventually roused back to awareness by Warrick, still pinned beneath him and wheezing quietly and unobtrusively. After a couple of attempts he managed to roll off him. Warrick filled his lungs and let the air out on a long breath. Then he rolled over onto his back, sucked his breath in sharply through his teeth and moved onto his side. Toreth thought back, decided he ought to ask. "Did I hurt you?"

"Yes. Not much."

"Sorry."

Warrick shook his head. "Heat of the moment. I understand. Still, I'd rather you didn't do it again. It takes the edge off, somewhat."

Toreth looked down and realized Warrick was still half erect and nowhere near sticky enough to have come. He didn't want to move, but pride forced him to. Without saying anything he wriggled down the bed, steadied Warrick's hip with his hand, and took him in his mouth. Warrick gasped sharply, and his fingers tangled in Toreth's hair before sliding down to his shoulder. It was something he'd never done to Warrick outside the sim, Toreth reflected, and wondered why. Warrick tasted different from the sim, which was strange at first. But, of course, this was really him, not a statistical average or an old memory electronically stirred into life. Real and better.

He pushed the thought aside and concentrated. He kept it light and shallow until Warrick was hard again, and breathing hard, and then he finally moved to take him more deeply into his mouth.

Warrick moaned and his hips pushed forwards. "Ah. God, yes."

Toreth found that, although this was something that usually bored him a little, he was enjoying himself. It was incredibly satisfying to do this and listen to Warrick's reaction, to his rich, low voice, still a little hoarse from earlier and getting ragged again now. The realization nearly made him laugh, which might have had unfortunate consequences. He pulled away, relishing Warrick's protest and the hand tightening reflexively on his shoulder, pushing him down. Obeying the direction, Toreth closed his eyes, listening, trying to drive the dark voice past words.

Warrick's fingers dug sharply into Toreth's shoulder, his other hand clawing handfuls of the sheets behind him. "Yes. That's good. That's *good*. That's . . . mmh. Don't stop. Don't . . . "

And he didn't.

Toreth woke up (or almost woke up), turned over, and groped out with one arm. The bed beside him proved to be empty, which pushed him close enough to real wakefulness that he registered the shower starting to run. He moved over further, onto the other side of the bed—still warm—and wished he'd woken up a few minutes earlier.

For a moment, he felt a flutter of something like panic starting. Fuck off, he told it firmly. I was only stretching. And it's just a coincidence that I've got my face in his pillow. Happy now?

Happy or not, the feeling went away. He lay for a while, wondering whether it would be a good idea to follow Warrick into the bathroom. From what he remembered, it had a fairly spacious shower. After last night, though, he didn't think he'd be able to put any of his pleasantly hazy plans into action. By the time Warrick came back into the room Toreth was nearly asleep again. All except his stomach, which growled loudly enough to make Warrick look over. "Was that you?"

With an effort, Toreth propped himself up on his elbows. "Mm-hm. I'm starving. What time is it?" He couldn't be bothered to move any further and look for himself.

"Probably too late for breakfast, although we might manage it if you can be a little late in."

"No. I have to be there before Sara."

Warrick finished dressing. "Well, if you need to get going you should probably get up before I leave. You'll be asleep again in a minute. Everything's paid for, by the way," he added.

He came over to the bed and looked down at Toreth while putting on his watch. "You really aren't a morning person, are you?"

"I'm barely a fucking afternoon person." Toreth finally managed to drag himself upright and sat on the edge of the bed, trying to summon the energy to have a shower. He could happily have stayed in bed all day, and that thought made him remember that the next day was Saturday. Fuck his case, he deserved a day off. "What are you doing tomorrow?"

Warrick grimaced slightly. "Nothing too strenuous. Why?"

Just say the words, don't think about them too much. "I thought I might invite myself round for pancakes."

Warrick smiled. "Why not?"

When Warrick let himself into his flat he could smell something burning, so he knew Dilly must still be there. He found her in the kitchen, using a boning knife to scrape the carbonized remains of something from the bottom of a pan. She looked around as he came in and smiled sheepishly. "Sorry!"

He removed the abused utensils from her hands without comment. With more optimism than expectation, he ran them under the tap and inspected the damage more closely. The knife had suffered nothing that a good sharpening wouldn't cure, but the pan looked to be a fatality. Whatever she'd been cooking was both unidentifiable and welded to the surface. "What were you trying to make?" he inquired.

"Scrambled eggs."

"Scrambled...I'd ask how this was possible, but as I know from experience that you can burn water, I won't." He took out another pan. "Why don't you make some coffee and I'll do breakfast? Assuming you can do that without immolating anything else."

"I'll do my best."

They worked in silence for a while, then he said, "I thought you had a meeting."

"The office left a message to say they'd rescheduled. Just by a couple of hours, in fact, but long enough for me to wreck your kitchen."

"Apparently. Right, done." He set the plates on the table, then, forgetting, sat down altogether too hard and winced. Dillian unsuccessfully attempted to change a laugh into a cough. "It's not funny," he snapped, bothered as much by the speed of her deduction as anything else.

"No," she said with an almost straight face. "Of course not."

He kept the glare up for a moment, then started to laugh. She sat down opposite him, also laughing, and poured the coffee. "No need to ask if last night went well, then," she said.

Fortunately, he'd only picked the cup up, not taken a sip. "Dilly!"

"Oh, honestly, Keir. How old do you think I am? I mean—taking him to a *hotel*, for goodness' sake! I should hope you had fun after going to all that trouble." She poked the scrambled eggs with her fork. "They're sloppy."

"They're supposed to be. We go through this every time. Just eat them and stop..."

She paused, fork raised. "Stop embarrassing you?"

170

"Yes."

She tried a mouthful of egg, and nodded. "Mmm. Good."

"Of course they are. Finish them before they get cold."

"You never blush, you know," she said thoughtfully, buttering toast. "Mother either. Aunt Jen does, and I do. Do you suppose it's genetic?"

"No. Actually, I'm sure I used to. It must've worn out over the years, thanks to you." Warrick counted nine seconds until she looked up again. He sighed. "If I have to. Yes, everything went very well. Yes, we sorted everything out. Yes, we—"

"Fucked like rabbits," Dillian supplied, in her most refined voice.

The embarrassment, which had been fading, returned in full force. "Where do you get that language?"

"It's a hazard of the profession, I'm afraid. Talking to construction workers." Her expression became more serious. "Are you sure about this, Keir?"

"What?" he said, hedging and hoping she'd take the hint.

"Him." Her mouth twisted slightly. "Toreth."

"What's to be sure about? It's not that serious. We just..." He looked at her patient, concerned face. Damn her. "Yes, I am sure. Don't you approve?"

"Honestly? No, I don't." She shrugged. "But you knew that, and it's not my place to approve or disapprove of who you choose to sleep with. If you're happy, I'm happy for you. You know that, too." He nodded, because he did. "So the real question is, *are* you happy?"

"Yes." The speed and confidence of the answer surprised him a little.

"Then just be careful with him. Please?"

He'd heard that before. From Sara, who didn't want him to hurt her friend. And Marian—murdered Marian—who had worried about quite the opposite. Now Dilly made it two to one in favor of Marian's view. Warrick looked down at the scrambled eggs congealing slowly on the plate in front of him. "Oddly enough, people keep saying that to me," he said, trying to keep his voice light.

"Then, well...maybe you should listen to them."

"I am careful. Always." Because I know he's dangerous, which is at least part of why I want him. He thought of the chill he'd felt when Dilly told him Toreth was charming. If his and Dillian's positions had been reversed, what would he say to her? "Be careful with him" would be the mildest possibility.

Fortunately, Dillian couldn't read minds. "Then everything will be fine." She reached across the table, touched the back of his hand. "And if you ever need me..."

He looked up again, smiled. "You'll be on Europa."

"I'll come back, for you."

"Thanks."

"Don't worry about it. I love you, that's all."

She finished her eggs, then looked at her watch. "Oops. I have to go."

"Good luck with the meeting."

171

She stopped in the doorway and looked back, her eyes twinkling. "Before I go, do you want me to get you a cushion?"

Before he could find anything to throw, she had gone.

Sara was late for work. She'd woken up early, but then spent an hour composing a transfer request. It had been successively revised down in tone until the screen no longer blistered, but it was still somewhat forthright. Once she got in she'd have another go at it until it was suitably bland, and then send it to Tillotson. Considering all the times she'd covered for him in the past, she'd better get a damn good transfer reference from Toreth.

She was so busy enjoying her foul mood that she didn't see the flowers until she was halfway across the office. The rest of the senior para admins in the section were watching her expectantly. She said a general hello and went over to her desk. It was a huge bouquet and every single blossom was real. The calculation of cost was fast and automatic and gave an impressive result. It took her a while to find the message among the profusion of flowers. When she did it read, "Sorry."

Hands landed on her waist. She looked down and saw the vivid scratch marks on his skin. "For calling you a lying cunt, that is," Toreth whispered. "Really, very sorry."

The rest of the room watched the scene with undisguised fascination. Sara looked up at him over her shoulder. She knew he wasn't sorry, of course, and that this was just a belated realization that he'd gone too far. That didn't matter, though. "You're forgiven," she said.

He grinned and let her go. "Excellent."

She turned and examined him more carefully. God, he looked pleased with himself. There could be only one reason why. "And I'm sorry," she said, "about the tickets."

The grin broadened. "No need. In fact, call the flowers a late thank you for that, as well as an apology."

"Oh?"

"Yes, 'oh.'"

Sara decided that, thank God, she wouldn't be needing the transfer letter. As Toreth turned to go back into his office she asked, "Do I get to hear all about it at coffee?"

He paused. "No. No, I don't think so." Another pause, another smile. "Well... maybe," he said, and the door closed behind him.

Surprises

❖

Part One: Conversation

Sara had taken a long lunch, even by her standards. She'd been gone from her desk when Toreth came back upstairs from the morning's interrogation and he didn't see her until well over an hour later, when she breezed into his office, grinning from ear to ear. "Where've you been?" he asked.

"The AERC." She sat on his desk, kicking her heels against it. "You remember you asked Warrick if he'd let me have a go in the sim? He called this morning and said someone had canceled something and I could do it but it had to be today. I would've told you, but you were busy. I asked Kel to cover for me."

"What did you think?" Toreth asked, even though her expression told him that she'd been as blown away by the experience as he had been the first time.

"Fucking *incredible!* I couldn't believe it. He took me through all these different settings, rooms, whatever they call them. It was so *real.* I know you told me about it, but...unbelievable. And Warrick...the stuff he can do! So weird. There was this beach—"

Suddenly Toreth couldn't hear her any more. *The stuff he can do.* He knew all about that. Had Warrick done any of it with Sara?

Sara was still chattering away happily. "—breathing underwater. It was so *weird.* Warrick said I was pretty good at it. Lots of people choke the first time, or they just can't do it at all. God, I hope I can get another go. I think I might volunteer for trials. There's a list a mile long but maybe you could put a word in, hm? Hm? Toreth?"

For some reason, despite their many past conversations about fucking, he couldn't think of a good way to ask her. "Did you do anything else?"

"Yeah, loads of stuff. He did this thing—" she clapped her hands, "—for drinks, yeah? You've seen him do it, I'm sure. Outrageous showoff, but it was pretty impressive, I admit. They tasted great. There's an alcohol feed, but he wouldn't turn it on. He said he wasn't sending me back here pissed after lunch because

173

you'd think he'd been trying it on. He—" She stopped dead, maybe seeing something in his face. "You don't think that, do you?" she asked after a moment.

Toreth shrugged, aiming for casual and composed. "I did wonder."

"He was only joking. Why would you think I'd do anything with him?" She shook her head. "Why would you even think we'd want to?"

"You've been flirting with him," Toreth said tightly.

Her eyes widened incredulously. "I've been what? When? I kissed him a couple of times to say hello. That's not flirting. What you did to his *sister* right in front of him, that was flirting. Anyway," she continued in a harder voice, "I'm not the one who goes for other people's partners."

He heaved an exaggerated sigh. "Aren't you ever going to give up on that?"

"Of course I'm not!" Her voice rose in theatrical outrage. "You screwed my boyfriend!"

"Once. Six years ago." He felt far more comfortable with this old, familiar argument. "And you'd split up with him before I laid a finger on him. Or in him."

"That was a tactical breakup and you bloody well knew it."

Toreth shrugged, affecting disinterest and not having to try so hard now that they were away from the topic of the sim. "I don't know what you were so upset about. He was a lousy fuck, anyway."

Sara glared for a moment, and then sniggered. "Yeah, you're right. He was. And, Christ, talk about hard to get rid of. Served you right, didn't it?" She cocked her head thoughtfully. "I don't know why you're making such a fuss. About Warrick. I mean, he does other people in the sim."

"He doesn't," Toreth said, without thinking. Without really letting himself hear what she'd said.

"Of course he does. He was explaining to me they'd had a problem last week with one of the...*oh.*"

"He—" With an effort Toreth pulled himself together. "It doesn't matter what he does."

Sara peered at him closely. "You're jealous!" she said delightedly. "You're getting all possessive."

His stomach dropped a couple of floors through the building, leaving him stranded in the suddenly stifling office. "Don't be stupid."

"Then you should sue your face for libel."

"Slander." Automatic correction while he thought about what she'd said.

"Well, it's written all over it." She grinned. "I feel like I should mark it on the calendar. You'll be picking out curtains with him next."

Oh, God, she was right. "Just get out of my office and do some fucking work for a change."

She swung herself off the desk. "Yes, Para, *sir.*" He could hear her laughing as she closed the door.

174

Oh, God, she *was* right.

Toreth sat at his desk, feeling one part angry—at Warrick or Sara he wasn't quite sure—and two parts horrified. "Jealous." He hated the word—one of a whole set of words that only ever applied to other people, never to him. The strange part about it, the part he couldn't understand at all, was that he'd known about the sim already, before Sara had said anything. He'd known that it was part of the development. But he'd somehow managed to push the fact out his mind and he didn't even remember when he had done it. Now it was back and screaming for attention. Warrick in the sim with someone else, someone from SimTech, someone Toreth had met...

He knew what he ought to do, which was go see Warrick tonight and...say something. Something he couldn't even begin to think through. And he knew what he was going to do, which was go out, get drunk, and find someone to take his mind off the whole thing.

Four days later, as he came out of the I&I main entrance, he saw Warrick sitting on the grass near the imposing statue of Blindfold Justice. He had a handful of gravel and was throwing pieces up at the statue, trying to get them into one side of the level scales. A security guard was watching him, but Warrick would have had to scan his ID to enter the Int-Sec complex, and he'd be marked as a harmless corporate director, someone not to be harassed over a little pebble-throwing. Toreth thought about ignoring him, but, while he hesitated, Warrick turned and caught sight of him. As Toreth reluctantly walked over, he got to his feet and brushed off his hands. "The scales of justice don't seem to be very finely balanced," Warrick said.

"They got sick of people doing what you were doing. Now they're fixed."

"Really? How wonderfully symbolic."

Toreth shrugged, and started to head in the general direction of home. Warrick fell into step beside him, not apparently feeling the need for further conversation. After two hundred meters of silence, Toreth said, "Did Sara call you?"

"No, I managed to spot this one all by myself." He smiled, a brief flicker. "You could say that the predictive power of my model is improving as the dataset grows. I did call her, to inquire after your whereabouts, but she was uncharacteristically reticent. So, what have I done?"

"Why the fuck should you have done anything?"

"Well, one—" Warrick held up a finger. "You haven't called for four days. Two, you won't accept my calls at work, and three, you aren't at home at night." He let his hand drop. "Sara wasn't very forthcoming about the details of where you've been instead, but I think I have a sound general idea. Nor would she tell

175

me what had provoked it, which of course just told me that it was me. She can say a lot while not saying much, when she puts her mind to it. Well?" No sound except the breeze in the leaves. "No?" Warrick asked. "Very well, I shall guess. Leaving the possibility of coincidences aside, I assume it must be connected to Sara's visit to SimTech?"

Why couldn't he be fucking someone a bit less intelligent? "It's nothing."

"Oh, no. It's 'nothing' if things return to normal. Will they? I shall take that as a no." Warrick stopped walking and turned to face him. "I'm going to ask once more, and then I'm going home. After that, you can call me, or come round, or not, as you like. And if you don't, I won't be back." Not a threat, but a simple statement of intent. "Now, Toreth, for the last time, what's the matter?"

Toreth had faked this kind of conversation before, or at least similar ones, and he'd heard it dozens of times. How much harder could it be when there was some truth to it? "Sara mentioned that you'd been fucking other people in the sim," he said in a rush, hoping it wouldn't sound so petty if he said it quickly.

"Did she?" Warrick waited for a moment, and then said, "That's it?"

For a second, Toreth wanted to hit him. He laced his fingers together behind his back. "Yes."

"Oh." Warrick seemed taken aback by that. "I could say that depends on what you call fucking, but assuming the broadest definition, yes, I do sometimes have sex with people in the sim. Something that you already knew."

"I thought..." Toreth wasn't quite sure what he'd thought. That he wasn't doing it anymore. That Warrick was *his*. Now he could hear Sara laughing again. He took a deep breath. A flat demand would do no good with Warrick. "I'd rather you didn't."

"You would?" Warrick turned away and started walking again. "Well, that's a pity. Firstly, it's my job. I don't do it often—very occasionally indeed nowadays, as I unfortunately find less time to spend on proper work. But sometimes I have to. If there are problems, I have the most experience in certain areas. We have tight schedules, and limited sim time." Warrick paused, hunting for words. "I'm not pretending that I don't enjoy it, sometimes, but that's not why I do it." He smiled wryly. "It's work, not pleasure."

Which all boiled down to, I can't stop. Or maybe, I won't stop. "And secondly?"

"Secondly, that isn't something that works one way. Can you honestly say that I could expect the same—" another pause, "—concession in return?"

Toreth wanted to say yes, just in the hope that it would banish the images of Warrick in the sim that he'd had ever since talking to Sara. He'd be lying, though, which was fine except that they'd both know it. "No."

"Quite. No. So where does that leave things?"

Toreth shrugged. "You don't like part of my job; I don't like part of yours. I don't like you fucking other people in the sim; you don't like me fucking other people anywhere."

"Seems like an accurate summary. What do you want to do about it?"

Toreth thought about it as they walked on through the grounds. It didn't take long, because the conclusion was surprisingly obvious—he wanted to keep fucking Warrick more than he cared about test fucks in the sim. When he was quite sure he could persuade himself that that was true, he said, "My place is closest."

Warrick smiled. "Sounds good to me."

As conversations went, Toreth thought, it hadn't been too bad.

Part Two: Taste Test

When Toreth needed to butter Sara up, or apologize, he bought flowers for her. A simple system, but it had always worked well to smooth over difficulties. A few days after the conversation about sim fucks, Toreth found himself wondering whether it would work with Warrick, too. Flowers were clearly out of the question, but what about something else? Fucking seemed like an obvious choice, but they had great sex all the time, and even a really well-orchestrated evening wasn't the same as a tangible gift. The question stumped him completely. He tried ignoring the idea for a while in the hope it might go away. It came back, though, resurfacing with sufficiently irritating regularity that after a few weeks he decided to consult Sara. As it happened, she'd invited him around to her flat, so there was no need to broach the subject in the overly public atmosphere of the I&I coffee room.

To his surprise, when he arrived he found Sara cooking. Even more oddly, she was doing it in the living room. Admittedly, her kitchen was cramped, but even with his limited culinary experience, he thought kitchens were more traditional. She had a self-heating fondue bowl, a pile of ingredients, and a handwritten recipe on a piece of paper which looked as though it had already suffered through one or two attempts at completion. While he talked, Sara nodded and uh-huhed, breaking pieces of chocolate into the bowl. He didn't mind. It seemed easier, somehow, to start the explanation while she wasn't quite paying attention, and he felt less of an idiot for having to ask her at all. He finished with, "—so I thought you might have some ideas."

"Well, what kind of thing does he like?" she asked absently, as she consulted the paper and frowned. "And what the hell does 'add to taste' mean, anyway?"

Toreth thought it over as he watched her stirring the bowl. He opened the bottle of wine with a *pop*, which caused the huge black cat on the chair opposite to growl and flatten its ragged ears. Toreth gave Bastard the finger, while Sara wasn't looking, and the cat stared back, balefully unimpressed. He returned to the problem in hand. "Cooking," he suggested, ignoring her second question.

"Buy him something kitchen-y, then."

Immediately he regretted telling her about his sudden gift-giving impulse, but it was much too late. Something kitchen-y. Something nice and domestic. For a moment he actually felt sick, the overly sweet smell of melting chocolate catching in the back of his throat. "I wouldn't know where to start," he said, when the feeling passed. "And besides, he's got everything already. You should see his kitchen—I don't even know what most of the crap in there is for, never mind what it's called."

"Okay, what else?"

"Fucking. Being topped. And, well...shiny tech, I suppose. The sim. I don't really know what else. I just fuck him."

"Well, there's your answer." She added a lump of butter and began stirring the pan slowly, picking up a marshmallow with her free hand.

"What?"

"Shiny fuck tech," she mumbled around the mouthful of sweet.

Perfectly obvious, when you thought about it. "You're a genius. I knew you'd be better at this than me."

"It's easy. I love buying presents—almost as much as I love getting them. Do you want me to help you pick something?"

It certainly wouldn't hurt. With an unexpected sense of excitement, he fished his hand screen out of his jacket, expanded the screen, and spent a couple of minutes searching. "Okay...here we go," he said. "Catalogs."

They sat together on the sofa, paging through screens, while Sara stirred the fondue, adding cherry brandy in splashes. "Jesus, some of this stuff is *weird*," she said after a while. "And I say that as someone who knows some fairly weird people."

"I set it on random selection. Just to get some ideas." He was certainly getting plenty of those.

She speared a marshmallow on a long fork, dipped it into the mix, and blew on it to cool it before she ate it. "Mmm. Not bad. That'll do for *to taste*. You know, maybe it's just me, but I have to say I can't see him wearing—wait. There. Go back. Further down." She pointed. *"Those."*

Toreth looked at the screen, where a sugary fingerprint marked her selection, and then nodded. Perfect. "Yeah. Yeah, you're right."

"'Course I am. Like you said, I'm a genius." She consulted her recipe, adjusted the controls on the pan, then started pouring cream in very slowly as she stirred. "Don't curdle this time...please don't curdle..."

"They're made to measure," he said after a while. "And...fucking hell. Have you seen how much they *cost*?"

"Well, it's got to be something expensive, hasn't it?" Holding a cherry by the stem, she dipped it in, shook off the excess chocolate, and ate it. "Something good. I mean, it's Warrick."

"I suppose so." It wasn't actually an enormous amount of money, just more than Toreth would normally think of spending on toys. It seemed less every second, though, as he imagined Warrick's face when he saw them. Oh, yes. Cheap at the price.

"There you go. Sorted out." She spat out the stone. "Try some of this. It's fantastic."

He'd been hoping she wouldn't ask. It looked horribly, sickly sweet. "I ate before I came over."

"Oh, go on. Please. I need a second opinion."

"Try the cat."

"Bastard will eat *anything*, whatever it tastes like. You ate half a twenty-euro tub of moisturizer last week, didn't you, sweetheart? *And* threw it up on mummy's bed."

Recognizing she was addressing it, the cat started purring like an asthmatic generator. Toreth regarded it with deep loathing. He had a fresh set of scratches on the back of his hand to remind him exactly why he'd named the cat You Fucking Evil Bastard.

Sara proffered the bowl of cherries. "Come on."

Toreth dipped in a cherry and tried it dubiously. Ready to fake appreciative noises, he found it less sweet than he'd imagined. The bitter chocolate went surprisingly well with the fruit; the contrast made the cherry taste fizzy. "Oh, hey. That's pretty good."

She frowned. "No need to sound so surprised."

"Come off it. You're usually about as housetrained as I am. What brought this on?"

"I'm supposed to be taking something to a dinner party tomorrow and I thought I'd make an effort. Pretend to be a grownup for once. Warrick lent me the fonduing thing and gave me the recipe. He gave me the cherries, too—enough to try now and plenty to take tomorrow. Pretty nice of him, hm?"

Yes, it was. "When did you get them?"

Sara looked at him sidelong, and then smiled. "Yesterday evening at SimTech. I was doing a volunteer run on the sim."

She was doing it deliberately and he knew she was, but he couldn't help responding. "Oh?"

"Oh?" she mimicked.

Before he could think of anything to say, she laughed. "All right. Sorry. He wasn't in the sim. He wasn't even in the building. He left the stuff at reception with a note. Happy?"

Now he could relax. "Why would I care whether he was there or not?"

She shook her head. "Like I said, weird people. Have another cherry. Are you going to the SimTech do?"

179

Toreth ate the cherry, without chocolate, while he thought about it. Warrick had said something...what was it? Eventually he gave up. "Probably. I don't remember. Was it an anniversary or something?"

Sara rolled her eyes. "God, sometimes you're hopeless. It's *on* the anniversary, but it's because they passed the, um, third round safety trials."

"Meaning what?"

"No idea, except they're splashing out for a huge bloody party, so it must be something good. It's for the staff and sponsors, but they did a lottery for volunteers and I got an invite. Or Warrick fixed it for me—I didn't ask. It sounds like it's going to be fantastic: food, drinks, dancing, sim demos, you name it. Formal, though. I'll have to find something to go in. You've got a dinner jacket, haven't you?"

"Well, there's the one I bought back when I was seconded to Corporate Fraud. You remember—when Liz Carey and I were working that undercover corporate case." Catching her expression, he said, "You're right. I'll get a new one. When is it?"

"Three weeks. Plenty of time."

Yes, plenty of time. Toreth returned his attention to the catalog. Plenty of time indeed.

Part Three: I May Forget Birthdays, But...

Toreth had been waiting in a state of strategic unreadiness for fifteen minutes by the time the car arrived—five minutes early—and Warrick called up from the entrance. "I'm running a bit late, I'm afraid," Toreth told him. "Come up to the flat." Then he cut the comm before Warrick could refuse. Planning these things out was almost as much fun as doing them. Almost.

Toreth opened the door wearing trousers, socks, and an unbuttoned shirt, with his untied bow tie draped around his neck. His dinner jacket and shoes were ready in the hall. On Warrick's face he caught a flicker of irritation at the fact that he wasn't even dressed, only partly countered by a flicker of appreciation. So far, so good. He offered an apologetic smile, which Warrick wouldn't believe for a second. "Sorry about this. I won't be long. Come in."

Warrick brushed past him without comment and leaned against the wall, arms folded, fingers tapping his biceps impatiently. Toreth closed the door and started to fasten his way down the buttons on the front of his dress shirt. "I don't suppose there's any chance of you missing this thing, is there?"

"No. All the major sponsors will be there, and I have to make a presentation and a speech. I can't be late." Warrick frowned. "I thought I'd explained all this?

180

Of course, you don't have to come along, if you don't want to. If you'd mentioned it—"

"No, no. Just wondering. I'm looking forward to it." He tucked in his shirt and began on the buttons at the wrists. "But while you're waiting—I bought something for you. It's over there." He nodded towards where he'd left the box on the table in the hallway. Beneath the mirror, so that when Warrick opened it Toreth would be able to see his face.

Warrick raised an eyebrow, surprise replacing irritation. "What is it?"

"A present."

"What's the occasion?" Warrick asked as he crossed to the table.

"Nothing in particular." Toreth stood behind him, tying his bow tie. "Go on. Open it."

Warrick looked at the box for a moment longer, and then lifted the lid. He moved aside the covering layer of packing foam, and then his eyes in the mirror went wide. "Oh, my God," he breathed.

Toreth smiled. Exactly as he'd imagined it. "What do you think?"

"What do I...?"

After a few seconds, Warrick reached into the box and took out the manacles, one in each hand. Made from silky, brushed steel, they gleamed dully in the hall light. As he lifted them, the oval links of the chain joining them slid over each other with a cold, metallic music. Their hinges moved easily as he turned them over in his hands. They were beautifully made, Toreth thought. Beautiful toys. Smooth, rounded edges, which wouldn't cut. Solid, old-fashioned-looking locks, which hid an electronic timer release. He'd played with them for a while when they'd arrived, and he'd been tempted to call Warrick then. In the end, though, he'd put them away and waited, because it would have been a waste. *This* was infinitely better.

"Next layer," he said quietly. Without letting go of the manacles, Warrick moved the packaging beneath and his lips parted silently. The steel collar lay in a hollow in the foam, the attached chain curled in a spiral within it. "Do you like them?"

Warrick looked between the silvery gray bonds and their reflection in the mirror in front of him. Toreth thought they contrasted beautifully with his black evening suit. "I had them made specially," Toreth continued. "Especially to fit you."

"They must—" Warrick cleared his throat. "They must have been expensive."

"Fairly." Stepping up close, Toreth reached around him and took the manacles. He fitted them around Warrick's wrists and closed them, without locking them. Warrick's eyes closed, too, and he shuddered against him. "They suit you," Toreth murmured into his ear. "Very nice."

He reached down for the collar, flicking the lock open easily, and fitted that as well. Warrick swallowed as the cool metal fastened around his throat. Excited, and perhaps a little afraid? "Open your eyes. Open your eyes and look at yourself."

Just as Toreth thought he was going to have to repeat the instruction, Warrick's eyes opened and he stared into the mirror. And simply stared, for endless seconds. Then he touched his dry tongue to dry lips, and nodded. His hands were trembling, the chain shifting quietly. Toreth looked, too, drinking him in, barely seeing himself in the background. Silver and black. Pale face, flushed lips, eyelids closing again. Rapid, uneven breathing. God, he looked good—the first reward from his careful planning. Taking hold of Warrick's hands again, he ran the chain through them, stopping when his fingers closed over the single large, round link exactly halfway along. "Feel that? That locks to a bolt in the wall."

Warrick's body went rigid against his, his breath catching in his throat.

"I've put three in the bedroom here," Toreth continued, when Warrick seemed to be listening again. "One for standing. One for kneeling. One at the head of the bed. Probably violated the hell out of the tenancy agreement. There are a couple still left over. For your flat, if you like. I thought—"

"Toreth." Warrick had wrapped the length of chain around his hands, pulling it taut, knuckles whitening. "Fuck me. Fuck me *now*."

Too utterly perfect. Toreth pressed against him, pinning him up against the edge of the table, and said, "You like them, then?"

"God, *yes*, I like them. Yes."

"Then tell me again what you want. Say it for me." Start of the familiar game.

"I want you...I want you to fuck me."

Toreth took hold of Warrick's hips and dug his fingers in hard, rubbing hard against him, tormenting them both with the contact through too much cloth. "No," he whispered.

Warrick gasped. "Please—"

"No." Toreth pulled back, just a fraction, while he still could. "Because we have your very important event to get to where—" he kissed Warrick's neck, feather light, "—you have to make a presentation and a speech for which—" kiss, "—you will be late—" kiss, "—if we don't go right now." Then he bit him, once, hard.

The response was something perfectly balanced between a moan and a whimper, wonderfully desperate, which sorely tested the strength of his resolve. Here, in the hall, watching Warrick's face in the mirror while he...no. Dangerous line of thought. Instead he focused on how very much better it would be with a few hours of anticipation added to the experience. On how Warrick would look for those few hours, knowing what Toreth would do to him when they got back.

Taking a deep breath, just about convincing himself, Toreth forced himself to let go of Warrick's hips and lift his hands to unclasp the collar and return it to the box. He took his time, coiling the chain neatly back into the hollow in the foam.

Then he removed the manacles, uncurling Warrick's hands, finger by finger, to free the chain, and carefully packed the whole thing away. Finally he stepped back. "Time to go."

Warrick leaned heavily on the table, his breathing ragged. "No. You can't . . . *I* can't." He looked up at Toreth's reflection in the mirror, his eyes hot and his voice thick with need. "I *can't.*" Then a tiny smile creased the corner of his mouth, acknowledging the perfection of the plan. "*Bastard,*" he said, with feeling.

Toreth couldn't have asked for more. He laughed as he slipped his shoes on. "Flattery won't get you anywhere. But I promise I'll remember it later."

Toreth had attended a couple of SimTech events before; both times he had brought Sara along with him for company and arrived with her, separately to Warrick. Not exactly Warrick's idea, or his—he'd never given it much thought, in fact. Tonight would be a slight variation on the theme, because Warrick had arranged to pick Sara up on the way. A good job, Toreth thought, that he seemed to have pre-programmed the route, because Warrick didn't look up to remembering his own name, never mind an offer of a lift. For the first ten minutes in the car, Toreth did his best to make the situation worse, until Warrick finally moved from the seat beside him to the one opposite. "Please," Warrick said.

"What?"

"I—leave it for a while. It's an important evening. If I turn up like this . . . " He looked out of the window and shook his head sharply. "No more."

"Sure. Whatever you want, of course." The ready agreement made Warrick look around again, openly suspicious, but Toreth merely smiled at him and sat back. Warrick could stop this—or any game—whenever he chose, but pushing it so far that he needed to wasn't as much fun as keeping it on the edge of the acceptable.

When they reached Sara's building Toreth volunteered to fetch her, to give Warrick a chance to compose himself. She must have been waiting in the entrance, though, because by the time he had the door open, he saw her coming down the steps. She wore a dress that, on a per-square-centimeter basis, was probably astonishingly expensive. Lucky, from that point of view, that there weren't that many square centimeters involved. What fabric there was seemed to be mostly at the sides, held together across front and back by a web of strategically placed strips of gossamer fabric that gave the teasing impression they could be translucent if you caught them in just the right light. Her golden skin tone, peeping through the gaps in the web, made a beautiful contrast to the pearly fabric.

"Nice frock. What's your hourly rate?" Toreth asked as the car started again.

She glared. "I borrowed it from my sister."

"What does she charge, then?"

The glare intensified. "It's a handmade indi." When he looked blank, she elaborated. "Independent. Noncorporate freelance designer. Fee could only afford it because she knows someone who works for him. She said if I spilled anything on it, she'd kill me."

Warrick examined her with care, and then smiled. "Don't worry. If you do spill anything, I expect it will miss."

Sara managed to keep the indignation going for another few seconds, and then laughed. "Yeah, probably. Is it all right? Not too much?"

"It's delightful," Warrick assured her.

"Yeah. Eye-catching." Toreth reached out and straightened the thin strap threatening to slide off Sara's shoulder. "And the last thing you could accuse it of is being too much."

The flying insults lasted until the car began to slow in front of a large, brightly lit building, and Warrick said, "Now, children, be good. We're here."

They walked through the impressive entrance together with Sara between them, and stopped for Warrick to speak to the manager waiting there for them. The atrium wasn't as large as it looked at first, Toreth realized, as one entire wall was mirrored in a single, flawless sheet, doubling the apparent size. Toreth studied their reflections, watching himself smile. The back of Sara's dress was as revealing as the front, appearing even more nearly translucent in the brighter lights. Her glossy black hair made a startling contrast to the fragile-seeming fabric. The ten-centimeter difference in his and Warrick's heights gave the picture a pleasing asymmetry as they stood flanking Sara, blond and dark. I'd fuck us, he thought. Any of us. Hell, all of us.

Then the manager, all smiles and attentiveness, escorted them through the corridors of the corporate entertainment complex. SimTech was obviously splashing out; normally, Toreth only saw this kind of place when he was on duty. The suite of rooms included a large hall decorated in swaths of fabric in tasteful, muted metallic shades of the SimTech logo's blue and gray. The gray reminded him of the manacles, and from the way Warrick caught his breath as they entered, he wasn't alone.

Toreth knew many of the SimTech employees and a few sponsors by sight from the investigation. If that made any of them uncomfortable, Warrick had never mentioned it, and Toreth didn't care. Asher Linton and Lew Marcus were already there, and Linton at least greeted Toreth's appearance with politeness, if not exactly enthusiasm. Marcus nodded to him, and then remembered something he had to do elsewhere.

They'd arrived early, before the majority of the sponsors and other guests, in order that Warrick could be there to greet them. Therefore, the first part of the evening went as Toreth had expected, with him rapidly growing bored while Warrick was occupied with corporate business.

After a while, he went off with Sara to try the sim demos before too many of the important guests turned up and sessions were limited to a few minutes. They were in luck. The technicians setting up the equipment were running late and looking for experienced volunteers to test the system. Toreth had seen all the demo rooms in use before, so the most entertaining part was watching the attending technician fitting the sim couch straps onto Sara while trying not to touch too much bare flesh. Still, the sim killed half an hour or so. When the technician in charge finally kicked them off the machines to make way for sponsors, they acquired some drinks and went in search of Warrick again. They found him in the main room, on the otherwise empty dais at the end where the speeches and presentations would take place, leaning on the ornate balustrade and surveying the crowd.

Leaving Sara down on the main hall floor and in charge of his glass, Toreth climbed up to stand behind Warrick. Careless of witnesses, he put his hands on Warrick's waist—it wouldn't be too obvious. Warrick made no objection, so Toreth said, "The sponsors'll be impressed—it all looks very good."

"Yes. I'm very pleased with—"

"Not as good as you in that collar, mind." Toreth leaned in a little, pressing against him, and whispered, "If I'd brought the chains, I could cuff you to that rail and fuck you right now."

He felt the shiver. "Not here," Warrick said quietly.

"No one would know. I could blindfold you."

"There is a difference between . . . between not seeing and not being seen."

"You want it, though, don't you?"

Long, low intake of breath. "Yes."

"How long before we can go back to the flat?"

"Toreth, we've only just—"

"How do you want to do it, for the first time? Standing? Kneeling?"

"Oh, *God.*" The helpless desperation in Warrick's voice was so perfect, it actually hurt, a pain in Toreth's chest that left him breathless.

"Shall we use a mirror?" he asked when he could speak again. "Or a mirror for me and a blindfold for you. Not seeing and being seen. I think—" He tightened his hold. "I think I'd like to watch you come while I fuck you."

"I—" Warrick stood up abruptly, taking a pace away from him. "Dillian should be here, somewhere. Can you see her?"

Toreth grinned and looked out over the crowd. He was good at faces, especially Dillian's, and it took only a few seconds before he said, "Over there."

Collecting Sara, they crossed the room. The crowd was an interesting mixture

185

of the humbler SimTech employees and volunteers, and the obviously wealthy corporates. SimTech was a great deal more egalitarian than most corporations were, although Toreth thought that might be due more to size than any deliberate policy on the part of the directors. As they came up to Dillian, Toreth noticed a woman standing beside her he didn't recognize, which was a pity. Early to midthirties at a guess, rich brown hair, trim figure in a flattering dress, glass of something clear with ice in one hand. Certainly not someone he'd turn down in a bar.

Dillian smiled at them. "Sara. What an incredible outfit—it's beautiful! Nice to see you, Toreth."

After greeting Dillian, he turned to the stranger, who offered her hand. Toreth approved—slender, strong fingers, with squared-off nails and natural polish. No wedding band, he noted automatically, feeling the first prickings of interest despite the fact, and despite Warrick's presence beside him. He noticed her returning his appraisal intently, and wondered if she was returning his interest, too. Dillian began the introduction, but before she got any further than "Cele, this is Val—" the woman grinned.

"We've met before."

News to him. For a moment he wondered if he'd interrogated her, but the smile made that unlikely. He looked at her more closely but his memory remained stubbornly unhelpful, which probably meant he'd fucked her. He was trying to frame a tactful way of asking, when she continued, "Well, I grant you, it was ten years ago, and you called yourself Marc then, but I remember distinctly that you have a faint scar on your left temple—" She reached up to him and traced the mark with her finger. "—like this. Got it in a bar brawl, you said." She looked over at Warrick and winked. "He was colossally intoxicated at the time I discovered it, you see. So was I, for all that."

Tact didn't seem to be a requirement. In any case, ten years made it ancient history. Toreth took a sip of wine and smiled. "I'm sorry, but I still don't remember. Maybe you met my evil twin."

Warrick raised an eyebrow. "Are you suggesting that you're the good one?"

"I found the scar when I was licking you all over," Cele said. "Does that help?"

"Cele," Dillian said, with a warning note in her voice. Sara appeared frankly intrigued.

Cele pulled a pencil out of her bag and flourished it, looking around the group. "Are we having a problem here? No? Good. Shall I draw your erection, Marc?"

Toreth blinked, stuck for an answer. He glanced at Warrick, but he still seemed amused rather than upset. Clearly, this was standard behavior for Cele.

She picked up a paper napkin from beside a tray of canapes. "Everyone's is different, you know, and yours is quite attractive. Seven inches—"

"Well, there you go, then," Toreth interrupted.

She paused, pencil raised. "What?"

186

"Must have been my evil twin." He grinned at her. "Far too small to be me."

Warrick closed his eyes, Dillian rolled hers, Sara yelped delightedly, and Cele's smile got bigger. "You know why women are such poor judges of perspective?" Cele asked them all. After a suitable pause, she held her hands up, palms facing each other, about a hand's breadth apart. "Because all our lives we've been told this is eight inches."

This time Sara's laugh attracted attention from all around them. Dillian snorted wine out of her nose and choked. Warrick thumped her on the back until she could stop coughing and stand up again. Cele offered her a glass and the napkin. "Sorry, sweetheart," she said, and then smiled at Toreth. "It's all right, Seven Inches. I forgive you for not remembering—it was just fucking, after all."

Woman after his own heart. Toreth was perfectly willing to concede that he had, indeed, fucked Cele at some time in the past. He wished he could remember; she looked fuckable enough now that he could imagine ten years ago he would have homed in on her like a heat-seeking missile. He'd have to try to get her alone at some point to continue the conversation. If nothing else, she could tell him if they'd had fun.

With order finally restored, Dillian looked at the glass Cele had given her and asked, "Water?"

Cele nodded. "May not look it, but I'm hard at work here. Guided tours of my work later, for the sponsors."

"Work?" Toreth asked, feeling a stupid, infuriating twinge of unease at the idea of Cele at SimTech. She hadn't been on the staff during the investigation.

"I've been contracting for Keir," Cele said, mildly impressing Toreth with the intensity of innuendo she crammed into such a short sentence. "He took pity on me. For I am An Artist—poor and starving in a garret—and he's stinking rich."

Warrick shook his head. "Don't listen to her. She's designed some sim rooms for us, and they're beautiful work. The sim can do a lot, but if we're not going to be confined simply to what we can generate from templates or copy from the real world, creativity is still required."

"And she's not poor, either," Dillian added. "She's very talented, and in a lot of demand."

"Ah." Cele waved her hand. "You're embarrassing me. But Dilly—if I'm so good, are you going to have a look at my rooms?"

"I, er..." Dillian glanced around, as if seeking inspiration. "I saw the drawings."

"Not the same thing, sweetheart. Go on—go in this time."

"Maybe."

"Haven't you been in the sim yet, Dillian?" Sara asked.

"No." Dillian glanced at Warrick. "I know, I really ought to. But I don't like the idea."

187

"Are you claustrophobic?" Sara asked. "I didn't like the visor much the first time, but after that it was fine."

"Good Lord, no. I could hardly spend so much time on sealed-environment constructions if I were. It's hard to explain why. It's the idea of . . . of my body being in one place and my mind being somewhere else."

Warrick sighed. "It's nothing at all like that. I've explained the principle a hundred times."

As Warrick started to explain the principle again, Toreth turned to Cele and said, "I suppose you had to spend a lot of time in the sim." Starting an oblique approach to a question.

"A fair bit. Finding out what it could do, building the rooms. You?"

He nodded. "I've helped out in a few trials. Mostly I just use up Warrick's personal sim time for fucking."

"Oh, yes. You can do some *weird* shit in there." She grinned. "But I haven't done any of it with him, Seven Inches, so you can stop looking at me like that."

Toreth hadn't been aware he'd been looking like anything. "I wouldn't mind," he said evenly. "It's his job."

She laughed. "Of course it is. And of course you wouldn't. But if you were going to mind, there isn't any need. He's my unofficial adopted big brother, at least when he can spare the time from big-brothering Dilly."

He shrugged, feeling at least somewhat reassured. "Like I said, it doesn't matter."

Cele didn't answer. She was staring past his shoulder. After a moment, she nudged Dillian and said, "My God—look!"

"At what?" Toreth asked as he followed her gaze. Nothing notable caught his attention, but out of the corner of his eye, he saw Warrick putting his glass down. He looked . . . shocked, as if he'd seen something totally unexpected.

"Excuse me," Warrick said, striding away before Toreth could ask what or who he'd seen. Toreth watched, wondering, until Warrick halted beside a dark-haired woman, apparently interrupting her current conversation without ceremony.

When the woman turned towards Warrick, she seemed faintly familiar to Toreth. "Who's that?" he asked Dillian, who obviously knew.

"It's the b—it's Mel. Melissa. Keir's ex." Of course—her hair had confused him. The color must be recent because she'd been blonde in the security file.

"Ex-*wife*?" Sara asked, catching up with the conversation.

"Yes." Dillian frowned thoughtfully. "I wonder what she's doing here?"

"Looks like we'll find out in a minute," Cele said, as the woman turned and started towards them, Warrick a step or two behind her.

"Cele," Melissa said as she reached them, and kissed Cele's cheeks. "Lovely to see you again."

Cele returned the greeting, adding a hug. "You look great, Mel. It's been too long."

"Yes, it has. And Dillian." This time the single kiss was what Toreth would classify as insultingly perfunctory, missing Dillian's cheek by about three inches. Dillian didn't reply.

Warrick didn't appear to have had the time—or possibly inclination—to mention Sara or Toreth, because Melissa looked between them, obviously trying to work out the relationships. Since Warrick didn't seem inclined to do anything, Toreth offered his hand. "Val Toreth. And this is Sara Lovelady."

Her hand was cool, the grip brief but firm. "Melissa Aetherford." After a moment's silence, she asked, "Are you a friend of Keir's?"

Toreth smiled. "Not really." Sara stepped on his foot and he ignored her. "Actually, I'm fucking him." This time, Warrick went paler, Dillian went pinker, Cele grinned openly, and Sara turned away hastily, adjusting the strap of her dress.

Melissa looked back at him steadily, matching his smile. "Lucky man."

He thought about the obvious question, but he didn't feel like playing to her feed lines. "I think so." Her smile went slightly frosty and he chalked up a point.

"What are you doing here?" Cele asked Mel. "Not that there's any reason you shouldn't be, of course, but Keir didn't mention."

"I'm here with a client," she said, still looking at Toreth.

"You should've let me know, Lissa," Warrick said.

So you could've kept me out of the way? Toreth wondered.

Melissa turned to her ex-husband, her smile melting into something Toreth had to admit was quite charming. "I would have done, of course, but I didn't know myself until very last thing this afternoon. I'm filling in for someone with sick children."

Dillian, out of Melissa's line of sight, rolled her eyes and mouthed, "Of course."

"I'm sorry if I startled you," Melissa continued.

"Not at all." Warrick's voice had a brittle edge, as though he were running a strict internal censor on every word. "It's very good to see you again. It's been a while since we...since we spoke. What are you doing these days?"

"Sales—market projections, primarily. Not my first choice, but there are only so many jobs for statisticians."

"Researching markets for sim applications?" Cele asked.

"Broadly, yes. Demand estimation. Nothing very exciting."

"It's not P-Leisure, then?" Dillian asked.

"Hardly." Mel lifted her head slightly, as though an unpleasant smell had drifted past. "Training simulation systems, primarily. Specialist environments: radiation hazard, low gravity, deep sea—that kind of thing."

Cele chuckled. "I'm sure you could combine the two."

Warrick cleared his throat. "Sex isn't the only application for the sim, Cele."

"It's the most popular one, though," Dillian said. "And the most potentially profitable." When Warrick fixed her with an icy stare, she smiled sweetly. "Well, it is. I *am* a shareholder. I do have to think of my investment. It wouldn't surprise me if three-quarters of the people who've been through tonight weren't looking at Cele's scenery. It's full of corporates taking their mistresses in there. In all senses of the word."

"Dillian!" Warrick said, and Toreth frankly stared. He'd never heard Warrick so defensive. Almost embarrassed, which in the context of the sim was something new.

Dillian glanced at Mel, then back to her brother. "Oh, am I being discriminatory? There *were* a few women with rather attractive escorts."

"They're only running ten-minute slots," Sara said.

Cele snorted. "Sounds about five minutes too long for most of the corporates *I* saw in the queue."

Mel shook her head. "Surely people wouldn't—not right here?"

"You should put a screen up next time, Keir," Dillian suggested. "So we can see who's right."

"Public sex?" Mel looked around the group, her gaze ending up on Warrick. "Well, I suppose it's only to be expected."

"It's not in public, though, is it?" Sara said. "The sim's about as private as you can get."

Warrick took a breath. "I don't—"

"Oh, come on, Mel," Cele interrupted, and Toreth wondered what she'd thought Warrick might say. "Dilly's only joking. Nobody would do that at an official event."

"Actually, I know someone who has," Sara said. "Toreth, do the buffet story."

He was about to refuse, when he caught Mel's expression. She looked to be on the brink of walking off anyway, and a push wouldn't hurt. Toreth couldn't resist. Cele and Dillian would probably find it funny, if no one else did. "This is back when I was a trainee. They laid on a party after the final set of exams and . . . so on. Buffet, which they did every year, but our year was the first one they had a free bar, which considering how tight they usually are was a miracle. Probably splashing out because it was the last one before the reorganization."

Eleven years ago. He paused for a moment, thinking of security files and trying to remember whether Warrick had been married to Melissa then. "Anyway, it was a *good* party, especially when you've spent a year on trainee pay. There was this woman there—one of our intake. Don't remember her name, but she was *very...*" He mimed curves in the air. "Which was a waste, really, because she didn't drink, didn't date, didn't do anything except pass exams. I had a few bets on that I'd get her before the end of the year, and the party was the official end of training, so that was the last evening."

He glanced around the group, assessing. Sara, who'd heard this a million times, was looking around, too. Cele seemed amused, as did Dillian, although Toreth suspected Dillian's appreciation might be due partly to Melissa's reaction.

She looked positively arctic. Warrick, his eye on Melissa, didn't appear too happy either, but Toreth decided the payoff would probably be worth it. "The later it got, the more people kept coming up, asking me if I'd got the money with me. I managed to persuade her to have a glass or three, since we were celebrating, and finally, ten to midnight, I got her—on the buffet table."

"Didn't anyone *notice*?" Dillian asked.

"Pretty much everyone who was still sober enough to see straight. So about half of them. I didn't want anyone claiming I'd missed my deadline and wriggling out of paying up."

Cele laughed. "Not to mention that you were drunk enough that you've forgotten *her* name as well."

"No, that's my normal awful memory." He grinned. "Nothing personal. I was pretty sober. *She* was hammered, mind—she ended up sitting on a meringue. Someone took a picture of her on the table with her legs round my waist. Cream and fruit everywhere. Flew round the division systems, of course. Paper copies printed and stuck up everywhere, too. She never spoke to me again. God knows why—*I* didn't take the picture."

Melissa drew in a breath, so Toreth carried on quickly. "Anyway, back on the table, everything was going to plan, when someone put their hand on my shoulder. Five minutes to midnight, so I assumed it was someone trying to cheat and I told them to eff off, pretty colorfully, I'll admit, and—" he spread his hands, "—finished things with two minutes to go. And when I turned round—"

"It was the Chief Instructor for the Interrogation training course," finished Sara, interrupting in the usual spot.

Toreth nodded. "He'd come to announce who'd won the training debt partial refund awards."

Cele's eyes were sparkling with amusement. "Oh, God, no! You hadn't!"

"Oh, God, yes, I had. Most expensive fuck of my life. I collected two hundred and fifty euros from the bets, and it cost me eight and a half thousand when they stopped the award because I told McFarlen to go forth and multiply. Lucky, in a way, because if they hadn't been able to do that they might've thrown me out. First and *last* year they had a free bar, as well."

Cele shook her head. "I'm not sure I believe it."

"God's honest truth. There's probably a copy of the picture in a box under my bed. I'll dig it out and send you a file."

"How charming," Melissa said. She set her glass down firmly on the table. "If you'll excuse me, I have to get back to my client."

As she walked away, Warrick's glare swept around the group, and Toreth saw Sara actually take a small step backwards. Braced for a grade-A bollocking, Toreth was almost disappointed when Warrick ended up staring at Dillian. "Satisfied?" he asked icily, and without waiting for a reply, he strode after Melissa.

Dillian appeared unrepentant. "How dare she turn up without telling Keir!" she snapped, as soon as Warrick was approximately out of earshot.

Cele put her arm around Dillian's shoulders. "Calm down. You heard what she said. It's hardly Mel's fault if someone's kids are ill."

Dillian shrugged her off irritably. "She probably poisoned them," she said with every evidence of sincerity.

A voice from behind him pre-empted Cele's reply. "Dilly!" Toreth turned to find Asher Linton hurrying over to them. She smiled at him, distracted, and said, "Have you seen Keir? You'll never guess who's here."

"No need." Cele pointed across the room.

Warrick stood next to his ex-wife, with his hand on her elbow. As they watched, she moved her arm pointedly and stalked away. He stayed where he was, looking after her, his hand still raised.

"Oh, dear," Asher sighed. "Well. Can't be helped, I suppose."

Toreth found Sara's foot on his again. When he looked around, she wiggled her eyebrows in a generally Warrick-ward direction. From his expression, Warrick was probably in a foul mood. On the other hand, left to his own devices he might go after that bloody woman, and Sara's hints looked set to be persistent enough that it would be easier to do what he was told. "Be right back," he announced vaguely, then headed over towards Warrick.

When he got there, he hesitated. Warrick stood, still staring after Melissa, and Toreth couldn't come up with a decent opening. In the end, he said, "Warrick?"

Warrick turned around at once, looking no happier than he had when he'd walked off. "Thank you *so* much for your contribution to the evening. What the hell was all that about?"

"I didn't fancy spending the whole evening wishing I'd brought my thermal underwear. Dillian thought it was funny."

"Yes, Dilly would." That had a venom he'd never heard Warrick direct at his sister before. "But as things between Lissa and myself have nothing to do with you, I'd appreciate it if you kept out of it in future."

That, unexpectedly, stung. "You're the one who invited me. Changed your mind now?"

"Of course not!"

"So why didn't you tell her who I was?"

"I . . ." Toreth had never seen Warrick blush, but he had a postural equivalent—a defensive shrug, a way of lowering his head and looking up—which meant he'd been caught without a ready reply. "Well, to tell the truth, I didn't know what to say. I wasn't even sure what you'd want me to say. How would you prefer to be described?"

Warrick had an annoying habit of turning these things around by being logical and practical. Annoying in this case because Toreth had no idea. He'd never thought about it before, and nothing sprang helpfully to mind now. "I don't know," he said at length. "But something. If you don't want people knowing about me, don't fucking invite me in the first place. I'm quite happy with dinner and a fuck twice a week; I don't need to spend my evenings being bored into a coma by your ex-wives and corporate fucking friends."

Warrick glanced in the direction Melissa had gone. "Do we have to—"

His anger sharpened. "I'm not some fucking corporate accessory fancy dog you can drag around on a leash and not even mention to people."

"Now you're being ridiculous," Warrick snapped. "When the hell did I imply you were anything of the kind?"

"You—" With an effort Toreth reined himself in, and considered the options. Drop it, or let the whole thing spiral up into a blazing row, which would eventually force him to storm out. That would only make him look like an idiot and hand the whole game over to Warrick on a plate, not to mention wasting all his hard work with the present. Melissa had already ruined the mood completely. "Yeah, you're right." He couldn't quite manage gracious, but it sounded better than he expected. "I overreacted. Sorry."

As he'd expected, it stopped Warrick dead. After a moment, he nodded. "And I apologize for the lack of consideration. I'll try and think of something suitably noncommittal for future use."

Toreth nodded, although, now that he'd demanded it, the idea made him uneasy.

Warrick looked at his watch, and then laid his hand on Toreth's arm, which was interesting because he didn't usually touch in public. "As you said, I did invite you. There's the food soon, and then the official parts, but we have some time beforehand. What would you like to do? There are sim demos running."

Toreth considered. He might at least try to salvage something from the wreckage. The chains were still at the flat, and Warrick was coming home with him, not Melissa. "I did the sim with Sara. What I'd like to do is—" Toreth dipped his head slightly and finished the rest of the sentence in a murmur into Warrick's ear. Glancing up as he did so, he saw Melissa watching them from some distance away. She looked as if she had bitten into something unexpectedly sour. Good. He stepped back. "Well?"

"Mm." Warrick swallowed and then his smile widened, developing a distinct hint of mischief. "Come on."

"Where?"

"Just come on."

"Woof."

Warrick laughed. "Good boy. This way."

"So, did you ever fuck Cele?" Toreth asked in an undertone as they crossed the crowded room.

193

Warrick stopped for a moment, stared at him, and then shook his head. "Not that it is any of your business, but no."

They started walking again. "She's pretty tasty," Toreth said.

"You obviously thought so ten years ago."

Toreth shrugged. "I've fucked a lot of women and they weren't all that good-looking. Don't you think she's attractive?"

"Yes. But that doesn't mean I've ever slept with her." Warrick must have caught his disbelieving glance, because he added, "It's not compulsory. It may come as something of a shock to you, but it is possible to be acquainted with people—including attractive people—without sleeping with them. Or even wanting to do so. Technically, it's called 'friendship.'"

"Very funny. I've got friends I don't fuck. Sara, to start with."

Now it was Warrick's turn to look disbelieving. "Really?"

"Yeah. Did you think we did?"

"I hadn't given it any thought."

That was so clearly a lie that Toreth felt rather good. Good enough not to spoil the effect by mentioning that he had, in fact, fucked her once. Instead he asked, "So you never even wanted to fuck Cele?"

"Good grief . . . well, yes. In an adolescent way, I suppose I did. At the hormonally crazed stage when you're desperate for sex with anyone. But even then . . . I mean, she's Dilly's friend. I knew her when she was eight, for God's sake."

Toreth wasn't quite sure what difference that made. On the other hand, he no longer had any kind of contact with anyone he'd known when he was eight, so perhaps it did. In any case, he believed Warrick, who didn't lie about that kind of thing. Or not that Toreth had yet caught him at. The idea of Cele in the sim with Warrick still made him uneasy, though. However much he'd been telling himself it was Warrick's job and nothing to do with him, he discovered that he didn't want to meet anyone involved. Best not to think about it.

They'd reached the far side of the room. Warrick stopped at a set of double doors, glanced casually around, and then opened them.

Sara watched them go. She'd half expected a spectacular blowup, but the volcano seemed to have simmered down. The whole thing still surprised her on occasion. More than a year since they'd first met, months since things had become what you might call serious, and they were still at it. Strangest of all, she couldn't see any particular reason it shouldn't *keep* happening. Not much of a surprise for Warrick, maybe, since he'd apparently managed to get himself married—and she'd love to hear the circumstances behind that. On Toreth's part, though, it wasn't something she'd have credited without benefit of mind fuck. Just one of those things, she supposed. For now, the ex-wife presented a more interesting mystery. Especially with sources of information to hand. "Dillian, what did you start to call Melissa? When we first saw her, you said she was the b-something."

"The Bitch Queen," Dillian admitted after a moment. "Don't tell Keir, will you? Please?"

"Of course not." Telling Toreth was a completely different question. "So, when were they married?"

"The year after Keir left university. That's where they met. It lasted four years, which was four years too long."

"What happened?"

"She walked out on him."

Cele said, "They had a conception license application bounced."

Dillian sniffed. "That was nothing to do with it."

"But they did have the application turned down, didn't they?" When Dillian didn't answer, Cele turned to Sara. "Mel couldn't find a job, and the Department of Population didn't consider Keir's job to be stable enough to have the license granted."

Sara looked around at the reception. "Because of his *job*?"

"SimTech was nothing like this, back then," Asher said. "In fact, at that point we were still running things out of my attic. Keir and Mel were living on a loan from Kate—that's his mother—until the first sponsors paid up."

Cele nodded. "And the *hours* they all worked. Makes me glad I've never had a real job."

Asher smiled. "I was the lucky one. It was my house, so at least I still saw Greg. Mel hardly saw Keir, which can't have helped things."

"I don't know why you're both always so fair to her," Dillian said. "Sara, listen. She married Keir because she thought he was going to be rich and respectable. And then he turned down a very good corporate job to found SimTech. No money, and very much not respectable. She was spitting mad, although I don't think the sex side would have bothered her so much if it had been euros up front."

Cele shook her head. "She married someone who worked for the Administration in the Data Division. And then he ended up in partnership with P-Leisure, designing virtual fuck tech." Sara thought it had the sound of a very old argument. "How would you have felt?"

"I wouldn't have minded. I *didn't* mind it. Anyway," Dillian said to Sara, "she decided she'd backed a loser. The application was just an excuse. She could've waited. But instead she dumped him and sucked every cent she could out of him, like the spiteful vulture she is."

"Mixed metaphor, sweetheart," Cele said. "Leeches suck. Vultures..."

"Peck?" Sara suggested.

"Whatever they do, she did it," Dillian said. "She broke his heart. It wasn't funny."

Cele held her hand up. "Hey, whoa there, girl. Did I say it was? But she's not all bad. I always felt sorry for her."

"To be fair to Dilly," Asher said mildly, "there was the business with the shares." She turned to Sara. "During the divorce, Keir rather unfortunately signed everything her lawyers put in front of him. I did my best, but..."

Dillian nodded. "I was in the middle of my first contract on Mars, or *I* would've stopped him, but by the time I got back it was too late. Part of what he signed away was some SimTech shares. She waited a couple of years, and then demanded he buy them from her. She could do it, too—it was all in the damn settlement. But SimTech was broke, and she knew it. She's a bitch, she's always *been* a bitch, and she didn't deserve him."

"She did need the money, though," Asher said. "She'd remarried—"

Dillian muttered, "Quick off the mark."

"—and she'd got her license approved that time. It wasn't pure spite."

"Anyway, there's a happy ending," Cele added. "The heroine rides in from outer space and saves the day. Dilly sold her soul to some God-awful construction project and gave Keir the money to pay Mel off."

Dillian shuddered. "Two years on a deep-sea installation. They pay very well, because no one's mad enough to do it."

"So the shares are safe with Dilly—" Asher said.

"And *she's* sick because SimTech's so successful," Dillian finished, with great satisfaction. "She'll never get another cent from it."

Cele smiled. "The basic problem," she said to Sara in a confidential stage whisper, "is that *no one* is good enough for Keir, on whom the sun rises and sets."

"Rubbish," Dillian said unconvincingly. "I want him to be happy, that's all. You'd want the same thing, wouldn't you, Sara?"

Sara nodded, wondering how Toreth measured up to Dillian's standards. Probably not well—Sara would certainly be horrified if Toreth went anywhere near her sister.

Dillian looked around the room. "I wonder where they are?"

Toreth should have guessed. The doors Warrick opened, ushered him through, and carefully wedged shut behind them with a chair, led into a large room with long buffet tables laid out along two sides. Not surprising in view of the conversation, perhaps, but unexpected in an absolute sense. Fucking in public, with the attendant risk of discovery that Toreth was happy to admit he loved, wasn't in Warrick's usual repertoire. Even more surprising that it was at a SimTech event. Was it an apology for the missing introduction? Toreth grinned, pulled him over for a kiss to start things moving, and then said, "I don't see a meringue, but you could sit on a gateau."

196

"That wasn't quite what I had in mind." The alarm on Warrick's face made Toreth laugh.

"No? You just wanted me to admire the salad?"

"I was thinking of something rather more discreet. And involving removing fewer clothes."

Ignoring the objection, Toreth released him, and then headed for one of the tables. "Unfortunately, I don't keep lube in my dinner jacket pockets," at least not when he had other plans, "and I bet you don't, either. So we'll have to find something else first."

Warrick followed him. "I *really* don't think we should start pillaging the refreshments for immoral purposes."

"Hey, it was your idea to come in here. No one will notice. Aren't we supposed to be having an evening off? Having fun?"

"I'm not. Having an evening off, that is—this is work." Warrick paused, and then smiled. "However, I have no objection to some variations of fun."

Sounded more promising. "Good. How do you feel about mayonnaise?"

Warrick shook his head firmly. "Absolutely not. I am not spending the rest of the evening smelling of egg."

"You can always have a wash."

"True, but that removes half the attraction of the idea."

"Which is?"

"The prospect of walking around with you afterwards, knowing that you've fucked me. That you've come inside me. Feeling taken." He shrugged, managing to sound almost matter-of-fact. "Otherwise, we might as well return to the original plan, wait until we go back to the flat later, and do it there in reasonable comfort. Or preferably discomfort." Toreth swallowed, his mouth suddenly dry. Absently, Warrick picked up a prawn, dipped it in the mayonnaise, and ate it. Toreth watched him lick his lips and lost several seconds. When he tuned in again, Warrick was saying, "And it would be a shame to abuse such excellent mayonnaise. How about the butter?"

"Probably in a chilled dish." Toreth reached over to poke the block. "Yes. Good way to get chilblains somewhere it'd be tricky to explain."

"Mm. And in any case, rather hard." Warrick scored a nail across the butter, and then sucked the resulting slivers from his finger in a way that did nothing for Toreth's self-control. "Almost as hard as I am."

Toreth laughed. "You know you're asking to get bent over that table and fucked right now?"

Warrick turned around, raising an eyebrow, his eyes sparkling with sex and amusement. "And you've only just noticed?"

"No. But what about your present?"

"Mmh. Yes." When Warrick resurfaced from another kiss, he said, "But later. Now and later. If you're up to it," he added faux-casually.

197

"If *I'm* up to it?" Although he'd fully intended simply to tease again, to recreate the mood from the flat and leave Warrick desperate, Toreth suddenly changed his mind. Waiting was fun, but too much self-denial simply wasn't healthy. He cast a more serious eye over the table and said, "What about olive oil?"

"Rather runny."

"I'll be careful."

Warrick shook his head. "You'll get it everywhere."

"Well—" He planted a kiss on Warrick's throat, restraining himself from a bite that would leave a telltale mark. "It's olive oil, or spit and a promise."

"Mmh. What's the promise?"

That I'm going to take your mind off Melissa, if you were thinking of thinking about her.

Toreth picked up the bottle and moved behind Warrick, pinning his thighs to the edge of the table as a reminder of the flat earlier. Warrick wriggled against him, useless from the point of view of escape, exquisitely effective from Toreth's perspective. He leaned in close and whispered, "That I'm going to fuck you hard enough that you'll have to stand up for the rest of the evening."

He pressed forward, and Warrick shivered. When he spoke he was rather breathless. "I'll take the olive oil."

Toreth reached around to unfasten Warrick's trousers and pull them down before doing the same for himself. "Good choice. But first..."

He undid Warrick's bow tie, pulled it out from his collar, and said, "Give me your wrists." Warrick lifted his hands without hesitation, and Toreth wrapped the tie around them before knotting the ends. "There we go." He nuzzled the nape of Warrick's neck and then nipped it, making him jump. "Just a reminder. Now keep still."

Toreth uncapped the bottle and tipped it against his fingers. He misjudged it slightly, and the oil trickled down along them onto his palm, silky smooth, running towards his wrist. He decided not to mention to Warrick that he'd been right about it getting everywhere. In any case, there was no such thing as too slippery, as someone he couldn't remember had once told him. He wiped the excess onto his already aching cock, and then turned his attention to his pseudo-captive. Warrick shivered again as Toreth's fingers touched him, jerking his wrists against the tie, then said, "I don't do this, you know."

"What?" Toreth asked, knowing the answer.

"I don't fuck in public places."

Suddenly, he was acutely aware of the muffled noise of the reception and the danger of discovery thrilled through him. He worked in a finger and said, "I can tell. Relax."

"This is...mmh...this is the first and last time."

Toreth decided not to mention offices. "How much are you willing to bet on that?"

198

"I mean it. It's the only time. So get on with it."

"Now? Are you sure?"

Warrick nodded jerkily. "Yes. Before someone comes in here and—" A laugh cracked his voice as Toreth replaced his finger with his cock and pushed into him. "And finds us—*ah*." He gasped and said, "Careful!"

Muscles suddenly tight—uncomfortably tight—around him. Toreth froze, awkwardly halfway. "Shall I—"

"No! I'm fine. It's simply an unfortunate reflex." Warrick had a particular voice he used for practical discussions in the middle of fucking, serious and disconcertingly detached. Toreth suspected it had something to do with the sim. "Probably due to the prospect of an audience. Give me your hand."

Toreth offered the oily one, and Warrick murmured appreciative comments as he wrapped it around his cock, softened by the unexpected pain. "Sorry," Toreth said, stroking gently.

"No need to be. It's entirely my own fault."

"Yeah, that's exactly what I thought. I did ask."

Warrick shook his head, but didn't reply.

"I don't know why you're worried about it," Toreth said after a minute. "What about the sim? That's fucking in public, if anything is. And recorded."

"That's not the same. That's work. This is most *definitely* pleasure."

Which, judging from the nicely hardening cock in his hand, was indeed becoming the case. A little longer, and Warrick started to move gently, back onto him and forwards into his hand, slowly speeding up as his body relaxed, accepting the penetration. Then Toreth remembered something. "Del Halford."

"Mm?"

"Woman on the buffet table. That was her name. Delanie Halford."

Warrick laughed. "For God's sake . . . I don't believe I'm doing this."

"Don't worry, you're not. You're imagining it."

"Ah. I seem to have a—mmh. An even more vivid imagination than I thought." A few more seconds, then he took a deep breath and nodded. "Now. Not too—oh, Christ, yes. Yes, like that. That's . . . perfect."

Still holding back, Toreth left most of the movement to Warrick, savoring the sight and feel as he quickened the pace. In fact, Warrick seemed in a distinct hurry—a combination, probably, of arousal and a desire not to spend too long here. Toreth followed his lead. He had to admit that the danger of discovery was more appealing than actually being caught, however funny Sara would find it.

Over his own breathing, he heard Warrick panting. He had his head down now, bound hands gripping the table edge, pushing back hard. Toreth ran the heel of his oilless hand down Warrick's spine and back up, again and again. Moving with him easily, relishing the feel of his own orgasm building, listening to the rising moans, until he realized how much of the noise he was making himself. Slipping his hand around Warrick's chest, Toreth pressed him close, burying his face in Warrick's shoulder. Thinking that, even with the overtone of olives, he still smelled better than any other man he'd ever fucked. Close now, so close, and he had only a very faint awareness of something on the table falling over with a crash. Then, far more distinctly, he heard the handle of the door turn, and a muttered exclamation of annoyance.

Warrick's head came up. "Oh, no!"

Stop or not? Toreth wasn't even sure he could, and he certainly didn't care.

"Toreth, stop it," Warrick hissed, bound hands scrabbling awkwardly at the arm around him. "Plastic duck. Plastic *duck*. Toreth!"

Wanting so badly to finish, Toreth pulled out instead, leaving Warrick to pull up his trousers, and grabbed a handful of disposable napkins, wiping oily fingers before he fastened his own clothes. Was that another noise outside?

Warrick said something.

"What?" Toreth asked.

"My hands—untie my hands!"

The frantic note in his voice made Toreth laugh and then he found that he couldn't stop, despite Warrick's furious whispers. He kept laughing—giggling, Sara would no doubt call it—while he struggled with the tightened knots, until by the time they were ready to go he'd given himself hiccups.

When they reached the door and moved the chair, Toreth heard sudden, clear voices on the far side. "I told the girls to leave it unlocked, sir, and they said—"

"*Fuck,*" Toreth said, almost too loud. Beside him, Warrick had gone rather pale, and appeared to have taken root. Toreth grabbed his hand and dragged him to the far end of the room. They ducked behind a screen as the door opened.

"See? It's not locked at all. I have better things to do with my time than—my God! Look at the state of the buffet. What precisely are your staff playing at? The *mess*. It looks as though someone's been shaking the table."

The urge to laugh again was so strong it hurt; the sight of Warrick beside him, now also quivering with suppressed laughter, didn't help. Then there were the hiccups that, somehow, he kept quiet enough that the outraged catering manager didn't hear them.

"You are paid to check these things—that is your *job*."

"I'm sorry, sir. I don't know what's gone wrong. I'll get them back in here straight away."

"I suggest you do that. The doors open to the guests in ten minutes. If the room isn't ready, then you won't have a job to come in for tomorrow."

"Yes, sir."

Footsteps retreated, and Warrick peeped quickly around the edge of the screen. Then he put his mouth to Toreth's ear. "One of them's still here. And stop that bloody *noise*."

Toreth hiccupped again. "I can't."

"Hell." Warrick looked around, and brightened. "There's a door to the outside. Through the curtain."

Keeping a wary eye on the room behind him, Toreth crept forwards (and hiccupped), eased behind the curtain, examined the doors (hiccupping again), and went back to Warrick. "Alarmed. Can't tell if it's switched on." And he hiccupped. Twice.

"For Christ's sake."

Warrick pulled him forward, and kissed him, firmly and deeply. It went on for rather a long time, and gave Toreth plenty of time to decide that not only did Warrick smell better than anyone else did, he tasted better, too. When Warrick finally let go, Toreth waited, but the hiccups seemed to have gone. "Fucking hell."

"Guaranteed patent cure," Warrick whispered, then smiled wryly. "Lissa taught me that."

A stupid stab of jealousy, before he pushed the feeling firmly away. "I'll make sure I get hiccups more often. Has he gone yet?"

Another glance, and Warrick returned, his expression a strange mixture of amusement and unease. "No. And there are two young women examining the table with great suspicion."

"We'll just have to wait until the crowd comes in. Then we can slip out, mingle, and no one will know a thing. Come here."

Warrick handed him off, looking wary. "Why?"

"Because I want to make sure the hiccups don't come back."

"...but if we're not to be confined simply to what we can generate from templates or copy from the real world, creativity is still required. We—every one of us here tonight—are the source of that creativity and the source of the future success of SimTech. Not simply technical creativity, or sim room design, but creativity in finding new applications, new markets, new opportunities for that technology to shine—to show the world what it can do. No single person..."

"He speaks nicely, doesn't he?" Dillian murmured.

Sara nodded, which made the room tilt alarmingly. That was the problem with free alcohol, especially when there was seemingly invisible staff circulating with the endless bottles. How many times had someone refilled her glass without her noticing? It was full again now, of champagne, and she had another sip while she listened to Warrick. He did have a nice speaking voice, although she was having trouble with the words. Smooth, commanding, really rather attractive. Almost made her regret her principles about friends' boyfriends.

"Where's Toreth?" Dillian asked after a while.

Sara looked around, discovering that the two of them were alone. Of course—Asher, as a director, would be on the podium. Cele must also be somewhere at the front, because Sara had a vague idea that Warrick planned to mention her in the speech. But Toreth...Toreth was nowhere in sight. "Dunno." She shrugged. "Probably screwing one of the waiters against a wall in the back."

At first Dillian smiled. "I should hope not."

Sara waved her glass. "Don't worry about it. Happens all the time. 'S just Toreth."

Her matter-of-fact tone must have registered, because Dillian's smile vanished. "Are you serious?"

Oops. "No, 'course not."

"Yes, you are. He's cheating on Keir?"

She would have denied it again, except that the idea of Toreth managing to sustain the kind of relationship that involved keeping secrets and cheating made her giggle.

Dillian's expression hardened. "Is he or isn't he?"

"No. He's not cheating, he's screwing around." She frowned, because that hadn't come out quite how she'd expected. "I mean, it's all okay. It's just Toreth. Warrick knows about it, so it isn't *cheating* cheating. He just...does other people."

"I don't believe you. Keir wouldn't put up with it."

God, she sounded like her brother when she was pissed off. "It doesn't mean anything. He's always done it. He—" He couldn't stop if he wanted to. "Look, they're both grownups. If Warrick doesn't like it, he can leave, can't he?"

"And if I asked Keir about it...?"

Not very subtle. Sara shrugged. "He'd tell you the same thing." Movement, and a rise in the noise level in the large room, caught her attention, and she looked around. The presentation had ended. Now, as the crowd began to fragment, she caught sight of Toreth heading towards them, with a glimpse of Warrick's dark hair beside him. "Look—they're both here," Sara said with relief.

When the pair reached them, Warrick looked flustered, and Sara had a sudden, very clear image of Toreth standing right at the front of the crowd, watching. Smiling. Maybe licking his lips. God knows, he'd had Warrick worked up enough in the car when they picked her up. The present must have been a spectacular success. She wondered briefly what Dillian would make of her brother's taste for chains.

"How much longer before we can go?" Toreth asked.

Warrick checked his watch, then did it again, as if hoping he'd misread it. "An hour, at least. I have to be here to say goodbye to the sponsors."

Toreth grinned. "Good. Sara, want to see if we can grab another ten minutes on the sim?"

As she followed him across the room, she wondered if Dillian was going to say anything.

❖ ❖ ❖

It was, simply, torture. How Toreth, standing with Sara near the main exit doors, could look so relaxed was entirely beyond Warrick. Most things were, right now. Defenses crumbling under the onslaught of crashing waves of lust, he stood in the foyer and said goodbye to the departing sponsors. His eyes were drawn repeatedly to the vast mirror on the wall opposite. His reflection looked so calm, so collected. How Toreth managed it, he didn't know. His own calm came from years of practice in the sim.

This is my body, Warrick thought, my representation in the world, controlled by my mind. I can make it do what I want. What I tell it to do. This is my body.

Only it wasn't. It was Toreth's, willing and desperate and aching to be taken. Thinking about it, about bolts in the wall and blindfolds and Toreth fucking him in chains, blanked out the noise around him, leaving him scrambling for words when the next group approached.

He knew that Toreth must want it, too, after what amounted to six hours of foreplay: the scene in the flat; the taxi; the platform; the interrupted fuck; twelve and a half minutes of adolescent groping behind the screen in the buffet room, which had started off as nostalgically amusing and finished with him almost ready to follow Delanie Halford's example; the speech—

You really ought to think about something else, an internal voice noted dryly.

Thank God for the decorously buttoned dinner jacket. He must have felt like this before, sometime, but he couldn't remember when. Not since shaving was still a novelty, anyway. Hormonally crazed, indeed. Another glance at the mirror. Imperturbable, icy calm. It couldn't possibly be him. Would he guess? he kept wondering. If he shook his reflection's hand, would he guess that only the overriding importance of SimTech, his first and greatest love, held him back from going down on his knees and begging Toreth to finish it *now*.

Dillian had talked to him earlier, and he'd actually found it difficult to listen. The previous half an hour of watching Toreth do every damn provocative thing he could do in public hadn't helped. Sucking his finger. How the hell could the man simply stand against a pillar and suck his finger and make it look *natural*? Like someone with a slightly odd habit listening attentively to the speaker. He'd almost laughed, afterwards, because Dillian had asked him if he was sure about Toreth. Never more sure, he'd wanted to tell her. There had been something wrong, though, something she wanted to ask without saying it. Perhaps he should have tried harder to find out what, but after her contribution to the debacle with Lissa, he didn't feel particularly charitable towards her.

Another glance at his watch, another smooth farewell to another happy sponsor.

He ought to feel worse about Lissa. Under more normal circumstances, he would. How many years now of feeling guilty when he saw her? Every meeting

203

stirring up the lingering feeling that he'd failed her, that he could've done something different, tried harder, accommodated more. But he found that there wasn't space, between the aching need and the memory of steel on his wrists, for the usual unfocused, low-level unhappiness. Lissa didn't deserve to be embarrassed, and he was sorry for that, but nothing more. The surprise of discovering that distracted him temporarily from the gnawing desire. There was a feeling of finality, of something let go at last, which was novel and rather pleasant. Maybe Dillian had been right when she said he'd been hiding in the sim, avoiding his real life. Well, he had Toreth now (or at least, please God, soon), so that should make Dilly happy.

"Keir?" Asher approached, smiling. "I think that was the last one."

He returned the smile automatically. "Good. If I shake any more hands, my arm will fall off."

"I know." She flapped her wrist. "Me too." Looking around the room, she nodded. "It went well. A good evening, I thought."

"*Very* good." The slight edge of hysteria he thought he could hear in the emphasis didn't seem to register with her.

"I got a positive response from everyone I spoke to," Asher continued. "People always make promises they don't keep at events like this, but I think some of them will pan out. Have you got the list of calls to make tomorrow?"

"Yes—safely saved." Then it was goodbye to Asher, and next to the senior staff, thanking them for their efforts towards making the evening a success. After that, he spoke to the complex's management, with more congratulations and appreciation. It was almost a surprise when he discovered that his last duties had been discharged.

As he crossed the foyer again, he heard Sara laughing. Coming up behind the pair, he heard her say, still giggling, "—you in? I *can't.*"

Toreth must have spotted Warrick's reflection in the door, because he nudged her and she stopped. He wondered what it had been about. Nothing good—that much was obvious when Toreth smiled at him, his expression full of anticipation. What now? Then he realized. His duties weren't quite over, because they had to take Sara home. He would bet the cost of booking this hall that Toreth was trying to persuade Sara to help him drag the evening out even further.

"Ready to go?" Toreth asked, with an appallingly bad attempt at innocent inquiry.

"Oh, yes."

That turned the smile into a laugh, and Toreth said, "Don't forget we've got to take Sara home first."

Suddenly he didn't care about image or public propriety. "No."

Toreth blinked at him. "Sorry?"

"No." Warrick turned to Sara. "I'll call you a taxi. Don't worry, I'll pay for it."

She grinned. "You don't have to."

"I insist. I promised you a lift, and you'll get one."

A minute to call the taxi for her, another minute to walk to the car with Toreth, and then the door closed behind them. He sat down opposite Toreth, who stared out of the window, frowning slightly as Warrick gave the address to the system. If Warrick leaned forwards, he could touch Toreth. Could do anything he wanted, now that the evening was over. Or, from another perspective, about to begin at last. "Toreth," he said as the car moved off.

"Quiet."

Fuck me. Fuck me *now*. "Toreth—"

"What did I say?" The voice thrilled through him—game voice, cold and frightening. "Well?"

"Be quiet." Shivering breath. "I'm sorry."

Toreth shook his head. "That's not a very good start, is it?" He sighed. "Kneel down."

Pulse racing so fast he couldn't distinguish one heartbeat from the next, Warrick obeyed, the carpet of the car floor cushioning his knees. He put his hands behind his back, clasping his wrists. Imagining chains.

Toreth smiled. "Close your eyes."

The world changed to sounds and skin—his own quick breathing and Toreth's touch. Fingers held his face gently, positioning his head, thumb brushing over his lips, parting them. Even as he opened his mouth, the hand lifted away. "I told you to do something," Toreth said quietly. "You didn't do it." Then silence, stretching out. He struggled to keep his eyes closed, fighting the temptation to look, because he knew what was coming. Even though he was expecting it, when Toreth hit him he couldn't bite back the moan. "Now stay there, shut up, and wait."

After the flat door closed, they stood in the hall for a long time, Warrick staring at the box still lying on the table. All exactly as it had been when they'd left the flat. In the aching silence of the car, he'd begun to wonder if it had been real after all. From the corner of his eye, he could see Toreth watching him. Finally Toreth said, "Fetch me the cuffs."

Lifting the foam, Warrick uncovered the manacles and stopped, hypnotized by the sheer beauty of the metal, until Toreth said, "Don't you want it? Do you want me to put them away again?" No hint in his voice that he might not mean it. Warrick snatched up the cuffs and offered them. Toreth held them up by the central ring, his head tilted to one side as he contemplated them. "Pretty, aren't they?" he murmured.

Warrick took a deep breath. "Please."

A few more unbearably long seconds before Toreth looked up. "Did you say something?"

"Please, put them on me."

Slow smile. "Turn round. Hands behind you."

Soon...soon...oh, God—now. The steel closed around his wrists, even better than it had been the first time. His hands—his whole body—shook and, distantly, he heard Toreth swearing at him, telling him to stop fucking around. Clenching his fists, he managed to still them long enough for Toreth to secure the locks. Toreth's hands slid up his arms, over his shoulders, and unfastened his bow tie. It fell to the floor, and then his shirt collar was loosened. "Tell me." A whisper, lips pressed against his ear. "Did you do this with Melissa?"

"No."

"Never? Tell me the truth—I'll know if you're lying."

Warrick swallowed, trying to pull his scattered thoughts together, to marshal them into something like a coherent sentence. "Sometimes. Sometimes we used to play with belts or scarves...with blindfolds." Always a treat for him, not because Lissa wanted it. "Or—but she didn't really...no. Not like this. Never like this."

"Good." Toreth's hands moved down again and circled his wrists above the metal, fingers digging in. "Did she buy you chains?"

"No."

"Did she hurt you?"

"No." Not like this.

"Good. Very good." Almost inaudible, a caress of breath. Then Toreth let go and stepped away. "Now, close your eyes."

Anticipation thrilling through him, he tried to listen, to work out where Toreth was, but he didn't hear even a hint of movement, or a clink of chain. The touch of metal on his throat, shockingly unexpected, almost sent him to his knees—might have done so, in fact, if a hissed, "Keep still!" hadn't frozen him, trembling, in place.

Click of the lock. Tug of the manacles behind him and the band around his throat dug in a little as the chains locked together. Then it was finished—complete—and the world slid away from him for a moment. Hands on his shoulders again brought him back to awareness, fingers digging in and pushing him down to his knees. "Open your mouth."

At that moment, he honestly didn't care, but part of his mind, still not fully subsumed in the game, noted that Toreth must have washed at some point since the buffet, because he tasted clean and smelled of only a faintest hint of olive oil. Then he forgot everything as Toreth's hands tangled in his hair and pulled him forwards. He struggled to keep his balance, awkward with bound hands, the collar and the cock filling his mouth combining to choke him. Panic rose briefly until Toreth eased away, giving him a moment's respite before he thrust in again.

Breathe—find the rhythm, each stroke easier to take than the last. Accepting it. Letting Toreth do what he wanted, because that was what *he* wanted. Surrendering. Submit and be taken. Falling deeper into the game until it was easy and natural. Even when Toreth's hands tightened in his hair, crushing him close as he came hard and deep into his throat, Warrick didn't choke. He swallowed, remembering not to try to breathe—performing perfectly. It brought a flush of triumph, pleasure at success, which surfaced briefly though the dizzying arousal before sinking away.

When Toreth released him, Warrick leaned against his leg, panting, twisting his wrists to feel the strength of the steel. Perfect, wonderful, never better, and it had never been this good with Lissa. Unfair but undeniably true. If she'd known—if *he'd* known—what he needed, would she have bought him chains?

"Not bad," Toreth said. His voice was almost level, barely out of breath. "You're learning. Almost good enough to deserve something in return."

"Please." All he could manage.

"Please?" He pulled Warrick to his feet, and pushed him back—two, three steps and he collided with the wall. Toreth moved in close, resting his cheek against his, the slight roughness a further excitement. Pinning Warrick against the wall with one hand, the other roaming over his body, finally settling against his crotch, rubbing in short, fast movements. Somehow, Warrick formed the words. "Mmh . . . no." His body, with ideas of its own and hungry for the contact, pushed forwards against Toreth's hand. Yes, yes, yes, please. No. He wanted . . . "You promised—the bedroom."

Toreth laughed. "And what the fuck does that matter? You come when I say, where I say."

"No. No, please." Fighting it for real, struggling in the unyielding chains, because he didn't want to come now, didn't want it to finish yet, here in the hall when there was so much . . . but Toreth held him easily, and that alone was almost enough to tip him over the edge, even without the skillful hand stroking him towards orgasm. He was still resisting when the sensation ripped through him, wringing a scream from him that, for once, he heard. God Almighty. Was he always that loud?

A minute passed, and Warrick found he still couldn't breathe properly, the high not fading. Toreth's hands on him—the words coming back to him from the start of the evening—the manacles around his wrists—the tightness of the collar—the bolts waiting for him in the bedroom. If Toreth should walk away from the game after tonight, walk away from him, the memory of this evening might be enough to last the rest of his life. He opened his eyes to find that Toreth had stepped back and stood watching him intently, calculatingly. When Warrick could manage the words, he said, "Don't stop. Keep it going."

That brought out a satisfied smile. Toreth caught hold of the collar and tugged him sharply forwards. "What makes you think I'm *ever* going to stop?"

207

Part Four: Conversation (Reprise)

Warrick's voice woke Toreth from the middle of a complicated dream involving chains made of meringue. "Are you *still* asleep?" A loud closing of the door followed Warrick's question, then a wash of light as the windows cleared.

"Doesn't look like it, does it?" Toreth considered rolling over and sticking his head under the pillow, but he didn't think it would help. It seemed particularly unfair, since it was his own bed. He heard Warrick cross the room, and then the noise of something being set down on the table by the bed. Surrendering to the inevitable, he opened his eyes. "What is it?" he asked, blinking at the light.

"Breakfast. Or, possibly more accurately, a very early lunch."

"Lunch? What time is it?"

"Half past eleven."

Toreth closed his eyes again. "That's not fucking lunchtime. Especially not on Sunday. I'm going back to sleep."

"Suit yourself. You might want to have a look at the tray first."

He was about to express his opinions a little more forcefully, when a rather appetizing smell drifted across the bed. It smelled like ... He sat up and found Warrick waving his hand over the tray, wafting the aroma towards him. "Steak?" Toreth asked.

"Steak sandwiches, with onions. Fresh juice. Coffee. Pancakes under the cloth."

Propping himself up on the pillows, Toreth took the tray and wondered where the contents had come from. Not from his kitchen, that was for sure. His flat didn't hold anything edible or drinkable that hadn't been thoroughly preprocessed, or fermented and distilled. Toreth tried a bite of sandwich. "Good," he said, unnecessarily, because it always was.

"Thank you," Warrick replied gravely. He took off his borrowed shirt, looked around for somewhere to put it, and then settled for dropping it where he'd probably found it, on the already crowded floor. Toreth made a mental note that he ought to have some laundry done at some point in the next week.

"Sorry about the mess," he said with his mouth full, as Warrick went to lie across the foot of the bed.

Warrick raised an eyebrow. "No apology required." He surveyed the room, the clutter of dirty clothes on the floor contrasting with the clean ones neatly hung. "I couldn't live like this, but then I don't. And although I do admit to a faint curiosity regarding the color of your carpet, I think I'd be rather disconcerted to come here one day and actually find out."

Toreth ignored him. "Did you have all this in the car last night?" he inquired, waving his hand over the tray.

"No. I went out and picked it up this morning, along with the griddle to cook it on. You never have anything fit to eat, so I thought it'd be a change. I also thought I might leave the griddle here, if that's all right with you."

"Yeah, fine." Except for a faintly horrifying implication of...nothing he wanted to spoil the morning by thinking about. At least it wasn't curtains. "What about yours?" he asked, as a distraction.

"I had *my* breakfast two hours ago. I had some calls to make. By getting up at eight, I finished everything. So now...I'm at your disposal."

"*Eight*? After last night?" He picked up a pancake and folded it in half, melted butter dripping onto the tray. "When did we go to sleep?"

"Three, I think. Perhaps half past. However, that still means you've been asleep for almost eight hours, which is plenty."

"Easy for you to say." Toreth licked butter off his fingers, reached behind his shoulder, and tapped the chain hanging from the bolt, making it clink gently. "The trouble with this is that I'm the one who ends up doing all the work."

"Mm." Warrick closed his eyes for a couple of seconds, and then opened them halfway. "True. However, I'm not to blame for your lack of imagination."

"No, maybe not." Balancing the tray with one hand, Toreth pulled the sheet aside. He ran the ball of his foot over Warrick's shoulder, then pressed it between his shoulder blades until he went down flat on the bed, his breathing already quickening. Toreth smiled, working a thread of danger into his voice. "After all, I can do anything I want...and you'll do whatever you're told. Won't you?"

"Yes." He felt Warrick shiver.

"Well...I'll have to think about it." Toreth considered putting the tray down, but he hadn't finished yet and he didn't fancy ending up fucking in a bed full of crumbs. So he settled for moving the juice and coffee to safety on the bedside table, and then shifted his foot higher while he started another sandwich.

There were faint red marks on the back of Warrick's neck, reminders of the collar last night, which would, in Toreth's judgment, fade by Monday. He pressed his foot down, a little too hard to qualify as a massage, but not hard enough to hurt. Not yet. Warrick had turned his head away, but his breathing was a perfect telltale. After a minute, he saw Warrick's hips start to grind down into the bed. "Keep still," Toreth ordered.

He kept playing as he continued his breakfast, circling more firmly into the nape of Warrick's neck, down and up his spine, watching as his hands began to tighten on the edge of the mattress with the effort not to move. Lazy Sunday morning fun, which still had an enjoyable novelty for Toreth. He wondered if Warrick had done it before with anyone. Relaxed weekends spent fucking with Melissa, maybe. Or on reflection, maybe not. On the brief meeting last night, she'd struck Toreth as a withholder, doling out sex as a bribe or a reward for good behavior. One kind of domination, he supposed. This was more fun.

By the time Toreth finished eating, Warrick's breath was catching on a whimper every half dozen breaths. Toreth's own breathing had become none too steady. Still, he realized, once more he was putting all the effort into the proceedings, even if it wasn't very much effort in an absolute sense. And even if was reaping a rather gratifying return on investment. Besides, something Warrick had said earlier finally sparked a question in his mind. Without taking his foot away from Warrick's neck, he lowered the tray onto the floor. "Turn over."

"I can't. Your—"

"Not interested." Toreth didn't release the pressure. "Turn over."

Despite the difficulties involved, Warrick obeyed, ending up with Toreth's foot against his throat. With experimental care, Toreth pressed down until he saw Warrick's eyes go wider and his lips open to stop it. Then he lifted his foot away and sat up. "At my disposal?" he asked, dropping the edge from his voice.

Warrick shook himself, shedding the role if not the arousal, and then rolled onto his side and looked up at him. He rubbed his throat, and coughed carefully. "That's what I said. Anything you like."

Adding that to the breakfast, Toreth came up with another question. "Okay. What do you want?"

Warrick smiled sheepishly. "That obvious, is it? Well...to ask you a favor."

Toreth laughed; he'd only been half sure of his guess. "Fuck. Really? What?"

"Sorry. I should just have asked. But I didn't think it would hurt to get you in a good mood first."

"Feed me, fuck me, and then ask me when I'm half asleep?"

"Something like that. Would you prefer me to ask while you're awake?"

"Ah...yes. Ask first, fuck afterwards. Or during, if it's going to be a long question." He slid down the pillows and closed his eyes. "I'm listening."

"All right." Warrick moved around to lie next to him and placed his hand flat on Toreth's stomach. Toreth tensed the muscles as Warrick dug his fingers in.

"Mm. Very nice," Warrick murmured.

"Favor?"

"Yes, of course. There's another SimTech event coming up in a few weeks' time." The fingers wandered off, gentle and only mildly distracting. "It's only a small thing. A social dinner for the directors and a few sponsors and partners."

"And?"

"And I'd like you to come to it."

"That's a favor?" For a moment, Toreth was nonplussed. By the time he'd made the connection to "and partners," Warrick was speaking again.

"I'd like you to come to it, with me. Just you. As my...as in—arrive with me, leave with me. Be with me."

It was odd how he was growing used to this. He waited out the irrational rush of fear—expected and therefore not so disconcerting—then said, "As your what?"

"I, ah, didn't think of anything. Did you?"

210

"Um . . . no." He thought about it again, but everything serious seemed terribly wrong. "How about 'regular fuck?'"

"Regular f—" Warrick spluttered, then started again. "I can't introduce you to people—sponsors—as my regular fuck!"

Toreth smiled, his eyes still closed. "That's your problem. Works for me."

Warrick sighed and then said, "I can't promise it'll be very exciting, and there'll definitely be no sex in the food this time. But will you come?"

"Sure. Doesn't sound too taxing."

"Oh . . . well, good."

He put his hands behind his head, deliberately relaxing, and opened his eyes to find Warrick watching him with a mix of surprise and wariness. "What?" he asked.

Warrick shook his head. "Nothing."

Oh no, not nothing. You were expecting me to panic because you mentioned something that had a hint of . . . and you were right. Before he could finish the thought, the adrenaline kick washed back through him. Fight or flight, he thought. Or . . . "So is that it, then? I said yes, so I don't get the fuck?"

Warrick grinned. "No, you get the fuck. Anything you like, as I said."

"Mmm." Toreth stretched out, anticipation chasing away the lingering unease. "Surprise me."

Family

❖

Dear Val,

Thank you for your presence at George's funeral yesterday. I&I was always the biggest part of his life, and I know he would have been touched that so many from I&I and especially the General Criminal section chose to attend.

I'd like to thank you especially for your kindness in the days after George's death. I won't say thank you for last night. That was something that I don't have the words for. To have someone spend that difficult night with me, to wake up and have someone beside me to comfort me and take the pain away, if only for a while, meant more than I can say.

But I hope you'll understand that I can't rush into something now. Thank you for being so understanding last night, and for suggesting that a letter might the easiest way for me to let you know what I decided about us. It has been, and your kindness is, again, so much appreciated.

Yours with love, and friendship,
Jillian

Mike Belkin looked up distrustfully as he finished reading the note aloud. "And if I get my admin to run it through the system and verify the sender's signature?"

Toreth gestured expansively around the coffee room. "Go right ahead. It'll probably save me time later. I've got a dozen more people to collect from and some of them are bound to be suspicious, welshing bastards, too."

"Okay, I believe you. I should know better. 'Your kindness in the days after George's death'?" Belkin snorted in disgust. "You set it up, didn't you?"

"Pays to plan ahead, if you know what I mean."

There was general grumbling from the seniors gathered around Toreth—he caught the odd word that sounded like "cheating"—but most were already reaching into their pockets. Chevril, sitting at the other end of the coffee table, was the only one smiling; he'd refused to risk a cent on the strength of Jillian Lewis's virtue, and was obviously reaping the satisfaction of an unopened wallet.

"Fifty, wasn't it?" Belkin sighed, then handed over the folded notes. "And I thought I'd be safe by asking for written evidence."

Hepburn shook his head. "And having to do her on the day of the funeral, too. What did you do, slip something in the sherry?"

"I don't make you take the bets, I just take your money." Toreth pocketed the notes and grinned. "That everyone? Tell you what, I'll buy you all a drink this evening to celebrate. In memory of good old George."

"The useless tosser," Belkin added. That produced some laughter, but most of the seniors were still smarting from their losses. Looking around, Toreth decided it would be a good few months before he'd be able to pull another stunt like that. But they'd forget. They always did.

Half past ten. Watches were checked, coffee mugs drained, and the group broke up, the paras heading back to their offices and interrogation rooms for the rest of the morning.

Back in his office, Toreth read the message for the thirtieth time. It had been waiting for him when he'd arrived at work, but he'd left it, hoping vaguely that it might have gone away by the time he'd had coffee and collected his winnings.

"Sorry to decline, but I'm spending New Year with the family. However, you are welcome to come with me. Let me know yes or no as soon as you can."

His first impulse had been "no." Which, he supposed, was why it was a mail and not a call.

December was never Toreth's favorite time of year. Someone had already tacked cheap and nasty decorations up in the coffee room, and the shops were full of holiday crap, had been for months. Now this unappealing invitation: a New Year holiday spent with someone else's family. Toreth tried to imagine introducing Warrick to *his* parents. His mind slid away from the sheer awfulness of the concept, so instead he imagined fucking Warrick in their flat, good and loud. That was easier to think about, and the idea of his mother's face the next morning almost made him smile. That would really give the bitch something to complain about. But happy as that idea was, he was avoiding the issue. Unusually, he felt the need for advice, so he called Sara in and showed her the message. "Do you think I should go?"

She read it and frowned. "What the hell are you asking me for?"

He sighed. "Forget it."

"No, sorry. I, er...yeah, why not? Dillian's a laugh, and she makes the rest of them sound okay."

That was a surprise. "I didn't know you knew her that well."

"I've been out with her. Well, with Cele, actually, but Dillian was there a couple of times. She's okay. Anyway, why not go?"

"It just seems a bit..."

"A bit what?" Sara rolled her eyes. "God Almighty, not again. It's just an invite for New Year—he hasn't bought you a bloody ring."

He stared at her in bemusement. She was in a bitch of a mood about something. Come to think of it, she hadn't been in the coffee room earlier. "What the fuck's wrong with you?"

"Oh, nothing." She looked down at her hands. "Bad evening. Bad morning. Bad breakup in between. Basically not a good time to see happy people. Especially not happy people acting like idiots."

"No need to take it out on me—I only asked a fucking question. Forget I ever mentioned it." He reached out and touched the screen, and the message disappeared. "Do you want to go out somewhere tonight?" He saw the refusal coming, so he added, "Just you and me. I'll buy." It would give him an excuse to get away from the others after only one round.

She hesitated, then shrugged. "Yeah. Yeah, sure." She looked up and smiled faintly. "Thanks." On her way out she said, "Go do the family thing. You might even enjoy it."

So, on the strength of that, he said yes.

After he'd sent off the reply saying yes, he nearly sent another saying no. He decided the most relaxing way to spend the next few days would be simply to pretend that it wasn't going to happen. Consequently, Toreth felt almost surprised to find himself sitting beside Warrick as the SimTech car drove them through New London.

He'd been seriously delayed at work (not his fault, but that didn't matter), and although he'd been able to give Warrick plenty of warning, it made an inauspicious start to the trip. There had been another bad moment when he'd come down from his flat into the chilly afternoon air and seen the presents stacked in the back of the car. He had something for Warrick, which he'd bought weeks ago, but he hadn't even thought about anyone else. "I didn't buy anything," he'd said.

"Bought, wrapped, and labeled. I'll send you the bill when we get back." He should've known that Warrick's efficiency would be up to the job, but he'd had a fleeting feeling of disappointment at not having an excuse to back out.

Rather than sit with nothing to do, Toreth had brought some work along. As he was officially on holiday, it wasn't anything too taxing, but he managed to pass the time easily enough in assessing interrogation transcripts from trainee sessions. He'd volunteered to do it because he liked to keep an eye on the upcoming juniors. This year's intake was shaping up quite well. He made a note of the names of a few of the more promising recruits. After New Year he'd see about wangling their assignment to his team during their hands-on training, to take a closer look at them.

Even with full traffic guidance on the crowded roads, the New Year exodus slowed their progress. But eventually, deep into the suburban hinterlands of New London, they moved off the motorway. In the combination of street lighting and a light evening mist, the endless expanses of housing looked vaguely sinister. "How much further?"

Warrick looked up from his own screen, where he was reading something technical-looking. "Mm?" He glanced out of the window. "Oh, nearly there. Few minutes."

Toreth looked out of the window as well, trying to remember if he'd ever made it to this particular area during any of his investigations. Out of the corner of his eye, he caught Warrick looking at him and smiling. "What?" Toreth asked.

"Nothing. I can't believe you're here."

Toreth laughed, sounding nervous even to himself. "Me neither."

"I owe Sara an apology, you know. She said you'd do it. I told her you'd disappear at the last minute. I did wonder, to be honest, when you left the message saying you were going to be late."

Toreth felt a glow of satisfaction, not much spoiled by the fact that Warrick was almost certainly saying it precisely for that effect. "So you don't know me as well as you think."

"Apparently not."

The car made another turn, into a narrower street lined with large houses, not flats. They were tightly packed, but they had spaces for private cars and a hint of small gardens behind. It looked very middle-class suburban and respectable and not at all somewhere Toreth felt at home. "What are they like?" he asked.

"Like? Well..." Warrick hesitated, and it occurred to Toreth that *he* might have grounds for unease as well. That made him feel a little better. "They're fine," Warrick continued. "They're—ah. You can see for yourself soon. We're here."

It wasn't until Dillian opened the door that Toreth wondered how many people "family" was. He was moderately sure that Warrick's father was dead, and he remembered Warrick mentioning a niece during the Selman case, so presumably Dillian wasn't his only sibling, but beyond that he had no idea. It had all been in Warrick's security file, of course, but he'd long forgotten the details. It wasn't the kind of thing that interested him. He ought to have asked, or looked up their files, but he hadn't done either. Warrick didn't as a rule offer up unrequested information.

Dillian looked delighted to see Warrick, and then somewhat less pleased to see Toreth standing next to him.

"Come in." She gave Toreth a polite peck on the cheek and then a warmer hug to her brother. "We were wondering where you'd got to."

"Sorry," Warrick said. "Unavoidable delay."

Dillian looked at Toreth, but didn't say anything. The last couple of times Toreth had seen Dillian, which had been brief enough meetings, he'd gained the impression that his continued presence in Warrick's life was becoming unwelcome.

As the door closed behind them, half a dozen children spilled into the hallway, heralded by a thunder of footsteps on the stairs and a shrieking chorus of "Uncle Keir!"

Toreth looked around in what was nearly a bid to find an escape route only to see Dillian standing in front of the door, watching him with a slight smile. He must have looked as uncomfortable as he felt. Fortunately, the initial target of the attack was Warrick, who seemed remarkably unperturbed by it. After a short while, though, the presence of a stranger registered and the group clustered together for mutual protection. Six pairs of inquisitive eyes fixed on Toreth. "Who's *he*?" demanded a girl of about six, who looked as if she would grow up to be a clone of Dillian.

"'He' is a friend of mine," Warrick said. "And 'his' name is Val Toreth."

Her eyes widened. "He can't be. That's *my* name!" she exclaimed, somewhere between delight and indignation.

"I shall endeavor not to get the two of you mixed up. Although that means I shall have to call you Valeria."

The girl frowned. "No." After a moment's consideration she decided, "He can be *Uncle* Val." Toreth didn't look at Dillian, who sounded to be having trouble breathing.

Warrick handed his bags to Dillian and picked the girl up, provoking a chorus of disappointment from the others. "I think that sounds like a very satisfactory solution," he said seriously, then addressed the rest of the flock. "Now, we really ought to go and say hello to the grownups. Why don't you show me where they are?" The pack closed in around the three adults as they went down the hallway.

"Did you have to say that?" Toreth muttered, trying not to trip up over any of them. Valeria hung out of Warrick's arms, practically upside down, pulling faces at the other children.

"Trust me, it's far, far better than letting her think you don't like it."

"If you tell Sara, I'll kill you. And her." Although he might have to kill Sara anyway for talking him into this.

Warrick grinned. "I wouldn't dream of it."

They reached a half-open door, and Warrick deposited Valeria back into the seething horde. To Toreth's intense relief, Dillian shepherded them away somewhere and relative silence fell. Now he could hear voices from beyond the door.

216

When they entered the room, he couldn't decide if it was better or worse than the earlier scrutiny. The looks weren't quite as intent, but there was a lot more knowledge behind them. Who he was, what he did for a living, and what he was doing here, with Warrick. He wondered what Dillian had told them. There were far more people in the room than he had expected. Some of them were easy to place, like the woman who stood first and came over to greet them. She had graying dark hair and a determinedly friendly smile, and she simply had to be Dillian's mother. It was like looking at an age-enhanced picture in a long-standing open arrest file.

"Keir, darling." She hugged him, and he returned it warmly. "We were starting to wonder if you were going to make it."

"I'm sorry. Unavoidable, but we're here now." He let her go. "Mother, this is Val Toreth."

"It's wonderful to meet you, Val." She took his hand in both of hers. "I'm Kailynna Avens, but please call me Kate. Let me introduce you to everyone."

The rest of the introductions went past in a slight blur, and Toreth concentrated on getting the more important names stashed in his memory. Slightly to his surprise (and relief), he recognized two of the faces: Asher Linton and Cele. Asher smiled at him, and Cele waved and winked when Kate said her name.

"I'm afraid it must be a little intimidating, meeting us all at once like this," Kate said at length.

"Not at all," Toreth lied.

"Good. I'm so sorry we haven't met before, but it's a long way, I suppose, and Keir's always so busy and, well..." The sentence trailed off and Toreth noticed Warrick's pained expression. "But you're here now," Kate finished decisively. "Have a seat. Can I get you something to drink?"

Please, God, yes. Just give me the whole fucking bottle. "That would be lovely, thanks."

She reeled off a surprisingly long list of options and he picked something to fit in with the drinks he could see in evidence around the room. After supplying the gin and tonic, Kate disappeared somewhere with Warrick. Toreth braced himself for a barrage of questions about his life and work, but it didn't happen. The conversation simply returned to what he presumed had been in progress when he entered. At the same time, he didn't feel particularly excluded. The family seemed to be content to let him join in or not, as he pleased.

The room, like the rest of the house he'd seen so far, was tastefully, if not recently, decorated. Light, plainly painted walls, dark floor. A few pictures that looked moderately expensive but not new, with the exception of a recent family portrait over the mantelpiece. The only other notable feature was a large rug, a thick pile with a simple geometric design in dark colors. Toreth guessed it was made from natural, undyed wool and hence more expensive than the rest of the décor. A gift from Warrick, he suspected.

217

Professional assessment over, he looked around, fixing the names to faces. The woman Toreth had sat next to was Jen, greeted by Warrick as Aunt Jen, and clearly Kate's sister. A few years younger, Toreth guessed, and with a sardonic smile that reminded him of Warrick. He caught himself starting to think she was attractive for her age, and stamped firmly on the idea. At least he could try to limit the trouble he could get himself into. She seemed friendly, but he had the distinct feeling of being carefully assessed. After shaking his hand, telling him to call her Jen, and inquiring whether he would mind if she called him Val (something Kate hadn't done, making him feel obliged to say it was fine), she said, "Have you met any of the family before?"

"Only Dillian. And I know Asher Linton and Cele." She nodded, apparently unsurprised, and he felt suddenly certain that Dillian had been talking about him. Nothing to be done about that, except to make the best impression he could now. Although, briefly, he wondered why the hell he cared.

"Did you know Cele is an artist?" Jen asked. When he nodded, she added, "She painted the portrait over there." She waved towards the family portrait and, obediently, he examined the picture more closely. Warrick, Dillian, Kate, and Jen, posed to emphasize the startling family resemblance. Toreth didn't know or care a great deal about art in general, but he had a lot of experience with likenesses, and the portraits were superb—not only accurate, but also capturing the personality of the subjects. Witnesses would find it easy to identify any of the four from the picture.

"It's very good," he said.

Jen nodded. "Cele is extremely successful these days." She smiled. "I certainly couldn't afford any of her work, but that was a gift for Kate's birthday."

"From Warrick?"

There was a brief pause, and then Jen nodded. "It was a joint gift from Keir and Dillian, actually." The name caused the hesitation, he decided. Warrick, here, clearly still referred to his late father. Well, they'd have to cope. Some compromises were out of the question. After a moment Jen said, "Did you get all the names, or would you like me to go round everyone again?"

"Please."

Within the family, the most surprising face belonged to a man identified as Warrick's brother. He looked so unlike Warrick and Dillian that Toreth wasn't at all surprised that he didn't share a surname with either of them. Tarin Marriot. Vague memories of the security file stirred, but failed to produce anything concrete. Had their mother remarried after Warrick's father's death? But Tarin looked older than Warrick and Dillian. He really ought to have looked at the file again. For one thing, even across the length of the generously sized room, he could feel the hostility coming from the man. He'd barely even nodded when Kate introduced them. Now he was concentrating on his conversation, ignoring Toreth pointedly.

218

There were two other couples around Toreth's age, cousins of some kind, who turned out to own three of the six children between them. Valeria was Tarin's daughter, although his wife wasn't present, for reasons unknown (or at least unrevealed to strangers). Toreth found himself wondering why Tarin wasn't included in the family portrait. He considered asking Jen for some background, but decided that the question had the potential to cause far more trouble than it was worth. An older couple had also been introduced as an aunt and uncle. One of them was probably a sibling of Kate's, or of one of her husbands. The man looked a little like Tarin, so say a brother of his father.

It seemed somehow absolutely like Warrick that he would have an inconveniently complicated family. By the time he had a first approximation of the family arrangements fixed in his mind, Toreth could feel a slight headache starting. Why hadn't he looked it all up? Why had he accepted the invitation at all? The room was large, but with nearly twenty adults present, it was beginning to feel crowded. Normally he liked crowds, but this felt too loud, too unfamiliar. Or possibly too familiar. No. He wasn't following that thought. It wasn't even as if the gathering was anything like New Year at home—or rather at his parents' home. For one thing, people were smiling. Drinking and smiling. Drinking, smiling, and talking to each other. Sara's suggestion that he might even enjoy it seemed unlikely, but the situation wouldn't be improved by starting with the assumption that he would have a fucking awful time.

One thing that set it apart from New Year with his parents was that only about half of the people present were relatives of one kind or another. The rest were assorted family friends, including Cele and Asher Linton. He wondered what a business partner of Warrick's was doing here, before he remembered that Asher was also an old friend of Dillian's.

After a while Kate and Dillian reappeared, with a subset of the children. To Toreth's relief they seemed to have the hang of sitting quietly and not bothering the adults. Surprisingly, Dillian sat down on the sofa between himself and Jen. Perhaps she wanted to keep an eye on him. He listened to the conversations going on around him, contributing from time to time. He paced his drinking carefully, because Kate seemed happy to refill glasses as soon as they were empty.

After half an hour or so, he even managed to coax a few sentences from Tarin, although, from his tone, conversation wouldn't be enough to fix whatever the hell his problem was. In fact, Toreth doubted anything would, short of a thorough m-f. Tempting idea. Warrick could have mentioned something, he thought irritably. But then, on that logic, he could have asked. He decided to write it off and simply ignore Tarin.

Toreth had been sitting in silence for a while when Valeria appeared beside him and, before he could fend her off, climbed onto his knees. He sat, frozen. She made herself comfortable, then turned dark, serious eyes up to him. "Tell me a story, Uncle Val."

Beside him, Dillian snorted with suppressed laughter and hastily turned away to talk to Jen.

"Um." Toreth's mind went blank. The only stories he knew were jokes, which were all highly unsuitable for six-year-olds. "I don't know any."

She gave him a withering look, which was obviously part of the family heritage. "You must know *one*."

He cast around, hit on something. "Do you know where Mars is?"

"Yes. It's a planet."

"Right. Well, I lived there for a while."

"Auntie Dillian went to Mars," she said, plainly unimpressed. "She's an en-gin-eer." She pronounced each syllable carefully. "Are you?"

"No." Perhaps it was the unaccustomed circumstances, or perhaps he hadn't been as careful with the drinks as he'd thought, but none of his usual half-truths came forward. "I'm a para-investigator."

She played with this fascinating new word for a while. "What's a para-'vesti-gator?" she asked at length.

Oh, Christ. I investigate crimes, cover them up for corporates, and sometimes I torture prisoners. Your uncle hates it, but he fucks me anyway because I can make him come so hard he practically passes out. "Er...I ask people questions."

"All *day*?" From her expression, Valeria considered that to be about the most wonderful job she could imagine.

"More or less." Time to change the subject.

Before he could even attempt it, the girl turned around and addressed the nearest adult, who of course was Dillian. "Auntie Dillian?" She reached out and tugged her sleeve. "Auntie Dilly? I'm going to be a para-'vestigator."

Unfortunate that the announcement coincided with a lull in the conversation. Dillian went ashen pale, then spots of color flushed high up on her cheeks. She stood up quickly, looking around as if desperately hoping that no one else had heard, then snatched Valeria up out of his lap. "Let's go help Uncle Keir with dinner."

Wonderful. Dillian even more pissed off with him, and it wasn't even his fault this time. She should have taken the little brat away earlier, instead of laughing about it. Before he could frame a suitable apology or explanation, she had left the room. A couple of the adults followed her out, including Tarin. He looked furious enough to choke. There was a brief silence, and then the conversation started up again, slowly. This time Toreth didn't try to join in.

He had just decided to go out—to get some fresh air, to find Warrick, or possibly to go home—when Warrick opened the door. "You'll all be glad to hear that dinner's ready."

220

In the dining room, he was mildly surprised to see the long table laden with food, but no place settings. A buffet, of course, because even considering the size of the table it would be too small for everyone to sit down. As a guest, he seemed to be expected to go first. Picking up a plate, he inspected the food. He'd thought that Kate might be the source of Warrick's enthusiasm for fiddly recipes, but instead the dishes on offer seemed rather plain, but looked good, with plenty of fresh bread. The main item was a couple of large heated pots filled with something stewlike. His memory eventually dredged up the name cassoulet. The last time he'd eaten it had been at an expensive restaurant to which he'd taken an Int-Sec Internal Investigator in ultimately fruitless pursuit of a career-enhancing fuck. There it had consisted of a tiny portion with unnecessary decoration. Here there was more than enough, even considering the number of guests. He filled his plate, and looked for somewhere to sit.

Warrick came over. "We usually go into the kitchen."

"We" turned out to be Dillian (who looked less than pleased to see him but didn't say anything), Cele, and Asher. Warrick uncorked a bottle of wine and filled glasses. Then he checked his watch and raised his glass. "Happy New Year, less three hours and twenty-seven minutes."

They toasted the time and sat down to eat. With Cele, Dillian, and Warrick at the same table, Toreth reflected, you couldn't fault the scenery. He tried a mouthful of cassoulet, then turned to Warrick. "It's very good. One of yours?"

He shook his head. "Mother. She does it every year."

"Everyone comes round for dinner tonight," Dillian said. "Friends and family. And then the family stays over for New Year's Day. We have a fancy lunch then. Keir and Aunt Jen do that." Setting it out for the outsider.

Warrick turned to Dillian. "Mother said you'd been offered a job at the university?"

She nodded. "Visiting lectureship. I've decided to accept."

"Won't you get bored, stuck here on Earth?" Toreth asked, wondering how much more of her he'd get to see. In terms of time, that was, obviously.

"It'll make a nice change of pace, I think. And being at the university, I'll be able to see Keir. And the two of you," she said to Asher and Cele. No mention of him.

"What about Europa?" Warrick asked.

"The main contract's sunk without trace in a bureaucratic quagmire somewhere in the Department of Planning and Development. As far as I can tell, because it'll be the first European installation there, no one can work out the procedure for licensing it. Either that, or there's another corporation trying to steal the contract." She shrugged. "Not my problem, anyway. If it ever resurfaces, the university will release me, but I doubt it'll happen now."

Asher shook her head. "I hope you had decent penalty clauses."

"Oh, yes. They'll be paying *my* fees, whatever happens in the end. Best kind of job, actually."

The conversation turned financial, a topic that bored Toreth intensely. Cele didn't seem to have much of an interest in it, either, because she turned to him and asked, "How's my favorite Seven Inches?"

"You're still short."

She laughed. "If you say so."

"They're very well. And so am I. You?"

"Not bad, and better for seeing you." She looked around the table. "My God. Between you, Dilly, and Keir there are so many beautiful cheekbones here I could die and go straight to heaven. Don't suppose I could persuade you to commission a picture of the three of you, so I could justify spending the time on it?"

"Jen said you were expensive."

She grinned. "The pictures aren't cheap, either. But I'll give you a discount."

"I'll think about it." Apart from the expense, it wasn't actually a bad idea for a future New Year present. Warrick would probably love it. Just the two of them, without Dillian, would be better, considering the poses that sprang to mind. Or, on the other hand, maybe not. He'd always liked the idea of Dillian...he caught the thought, which wasn't conducive to his resolution to behave. "Do you come here every year?" he asked Cele, as a distraction.

She nodded. "Hardly missed one, ever since I first met Dilly."

Someone else who called her Dilly. He'd never dared try it. "Where did you meet?"

"School. Ash, Dilly, and me. Ash's rich parents were always off God knows where, and mine are Service, so Kate started inviting us here. Now it's one of her family traditions, like Dilly said."

Dillian looked around. "Sorry?"

"Not you, gorgeous. I was just telling Seven Inches here that Kate's big on family traditions, bless her." She winked at him. "You'll turn into one before long, you wait and see."

The idea didn't appeal, and from the brief expression of dismay on Dillian's face, she felt the same. So it was purely to spite her that he said, "I'll look forward to it."

Cele nodded approvingly. "Keeps the numbers up. *Some* people have been slacking off lately."

That seemed to be directed at Asher, who shook her head while she dealt with a mouthful of food. "Unfair," she said finally. She held up her left hand, displaying her wedding ring. "We can't all do what we want every year. And I only miss when Dilly's off-world, like last year."

"*I* was here." Cele looked mournful. "I get lonely, you know."

"And I'm always here," Warrick said. "Even if no one else is."

"I see you at work almost every day. That's more than enough." Asher took a mouthful of wine, held the glass up to the light. "This is awfully good."

By the time they'd finished eating, Toreth decided that he'd done very well. He was still passably sober, which was no mean achievement with the available quantities of wine. He hadn't said anything to Asher that could conceivably cause offense, and it was hard to imagine anything that *would* offend Cele. He hadn't even made any excessively suggestive remarks to Dillian. Except for the fuckup with Valeria earlier—not his fault—things weren't going too badly. Now all he had to do was keep it up for another day and a bit, and he could go home.

Toreth started the night with good intentions.

The house was crowded and he wasn't too sure how thick the walls were. He didn't fancy the idea of sitting through breakfast with Kate—and more especially Tarin—after one of Warrick's more vocal performances. Their sleeping together without fucking wasn't such a rare occurrence these days. Sometimes they were even sober enough that it had to qualify as deliberate. This, Toreth decided, would be one of those nights. Kate had given them a room together, complete with the double bed in which Toreth was lying. Nice arrangement, if slightly disconcerting. Of course, Warrick was thirty-four, and so it wasn't really any of her business who he had in bed, but still, it was vaguely unsettling to imagine her making the decision, choosing the room. Thinking about them as...

Maybe she hadn't. Maybe this was the room Warrick would have had anyway. Maybe even his old room, from when he'd last lived here. Toreth looked around it. Dark carpet, light walls, bed, two chests of drawers, and a wardrobe in an unobjectionable dark blue. Nothing said "teenage boy's room." On the other hand, that just meant Kate had redecorated the place. There could still be other clues lying around.

He slipped out of bed and started opening drawers. Most were empty. Some held old pairs of curtains, carefully pressed. He decided against searching underneath them. A couple of drawers held the clothes they had brought, neatly folded— Warrick's handiwork. The presents had already been added to the pile in the living room. Finally he opened the wardrobe. Empty, apart from their hanging clothes and a dusty box of unpaired shoes. All of which left him no closer to discovering whether this was Warrick's old room or not. Of course, he could just ask Warrick. He thought about it for a moment longer, then dismissed the idea. No point getting into long, boring family history crap. He couldn't even remember why he might have cared. He heard Warrick's footsteps in the corridor, closed the wardrobe, and jumped back into bed. Before Warrick opened the door, Toreth heard Dillian's voice.

"Keir? Have you got a minute?" The footsteps halted, then grew fainter. Dillian's room must be somewhere nearby. Minutes passed, and Toreth wondered what the two of them were talking about. Voices raised in indistinct laughter and then faded out again. He imagined them sitting together, side by side, dark hair and dark eyes. On the bed, maybe. Warrick in his dressing gown, Dillian in...a dressing gown as well? A nightdress? With her generally excellent taste, he'd be willing to bet she owned some nice nightclothes. Satin. Plain, probably, as she wasn't the lacy type.

Starting to think about Dillian was dangerous, but she was so intriguing and attractive that it was difficult not to. Not that Toreth ever intended to do anything about it. For one thing, she wasn't interested in him, and at the moment the disinterest seemed to be verging on hostility.

Which just made the whole idea more fascinating. What would it take, he wondered, to change her mind? Stopping having anything to do with her brother, for a start. Practical, but dull. Beyond the fact that she was perfectly fuckable in her own right, the idea of having her was so compelling only because of Warrick. They were so alike, it would be a fascinating comparison. Fucking her, then Warrick. Warrick, then her. Or, as Sara had told him once, what he really wanted was to have them both at the same time. Cele's comment at the table had brought the idea back in full force. God, talk about things to regret on your deathbed that you'd never done.

Spending too much longer on this train of thought would wreck his plans for a quiet night, providing Warrick ever turned up. Although of course, on his own, he could be perfectly quiet. Nothing wrong with that. He was hard already, thinking about her. Them. Imagining bodies captured on canvas: dark hair, pale skin, deep eyes. All the time in the world to look at limbs and faces. He propped himself comfortably on the pillows, arm behind his head, and started to touch himself. Just lightly at first. Make it last nicely. He had plenty of time, because when Warrick and Dillian got talking they could be hours.

Warrick and Dillian. She was so like her brother and so different. What would she enjoy? What would she want? What would make her want *him*? As usual, though, the speculation was turning him on too much to waste time lingering on the setup. Simply begin from where she'd agreed. Moment of surrender—his favorite point in the hunt. Sometimes the fuck itself was a disappointment, although he bet it wouldn't be with Dillian. He started off with her clothed, couldn't be bothered, and stripped her instead. It wasn't difficult to imagine her body. He'd seen her in a few tight evening dresses, and once at the swimming pool, skin shining with water. Then he had to decide where. He toyed with a few options before settling on Warrick's flat, because the bed was a good size, and because it was easy to imagine. No need to waste time on creating the detail. And because it was easy to picture Warrick there as well.

He'd never bothered trying to come up with a how or why, however implausible. By this point in the fantasy he never cared anyway. He was simply there, with them. Warrick, naked, he could call to mind any time. Warrick in any number of states and positions, in fact. A never-ending source of entertainment in boring meetings and interrogations.

The picture changed from pure imagination into the memory of fucking Warrick over the desk in his office at I&I the day they'd dealt with Marian Tanit. One of his favorite fantasy fucks. Warrick hadn't wanted it, or rather hadn't wanted to want it—he'd been keen enough in the end. He changed the picture around, Warrick fucking him, hands holding him tight from behind. Now it was easy to slip Dillian into the scene, on the desk in front of him. Yes. Slipping into her easily and her head going back, offering her throat, exactly like she did sometimes when she laughed. Getting close. Warrick hard and deep inside him, arm around his chest (he moved his own arm to mirror the embrace), and Dillian . . . yes . . . Dillian . . .

"Couldn't wait for me?"

Toreth's eyes flew open, but between shock and desperate arousal he couldn't produce a word. In fact, it took a few seconds for him to be able to focus on the speaker. Warrick leaned against the closed door, arms folded and expression utterly unreadable. What had he heard? Had he said anything out loud? Fuck, he had no idea. He couldn't even manage to think what was likely. Dillian, probably, which was unfortunate enough. But, he hoped, not Warrick's name at the same time. That would be tricky to explain. No, actually, the explanation would be very, very obvious. And right. He doubted Warrick would approve. Eventually his language processing functions came back online. "How long have you been there?" he asked, praying for a clue.

"Long enough."

Bastard. What had he *heard*? "Was I being too loud?"

"Not at all." Warrick smiled slightly. "I couldn't hear you from outside. Or in Dillian's room, which is probably a good thing, or she might have wondered what you wanted her for."

One out of two, anyway. Fuck. Warrick sounded remarkably calm, considering, and that was rarely a good sign. The silence stretched out until he decided to try starting a sentence, without having any idea of where it was going, and hope for a helpful interruption. "Sorry, I didn't—"

Warrick shook his head, the faint, impossible-to-interpret smile still in place. "It's hardly a surprise. I've heard it before. You talk in your sleep occasionally, you know."

"I do not!" Not so much a denial but a protest at the very idea.

"How the hell would you know? It's not often, and it's not usually particularly interesting. In general, it's more of a request list, and I've heard most of it before, when you're awake, so from that point of view it lacks novelty." His tone was pure disdain, but one of the drawbacks of thin dressing gowns is that they make it difficult to lie about interest. At least for certain definitions and consequences of interest.

Toreth smiled at him, stretching a little, watching Warrick's eyes follow his movements. Might as well take every advantage he had. "I dream about turning up to work naked sometimes. Doesn't mean I'd do it. Don't you trust me?" he added, with a stab at innocent inquiry.

Warrick laughed. "*Trust* you?" There was, Toreth thought, such a thing as overdoing the disbelief. Warrick looked at him for a moment, then shook his head. "With some things. But with Dilly? Not this side of clinical insanity. Luckily, I do trust *her*."

No closer to knowing whether he'd said Warrick's name as well or not. If he had, it would probably need an apology, or something. But if he started the apology and Warrick didn't know...but if Warrick did know and he didn't say anything... Fuck it. He didn't care anyway. "If you don't want me to think about her, you'd better come over here and distract me," Toreth said.

Warrick's eyebrows shot up. "Don't we usually *finish* the argument before we get on to the make-up fuck?" he asked, although he sounded far from averse to the idea.

"Are we arguing?"

"I thought so." Warrick switched off the main light, leaving the dim glow from the bedside lights. Then he shed the dressing gown, walked over, and stood by the bed, looking at Toreth looking at him. "But I'm willing to consider that I might be wrong."

"Makes a fucking change." Toreth pulled him down into bed, rolled him over and pinned him down just long enough to feel him start to react to the restraint, then reluctantly let him go.

"How would you like to be distracted?" Warrick asked, somewhat breathless.

Holding Warrick down and fucking him until he screamed the house down would do the job nicely. With a display of willpower he found mildly impressive, he said, "Quietly."

Warrick's blinding smile almost made him change his mind. "I'll do my best. No promises."

So they practiced quiet fucking. Face to face, pressed together, delicious friction of skin on skin. Moving slowly and then not so slowly. Not-quite fucking, as Toreth thought of it. But even if it wasn't quite, it felt good, and Warrick smelled good—he always did, of course—and tasted good. And looked good. Not shifting his gaze for a second, he slid his hand down and took hold of Warrick's cock. Watching his face, hearing him gasp.

Somehow he always forgot how much he enjoyed this. They should do it more often. They'd shifted so that his own cock wasn't getting the contact that he needed. On the other hand, it was good to have the slight detachment to enjoy watching Warrick's reactions. And with one of them holding back there was at least a chance of keeping the noise down. A small chance. Warrick was biting his lip hard enough to whiten the flesh around his teeth, but also moaning deep in his throat, a steadily rising note in time with the movement of Toreth's hand. Toreth was so used to the sound he hadn't noticed how loud it was getting.

They were still lying on their sides, but with a bit of an effort he managed to get his other hand free and pressed it lightly over Warrick's mouth. He felt him shiver in response, arching into him. Warrick's head went back and he moaned again, louder. Then he shook the hand away. "Don't do that," he gasped.

"You're making a lot of noise."

"I don't...mmh, yes, don't stop...but that's...that won't help."

Irresistible impulse. Toreth leaned forwards, without losing the rhythm, and pressed his mouth firmly against Warrick's ear. "It will," he whispered, "if I do it harder."

Warrick shuddered again, moving faster, pressing closer. "Oh, yes. Yes, do it. Do it. I—" Toreth got his hand back in place just in time to muffle what was nearly a shout.

Afterwards, he lay still, listening to Warrick's breathing slowing, trying to be patient. He licked his fingers clean and wondered vaguely whether there was much of a mess. He should probably find some tissues or a towel or something before it got everywhere and... The fact that he was worrying about the state of the sheets suddenly struck him as terribly funny. The hastily stifled laugh roused Warrick, who looked up, then grinned. "I know," he said. "I feel as though I ought to be sneaking back to my own room afterwards. It's like being sixteen again."

"Fourteen." Although Toreth bet the circumstances were very different.

Warrick shook his head. "You're so damned competitive," he said, without heat.

"Whereas you, of course, are happy to come second every time."

Apparently stuck for a reply, Warrick changed tactics. He shifted around and began to rub his hip against Toreth, who moaned appreciatively. There were worse ways to lose an argument. Toreth thrust back hard, holding Warrick close. He still wanted to fuck him, really, but Warrick clearly wasn't in the mood yet and he couldn't wait. He needed to... to get it over with. While he was locked in his fantasy he hadn't thought about where they were. Now things were all too real and he was too aware of the crowded house. He could almost imagine that he heard distant breathing. If he hadn't been so hot and so desperately unfinished, he might have given up. But he needed it, wanted it so much that it couldn't take long and... who *was* in the next room? This was ridiculous. He'd fucked people while their *partners* were in the next room. Once, years ago, he'd fucked a girl in the dark at a crowded party, and he'd been able hear her boyfriend talking to his friends a few feet away. There was no reason, no earthly reason, for feeling like this now. But he simply—

He stopped moving, panting and frustrated. Warrick pulled away a little and pushed his sweat-damp hair back from his forehead. "What?"

"I... can't." He felt his face heat and hoped the light was too dim for it to show.

Warrick raised an eyebrow and smiled, white teeth in the semidarkness, wickedness incarnate. "Can't?"

"Look, it's just being here... no, hang on, don't—"

Warrick had already disappeared beneath the sheets. "Shh. I'll bet you tea in bed tomorrow morning that you can," he said, somewhat indistinctly.

Oh, God. Mouth and hands working on him, passionate and skillful. After a couple of minutes, "can't" began to seem less likely, and so did "shh." He grabbed for a pillow, pressed his face into it, and tried not to think about noise or about anything else except the exquisite tension pulling tight inside him, almost painful.

Yet he couldn't banish the awareness of the house around them and the people there, holding him back. Dillian. He focused on her. It was Dillian next door. Dillian lying in bed, just the thickness of the wall away. Dillian listening to them fucking. Yes, this was better. Dillian, trying to ignore them at first. Turned on by it, of course, and knowing that she shouldn't be. Giving in at last and...he stumbled briefly over naked or nightdress, then brushed the detail aside. Hand between her legs, thighs tensing, hips lifting. Other hand over her mouth so that *they* wouldn't hear *her* guilty excitement ...then a saliva-slicked finger slipped inside him, and a few seconds later the heat washed through him, driving away any thoughts of "can't." A groan turned into an almost surprised-sounding cry as he could and did. Thank God for the pillow, he thought hazily, not caring that much in the warm afterglow. And then: I wonder if she *did* hear?

Warrick resurfaced, licking his lips. "Told you," he murmured.

Toreth returned his pillow with more force than was strictly necessary. "Yeah, yeah. You're very good." Trying not to sound as if he meant it, because one thing Warrick didn't need for New Year was a larger ego.

"Mm." Warrick stretched out beside him and closed his eyes. "Don't forget my tea in the morning."

"Don't worry, I won't."

As he dozed off, Warrick warm against him, he decided he might as well make a cup for Dillian while he was at it. Then he'd be able to find out what she wore in bed.

The answer proved to be, disappointingly, that Dillian got up earlier than he did. When he went downstairs to pay off his debt he found her alone in the kitchen, fully dressed, having breakfast. "Good morning," he offered.

"Morning."

He looked around the kitchen, out of his depth as usual. Far too many cupboards. "I'm supposed to be making tea."

She pointed around the room. "Water. Pot. Tea. Cups. Milk. Sugar."

Very friendly. Even less friendly than yesterday. He tried to think back to work out what the hell he'd done. Probably nothing more than outstay his welcome with Warrick. On that score, last night might not have improved her mood, although she'd never seemed that prudish, at least not from Sara's description of their occasional evenings out. Maybe it was a family thing.

After delivering the tea and giving the matter some thought, Toreth decided to spend the rest of the morning in bed. He was, after all, theoretically on holiday. Early rising was for work. He had no idea whether he'd be missed or not—he suspected not—but he didn't care anyway. After making a halfhearted attempt to persuade Warrick to stay with him, he set the alarm to give him time to get ready for lunch and fell asleep at once.

When the alarm rang he canceled it, rolled over, and went right back to sleep without even noticing that he wasn't at home. A knock on the door, some time later, barely registered. It wasn't until the knock was repeated more loudly and the door opened and closed that he almost woke up. The bed jolted as someone sat down. "Fuck off," he mumbled.

This elicited a giggle, which most definitely did not belong to Warrick. "Mummy says that's a very naughty word," Valeria informed him.

Toreth groaned. *I bet mummy fucking does.* "What the—" He groped for something that wasn't a naughty word, gave up, and started again. "What are you doing in here?"

"Uncle Keir says to say that it's nearly lunch and it's time to get up," she said, parrotlike.

Uncle Keir was going to get his fucking neck wrung when Toreth found him. "All right." He finally managed to open his eyes, only to find her staring at him solemnly from the far end of the bed, with an expression that reminded him unnervingly of Dillian. "Thanks. Well, go on, then. Out." He made vague shooing gestures until she went away.

She was nowhere in sight when he came back from the bathroom, but after he'd dressed he found her on the stairs, obviously lying in wait for him. *Jesus, didn't she have anything better to do?* It was like having his own, somewhat undersized stalker. He stopped on the stairs beside her. She was doing something with some dolls, and when she saw him she stood up, dropping them. They strewed themselves over several steps, presenting, in the current piss-take safety phrase at the office, "a present and avoidable hazard to the well-being of personnel."

"I think you ought to pick those up," he said.

"Why?"

"Because someone will trip over them." She opened her mouth to start a protest and he continued in one of his more emphatic professional voices, "And because I'm *telling* you to."

He thought he might have overdone it rather, because her eyes went wide and she started gathering dolls with speed. Good. Maybe she'd stay the hell away in future. While she was busy, he made his escape.

When he found the rest of them, gathered in the living room, he discovered he had been holding up yet another family tradition, the opening of New Year gifts before lunch. There was clearly a well-established order of precedence, and once again he felt somewhat lost. So he sat quietly, opening gifts as they were offered by Dillian, who seemed to have responsibility for present distribution. Not that he had many: a pair of thin leather gloves from Warrick, perfect fit (and carefully pitched as expensive but not excessive), a bottle of spirits from Kate, and, to his surprise, aftershave from Dillian. He wondered briefly what message that was supposed to convey, finally settling on "I had no idea what to buy you, but I felt obliged to get something."

In any case, he wasn't interested in his own gifts. He was waiting for Warrick to open one particular box. Neatly wrapped in red and cream paper, it blended innocuously with the other gifts, although Toreth hadn't wrapped it himself. By a happy coincidence, the assistant in the shop had asked if it was a gift, and then wrapped it without further comment. It took quite a while for the box to be handed to Warrick. He read the label, then looked over to Toreth. He could read Warrick's mind, as clear as thirty-two-point font. *Please, whatever it is, just tell me that it isn't chains.*

Then he could hardly stop himself from laughing as Warrick shook the box slightly, relief evident when it made no sound. Toreth smiled, not aiming to make it reassuring. "Go on." He watched as Warrick unwrapped the paper and opened the box, his face still revealing more apprehension than anticipation.

The present had been something of an inspiration and, coincidentally, supremely suitable for this occasion. A dark brown leather belt with an old-fashioned buckle in silver. Dressy, but not excessively so. The only unusual feature was the holes for the buckle, which continued along the whole length of the belt. From his expression, it took Warrick almost three seconds to grasp the implication. "Very nice. Thanks," he said. He coiled it up again, slowly, his fingers lingering, unwilling to release the leather.

"I thought you'd like it." Then, as the group's attention turned to where one of the children had begun to unwrap a present, he caught Warrick's gaze and mouthed, *Later.*

Warrick swallowed and looked away, but he was smiling. Toreth smiled, too, thinking of the journey back the next day, and of more fun ways to pass the time than reading. He was just about to count the gift as an unqualified success when he glanced around and saw Tarin watching them. He was almost shocked by Tarin's expression: unconcealed anger, bordering on hatred. For Warrick or for him? What *was* his fucking problem?

Lunch was the thing he'd dreaded most since agreeing to come here. The point in the New Year proceedings that stirred the worst memories, of being trapped at the table with no escape. Old memories, now, but no less unpleasant for that. There were no names at the places, but everyone headed automatically for seats. Family tradition, no doubt, he thought sourly. He'd decided to wait until everyone else had sat down when he felt a touch on his arm and turned to find Kate smiling at him.

"Sit here, Val." She indicated a place near the head of the table and, for a moment, he thought she was suggesting he sit next to Tarin. Frankly, he'd rather starve. Then he spotted Tarin at the far end of the table and sat down, quickly and gratefully. Kate herself took the seat at the end beside him. He was also relieved to find Warrick seated next to him, and even happy to see Dillian opposite him. She still looked pissed off to have him there, but at least she was familiar. He'd thaw her out again, and it would give him something to concentrate on.

For the moment, there was also the food, the starters already set out and showing evidence of Warrick's meticulous handiwork. He complimented Kate on them anyway, giving her a chance to pass the praise on to Warrick and Jen. In doing so, she called him Val again. He'd had one moment to correct her, at the first introduction, and now it was far too late. Only his parents called him Val, and it had a kind of inevitability that Kate would as well. It didn't matter, though—not really.

"I hope your mother doesn't mind my stealing you away for New Year, Val?" she asked, with an almost miraculously bad choice of topic.

Out of the corner of his eye, he caught Warrick's sudden stillness.

"Hardly, since she doesn't know I'm here," Toreth said, keeping his voice dispassionate. "I haven't spoken to her for, um, five years. Five and a half."

Sometimes he didn't know why he didn't just lie and say they were dead. There was a long moment of silence before Kate managed a rather glassy smile and said, "Well, good. I shan't have to feel guilty, then."

He expected another silence after that, but Warrick stepped into the gap and began relaying the latest developments at SimTech to his mother, who apparently knew about the corporation in some detail. More than Toreth did, by the sound of it. After the investigation had finished he'd forgotten the specifics as quickly as he forgot technical details he learned for any case. At least it meant that for the moment he could listen, make the occasional comment, and not have to say too much. But at some point he would have to talk to Kate, since he doubted he'd put her off permanently. She wanted to talk to him, or even if not actually wanted, then she'd set herself the task of ensuring that he was made welcome. What the hell could he say to her? Trying for a measure of detachment, he applied himself to the problem. What could you talk about to your regular fuck's mother? The fucking itself was obviously out, which was a pity because it covered more or less everything he and Warrick did together.

I chain him to the wall, and we—Don't even think about it. Warrick would kill him. The sim was safe. I&I was probably dangerous—he certainly didn't plan to bring work up himself. He didn't mind answering questions about it, but most people didn't want to hear the answers, even if they'd asked in the first place.

Eventually Kate turned to him, obviously determined to try again. "Have you spent much time in the sim, Val?"

"A little." Fucking your son, mostly. Turn the question back—listening was easier and safer than talking. "Have you tried it?"

231

"Once, yes. I'm afraid I was terribly ill. Motion sickness. I've never been very good with that sort of thing, ever since I was a little girl."

"You could have tried again," Warrick said. "It's nothing more than a question of habituation. We've never had a subject yet who couldn't be acclimatized."

"Keir looks on me as a challenge." Kate smiled, leaning towards Toreth a little, confidential. "Or possibly an experiment."

"I don't like wasting an interesting piece of data, that's all," Warrick said.

Kate rolled her eyes. "Never have children, Val. You give birth to them, you bring them up, and then in the end you find you're 'interesting data.'"

This was definitely getting easier. "I know that one. The first time I met him I was data, too." Then he thought, Jesus, as long as she doesn't want to know what kind of data.

Fortunately, Warrick spoke before Kate could ask him to elaborate. "Rubbish." He didn't seem at all put out. "Come down and stay with me, Mother, why don't you? You always pretend you don't see enough of me. The sim will only take half an hour or so a day. You'll have plenty of time to do other things."

"Perhaps I will, darling, if you'd like me to." She smiled at Toreth, including him in the semiquestion.

What the hell did it have to do with him? He returned the smile automatically. "It'd be a pleasure to see you again."

Tarin remained silent for most of the meal, but the rest of the family was more than capable of making up for him. Toreth found himself dividing most of his time between Kate and Warrick. Then, towards the end of the meal, while everyone else ate dessert and he nibbled cheese and biscuits, he happened to catch Jen's voice, calling up from the end of the table. "I thought you were going to Europa in the New Year, Dillian? Didn't you have a contract?"

Dillian sighed. "Everything's on permanent hold. We were ready to go and then there was trouble with the Department of Development. Something to do with off-world investment regulations."

"The bureaucrats triumph again," Tarin said. "It wouldn't be such a problem if the Administration wasn't so chronically corrupt. The whole system needs reform."

Silence. It wasn't that everyone looked at Toreth; it was that everyone didn't. He sighed silently. This was one of the reasons he didn't socialize much outside work. Even if he made a habit of reporting essentially harmless comments of that kind—which he didn't—he didn't do it when he was on bloody holiday. But since there was nothing he could say that wouldn't make the situation worse, he simply sat and sipped the remains of his wine until Kate gathered herself. "Would anyone like coffee?" she asked.

The question generated an unwarranted amount of discussion, but at least the conversation started up again. Kate started to rise, but Warrick beat her to it. "No, don't get up. I'll make it." After a minute or so, Tarin followed him out of the room and the atmosphere around the table eased noticeably.

Kate stood up again and started to gather plates. Toreth thought a show of willingness might be politic. "Let me."

She returned his smile. "Thank you, Val." Unnecessary name use. Her continued determination to make him welcome left him, again, uncomfortable. Taking the plates from her, he gathered the rest up quickly. He had a moment's worry that Valeria would follow him but her attention was fortunately engaged by a second helping of trifle.

He stopped outside the kitchen door, trying to open it without dropping the plates, when he heard the voices from within. Warrick and Tarin. He stood still, not letting the precariously balanced stack rattle.

"You've been avoiding me," Tarin said.

"Don't be ridiculous. I've been in the same house since yesterday."

"Avoiding speaking to me, then."

"Now, why would I want to do that?"

"You know perfectly well why. *Him.*"

"That rather presupposes I care about your opinion of 'him.'" Toreth could imagine the sneer accompanying that tone of voice. It might have made even him think twice about pressing on with a conversation.

Tarin seemed to be immune, or oblivious. "Why did you bring him here?"

"He has a name, which, in case you had forgotten, is Toreth. Use it."

"Don't think that'll shut me up. Why did you bring *Toreth* here, then?"

Brief pause. "Mother suggested I might like to invite him."

"I don't believe you. She wouldn't."

"Well, if you don't believe me, there's very little point in your talking to me, is there? I would suggest that you go and ask her if it weren't for the fact that it is none of your concern. Not who I choose to be with, and not who gets invited to this house. Which, incidentally, is still Mother's house." Warrick's anger rang through every syllable of his brittle, overarticulating voice. Tarin sounded exactly the same, to a degree that nearly made Toreth smile. The physical resemblance might not be there, but the temperament clearly was.

"The house may belong to her, but I live here, too. *If* she did invite him, you should have said no. I cannot believe you could do it—not even you. It's bad enough that you're, well . . ."

"Fucking him," Warrick supplied icily.

"Do you have to be so—yes, that's bad enough. But here? Did you hear what Val said yesterday?"

"Yes. That wasn't his fault."

"He told her what he does!" Tarin's tone was pure outrage now. "She's six years old, Keir, and he told her what he does for a living. My daughter."

"It's just a job," Warrick snapped, defensive.

233

Toreth held his breath through a long silence. "Please tell me you don't mean that," Tarin said eventually, so quietly that Toreth could barely hear him.

"No. No, I don't. And I didn't . . . to be honest it never occurred to me that he'd accept the invitation." Toreth could hear the wry smile in Warrick's voice. "I don't know which of us was more surprised."

"Don't try to get away from the point. You can do whatever the hell you like away from my house, however disgusting. I don't care and I don't want to know. But you had no right to bring him here."

"For the very last time, it's none of your fucking business." Warrick sounded furious now, struggling not to raise his voice.

Then Jen's voice right beside him said, "Val?"

This time the plates almost went, but she caught the stack as it started to slide. From inside the kitchen, he heard Tarin's voice, on a rising note of fury. "I will not tolerate being unable to express my opinions in my own house without having to take into account the presence of some psychopathic Administration torturer who—"

Jen reached past Toreth and pushed open the door. Tarin's voice cut off in midsentence. "After you, Val," she said clearly.

When he stepped into the kitchen the two of them broke off their confrontation to look at him, Warrick hiding the anger almost straight away, Tarin taking a moment longer. Jen followed him in. "Is the coffee ready yet?" she asked as Toreth set the heavy plates down, glad to be rid of the weight. His hands shook slightly from the strain of holding them still.

"Yes, nearly," Warrick said in a voice so calm as to be disconcerting. "I was looking for the cups. You've reorganized all the cupboards."

"They're over here," Jen said.

Tarin turned and walked out without a word. Warrick and his aunt exchanged looks, making Toreth feel suddenly excluded. "Sorry," Warrick said.

She smiled. "No blood on the floor this time. That's a good start."

Jen turned to Toreth. "Kate tells me that we got through more wine than she expected last night. I volunteered to hunt down some more. Would you like to come with me?"

Technically it was a request, but the tone made it more of an order. Toreth didn't particularly fancy the idea, but it seemed preferable to where he was right now. Warrick's expression suggested he wanted to say something—probably to ask what he'd heard—and Toreth wasn't in the mood. Not looking at Warrick, Toreth said, "Of course."

They took the SimTech car, and they traveled in silence for a minute or so before Jen spoke. "I feel I ought to apologize for Tarin. I'm sorry you had to hear that.

I only caught the end but I can't imagine whatever went before was any better."

"It's my own fault for listening," Toreth said in his blandest talking-to-management voice.

She smiled slightly. "Well, I suppose you've got a point there, but I'm still sorry."

"Please, there's nothing for you to apologize about. You didn't say it." He spread his hands. "I assure you that I've heard a lot worse."

Her expression frosted slightly. "No doubt."

"I'm sorry if I've caused difficulties by coming here." He wanted to say that Warrick hadn't warned him, which was perfectly true, but even an appearance of trying to shift the blame in that direction would antagonize her further. He smiled apologetically. "Kate ought not to have to spend New Year keeping the peace."

That brought a thaw. "There'd be plenty of peacekeeping whether you were here or not, I'm afraid." She hesitated for a moment, poised on a question, and then asked, "I wondered if Warrick had . . . said anything to you? About Tarin."

He went for the only practical response, which was honesty. "He's never even mentioned his name."

Jen sighed. "No surprise there. Tarin was never very close to Keir or Dilly. Just before Keir went to university things grew a lot worse, and I've never really understood why. Would you be interested in hearing a bit of family history?"

Toreth thought the odds were quite low, particularly if Tarin was heavily involved. "If you'd like to tell me."

"Not *like*, no, but . . . I thought it might help. I'll try to give you the short version at least." She fell silent for a few moments, obviously organizing her account. "Kate married quite young to Marriot, Tarin's father. They had Tarin and then they simply drifted apart. He had, ah, political interests. Kate was never interested in that sort of thing. And then, when Tarin was six—no, seven, I think—his father died. A car accident."

There was a brief pause, which he filled by saying, "I'm sorry."

"So was I, which rather surprised me at the time. I'd never really liked him, to be perfectly honest. But then, very soon afterwards, Kate met Leo—Keir and Dillian's father." She shook her head. "It was one of those things. Kate would tell you he asked her to marry him the first day they met, which isn't quite true, because it took a week. But I won't bore you with the details. Keir was born, and then Dilly only a year later. I moved into the house with them, to help with the children." She smiled. "There are some photographs I must show you, when Keir isn't around to stop me."

Toreth had difficulty imagining anything less appealing than baby pictures of someone he was fucking. The thought must have escaped onto his face, because her smile grew slightly wider, with a hint of mischief. She wasn't at all bad-looking. "I hope I'm not boring you," was all she said.

"No. Not at all."

She shook her head, serious again. "Other people's families are never as interesting as they think they are."

"Please, carry on." He had to admit he was more interested than he'd expected to be. Some things you could never find out from security files, and he felt a professional curiosity to find out what, in this case, they would be.

"I knew Leo better than anyone did, except Kate. He was a wonderful man, kind and generous. Accepting. Tarin adored him." She looked away, out of the window, back into the past. He read a lot more in her half-averted face than she probably thought she was showing him. Either she'd fucked Leo, or she was wishing now that she'd done it.

"What happened?" he prompted.

She sighed. "There were some old friends of the family. Friends of Marriot's, originally. They were . . . idealists."

She looked at him, and he nodded, keeping his expression neutral. "Idealist" was the term anti-Administration political criminals used when they wanted to pretend they weren't doing something dangerously illegal.

"I don't know all the details, obviously," she said, "but they were arrested, quite suddenly. And Leo was arrested with them. There were never any charges against him, ever. It was *just* an association, nothing more. He hadn't done anything." Toreth nodded again, colluding passively in what was almost certainly an old, well-worn lie. He suspected where the story was headed.

"Not long after the arrest, he . . . died." She paused. "Under interrogation. An accident, Kate was told. They were married for almost exactly three years."

He'd guessed right. Fucking hell. Explanations clicked into place. The only thing he didn't understand was why she was telling this to him at all. It wasn't necessary. She'd seen him outside the kitchen, so she must know he was unlikely to give in to any urges to hit Tarin in the next couple of days . . . and then he realized. She knew it would all be in I&I records. He could look it up, once he got back to work, and probably would, given Tarin's behavior. She was giving him her version first, before he could see the cold, official accounts. Or maybe she hoped that it would stop him from reading the files at all. Was she trying to protect Tarin, or Warrick? He couldn't tell—she ran an impressive game. Now she was watching him, clearly expecting a response.

Toreth asked the first question that came to his mind. "Does Warrick know?" It hadn't been in Warrick's file, because some things he was quite certain he would have remembered.

"I . . . well, to be perfectly honest, I don't know. You would have to ask Kate. It was the one thing she forbade me to talk to the children about. I imagine he may know some of it, as may Dillian. Perhaps not the exact circumstances, but then none of us do." Not as well as you might, her expression said clearly, resenting him for something he hadn't done yet. "Tarin—well, he was old enough at the time to

236

know something about what was happening." She looked at him measuringly. "I don't know if you can appreciate it, but it was hard for Tar. Losing two fathers in such a short space of time."

"And for Kate. And for you."

She nodded. "Yes. It was." She glanced out of the window as the car drew to a halt outside a small collection of expensive-looking shops. He thought she had finished, but she didn't open the door. Instead she spoke again, looking at him directly. "Val, Kate is not political. She never has been and she's tried to bring her children up to be good citizens. How well she's succeeded... But I hope you can understand that you—that your job—presents something of a difficulty for Tarin."

Hence implying that he was supposed to let Tarin's anti-Administration sentiments pass without report. Or possibly she was simply asking him to put up with his rudeness without punching him. Neither interpretation was worth commenting on. "What about you?" he asked instead.

She looked at him calmly, any emotion now hidden and absolutely unreadable. "It was all a long time ago."

He nodded. "Thanks for letting me know. I'll try to keep out of Tarin's way."

"That would be a big help with the peacekeeping."

Since the conversation seemed to be over, he opened the door. "After you."

Warrick sat on the bed, running the belt through his hands, the rough back of the leather rubbing against his fingertips. The present was one good part of a not particularly enjoyable day, although after all this time he ought to know better than to let Tarin get to him.

Someone knocked on the door. While he debated whether to say anything, the knock was repeated. "Keir, it's me," Dillian said.

"Come in."

She put her head around the door. "Sulking?" she asked brightly.

He smiled. "'Looking for a bit of peace and quiet,' I would have said. But you may have a point."

She shut the door behind her and came over to sit next to him on the bed. He coiled up the belt and put it down. "Do you know where Toreth is?" he asked.

"Still out with Aunt Jen somewhere."

He didn't say anything, but he must've looked alarmed, because she laughed. "He'll be fine. What do you think she's going to do to him? Even Jen. Mind you, I was surprised that you got him here at all. New Year and family. I don't think he knows how to cope with it."

A slightly surprising comment, because recently Dillian had been pursuing a strict policy of no comment regarding Toreth. "You might be right."

She looked straight ahead, apparently studying the view through the darkening window with great concentration. "I wanted to talk to you about him."

"Well, I can't stop you."

"Please, don't be . . . I don't understand why you're with him at all, Keir. Sara told me about him—about what he does."

Warrick felt a prickle of something that wasn't exactly fear. Not yet. "She told you he does what?" he asked, managing to keep his voice level.

"That he's been—being—unfaithful. She didn't tell me as such, she just let it slip. But when I cornered her about it, she said you knew."

"Yes, I do." It could have been so much worse than that. "And we are now definitely entering 'nothing to do with you' territory."

"Don't you *mind?*"

It didn't help that he wasn't sure of the answer. No, and yes. Sometimes. "Please, just drop it."

She seemed to take that as a yes. "Then why are you still with him?"

"He's an incredibly good fuck?" he said, without much hope that it would actually shut her up.

It did at least produce a slight smile. "I guessed that part. I'm in the room next to yours, remember? And I've stayed at the flat."

Now he wished he hadn't said it. "Oh, God."

"That's why I suggested to Mother that she should put you at the end of the corridor. It was loud, but not *that* loud. I just put my fingers in my ears." The smile turned into a grin. "Actually, I thought you were quite restrained by—"

"Dilly," he said in a strangled voice.

"You're the one who brought it up." There was a silence for a while. Finally she looked away from the window, her gaze uncomfortably direct. "But is a good fuck *all* he is?"

He thought about all the tangled consequences of the investigation at SimTech. Things he couldn't explain and things that were too dangerous to explain. "Why the sudden inquisition?"

"Because if that is all there is to it, I think that . . . maybe you shouldn't have brought him here."

Just what he needed to brighten his day. "Oh, you as well."

"Me as well what?"

"I've already listened to Tarin expressing his views on my choice of guest and, frankly, once was more than enough."

She sat up straight, looking at him closely. "Oh, God. I'm sorry—I didn't know. You didn't hit him, did you?"

"Of course not!"

"Well, there was the time—"

"Dilly, for God's sake. I punched him *once,* at *one* New Year. I don't make a habit of it." The problem with families was that nothing was ever forgotten. "In fact, I was inhumanly restrained, although I don't think I could have kept it up much longer. I just told him to mind his own business."

"And I should do the same?"

"Mm. From you it sounds so much better. Or at least so much less self-right-eous. And I'm beginning to think you're both right, anyway."

"No!"

The emphatic reply made him smile. "Because then you'd be agreeing with Tar?"

She grinned sheepishly in response. "Well, yes. Basic rule of life."

"And what about Mother?"

"She can cope with Tarin sulking. She wouldn't have invited Toreth if she didn't mean it. You know that. And Tarin knows it, too. He's just scoring points— I doubt he really cares."

"No, he does care." He grimaced. "Too much, about some things. He'll really get himself into trouble one of these days. Not," he added, "that Toreth will say anything to anyone." And, damn it, he didn't want to feel the need to defend him, especially to Dilly. He was so used to having her as an ally that her dislike of Toreth left him feeling lost.

She didn't seem to be listening, though. She sat, fiddling with the seam of her sleeve, then said, "Can I ask you something?"

Automatically, because they were at home, he said what Jen would have said when they were children. "I don't know, can you?"

She didn't smile. "I do *know* he really isn't any of my business."

"I hear a 'but.'"

"But..." She frowned. "I'm worried about you, and he's the reason why I'm worried."

"Didn't we have this conversation before? There's nothing for you to worry about, I promise."

"I wish I could... Keir, when you came in to say goodnight, I saw a bruise. Here." She touched his shoulder, just above his collarbone. "And I've noticed other bruises before—on your face. More than once."

For a fleeting moment, he thought about Marian Tanit. On his list of conver-sations he never wanted to have, this one was very near the top. When he didn't say anything, she asked, "Does he...did he do that?"

He took a breath and looked her in the eye, because he wanted her to believe him the first time, so they could get this over with. And because he had to know what her reaction would be. Her first reaction. "Yes. But not in the way that you mean. It was...he did it because I wanted him to do it. I asked him to." When we were having sex. But he couldn't make himself say that to her. "When we were in bed."

It took a long few seconds for comprehension to dawn. Then the bewilderment was washed away by relief, and then overwhelming embarrassment. Nothing worse than that.

"Oh, God." She laughed, and put her hand up to her mouth. "Oh, no, I'm sorry, it's not that it's funny. Not at all. It's just that I'd got myself all worked up for this—for *weeks*—waiting for the right time, and I was going to be so . . . but I just never thought there might be . . . oh, dear."

He didn't recall ever seeing her blush quite so much before. He felt an unsporting stab of satisfaction at the unexpected payback for all the times she'd embarrassed him. Which, oddly enough, didn't include now.

"I feel like such an idiot, Keir. I'm sorry. I'm sorry for prying."

"It doesn't matter," he said, trying to sound magnanimous rather then amused. "Don't worry about it. It was good of you to be concerned."

"Good of me." She looked away and, doing so, caught sight of the belt on the bed beside him and her eyes went wider. Now she really did have the giggles, doubled over, her face buried in her hands. He could see her ears, though, still bright red. "Oh, dear . . . oh, no. I mean . . . I'm sorry."

Eventually the fit and the blushing subsided, and she leaned back against the wall and rested her head on his shoulder. "Oh, dear, I *am* sorry. Thanks for not being cross with me. It was an awful thing to think, I know. About Toreth. You won't tell him what I said, will you?"

"Of course not. Although," he added, "I doubt he'd care."

"No?" She shook her head slightly. "No, I expect he wouldn't. That's part of it, you know. He can be so strange. And he's difficult to talk to. No, that's not right. Easy to talk to, but hard to reach. It's as if there's something missing." He didn't comment. "I don't believe . . . I still can't see why *him*."

Warrick shrugged the shoulder she wasn't occupying. "I can't explain it either, I'm afraid." Which, in a way, was true. There were lots of reasons, but none of them answered that fundamental question.

He felt her smile. "Except for the incredibly good fuck part?"

"Except for that."

"Is it really good enough to make up for all the other things?"

"Yes, it really is." And he realized he felt relieved that she knew now. It made one less secret between them.

"Keir?"

"Mm?"

"Do you love him?"

Coming out of the blue, the question shocked him. "Do I *what*?"

She looked as though the idea had occurred to her only that moment. "Because it's been a while now. You're seeing a lot of him. You brought him here to meet everyone. So . . . do you love him?"

Oddly, he'd never even thought about the word before. It was such an impossible concept to connect to Toreth in any way. Nor was it something he wanted to think about now, here. So he pretended to consider it, looking at their dim reflections in the window, mirror images inside a mirror. He tilted his head, resting his cheek against the top of her head to improve the composition. Finally he said, "Well, now, that would be an incredibly stupid thing to do, wouldn't it?"

She nudged him away and sat up. "Yes. Yes, I think it probably would." She sounded serious, but he hadn't said yes or no, and she didn't ask the question again. Instead she got off the bed. "Mother said to let you know she's starting supper soon," she said. "If you want to help."

"Tell her I'll be down."

She stopped by the door. "Keir?"

"Yes?" What would it be this time?

"You are ... when you and he ... oh, dear. What I mean is, it is *safe,* isn't it?"

He'd wondered how long it would take her to start worrying about him again, once the idea had sunk in. "Yes, perfectly." She looked at him doubtfully. "I promise." He hated lying to her, because she was always so good at spotting it. But in this case she merely hesitated for a moment longer, nodded, and left.

He picked the belt up again and fastened it into a loop. Then he slipped it over his hands and closed his eyes, tensing his arms against the strap. Thinking about Toreth: cold voice, strong hands holding him so easily, mouth bearing down bruisingly hard on his, chains, blindfolds, and sharp-edged pain. He had no idea why he needed it so much, only that he did. The honest answer to Dilly's question would have been: "Yes, I trust him, but it can never be entirely safe. If it was, I wouldn't want it." As long as he knew that, and remembered it, and remembered what Toreth was, it would be as safe as it could be. But Dilly could worry about him quite enough without hearing that.

To Toreth's relief, dinner was less strained. Whether Jen or someone else had spoken to him or not, Tarin seemed to have himself under better control. He didn't speak to or look at Toreth, but that was frankly a relief. Dillian seemed to be in better spirits and once or twice he caught her looking between himself and Warrick with an expression quite different to the one he'd become used to recently—friendly, or at least less unfriendly. Intrigued, almost. Toreth scented an interesting distraction. He always liked a mystery.

The largest trauma of the meal was at the end, when it was discovered that the dishwasher had broken. The family looked at Warrick, who put his hands up. "I'm a programmer, not a mechanic," he said. "I can do it the old-fashioned way, though."

"I'll help," Dillian said.

Toreth took the opportunity. "I'll do it—after all, you made dinner," he said, speaking to Warrick, making it quite clear which of the two of them he intended to replace.

Warrick looked at Dillian until she shrugged. Then he smiled. "Thanks. I'll help you carry things through."

"Wash or dry?" Toreth asked once he was alone in the kitchen with Dillian.

"I don't mind." A little put out, perhaps, but still in a relatively good mood. "You do whichever you prefer."

"I'll dry. You're very friendly this evening," he added casually.

"Not especially." She started to fill the sink with water.

"Yes, you are." He moved up next to her to clear a space by the sink. "The last couple of months the heating system's come on every time you walk into a room and see me. I can feel the frost forming. And now you're happy to spend time with me?"

"I offered to help Keir."

"Of course." He tried to catch her eye, but she was concentrating fiercely on the pan in the sink.

"Succumbing to my irresistible charms at last?" he asked.

Finally she looked at him. "You are completely bloody..." She searched for words. "Impossible," she finished.

Easy catch. "Actually, I'm a fairly safe bet."

"Look, if you must know—" And she stopped dead.

"Well?"

"Nothing. Just forget it."

He touched her arm, a brief, friendly contact, nothing more. "Tell me."

"I...oh, all right." She began to speak briskly, getting the conversation out of the way. "I saw some bruises on Keir and I thought...and I wondered how it had happened and today I asked him about it and—" She stopped, a flush creeping up from the neck of her dress. Nice to know which way she blushed.

"And what did he say?"

She was burning now, staring down at the floor. "He explained." It must have almost killed her to say even that much. God, she looked good like this.

"Explained what?"

"That you—" Then she looked at him squarely, anger overcoming the embarrassment. "You *know* what. I'm not saying it simply to amuse you."

"That's not why I asked." Calm and reasonable. "I just want to be sure that you understand that he's all right. That you know what's going on between us."

"I don't *want* to know!" she snapped.

Oh, but she did. He could see the curiosity hidden deep behind the surface emotions. Maybe this was a way through her defenses. Somewhere along the line his playful interest had turned serious; the insane impracticality of trying this here didn't matter. He wanted her. "You thought I was beating him up, didn't you?" A little touch of hurt at the assumption.

242

Her anger drained away as she looked down briefly. "Yes. I...I don't know if you can—well, maybe you can understand how it looked." She looked back. "I *am* sorry."

"It's a game, Dillian. We both play it. I don't make him do anything he doesn't want to—as if I could." He smiled, drawing a small smile from her in response. "And it's only when we fuck."

She blinked at the word, but she was listening. Of course she was. Warrick would never tell her. If she wanted to know, she'd have to get it from him. He savored the thought for a moment, then continued. "In fact, it's not even all the time then. But the rest of the time I don't order him around, I *don't* beat him up. I've never hurt him, and I never will." His calm, even tone was pulling her further into the conversation despite herself. The flush had retreated from everywhere except her lips and cheekbones, and suddenly he wanted to ask her, Did you hear us fucking last night? Did it turn you on? "You believe me, don't you?" he asked.

She didn't answer.

"No? Why not?"

"Maybe because it's too much like...taking your work home."

"It's *nothing at all* like my work," he said with a coldness that wasn't entirely manufactured.

"But you *hit* him," she blurted out, caught off balance by his reaction.

"Not too hard."

"Hard enough to bruise."

"Sometimes. And then it's still not too hard, because it's what he wants. But that's not what it's about." Remembering Warrick the first time they'd fucked, he said, "Give me your hands."

"What? No!"

"Come on." He smiled. "Just a small demonstration. No bruises, I promise." He waited out a long moment of silence, before curiosity won out and she offered her hands diffidently. "All right. Now close your eyes." A last look, still mistrustful, before her dark lashes swept closed. He circled her wrists with his hands, bringing them together. He didn't hold her tightly, but it was secure enough. "Now. Pull away."

She frowned slightly, eyes still closed. "What?"

"Try to take your hands away from me." She twisted her hands, tentatively at first, then more strongly, her frown turning to concentration. He held her easily until she gave up. "There. No bruises. And that's all it takes, sometimes." He lowered his voice, leaned closer, and she didn't back away. "It's not about pain, it's about giving up control to someone else. Everything beyond that is frills and fun. It couldn't work unless he trusted me. Can you see that?"

She opened her eyes and nodded slowly. "Yes. Yes, I think so."

"He can walk away from it any time. I won't try to stop him." Easy to say, because Warrick would never leave. "But as long as he *does* want it, I'm staying."

This time she didn't say anything, but she nodded again and smiled slightly, ac-

243

knowledging his point. Warrick's smile. Utterly and literally irresistible. He let go of one wrist and put his hand on her waist, leaning down to kiss her. And straight away, he knew he'd fucked it up. He got only the briefest contact of beautifully soft lips, a tantalizing taste of her breath, before she jerked away, her eyes blazing.

He didn't try to duck the slap, because that was a good way to catch a fingernail in the eye. Besides, standing there and taking it created a better impression.

"You..." She looked at her hand, as if she couldn't believe the reflex. "No one has *ever* made me do that before." Angry with herself more than with him.

"I'm sorry," he said evenly. "I thought you wanted me to."

"How can I put this?" Dillian pursed her lips thoughtfully. "If every other man in the solar system developed hideous boils over their entire body, I'd still have sex with every last one of them before I'd even *think* about you."

Toreth blinked, then grinned. "But you'd get round to me in the end? That's nice to know."

She studied him, and her voice hardened. "You don't care, do you? What about Keir? Do you care at all about *him*?"

The ice in her question stabbed right through him, because in the fun of the chase, he'd genuinely, utterly forgotten what Warrick would do if he knew. He'd talked about him, and he'd been nothing more that a tool to get to her. Surely she couldn't say anything? How would it look, if she explained what had happened between them?

Luckily, I trust her.

Warrick would believe her, obviously—believe whatever she told him. Fuck, if she said anything, Warrick would... He found he couldn't even think about it. Now where was his confidence that Warrick would never walk away? "Don't tell him, Dillian, please. I—" I forgot about him? No, the truth sounded too ridiculous, so he settled for abject begging. "Please. I was stupid, I'm sorry. I got...carried away. Please don't tell him." Dignity was a small price to pay for getting out of this.

A long, agonizing pause followed, and he knew she was really thinking about it. She might say no. When she finally spoke, her tone was still so cold that he was sure she would refuse. "What goes on between you and Keir is your business. What goes on between you and *me* is mine. You will never, *ever* do that again." She paused. "But I'm giving you *one* chance." Even relenting, her voice was like diamond. "If you try it again, I *will* tell him, believe me."

He looked into her pale, angry, beautiful face. With the reprieve offered, he found himself still not wanting to give up the idea of having her, but willing to let it go back into the realm of pure fantasy because he did believe her. "Thank you," he said quietly. "And I'm sorry. I didn't—"

She put her hand up. "Don't bother. Don't apologize, don't pretend. Just don't do it again."

Could have gone a lot worse. He took a deep breath and nodded, keeping the smile of relief firmly off his face. "Never again. Promise."

She studied his face for a moment, then shook her head and turned back to the sink. He wondered whether to stay or go, but in the end he picked the tea towel up again and continued drying. Not unsurprisingly, she didn't seem to be in the mood for conversation, so he passed the rest of the time in imagining fucking her over the sink in a slippery mess of washing-up foam.

They left the next morning. Kate, Valeria, and Dillian came out to say goodbye, and Warrick was disappointed, but not entirely surprised, to see that Dillian's attitude towards Toreth appeared to have cooled again. Tarin hadn't appeared, but that was no surprise, either. The holiday hardly qualified as a great success, but he supposed that it could have gone worse. The expression on Toreth's face when Valeria demanded a goodbye kiss was almost worth the trip by itself.

In the car he sat, time passing, waiting with something between impatience and unbearable anticipation. The leather belt was coiled in his pocket, the buckle digging into his hip. By unspoken agreement, the present had lain unused the previous evening. It was something that needed time and concentration to be enjoyed. Here, or not until they got back to the flat? He couldn't even remember whose flat they were going to. Toreth's, he thought. Toreth sat opposite him, reading something, occasionally humming. Once or twice he checked his watch. To keep up appearances, Warrick read, too, or at least looked at the screen and turned pages occasionally. Was Toreth doing the same?

Sometimes he did wonder whether Toreth got as much out of this as he did. Some of it he knew Toreth enjoyed. Hearing that Warrick wanted him, how much he wanted him—usually desperately, by that point in the proceedings—was something he never seemed to tire of. Making him wait for it, sometimes longer than he could bear. And the fucking—he didn't seem to mind that too much, either. If Toreth didn't get off on his part in the scenes, then presumably he wouldn't still be around. Happy coincidence of compatibility.

Finally Toreth touched the controls and the car windows darkened. "Give me the belt." Mouth suddenly dry, all he could manage was to sit and do nothing. Toreth leaned closer, took the screen out of his hands and turned it off. "I know you've got it with you. You couldn't put it down."

"Not here."

"Give it to me."

He handed the belt over and watched as Toreth ran the length through his hands. "Strip." Now the hesitation was genuine. Sex was one thing, this was another. The chance the car could be stopped was small, but real. Toreth gave him a few seconds to think about it, then spoke slowly and deliberately. "Strip, or I'll strip you."

He lowered his eyes and started to undress. He couldn't stand up completely in the space between the seats, but he managed. He could *feel* Toreth watching him, his gaze brushing over his skin like an invisible touch. The sim come to life.

"Now kneel. Close your eyes. Hold out your hands."

He obeyed and offered his wrists, held out together, waiting for the touch of the leather. So when the belt tightened around his throat he couldn't help opening his eyes in mute surprise. Toreth laughed and pulled lightly on the strap, fastening the buckle. "You're going to need your hands. Now—" He settled back in the seat, making himself comfortable. "Suck me. And do it properly this time. Good and wet, because—" the pull on the belt increased slowly, inexorably pulling him downwards, "—because when I'm ready I'm going to fuck you here, on your knees, until I hear you scream for me, and then when we get to my flat I'm going to chain you to the wall and do it all over again. Understand?"

Warrick barely managed a nod, choked and breathless, neither of which had anything to do with the belt. It didn't matter what Dillian thought, and far, far less what Tarin or anyone else might think. This made it all worthwhile.

The next day, even though the New Year holiday extended for another day, Toreth went in to work. There was only a skeleton staff at I&I, working on the most pressing cases. Most importantly, there was no Sara and no other source of interruptions.

It took him most of the morning to track the file down. It was as well hidden from casual searches as it could be without deleting it, but someone who knew the system thoroughly, and who had a good idea of what they were looking for, could still find it. Someone had set the storage descriptor to "deep archive," which should only apply to prisoner record files over fifty years old. As far as he could tell, the classification had been set at the time the file was stored, which disproved his first assumption that Warrick had something to do with it.

The file proved to be short and interestingly uninformative. Warrick's father had been arrested by Justice on the strength of reports about a network of resisters, obtained through interrogation of prisoners arrested in the process of being smuggled out of Europe. The information connected Leo Warrick to the creation of false shipping records; his company had been named, rather than him in person, but that had been more than enough to justify his arrest. Reading between the lines, there had been a strong suspicion of his active involvement. Before a confession had been forthcoming, however, he had died under questioning. As far as Toreth could tell, the others arrested at the same time had never been asked directly to implicate him. Kate had been picked up, questioned briefly and gently, and released. No other family members or friends had been brought in.

Details of the death were vague. There was a suggestion of suicide, and a brief note about the subsequent internal inquiry reeked of cover-up—the speedy conclusion had been an unexpected adverse drug reaction. The interrogator responsible had been reprimanded but not seriously disciplined. There were only two realistic possibilities. The first was that there had been a friend within the Administration at work, someone who hadn't been able to prevent the arrest but was still influential enough to shield Leo Warrick's family from the worst consequences of his crimes, at the price of his life. The second was that the prisoner had made a deal as soon as he'd been brought in, something common enough in a large case like this. He had given up the names the interrogators wanted and in return he had been offered a quick, clean death and safety for his family. If so, the Administration had kept its promises in spades. There had even been an informal apology and substantial compensation paid to Kate. All terribly by the book.

If a deal had been made there might be something on record, although since the main file had been so carefully mislaid that seemed doubtful. The other source of information would be the interrogator who handled the case. Toreth didn't recognize the name, but that didn't mean she hadn't made the transfer over from Justice. If she hadn't retired or resigned, she could be working somewhere in I&I right now. He briefly considered trying to track her down, but there didn't seem to be much point. He couldn't justify his interest and it didn't matter anyway. It was ancient history. All that mattered was whether that history could hurt Warrick and, by association, himself. Possibly, if it came to the attention of the wrong people. It was a close enough association to proven resisters to make sponsors and clients nervous, and hence to open Warrick to blackmail if he were the kind of person who would submit to it. He wasn't, of course—his tastes in submission were strictly limited. Any blackmail attempt would blow up messily and probably openly. One step further removed, Toreth's name wouldn't suffer as badly. But being the . . . to be closely linked with a situation like that wouldn't exactly help his career.

Sitting back in his chair, he paged up and down through the report, rereading sections without paying much attention. Then he altered the "deep archive" flag to "file obsolete/out of date" and authorized the change. The next time there was an automatic purge at Int-Sec the file would be gone, and a search would pull up nothing beyond the reason why it had been erased. If there was another copy in the depths of the archives it would probably remain inaccessible to anyone without the individual file number.

The file disappeared from the screen. The last thing his eye caught before it went was the name of the interrogator who would know the answers. Toreth made a note of it, just because. And, next to it, the number of the file.

The next day, Sara was back. She brought them both coffee in his office and they exchanged New Year stories. Sara had mended her broken heart in style, reeling back in the boyfriend who had dumped her, stinging him for an impressive

New Year present, and then replacing him with an apparently more satisfactory model. And she'd beaten by two last year's record of nine parties.

"How was *your* holiday?" she inquired eventually.

He finally settled on saying, "Okay."

"'Okay'? That's it?"

"What were you expecting? Like you said, it was just a family thing. Lots of food—reasonable amounts to drink, thank God. Little kids," he grimaced, "absolutely everywhere. Complicated-yet-dull stories from thirty years ago about people I'd never heard of and a few arguments to break up the monotony. Oh, and I got myself slapped by Dillian. It was okay."

"Sounds like fun." She looked at him closely. "You enjoyed it, didn't you?"

He hadn't actually thought about it in those terms. It was certainly better than the idea of New Year's Day at home, without Warrick, never mind the memories of grim days at his own parents' flat. "I suppose it could've been worse."

"Told you." She took a sip of coffee. "Did you do the fucking-quietly-because-the-house-is-full-of-his-relatives thing? That's usually my favorite part, unless there's a *really* good trifle."

"Yeah." He grinned. "That was different. Novel."

"Novel?" She shook her head. "Yeah, I suppose it would be."

The idea that Sara had done the same thing, more than once, proved unexpectedly disturbing. The first time he'd ever had a...the first time he'd ever been to anyone else's family New Year. Except Sara's, of course, but that wasn't the same thing.

"Although he'll probably want to go to your parents' place next year, you know," she continued, deadpan. She'd met them, and she knew he didn't see them anymore, although even she didn't know all the reasons why.

"Not in a million fucking years," he said.

"I bet your mother would love him." Her mouth tightened a little with distaste.

He didn't say anything. Much as he hated to think about it, she was probably right, and it only made the whole idea so much worse. The silence hung in the air for a few moments and then Sara said, "Oh, speaking of meeting people—" She scanned the desk and picked up the note he'd written the day before.

"I saw this, first thing this morning, but I couldn't find the file. I think there's a mistake in the number because it's coming up as ee-oh-oh-dee. But I found Dru Balfe. She's a senior psychiatric specialist with an office on level B. Did you want me to call her?"

"No." He'd meant to leave it alone. There was no possible reason to pursue it any further. "No, but...I don't suppose you know where she has coffee? And when?"

She shrugged. "No, but I can find out."

"Great. Let me know as soon as you do."

Sara's information network proved to be operating efficiently. Toreth caught up with Balfe in one of the Interrogation level B coffee rooms. He introduced himself and, without giving a reason, asked if she thought she'd remember a case back from the days when the Interrogation Division was part of Justice.

"Records lost in the reorganization?" she asked sympathetically. "I'll do my best."

"The name was Leo Warrick. Suspected resister." Toreth sketched in details without getting a response until, just when he was about to give up, she finally nodded.

"I remember him, yes. Thoughtless bastard died on me. Drug reaction. I got my record marked over him."

"That's the one."

"What about him? He was a bust. Didn't know anything."

"How could you be sure, if he died?"

She frowned. "I had long enough with him."

"Do you remember anything at all he said? Anything the other prisoners said about him?"

"No." Short and final.

"He cut a deal?" he inquired, as casually as he could.

She looked at him measuringly. "Why *are* you interested?"

"I found a link to an old case I'm looking at. Unfinished business I thought I had a chance of tying up. But if there's nothing in this, I suppose I don't have anything after all."

Balfe shook her head. "You won't find a body *there*," she said with odd emphasis, and left to wash her coffee mug.

Toreth felt a chill. He knew what the phrase meant: it was one of the I&I staffs' little codes, a way of keeping each other out of trouble. He understood now her reluctance to talk. Leo Warrick hadn't died on her—he had never even existed.

Back in his office, he cursed his charitable impulse. He'd put his name on the deletion of a file connected to a Citizen Surveillance undercover agent. Kate had made an ideal target. Vulnerable, newly widowed—how much of an accident had that been?—and with a social circle linking directly into the resister network. A perfect entry point for an agent who could become trusted, make himself vital to the resisters and then spend years passing their every secret along.

He would've bet a month's pay that the arrest had been a mistake. Just the sort of screwup that had eventually led to the reorganization. Justice and Cit Surveillance tripping over each other, with the former blundering into one of the latter's infiltration operation and arresting their agent. With his cover destroyed, Cit would have had no choice but to can the operation. Why had Kate and her family escaped the mess? Standard procedure would have seen them disappear, in one fashion or another; Kate at least should have been arrested. An idea that she might prove useful again, perhaps. Or an unlikely, stupidly sentimental urge on the part of "Leo Warrick," for which Toreth was about to suffer the consequences.

He took slow, deep breaths, trying to calm his racing pulse. The operation was over and done with thirty years ago. There was no reason at all to think anyone would care, or even remember. The agent in question, whoever he had been, might be dead, or retired. Even if he were now at Int-Sec, he wasn't likely to be keeping an eye on long-closed case files. All he had to do was keep away from the files in the future and talk to no one about it. Not even Warrick. No, correction, *especially* not Warrick, because God only knew what he might decide to do about it. Whatever it was, it would involve the Int-Sec systems, that was for sure, and that would be suicide for both of them.

He should have known better than to get involved with anything to do with families—anyone's family. He was going to forget he'd ever even looked at the file. As long as he did that there was nothing to worry about. Nothing at all.

The screen in the small office displayed the results of Toreth's searches and the record of the changes he had made to the status of the file. The file was gone now, deleted from the main Data Division records. Even so, other copies existed in other systems, secure from destruction by someone with Toreth's clearance. Easily accessible, however, to a valued and trusted Int-Sec agent with a long and distinguished career and a very personal interest in the matter.

The question that agent considered now was: what to do about the para-investigator's unauthorized exploration of the past? He had found and read the files. He had spoken to Balfe. He had a personal association with parties in the case file. It had the potential to jeopardize a long-standing resister infiltration, monitoring, and control exercise that had proved outstandingly successful. Not to mention the risk of destroying a long-established cover.

The safest countermeasure would be to have him arrested on some charge and to die under questioning once he had revealed the extent of any information he had found. Or rather, not the safest, but the most thorough. It might, in fact, create more problems than it solved. That was always the risk. After all, he might have found, or even deduced, nothing beyond the cover story in the files. In fact, that seemed the most likely situation. His questions to Balfe had revealed no deeper suspicions. The very fact that he had risked tampering with the file was nearly enough evidence to tip the decision in favor of letting the incident go past. Most importantly, he had made no move to report Tarin's careless remarks. On the other hand, simply because he had said nothing yet—

A soft knock at the door sounded. Someone who knew that interruptions were unwelcome. "Come in."

The door opened and closed noiselessly. "Are you still busy?" The voice was as quiet and respectful as the knock.

"I won't be long."

"How long?" A hint of reproach crept in. "You promised we could go and feed the ducks before it got dark."

Kate canceled the connection to Int-Sec and switched off the screen while Valeria waited semipatiently beside her chair. Then she stood, picked her granddaughter up, and carried her out, locking the door behind them.

What to do? She continued to mull the question over as she helped Valeria into her coat and walked with her along the road to the small park. Even after all these years, it was difficult to think about the organizational foulup that had caused their handlers to withdraw Leo from the operation. Their relationship had been far more than professional. For one thing, after so many years of tedious sham marriage while she established herself with the resisters, it had been wonderful to have someone who *knew*. One person in her life with whom she didn't have to pretend. Leo had been matched to the assignment by their superiors, but they had been so good together, in every way. No one had ever suspected them—not Marriot's friends, not even Jen. Together, they should have been able to control and monitor the resisters indefinitely. It had taken the Justice Department's bungling to destroy the operation just when it was beginning to provide useful information. Was she risking a repeat performance by allowing Toreth to go free? Would she risk more by having him silenced?

They had run Tarin for years now as a perfect, unwitting source of information, with his carefully nurtured ideals and careless tongue. If he were to be reported, compromised, it would be a disaster. From that point of view, extending an invitation to Toreth had been a serious error on her part. When she had suggested the idea to Warrick, she had never expected Toreth to accept—his psych file had suggested quite the opposite. However, also from his psych and security files, it seemed unlikely that, even if Toreth had found anything, he would tell anyone about it. The one person he might conceivably tell was also the one person least likely to let the information go any further.

By the time they had reached the pond, she had made her mind up. She would do nothing, for now, and continue to monitor the files. At least it had demonstrated that the monitoring programs were functioning efficiently. Having made the decision, she found herself unexpectedly and profoundly relieved. Before she had time to examine the feeling, Valeria tugged gently on her hand. "Granny?"

"Yes, sweetheart?"

"Are you done?"

"Done what?"

"Thinking."

Kate smiled. "Yes, I'm finished."

"I want to feed the ducks, please."

She knew it was unfair to have favorites—although she'd never been good at avoiding it—but she did like Val. Sharp and observant. Tarin's outraged report of her announcement that she wanted to be a para-investigator had nearly made Kate smile. She must try to get her an entry to Int-Sec when she was old enough. Not as a para-investigator, of course, but her acute intelligence shouldn't be wasted.

They threw pieces of stale bread to the ducks. The day was edging into twilight and the birds were more interested in roosting than feeding, but that probably wasn't enough to explain Valeria's serious expression. Kate expected that she looked rather serious herself as she considered the intensity of her relief that nothing needed to be done about the other Val.

Toreth. She liked the man, and she worried that the feelings had clouded her judgment. The part of her that deeply loved her children—Leo's children—was glad that Keir had finally found someone, if an improbable someone, who seemed to make him happy. Unfortunately, that part of her could endanger the operation. She wondered briefly if she ought to refer the decision, but she could find no flaws in her arguments. It was, she concluded, a happy coincidence of logic and desire. One of the few in her dangerous, delicately balanced world, and she should accept it and be grateful.

Eventually the bread was finished. They stood and watched the ducks pecking halfheartedly at the last pieces. "Granny?" Valeria asked.

Kate crouched down beside her, ignoring a protest from her knees. "Yes, darling?"

"Do you like Uncle Val?"

Kate looked at her sharply, but there was no reason to think the child could have anything other than totally innocent motives for her question. "Yes, I do. Actually, I like him a lot. Why?"

"Daddy doesn't like him."

There was precious little point in denying that. "Mm. How about you?"

Valeria smiled. "I like him. Even if he doesn't know any stories."

"Well...that's fine, darling. Sometimes people like each other, and sometimes they don't. But maybe it would be best if you didn't talk to Daddy about him, mm? It might upset Daddy, and that wouldn't be nice. Talk to me about him, if you like."

Valeria nodded. "Okay." Kate took her hand and they set off back home. "Why do you like him?" Valeria asked after a while.

The girl did come up with the damndest questions, because it was the one thing Kate hadn't asked herself. The answer came at once, though, unambiguous: because he reminded her of Leo.

"He's handsome," she said, and Valeria giggled.

252

Mirror, Mirror

❖

Warrick had been delayed at work. One damn thing after another, and by the end of it, he was ready to dismember the next person who came up to him with a problem that could easily have waited until Monday. When he finally escaped his office, the car was late, which meant another five minutes lost standing in the AERC atrium. If he'd been less annoyed, it might have amused him to once more notice the change in himself. Desperate to get away from SimTech. Asher and Lew had both commented on it in the past: Lew with a certain amount of silent disapproval, Asher with amusement tempered by occasional hints of concern.

Even as he thought it, Warrick saw Lew, emerging from the lift. Fortunately, the car arrived and Warrick hurried out to meet it. He didn't know if Lew wanted him, but he'd rather not take the risk. Lew stood in something of a glass house when it came to questioning other's tastes in sexual entertainment. Of course, he was probably more upset by the early departures. There was no reason to assume he had any inkling of what was waiting for Warrick. Asher had some idea, and that was the source of her underlying disquiet.

It's safe, he'd assured her, as he'd assured Dillian. Everything I do with him is perfectly safe. Or rather, acceptably safe, since absolute safety could never be guaranteed. That was the key to safety assessments, as he'd heard several times over the afternoon's meeting with the team from the Consumer Safety Division of the Department of Corporate Regulation and Consumer Affairs. To be deemed safe, a product only had to be safe enough, and that could be a flexible concept. Getting into a car, even one fitted with the most modern autoguidance, was more dangerous than staying at home. Taking approved recreational pharmaceuticals was more dangerous than abstaining. Playing the game with Toreth was more dangerous than settling down for the evening with a glass of wine and a good book, but, oh, how very much more satisfying. Fulfilling a deep, primal need as nothing else could. An acceptable degree of risk.

These days, meetings in hotels were a rarity, so when Toreth had left the message with a time and place, the usual Friday afternoon anticipation had doubled. Something special, something no doubt carefully planned. He loved imagining Toreth working these evenings out, building the scenarios for them both. By the time he reached the hotel and collected the keycard, the irritation at the delays had melted away into a delicious buzz of anticipation. The journey over had been quicker than he'd expected, so as long as Toreth didn't happen to hit the unusual side of his punctuality curve and arrive early, he'd even have time for a shower.

When he opened the door, though, something caught his eye at once. A box lay in the center of the bed, with a note scribbled on a piece of card.

Be ready by ten past. T.

Toreth was usually late, by a minimum of five minutes. Not today, though. Today he would be on time to the second. Toreth's minimalist approach to gift-wrapping was in evidence again—the box was plain cardboard. Warrick laid the contents out on the bed: several hollow black metal bars a little thicker than his thumb, four leather cuffs, a belt, and various pieces of chain, plus a small plastic bag containing an assortment of bolts, screws, and washers. The box had already been opened and, naturally, if there had been any instructions in there they were gone now.

If he'd arrived on time the task would have been easy, but Toreth wouldn't care about an excuse like a delay at work. He checked his watch. The simplest thing to do would be to look up the manufacturer and find instructions from them, although in a way it was cheating. On the other hand, if he didn't do it he might not be ready, and then Toreth wouldn't stay. The one real, dreadful punishment for not playing the game up to standard.

A quick examination of the box found only blank spaces where the labels had been carefully removed. No marks on the bars. The cuffs were equally uninformative, but the belt revealed the name on a tiny stamp on the leather, hidden inside. It took a couple of minutes to find the instructions before he expanded his hand screen, laid it on the bed, and started work.

Of course, Toreth hadn't left a screwdriver, but Warrick had an exotic penknife with a ridiculous number of gadgets—an old present from Dilly. Usually it did nothing except wear holes in his pockets, but when it did come in handy...he laughed out loud, imagining telling her about this latest instance. Probably better not to. He dismissed the image and concentrated.

What didn't help was that, perforce, he had to imagine the finished item as he picked up the pieces, trying to see how they fit together. It did nothing at all for his concentration. Cuffs on wrists and ankles. Wrists locked to the belt...behind him? Yes, that looked right. His legs held apart by the rigid bar. Immobilized for whatever Toreth wanted to—he dropped a bolt, and spent a panicky thirty seconds hunting for it. I'm an engineer, he told himself. I can do this.

He laid his watch on the bed so he could keep an eye on it while he worked. Two bars went together in the wrong order and he had to waste more time back-

254

tracking, swearing softly. Frustrated and, he admitted to himself with a wry smile, loving it. If this had been the sim, he could have conjured the frame up (once initially created) and locked himself into it with a few thoughts, which was precisely the reason why the game didn't work in the sim. Even if he didn't use the sim tricks, the possibility would always be there. Here, the limitations and problems were unavoidably and excitingly real.

Finally the thing was ready. When completed, the frame proved to be collapsible, the bars sliding together to make a neat package perfect for discreetly taking to hotels. He couldn't help stopping to admire it, even though he couldn't afford the time. Toreth could be surprisingly good at selecting presents, although they were hardly unselfish.

Now...how to get it on. He considered the possibilities while he undressed, then started with the simple things. Ankles were easy, and the belt, but the wrist cuffs posed a serious problem, because they were permanently attached to the belt. In addition, the fastenings were inconveniently and unnecessarily complicated, featuring three narrow buckles on each one. Chosen deliberately, no doubt, for that exact reason. In the end he loosened the belt, twisted around to strap his right wrist into the cuff and then refastened the belt. That left him only one cuff, which surely couldn't be too tricky, since he was using his right hand. One cuff, and no damn time.

His gaze fixed to the watch on the bed, he struggled with the buckles. It looked as if Toreth was late after all, which was fortunate because the straps *would not* fasten. If Toreth came in now, when he was so close—the buckle slipped from his fingers and he swore again—so close to being ready, it would be unbearable.

One buckle fastened, and he paused, trying to flex his wrists and stretch his cramping fingers. Not a good idea, because the sensation of restraint sent a shiver through him, then another. He forced himself to stillness and carried on. One more minute and another buckle—three minutes over, and so nearly there. Were those footsteps outside? With a frantic effort, he managed the last buckle, hissing at the unexpected pain as a sharp edge dug into his fingertip beneath the nail. When he rubbed his finger and thumb together, he felt the stickiness of blood. Nothing serious, though. Besides, what mattered was that he was ready and when—

"Not bad," Toreth said.

Warrick managed to stop the turn before he lost his balance completely. Carefully he looked to his left, to where Toreth stood in the bathroom doorway, hands in his pockets, utterly composed.

"How long have you been there?" Warrick asked.

"All the time. I was watching in the mirror." Toreth strolled across and lowered the lights, casting the room into shadow. The light from the open bathroom door spilled across the floor, lighting the space where Warrick stood and making the room around him seem darker, something more than a mere hotel room. Toreth walked around him, slowly, inspecting. "Not bad at all. Very nice, in fact. And just in time, too."

"Yes." Warrick kept his eyes away from the treacherous watch on the bed, which showed fifteen minutes past, its face barely visible in the low light. Perhaps Toreth wouldn't see it now.

Toreth stopped behind him and checked the wrist cuffs, tightening the straps. Warrick shivered again, lips parting as his breathing accelerated. Then Toreth paused and Warrick tensed, waiting for...something. He didn't know what was coming and the newness and uncertainly fluttered inside him.

"You've hurt yourself," Toreth said. Cool, dispassionate observation, not concern.

Warrick nodded. A feather-light touch stroked down over his back as Toreth knelt behind him. Kisses on his arm, down over his enclosed wrist, across his hand, and then Toreth took the bleeding finger into his mouth. He sucked gently, tongue licking firmly over and around, halfway between soothing and hurting, and Warrick closed his eyes. At the same time, Toreth's hands roamed over him, feeling to be in far more places at once than could be physically possible: ribs, stomach, legs. Up between his spread thighs, making him exquisitely aware of the vulnerability of the position the bars locked him into. His cock ached already, but Toreth's hands stayed clear of it, although they brushed close enough to make him moan with frustration.

Toreth released his finger and stood up. "Better?" Toreth asked.

Indescribably, wonderfully perfect. He nodded again, words lost somewhere back in the wash of sensation. Then Warrick heard a zip unfasten, and Toreth pressed up close behind him, bare skin and hair touching Warrick's fingers. "Don't just fucking stand there. You've got hands—use them."

Not easy, but he obeyed, twisting his hands around to enclose Toreth's cock. Smooth, hard flesh filled his hands and Warrick moaned again, empathy and need. It took him a minute to find a rhythm, conscious of the cuffs with every movement. He focused inwards, losing awareness of the room around him, the hotel beyond the door. Toreth took a firm hold of his upper arms, pulling his shoulders back and down. Warrick arched his spine as Toreth bit down hard in the angle of his neck and shoulder, the pain making him whimper. As Warrick worked, Toreth's grip tightened, his breathing gradually quickening.

"Keep going." Toreth's voice in his ear, harsh and passionate. "Keep it going or I'll break your fucking arms."

His hands grew numb from pressure on the nerves, making every constricted flexing of his wrists more difficult. Fortunately, Toreth was thrusting into his hands now, his breathing ragged. "Ah, fuck—*Warrick*."

Pain flared down his arms as Toreth's fingers dug in, and Warrick bit his lip to stop himself from crying out. High now, dizzied by Toreth's voice and the flooding endorphins and the feeling of Toreth coming in his bound, helpless hands. Finally Toreth's hands loosened their grip, the release from the pressure and the sting of blood flowing back into his arms making Warrick groan. Distinct, discrete dabs of pain lingered, telling him that there would be finger marks still visible tomorrow—bruises, beautiful reminders of how absolutely Toreth owned him at this moment.

He waited, shivering, listening to Toreth's breathing slowing. Then Toreth moved back a little, only a few inches, and still close enough that his low voice curled up and down Warrick's spine. "So...what shall I do next?"

Warrick gathered enough breath to speak. "Whatever you want."

"We've got all evening. Plenty of time." Toreth's hands stroked over him again, over his shoulders and down his chest. "Plenty of time and such a lot of things we could try. But—" He pinched Warrick's nipple, hard, making him gasp. "Did you really think I didn't see that watch?" Dismay robbed him of any reply. Toreth moved around in front of him, his sharp predator's face shadowed in the side lighting. "You were four minutes over the time I gave you to get ready. You know what that means."

"Don't go." The words escaped before he could stop them.

Toreth laughed. "No? Why not? I've had *my* fun."

"Please." The instinct to kneel, to beg, was thwarted by the rigid strength of the bars, and his cock twitched.

Toreth smiled. "Again."

"Please. Please stay. I—I need it."

Silence, stretching out, as Toreth pretended to think about it; Warrick knew that he must have decided already what would happen. Everything perfectly planned. "Okay. I'm going for a wash. I won't be long. If, by the time I'm done, you're on your knees and ready to say sorry properly, I'll think about staying."

Without waiting for an answer, he turned and headed for the bathroom. As the door closed behind him, Warrick was already struggling frantically with the tightened buckles, his fingers slippery with come. This time he didn't even notice the stab of metal in his fingertips. If Toreth had closed the door, he couldn't be watching—he really meant this one. Twenty seconds passed, then thirty, and the buckles still resisted. Water splashed in the bathroom. Good, because while it was running Toreth was still in there.

Warrick forced himself to stop, to think past the arousal and Toreth's threat. He didn't have time to do it like this. If he leaned back, though, and braced the bar between the belt and the floor, and then stretched his fingers as far down the side as he could...he could just reach the catch that unlocked the first collapsible section. He pressed as hard as possible, given the circumstances, and for a moment he thought it wouldn't be enough. Then the fastener clicked free and he nearly fell as the bar shortened suddenly under his weight. He caught his balance, and reached down for the second catch. This one gave more easily, leaving him crouching awkwardly, but the water had stopped and that meant he didn't have long.

One more section, and this time he could barely reach the release with the very tips of his fingers. Straining to force his wrists through the cuffs far enough to make the last millimeters he needed, leather creaking—

Then Warrick was on his knees, panting, the bar pressed against the base of his spine, locking him in position. Now he had no choice but to kneel, his ankles still held apart and his wrists pulled down towards the bar. Triumph and arousal flooded through him in equal measure, and he had only a few seconds to recover before the door opened.

"Well . . ." Toreth paused, and Warrick crossed his fingers, heart in his mouth, keeping his gaze fixed on the floor. Please. Please— "I suppose I'll have to give you a chance now, won't I?" Warrick looked up, blinking at the brightness, seeing nothing except Toreth's shape, haloed by the light. An unlikely angel, to put it mildly, but this was most definitely heaven.

"Go on, then." Dark voice like a molten caress, heating him to his core. "Tell me how sorry you are."

Toreth leaned on the window frame of the hotel room, watching the paved area before the main entrance, and sipping his drink. Good job he hadn't written the card when he got here, because Warrick was late. It didn't matter that much. The present would keep, and if Warrick didn't show, he could always pick up a fuck in the bar downstairs. It had looked busy enough. Still, after all the effort invested so far, and an afternoon of happy anticipation, that would definitely be second best. Where was he? Surely he'd have called if he couldn't make it? To his irritation, Toreth found himself wanting to check his comm again—stupid, because it would notify him automatically if Warrick left a message. Then, finally, the SimTech car drew up, and the dark-haired figure emerged. Hurrying, too, and Toreth smiled.

Time to finish the preparations. He checked his watch, did the calculation based on his own experiments with the cuffs, and added the time to the note. At least five minutes less than Warrick would need, if he had his sums right. He also checked around the room. It didn't matter if there were some signs of disturbance, since he had to have been here long enough to deliver the box, but he didn't want Warrick becoming suspicious. Everything seemed in order. Toreth downed the last of his drink. Then he rinsed his glass, dried it, replaced it on the side, and re-treated into the bathroom, hiding out of sight behind the open door. There was always the chance that Warrick would come into the bathroom, although Toreth didn't think it was very likely. The note should ensure that Warrick stayed focused on the task in hand.

After a minute or two, the main door to the room opened, and he held his breath. Footsteps entered the room, halting briefly before carrying on to the bed. Toreth kept still until he heard the clink of metal. Then he eased carefully forward to a spot where he could see Warrick's reflection in the mirror.

Before he started watching in earnest, he checked the visibility of his own reflection. The space behind the door was usefully shadowed, and he doubted Warrick would notice him. Not when he had so many other things to occupy his attention. What was he doing now? Examining the gear, apparently, with minute and methodical care. Checking each piece in turn, and then setting it aside. Finally he heard a soft "a-ha!" of triumph, and Warrick pulled out his hand screen. Clever bastard. Of course, Toreth knew that already, and he'd factored it into the calculations.

Now that Warrick had the instructions, he took his penknife from his jacket pocket and started work. Toreth thought the knife was absolutely the most ridiculous thing he'd seen in his life. Who the hell needed a penknife with comms, centimeter-accurate location mapping, and a mini foldout screen? Warrick would enjoy the chance to use it, though. He heard Warrick laugh once, and then he bent to the task with silent concentration. Toreth leaned on the wall, checking his watch from time to time. Warrick was doing well, and better than he'd expected, but probably still not well enough. In the end it would depend on how quickly he managed the final part.

Every so often Warrick would pause, a piece held in his hands, stroking the leather of a cuff, or running his thumb over the curve of a metal loop. Possibly he didn't even realize he was doing it. Toreth caught the glint of reflected light as something metallic fell to the ground, and he pulled back further out of sight as Warrick started hunting for whatever it was. Toreth could still hear him, though, and the low, frustrated swearing sent a spike of excitement through him. Warrick so rarely swore. He'd known Warrick would get off on this, on handling the gear, on the pressure of time and the fear of failure. But so far the effect was exceeding his highest expectations.

When he risked looking back, the lost bit must have been found or abandoned, because Warrick was bent over the belt, fastening bolts. He also kept looking at the bed—at his watch, presumably, which was gone from his wrist. He was hurrying now, making mistakes. No chance that he'd finish with enough time to spare.

At last, the assembly completed, Warrick laid the bars out on the bed and stood looking down at them. Toreth could see his smile, the profile view flattering him as usual. Next Warrick stripped, his eyes still fixed on the gear. Pale skin and dark hair quickly revealed—wonderful visuals, and Toreth's body began to send messages suggesting that waiting wasn't so much fun any more. His eyes might be enjoying it, but his cock felt sadly neglected. Go out there now, was the firm suggestion. Go out there, throw him on the bed and fuck him, hard and fast. He'll love it, you'll love it, and we can do the games later. Sucking in his stomach, he slipped a hand inside his waistband. Just a touch, nothing too firm, and he sighed in silent satisfaction. With that nagging distraction taken in hand, he turned his attention back to Warrick.

Toreth knew the task he'd set was possible, because he'd managed to get into the thing himself a couple of times, while he was investigating the timing. There weren't many ways it did work, and he grinned as Warrick started with a wrong one, taking the tempting route of doing up all the easy buckles first. He picked up the mistake fast enough, though, loosening the belt and turning away to fasten the cuff on his right wrist. Toreth risked edging forwards a little to get a better view. He stayed there as Warrick turned back, squaring his shoulders and fumbling to get the second cuff around his wrist. Toreth's occupied hand moved a little faster and he bumped his elbow on the door. Fortunately, at that exact moment Warrick swore out loud again, thereby missing the noise. Slipping buckle, presumably—Toreth had a scratch or two on his own fingertips.

Toreth eased back again. *Fuck.* Too close, when it was nearly done.

Shortly afterwards Warrick's arms stopped moving and he paused for a moment, fingers flexing, breathing quickly. One buckle fastened, by the look of it. Reluctantly, Toreth pulled his hand out from his trousers and checked the time. Warrick was well over time already, and two buckles left. Toreth watched, trying keep his breathing under control, as Warrick got back to work.

His gaze was locked to the bed, lips moving silently as he fought with the cuff. Toreth couldn't see his wrists clearly, but from Warrick's brief, tense smile he guessed another strap had cooperated. Then his head came up sharply, and Toreth's stomach flipped—had Warrick seen him? Apparently not, because Warrick craned his neck around towards the door, and his frantic struggle intensified. Some unwittingly helpful passerby in the corridor, probably. A short, sharp sound of distress and a final effort, then Warrick's shoulders suddenly relaxed.

Time for his big entrance. Straightening his clothes, he slipped out from behind the door and took up his position, in his best casual pose. "Not bad," he drawled.

Warrick started to turn, and Toreth almost jumped to catch him, but he managed to keep his balance. "How long have you been there?" Warrick asked.

"All the time. I was watching in the mirror." He crossed the room and dimmed the lights, turning back to admire Warrick, highlighted in the light from the bathroom. He walked around him slowly, enjoying the view. Warrick's gaze tracked him, his breathing still quick from the exertion. "Not bad at all," Toreth said. "Very nice, in fact." He paused, and then added, "And just in time, too."

"Yes." The way Warrick kept his gaze firmly averted from the watch on the bed told Toreth that he knew exactly what the time was.

He paused in his circling to check the cuffs. As he tightened the straps, the blood caught his eye. Red drops, welling on Warrick's fingertip. Saliva filled his mouth, and he swallowed. "You've hurt yourself," he said, managing to keep his voice cool.

Warrick nodded. Toreth knelt behind him, not meaning to touch him. But Warrick's skin was like a magnet, attracting his hands and mouth. He tasted his arm, his hand, and then, finally, sucked the fingertip into his mouth. His already hard cock tightened even more at the sweet, salty taste of blood. Warrick's blood. Something he'd never had the slightest urge to do with anyone else. Like other things, it was only with Warrick, one more facet of the occasionally unnerving urge to possess him utterly, own every part of him.

Giving up any idea of restraint, he let his hands roam at will, stroking Warrick's thighs, imagining them spreading for him later. Much later. Warrick kneeling for him, by then wound to a fever pitch of desperation, begging for him, *needing* him... *Mine.* Oh, God, yes. By the end of the evening, Warrick would have no doubts about who he belonged to. It took an effort to release Warrick's finger, to stand up, to pull away the few inches he needed to keep control. He mustn't waste the careful setup. "Better?" Toreth asked.

Warrick nodded again, breathing quick and shallow, and it was suddenly too much. Stop playing around, and just get on to the next part of the plan. Toreth tugged down the zip to free his straining cock, and pressed forwards. "Don't just fucking stand there. You've got hands—use them."

He couldn't help a gasp as Warrick's hands enclosed him, but Warrick's own, much louder, moan covered the noise. Toreth smiled, holding himself still, making Warrick do the work. It took him a little while, but soon he had it.

Now—hurt him. He took a firm hold of Warrick's upper arms, pulling his shoulders back and down, positioning Warrick's hands and at the same time making sure he wouldn't be able to ease away to escape the pain. Warrick arched towards him, his neck an irresistible temptation. The hard bite drew out a whimper.

Warrick's fingers had a skillful touch, even under the current circumstances, and he didn't need to remind himself to tighten his grip on Warrick's arms. The rhythm faltered for a moment. "Keep going. Keep it going or I'll break your fucking arms." Or possibly scream.

Digging his fingers in, aiming for nerves, pulling Warrick closer, he squeezed until his own fingers ached. He'd meant to drag it out until Warrick's harsh breathing slipped closer to sobs. In the end, he couldn't. Briefly abandoning the game, he started to thrust, obeying the driving need, feeling the pressure building inside.

Don't say anything. A distant thought. Stick to the game. Don't say—"Ah, fuck—*Warrick.*" Passion filling in his voice, uncontrollable and out of character, as if he cared through the heady rush of pleasure.

When it was over, he unclenched his fingers, and Warrick groaned. Toreth stepped back, still panting, admiring the vivid red finger marks he'd left behind. They'd bruise up nicely, and last for a while. Stamping his property. He took his time fastening his zip, taking deep breaths, until he knew his voice would be steady, and then said, "So...what shall I do next?"

"Whatever you want." Warrick's voice was hoarse, and the submission instant and unquestioning.

"We've got all evening. Plenty of time." This was what he'd looked forward to the most, the reason he'd gone through the elaborate preparations. He ran his hands over Warrick again, over his shoulders and down his chest, enjoying the rub of hair against his palms. "Plenty of time and such a lot of things we could try. But—" He pinched Warrick's nipple, hard, making him gasp. "Did you really think I didn't see that watch?"

A single, small exclamation of dismay, and then Warrick went absolutely still. He moved around in front of Warrick, savoring his stricken expression. Oh, yes. This was even more fun than the orgasm. Toreth smiled, keeping his voice unyielding. "You were four minutes over the time I gave you to get ready. You know what that means."

"Don't go." Desperate plea, blurted out, and the genuine fear in his voice delighted Toreth.

He laughed. "No? Why not? I've had *my* fun."

"Please." Warrick's shoulders moved, pulling on the belt, and his cock twitched as he felt the restraints.

Could anything be better than this? Yes—a lot of things, and they were going to do plenty of them. "Again," Toreth said.

"Please. Please stay." Warrick's tongue flicked over his lips, and Toreth imagined how dry his mouth must be. "I—I need it."

A good thing, really, that he'd included the handjob in the plan, because if he'd tried to do this without he didn't think he would've been able to stop himself jumping Warrick right this moment. Instead he stood for a while, pretending to think it over, soaking up the delicious sight of Warrick's flushed desperation. "Okay," he said finally. "I'm going for a wash. I won't be long. If, by the time I'm done, you're on your knees and ready to say sorry properly, I'll think about staying."

Without waiting for an answer, he turned and headed for the bathroom, metal already rattling behind him. He closed the door and turned on the tap quickly, not wanting to miss the show. Leaving the water flowing, he crept back to the door, eased it open a tiny crack, and peeped through. Warrick didn't notice the movement because he had his eyes squeezed shut as he struggled with the cuffs. With slippery fingers and tightened straps, it wouldn't be easy.

Toreth intended to stay, of course, but it was far more fun to leave the question in doubt. What mattered was that Warrick believed he would leave, and from his expression, there was no doubt about that. After all, Toreth had left before. Those departures had been necessary if frustrating training, with evenings like this as the worthwhile reward. Even as he thought that, Warrick stilled and stood, chest heaving, staring down at the floor. What now? Toreth wondered.

After a moment, Warrick lifted his head, and Toreth froze in alarm, but still Warrick didn't see him. He was frowning with concentration as he leaned back, putting his weight on the bar. His head tilted back, lips parting as he pressed against the cuffs. Wasting his time, Toreth knew, because there was no chance that the leather or steel would give way. Then Warrick arched even further, shoulders straining, and Toreth realized what he must be trying to do.

Shit, he could break his back like that. No fucking way in hell could they explain *that* one away in Casualty. Even as he put his hand on the door, the rod shortened suddenly with a click he heard over the running water, and Warrick nearly fell. Only nearly, though, and soon there was a second click and the bar collapsed by another section. Toreth grinned. Very, very clever, and the final effect would be fantastically fuckable.

Time to turn off the tap, although it was a pity to miss the last part. As he returned, he heard the muffled thump of Warrick's knees hitting the ground, and his heavy breathing. Toreth ran his hands through his hair, summoned up a cold smile, and opened the door. "Well..." He paused, partly to draw out the tension, and partly because the scene before him drove the words out of his mind.

Fuckable didn't do it justice, he thought, not anywhere near. Warrick knelt, head bowed, his dark hair curling with sweat, and in the light from the bathroom, more sweat gleamed on his chest and taut shoulders. The bar between his ankles spread his thighs, and his erection, lost during the struggle with the cuffs, was swelling again under Toreth's gaze. Jesus fucking Christ, what could you charge for a sight like this?

"I suppose I'll have to give you a chance now, won't I?" Toreth said finally. Warrick straightened, looking up at him, blinking, teeth bared in a mixture of triumph and relief. His. Absolutely and completely his. Whatever he asked at this moment, Warrick would do for him. Luckily, he had the right instruction prepared.

"Go on, then. Tell me how sorry you are."

www.ingramcontent.com/pod-product-compliance
Lightning Source LLC
Chambersburg PA
CBHW020746250626
47155CB00003B/942